The Hollow Sea

ANNIE KIRBY

MICHAEL JOSEPH

PENGUIN MICHAEL JOSEPH

UK | USA | Canada | Ireland | Australia
India | New Zealand | South Africa

Penguin Michael Joseph is part of the Penguin Random House group of companies
whose addresses can be found at global.penguinrandomhouse.com

First published 2022
001

Copyright © Annie Kirby, 2022

The moral right of the author has been asserted

Typeset by Jouve (UK), Milton Keynes
Printed and bound in Great Britain by Clays Ltd, Elcograf S.p.A.

The authorized representative in the EEA is Penguin Random House Ireland,
Morrison Chambers, 32 Nassau Street, Dublin D02 YH68

A CIP catalogue record for this book is available from the British Library

HARDBACK ISBN: 978–0–241–52209–7
TRADE PAPERBACK ISBN: 978–0–241–52210–3

www.greenpenguin.co.uk

For Satbeer

PART I

Strandings

The Woman and the Girl: Monsters

I think of them often, the woman and the girl in the dilapidated fishing boat with a mermaid painted on the deck, fleeing monsters of some kind or another. They would have left at first light, travelling south from Bride Island across the Hollow Sea, a stretch of water treacherous in more ways than one, then east towards the mainland, the greens and greys of the archipelago fading into mist behind them. Ahead, an endless barren sea and the hope of refuge beyond.

They almost made it.

Sometimes, in my imagination, the monster that catches them is a storm, conjured from the early-evening stillness. The woman remains a calm space, a breath-note of silence in the screaming tempest, bone-white knuckles on the wheel, her face lashed by sodden ropes of her own pale hair. Carried up, the fishing boat cresting on the peak of a wave, the woman a statue, focused only on sanctuary, keeping the girl safe. Then, plummeting, her stomach left behind, the boat hurled into a space existing between two monster waves, shattering her last illusions of control. Waves arch together overhead, a temporary shelter.

The girl crouches motionless in the cramped cockpit, dark curls poking out from beneath her rain hat, hands linked around a red satchel slung across her torso. Beneath her raincoat, she is still in her pyjamas. She was supposed to have a cake today, with buttercream and eight candles. She wants to ask the woman if there will be cake when they get to wherever they're going, but she doesn't dare. The woman wipes her face with her sleeve, mouths a few jumbled words of comfort to the girl, and the waves crash down on them.

There is an alternative version of their last few moments. It comes to me more and more, in those early sleepless hours. In this imagining, the sea is calm, the air around them quivering with silence, stirred only by the faint chug of the engine and the lapping of waves against the hull, the mainland in the near distance sinking into a twinkling spring dusk. The woman thrums her fingers on the wheel and dances from one foot to the other. She glances at the empty swathe of ocean behind them, squints into the setting sun, shoves a loose strand of hair behind her ear. In this imagining, she has no tender words for the girl, no tender emotions. She is consumed by thoughts of safety, the mainland.

Whatever it is that lurks in the calm – an uncharted rock, a ship, a monster – finds them.

Which of my imagined scenarios is true? Perhaps neither, but in both the woman and the girl go into the water. And when they do, my imaginings merge into one. The sea is freezing. The shock of it forces the air from the woman's lungs, water closes over her head, rushes in to fill the empty spaces. The islanders had called her *witch*, but she has no magic to save herself. There is a slow heartbeat of a moment when the woman is bitter and angry and grateful, hollowed out with loss and love. The girl is sinking beside her, their fingertips brushing, and the woman makes one last supreme effort to grab the girl's wrist and propel her upwards in a flurry of bubbles.

Now the woman is alone beneath the water, and the water is in her. Colours, all the colours. White noise fading into beautiful silence.

2

Scottie: The Haunted Room

We had a haunted room in our house, pale apple green with stencilled stars and a creaking sash window. We'd never decorated, the green paint and stars left behind by the previous owners when they moved their brood to a larger place. We renovated the rest of the house, steaming off wallpaper, sanding floorboards, smoothing plaster over Artex, but this room we left untouched, even though paint was peeling off the skirting boards and occasionally we would find moth eggs the shape of rice grains in the carpet. Our lack of attention to the room wasn't a conscious decision, nothing we discussed. Perhaps we were superstitious, worried about jinxing things. Over time, the air in the room had thickened with not-quite-ghosts, will-o'-the-wisps haunting us not from the past but from the future. Our childish superstition started to feel like a bad joke.

I woke in the early hours, a few days before we were due to start preparing for our next frozen embryo transfer, clawing myself up from the mud of a half-remembered dream. Jasminder was lying on his side, facing away from me, a thin strip of space between us, his breaths rattling on the cusp of a snore. I slid out from under the duvet, careful not to wake him, creeping along the stripped-wood floors to our little haunted bedroom across the landing. The blind was up, the room suffused with the amber glow of light pollution from the city and suburbs fanning out around our house. It smelt fusty, with a faint undertone of moth spray. Outside, urban foxes yelped, and the drone of a moped came and went and came again.

I wanted to return to my dream. I had the faint sense, in the few lingering strands I could still grasp, that the not-quite-ghosts who inhabited this room had been in the dream and I'd been able to touch them. I craved that touch, wanted it more than I'd ever wanted anything, so I closed the door behind me, curled up on the sofa-bed beneath a dusty throw and closed my eyes. I slowed my breathing, allowed it to deepen, as if I were still asleep, and willed myself to slide back down into the dream. For a moment, I thought I would succeed, sinking down, down, in slow-motion through dark, viscous liquid. There were faces all around me, faces I would have given anything to see clearly, to cup in my hands, to kiss, but then I was snapping awake as dawn glimmered through the open blinds.

'Bad night?' Jasminder was standing in the doorway, yawning and sleep-rumpled in his pyjamas.

'I'm sorry if I woke you.'

He rubbed his fingers across his stubble. 'I'm on earlies anyway.' He came and sat beside me, taking my hands. 'This is going to be the one, Scottie. The one that sticks.'

I shook my head at him, tried to retrieve my hands, but he held on tight.

'I *know*,' he said. He linked his fingers through mine briefly and let go. 'You look sad.' He glanced up at the stars on the wall. 'This bloody room, eh? Try to look forward, not back.' He touched his index and middle fingers to his lips, then to my forehead, a gesture he had made thousands of times before but never had it made me feel so sad. 'Try to go out today if you feel up to it. It's not good for you sitting inside all the time. And can you finish sorting out the house insurance? It runs out soon.'

'You don't need to task me. I'm not one of your constables.'

He looked hurt. 'I'm not tasking you. But this stuff needs to get done so we can focus on the FET.'

I thought about pointing out that his use of the word *we* wasn't entirely accurate. It wouldn't be him having injections and mood swings and hot flushes. It wouldn't be him having the endometrial lining of his uterus scratched to try to give the embryo a better chance of grabbing on. It wouldn't be him having transvaginal ultrasounds or inserting progesterone pessaries. But I swallowed my words, knowing they were unfair. 'I'm perfectly capable of organizing my own day.'

He retreated, knowing he couldn't win this battle no matter what he said. Moments later, I heard him in the bathroom, humming a little tune as he shaved, and I felt a simultaneous rush of affection and irritation for his knack of moving on from an argument when I would be fuming for hours.

Try to look forward, not back, he had said. But looking forward, conceiving of a future, was exactly what I couldn't do. I put my hands on my stomach, pressing against the hollow space there, wondering how on earth I could tell him I wasn't sure if I could face any more fertility treatment.

★

I waited for Jasminder to go to work then fetched the box of IVF supplies from the cupboard under the stairs and sorted through the contents, reminding myself of what everything was for, what I should take when, what needed to go in the fridge. Alcohol wipes, needles and syringes, vials, hormone patches, a sharps box.

It was hard to pinpoint when my emotions about IVF had changed. Jasminder's sister Sukhi had been pregnant when we started our first cycle and I'd been stupidly, naïvely optimistic, fantasizing about our children growing up together, more like siblings than cousins. For ten glorious days after our first embryo transfer, I was what my fertility chatroom friends liked to call PUPO. Pregnant until proven otherwise. A few days before the pregnancy test that would confirm it one way or the other, I'd started to bleed. Jasminder came home from his nightshift to find me crouched on the bathroom floor, sobbing as my uterus shed the lining so carefully built up with hormones over the preceding weeks to give our embryo something to burrow into.

When Sukhi's daughter was born a few months later I chose two gifts. For our niece, Lily, a tiny sleepsuit, and for Sukhi, special new-mother bath soak with coconut, aloe and sweet orange essential oils. As I held Lily, I smiled at Jasminder to let him know I was okay. I truly believed my time would come. One day I would hold my baby in my arms, and all the griefs and hurts and secrets of the past would be healed. Now we had a photo of Lily beaming proudly in her school uniform on our mantelpiece, and another of her baby brother Indy, and Jasminder and I were drifting ever further apart in our equally toxic bubbles of hope and dread.

Seeing all the IVF paraphernalia spread across the kitchen counter gave me a dizzy, spaced-out feeling. Sweat prickled my skin, my breaths becoming fast and ragged. I knew what my friends in the online infertility support groups would say. *FET is nothing compared to a fresh cycle.* It was true there would be nowhere near as many injections as when I had had egg retrieval, but still I couldn't shake the dread that crushed me a little bit more every day as we counted down to the commencement of treatment. I repacked the box and shoved it back under the stairs, so I wouldn't have to look at it any more.

I decided to go for a run, to try and get some headspace. It was a cold, bright day, the rag end of winter ebbing into spring. The salt marshes at the edge of our little island city reeked of mud, rotten eggs and decaying wood but I didn't mind. It was a peaceful place, a merging point of land and sea, and I settled into a pace that matched the soft slap of the waves against the sea wall and the breeze rustling through the salt grass bordering the path.

The run was working, the exertion and the steady *crunch-crunch-crunch* rhythm of my trainers on the stony path helping to clear my mind. The tide was out, small channels of glittering water left trapped in the mudflats. I glanced back at the path to see two women coming towards me, each pushing a bundled-up toddler in an off-road buggy. One was Andrea, who had been my last childless friend before I lost her to motherhood. When she had got pregnant in her first month of trying, after years of maternal ambivalence, it had felt like the worst kind of betrayal.

I bought her gifts when her son was born, the same sleep-suit and mother's bath-soak combo I had chosen for Sukhi. Andrea unwrapped the bath soak and laughed. *It's a sweet thought but I barely have time to shower. You'll understand one day. Why don't you keep it? You're lucky you still have time for luxurious baths.* The thought of stopping for a friendly chat, of having to coo over her son, was too much to bear, so I pretended I hadn't seen them and swerved off the path, cutting across a marshy field.

I upped my pace, passing rippling pools of wading birds and sparrows flitting in and out of wind-stunted trees, trying to outrun the sensation of dread that was sweeping throughout my body. A swan, its neck feathers stained green by the algae in the water, tracked my movement along the rim of its pool, making sure I knew I wasn't welcome.

We had kept our most recent attempt at frozen embryo transfer a secret. And there had been something, a will-o'-the-wisp that lingered, a paler than pale second line on the home pregnancy test. We held our breath for a week until the blood test, which was inconclusive, so we waited another week for another test, and it was confirmed as what was known in fertility chatroom parlance as a Big Fat Negative. On the same day, Jasminder was promoted to sergeant, and I had gone to the corner shop to buy a bottle of cheap sparkling wine. We sat on the sofa drinking it in silence, the only noise the fizzing of bubbles in the champagne flutes. I kept the little white stick with its precious second line hidden in a trinket box, and when Jasminder was at work, I would take it out and stare at it, as if doing so could transform the line into something tangible, something more than a ghost flickering into my dreams.

A few days later, the episodes had started. Jasminder came down from the bathroom one evening to find me wedged into the space between the sofa and the coffee-table, shaking and making a noise somewhere between screaming and howling. He called an ambulance. The hospital attached sensors to my head to monitor my brain activity and gave me a CT scan to rule out organic causes, and none were found. I didn't have epilepsy or a brain tumour. I was referred to a psychiatrist, a softly spoken middle-aged woman, who seemed pleased to have discovered such an interesting case. *Sometimes these symptoms, these psychogenic episodes, can be a response to severe trauma. If you were involved in or witnessed a dangerous or frightening event, your episodes could be a response to that.*

I had shaken my head, resolute in my denial. *You mean like PTSD? No, nothing like that has ever happened to me.* I didn't think to mention the line on the white stick, or my other will-o'-the-wisps. I didn't think to mention my lost past. I didn't think to mention the secret I carried deep inside the empty hollows of my body, the secret even Jasminder didn't know.

The psychiatrist prescribed medication to block the adrenaline whizzing around my bloodstream, to add to the anti-depressants I'd been taking since our first IVF failure, and referred me to a mindfulness counsellor, who taught me techniques to try to control the emotions that caused the shaking. *Count your breaths, Scottie. One-breathe-in, two-breathe-out, three-breathe-in.*

A snowy egret rose up startled, blending with the pale sky.

I was running fast, as fast as I could now, but still I couldn't think about anything other than the possibility of another failure, another loss. I didn't have room in my heart for any more ghosts. I'd already had a transvaginal ultrasound to assess my uterine cavity. In a few days I would start down-regulation – daily injections to suppress my natural ovulation – then oestrogen patches to help thicken my uterus lining, progesterone pessaries and then, if the thawed embryo was viable, it would be transferred into my uterus. My support-group friends had affectionate names for their embryos, frozen or fresh. *Frosties. Embabies. Snowbeans.* But I couldn't do that. Losing another embryo would be bad enough but the thought of losing a *snowbean* was unbearable.

I almost decided, at that moment, to tell Jasminder I couldn't carry on, but then I remembered our most recent visit to see Sukhi, Jasminder playing with Lily and Indy in the snow. He had come inside, held my face with freezing hands and whispered, *It'll be us soon, Scottie. Don't give up hope. We're almost there.* How could I deny him another chance? I had run almost a full circle around the marsh. Andrea and her friend were sitting on a bench overlooking the harbour, eyes glued to their phones as they gently rolled the buggies back and forth. I sprinted behind them, praying they wouldn't turn around, and jogged up the stony embankment that kept the sea from the main road.

When I was far enough away that I was certain they wouldn't see me, I sat on the sea wall, inhaling the muddy, sulphurous stink, staring out at seaweed, fragments of rotting boats, shopping trolleys, tyres, gulls swooping down, the incoming tide streaming across the mudflats, and I wept.

3

Charlotte: Snow

My first memory after going to live with Helen and Phil was waking up to snow. Phil bounced around with impatient excitement, as if he were the child, not me. Helen made me eat a bowl of Ready Brek, fussing over my hat and mittens, tugging on my wellies, fastening the toggles of my coat over my hated back brace. I stood on the kitchen doorstep, taking in the luminous ghost-light, the slight muffling of every sound, as if the world were suddenly not quite real.

Will the snow hurt us?

Phil's beaming face crumpled a little. *No*, he said, through frosty breath. *It won't hurt. I mean, you don't want to get a snowball in the face, but other than that . . .* . He took my hand and we stepped into the immaculate whiteness together.

By the time Helen called me in to warm up with a hot chocolate, we had made a snowman and kicked through a snowdrift by the far fence. I turned to look as I went inside and saw my footprints all over the formerly pristine blanket of whiteness. It was the first time, looking at the pattern my boots had left behind, that I conceived of having a past, a presence in the world that stretched back in history. Even if I couldn't remember what that past was.

4

The Woman and the Girl: Sand Horse

The day before they flee south across the Hollow Sea in the fishing boat with a mermaid painted on its deck, the woman and the girl sit on the breakwater at sunrise, legs dangling, eating buttered saffron buns. Something is coming. The woman knows. She pushes the knowledge down, deep down alongside her darkest secrets. It has become a particular skill of hers, honed since she came to this little island, to pretend bad things aren't happening. The girl feels it too, an intuition of something important waiting just around the corner. But her inkling has none of the foreboding of the woman's, so perhaps what she is sensing is only her birthday tomorrow, when she won't be seven any more.

The girl licks breadcrumbs and butter from her saffron-stained fingers. *May I go to the beach, please?* She goes down to the shoreline most days at low tide to collect treasure thrown up by the storms. Ossified driftwood, starfish, mermaid's purses, occasionally a dried-up seahorse or a whelk-egg husk. The woman always permits it, yet there is a daily ritual, a dance of sorts, that they must complete before the request is granted.

What's the rule, Little Fairy?

The girl dislikes it when the woman calls her Fairy. She prefers her given name, but for four years now the woman has called her only by nicknames, has forbidden the girl to speak her true name aloud. *Don't go beyond the tideline,* says the girl. *Stay on the dry side of the sand.*

The woman frowns. *What else, Fairy?*

The girl is bored of the dance, but she answers anyway. *The sea can burn. Stay away from the water.* The woman nods her assent, watching as the girl hopscotches up the slipway, her satchel a flash of red bumping against her hip.

The girl scrambles down to the beach, walking along the line of detritus left by the tide, taking care to stick to the dry side of the sand, even though the tide is out. *Stay away from the sea, it burns,* is a rule she has had drummed into her for as long as she can remember, for as long as she has been forbidden to say her own name. But in the last few months a seedling of doubt has grown in her belly, a tiny green shoot of disbelief unfurling, stretching up to the light.

She casts aside her doubt, content to wander barefoot along the soft, dry sand, searching for treasure. What does she find? A peach stone, a blob of red wax and a cuttlefish bone. Later, she will hide them in the curing house but, for now, she simply brushes off the sand and pushes them into her satchel.

She notices something further down the beach, an object on the shiny wet sand close to the sea. Something much larger than sea treasure, but it's hard to see what exactly. It blends with the sand, the sun bouncing off its surface. To go closer would require her to step onto the wet sand, a clear breach of the rules. But what if the object is a stranded porpoise, or a lost seal pup? They had cared for a seal pup once, when the girl was tiny. She remembers its fishy, musky, fearful scent, the crust of blood on its wounded flipper.

She squats on the dry sand, squinting into the haze towards the unknown object. She's a good girl, has never broken the rules on purpose. But accidents happen and there had been a time, not so long ago, when she had found herself in the sea through no fault of her own and had thought she was drowning and burning at the same time. But she hadn't drowned and after, when she had lain in the thin, winter sun, trying to dry her clothes before going home, she had observed the reddened, tender skin on her arms and legs. Wondered if she might not have scraped them against a rock. Wondered if the sea hadn't burnt her after all.

But the woman's warnings, repeated constantly over the years, have done their work, and the thought of deliberately breaking the rules makes the girl's stomach hurt. That shape on the sand, though, down by the surf. It calls to her. She shades her eyes with her hand and scans the beach, to make sure the woman hasn't followed, then rocks forward, brushing her fingertips along the sand on the forbidden side of the tideline, ready to snap her fingers back. Nothing bad happens. She stands, balancing on one leg, straddling the tideline, pushing her big toe into the damp sand. Still it doesn't burn. She holds her breath and steps across the tideline.

The wet sand feels damp, claggy, different from the silky dry sand she's used to. She takes another step, enjoying the sensation of the sand collapsing beneath her feet. She glances back at her footprints. She finds it pleasing to have left her mark. She allows her feet to sink into the sand a little, shifting her weight from heel to toe.

She's close enough now, to see. The object is not a seal or a porpoise but a horse, sculpted out of sand. Sculpture is not a concept the girl is familiar with, but she understands carving. Mr Sam, who used to bring the groceries by boat every fortnight, once gave her a doll whittled out of drift-wood. It had no face. *I'd get rid of it, if I were you,* the woman had told her, so the girl had knelt beside the tideline, stretching her arms over to the forbidden side, and buried it in the damp sand.

The horse is like that, whittled out of sand but, unlike her featureless doll, it has a face and mane, and wide, snort-ing nostrils. It rears up out of the sand, its forelegs shaped as if kicking, its tail fanning out across the beach, its haunches disappearing into the ground. Keeping a weather eye on the plashing waves, just a few feet away, she circles the horse, observing the smoothness of its flank, the sharp-ness of its hoofs, its pricking ears. She wonders how it would be possible to create such a thing, and who might have made it.

The tide is crawling in. It doesn't rush. It tickles her feet. Like the wet sand, it doesn't burn. She likes the coolness of it, likes the sensation of the sand being sucked away from beneath her heels. She completes her circuit of the horse and crouches beside it.

What if she touched it? Would the sand crumble away? She cranes her neck to get a better view of the beach, her stomach sick at the thought of what the woman will do if she catches her, but she is alone. She risks the briefest, gentlest of touches to the horse's neck. The sea is swirling over her ankles now, licking the hem of her dungarees. She feels the urge to lie down next to the horse, to squeeze her body up alongside it, to brush its coat with her fingers and nuzzle her face in its neck. She imagines she can hear the sounds of it snorting and whinnying in the urgent waves.

She can smell salt and sand, her nose to the horse's neck. But something else too, an animal scent, musky, like the seal pup, perhaps, but fresher, a scent that quivers tautly, a scent ready to bolt, to spring away. The tide is rushing around them, soaking her dungarees and hair. Does the horse move? Does it lift itself onto its knees? She tightens her hand in its mane, imagines her fingers are entwined in coarse hair. Will she be able to ride it? Where will it take her?

So many questions but one thing is certain. The sea doesn't burn.

The woman is harvesting limpets at rock pools exposed by the low tide, the spring warmth on her neck and arms. The tide is coming back now, swishing in, flooding into the outer pools, filling crevices, pulling back. As she works, she thinks about the girl, so long a cuckoo in her nest, and the cake she will make for her birthday, dozens of thin layers cooked one at a time in a pan, sandwiched together with buttercream, the only way to make a cake worth eating in this godforsaken place. She thinks about the gift she plans for the girl. An unusual pink spiralled shell the woman found while out kelping into which she has drilled a tiny hole and threaded a leather cord. It will be the girl's first piece of jewellery. She tries not to think about the other anniversaries tomorrow will mark, the losses she has tried to carry for them both. The woman pauses in her work, her knees and back creaking as she stands up. She is not old, but the harshness of the place has settled into her bones over the decades and there are needlepoints of pain along her spine as she uncurls.

She scans the beach where the girl should still be hunting for treasure. There is no sign of her. At first, the woman is not concerned. The girl has probably become bored and gone back to the cottage or headed up to the clifftop to pick sea campion. Then she spots a smudge of red, the girl's satchel, down by the surf, surrounded by the frilled edges of the incoming waves. For a few moments, the woman is utterly still as she tries to make sense of it. The girl is in the water. She drops her pail of limpets and runs.

A horse made of sand. The girl lying in the surf beside it, her arms around its neck. Horse and girl seem to shimmer in and out of focus. The tide is rushing in. The woman curses herself. She shouldn't have allowed the girl so much freedom, but she has never truly believed this day would come. She stumbles into the surf, grabbing the girl, pulling her up, knowing she is pinching the tender, fleshy part of the girl's arm, not caring, shoving her back onto the beach, to safety. The woman kicks and stamps at the horse, sand flying everywhere. The girl weeps as it is destroyed. *What have I told you? WHAT HAVE I TOLD YOU?* The woman continues to trample on the horse, and now the tide is helping her, breaking it apart, sucking it into the surf.

Finally satisfied, the woman retreats up the beach, grabs

the girl's wrist, drags her to the tideline. *What is the rule?* *WHAT IS THE RULE?*

The girl is inconsolable, barely able to choke back her tears enough to reply, *Not beyond the tideline,* through snotty, snuffling sobs. There is a long moment of silence when they stare at each other, the woman's face suffused with fury, the girl's tear- and snot-streaked. And then the girl says, softly, calmly, *But the sea doesn't burn. You lied.*

The woman raises her hand. She has never struck the girl before, but there's a moment, agonizingly long, when they both think she might. The woman lowers her arm and says, in a tight, angry voice, *Go. Back. To. Your. Bed. And. Do. Not. Move. From. There.* The girl flees.

In the morning, the woman hauls the girl out of bed at daybreak, throws a few belongings into the red satchel, bundles her, sleepy and recalcitrant, along the slipway to the little fishing boat. The girl doesn't even have time to collect her treasures from the curing house. She stands on deck, looking back at the island of her birth, as a dark, beautiful storm rolls in from the west.

5

Scottie: An Island of St Hía

Jasminder was on the sofa in the living area of our family-friendly open-plan space, watching a documentary, and I was in the kitchen sitting at the breakfast bar trying to sort out the house insurance, when I saw the photo of the island for the first time. I typed the name of our insurance company, Heatherlands Insurance Association, into the search engine, and among the resulting company logos and pictures of shiny nuclear families outside their recently insured homes, there it was, a tiny thumbnail image of grey and green.

Even then, even before I expanded it, I felt drawn to the image by something more than idle curiosity. I clicked on the photo, enlarging it to fill my laptop screen. It was a scan of a photograph taken from an aeroplane, in the vintagey blue-yellow tones of the 1970s, an island jutting up from a furious ocean. A perfect semi-circle of sand rose to a deep, grassy slope on one side, on the other a craggy cliff tipping at a precarious angle over the sea, its highest edges softened by swirls of mist. And, at the confluence of sand and grass, a tiny grey smudge: a solitary dwelling nestled between the sea and the slopes, dwarfed by the looming cliffs. The caption read: *An island of St Hía*. The name sounded familiar, but I'd have been hard-pressed to find it on a map.

I zoomed in, focusing on the stone cottage. The image was blurred at this size, but I could still picture it clearly in my mind. The rip-rap of stones in the wall, the moss-skimmed roof slates, a front door with flaking paint and sea holly, a garden nestled between the house and the slopes to shield it from the elements. My heart fluttered. I told myself to stop it. My back ached along the site of my surgical scar, which hadn't happened for a long time. I arched my spine to relieve the pain.

'Did you know that, Scottie?' Jasminder called from the sofa. 'About the British concentration camps in the Boer War?'

I couldn't reply. I could barely even breathe. The little cottage on my laptop screen was like a concrete block hurtling through the abstract jumble of my forgotten life, the life before I was matched with Helen and Phil and delivered to them, a fey and silent child, her body contorted into a back brace, her thumb glued in her mouth. Jasminder and his documentary slipped away. I could hear the steady beat of the sea. And music, a piano, the melody of a lullaby harmonizing with the hushing waves. A woman singing. On my tongue, the taste of sand, peaches, rain and salt. Jasminder swivelled round on the sofa.

'You look like death warmed up, love. Go to bed.'

There was a time when I would have shown Jasminder the photograph, shared with him the effect it had had on me. But I knew what he would say. That I was deflecting because I was worried about the FET. That it wasn't the first time I had manufactured half-memories to fill the gaps in my past. There was the school trip to the Brecon

Beacons when I was twelve: I'd become mesmerized by the rip-rap placement of the rocks in a cairn and almost got left behind. And on honeymoon with Jasminder in Truro, I'd eaten a saffron-spiced bun and burst into tears.

My occasional meanderings into an imagined past exasperated Jasminder. When I'd told him that my memories consisted of only a few scattered impressions of my foster family's dog and being taken to meet Helen and Phil at the contact centre, he'd been sceptical. *Nine years old, right?* he'd said. *You were nine when you went to Helen? And everything before that is just a blank? That's not healthy, Scottie. Shouldn't you have been given a Lifebook with all that information in it? You need to stop crying over saffron buns and find out the truth.*

He was probably right, but the one time I broached with Helen the idea of writing to the adoption agency the expression on her face induced a guilt trip of monumental proportions, even as she said, through a rictus grin, *Of course you must do what you think is best, Charlotte.* On the way home in the car Jasminder had asked me if I was seriously going to wait until Helen was dead before I looked for my birth family, and I had laughed ruefully and told him that was the plan. I wasn't being completely honest. It was partly about not upsetting Helen, but I was also afraid. Afraid there was a good reason why I'd blocked out the past. Afraid there'd be something in my history – alcoholism, psychosis, Huntington's disease, criminal tendencies – that would mean I shouldn't have children, or I wouldn't be a good mother. And I'd been a mother in my heart for so long that that possibility was too terrible to contemplate. So I never looked, not because ignorance was bliss but because I feared a terrible truth.

No, I decided. I would keep this discovery to myself.

'I'm fine.' I tore my eyes away from the laptop screen and smiled at Jasminder in what I hoped was a reassuring manner. 'Just a bit tired.'

'Have an early night, then. I'll clean up down here.'

My cowardice in never looking for my birth family hadn't stopped me wondering who they were, where I was from, why they had given me up. Something about the photograph of the island nagged at me, a thread pulling and twisting deep inside. Could this really be the place I was from or was I, as Jasminder would think, just searching for something to occupy my mind other than the looming FET?

I should have gone to bed then, as Jasminder had suggested, and tried to get some sleep, but my eyes drifted back to the laptop screen. The website, which consisted solely of images of islands from across the world, had no further information or contact details. My left hand twitched, a warning I should shut down the laptop and meditate or read a book or wash up and focus on the shape, scent and feel of the bubbles, the way my mindfulness counsellor had suggested. Instead I opened a new tab, searched for St Hía and discovered it was an archipelago in the North Atlantic, a string of fifty or more islands and skerries, nearly all of which were uninhabited but for birds and seals. On the map, the archipelago was a delicate bracelet of green strung out across a desert of blue.

St Mertheriana, Lugh, Sorrow, St Rozel, St Columba. I

studied the names of the islands, wondering which was the one in the photograph. *Eleven of the islands are known to be inhabited and can be usefully divided into two main groups: the 'on' islands, constituting Lugh (pronounced* Luck), *Sorrow and St Mertheriana, which have infrastructures of schools and medical clinics, and the more remote and scattered 'off' islands some of which have permanent populations of less than ten souls.* My arm jerked backwards. Not a good sign, but I was nearly at the end of the page. *Colonized at various times by Cornish, Scottish, Irish and Portuguese settlers, the influences of all these cultures are evident right up to the modern day.* The twitches moved to my upper body, intensifying, as if an invisible hand was reaching inside me and yanking on an invisible rope. I tried to track the finger of my right hand across the mousepad, to shut it all down, but I couldn't move. It was too late. The best I could hope for now was not to make too much noise. But the howling started a few seconds later.

My very own version of not-quite-PTSD. I thought I'd got it under control, that it wasn't a problem any more, but now it was happening again. The sound was ear-splitting, but also physically painful, ripping me apart inside. The invisible cord yanked me again and I fell off the stool, my laptop landing in an inverted V-shape beside me.

'Scottie. Fuck, Scottie.'

Jasminder knelt beside me, trying to take my hands, but the howls were still tearing through my body, jerking my arms. He lay down next to me, pressing his body against mine.

'Hush,' he said. 'Hush.' His breath warm on my cheek.

It seemed to last for ever, but eventually I fell still and silent. My chest hurt. I propped myself up with my back against the kitchen cupboards, counting my breaths. Jasminder squeezed my hand, then went to the fridge and poured me a glass of water from the filter jug, his face tight with concern.

'What brought that on?'

It was a question with an obvious answer. My first episode had occurred after the failure of our last FET, and now we were starting the cycle all over again and I was full of dread. Except that wasn't it, was it? Because I hadn't even been thinking about the FET when it had happened. I'd been looking at a photograph online, a blurred image of that beautiful, remote island, and all I could think about was the hushing of the waves and the taste of sand and peaches on my tongue.

'Who knows? But it's stopped now. Did I smash the laptop?'

Jasminder picked it up and inspected it. 'No. Just a tiny chip in the plastic at the edge.' He gave me his hand, pulling me up.

'Would you mind taking it upstairs when you go?' I said. 'It needs charging. I'm going to watch TV for a bit.'

I didn't want to risk the temptation of looking at the photograph again.

'No problem,' he said. 'Don't stay up too late.'

He ruffled my hair and went up, snapping the laptop closed and taking it with him. I sat on the sofa, channel-hopping with the sound turned down, thinking about St Hía, and its mystery island with mist-curled cliffs, the little stone cottage perched on a stack of rock and grass in the middle of the ocean.

6

The Woman and the Girl:
The Mother-of-Pearl Comb

A few months before the girl lies down beside the sand horse and discovers that the sea doesn't burn, the woman finds white horse hairs on the girl's dungarees as she gathers the dirty clothes for washing. I imagine her sniffing the hairs, which smell of salt, rubbing them between her thumb and forefinger, their coarse texture unmistakable. A sensation in her stomach she can't quite identify. Fear, perhaps, coiled in a tight ball. She pushes the fear down, blows the horse hairs away into the breeze.

She doesn't think about the horse hairs, what they might mean, as she stamps on the dirty clothes in the washtub, agitating the sudsy water, soap bubbles glistening on the sea-spurrey growing around the cottage. She doesn't think about them when she forages for sea lettuce, laying it out on plastic crates to dry in the thin winter sun, or when she repairs the well-cover damaged last summer in a storm. She doesn't think about them when she sits down at her piano and tries to write a song, filling her mind with music so there is no space to think about who might have come to their little island with a horse, or what it means that the girl had contact with it, or if they will be returning.

She plays a few notes on the yellowing keys, but they don't please her. The song, a draft of the lyrics already scribbled down in her urgent, haphazard script, is based on a local legend about a woman who married a blackfish. She can feel the beauty and tragedy of the song, can create the sense of it perfectly inside herself, yet she struggles to translate it onto the keys. *I must go down to the seashore, to where the blackfish throng.* Sometimes melodies flow easily from her fingers, but this song will have to be coaxed, turned inside out and upside down, revised again and again, and she will probably never be content with it. *On one night at midsummer, to hear my husband's song.* Perhaps it doesn't matter. There was a time when she created music for music's sake, but today the song is only a means to an end, a way to block out the thoughts running through her mind. To forget the past and the future too.

The woman hopes that the mystery horse hairs will join the list of things she never thinks about. Her error in taking the girl to the on-islands for the blackfish hunt, into the den of gossips. Poor old Sam's book of folktales. Uffa Denbigh's warning that one day *they* would come for the girl. The day she had considered letting the girl float to Heaven on the ocean waves. The face of her dead husband, her jeans stiffened with his blood. *He left me when he drowned, his soul a blackfish come.* Her creativity is faltering, rupturing, tearing open spaces for her thoughts to intrude. *I bore him seven children, in mists of song and sea.*

The girl is sitting beneath the kitchen table, playing with a macramé set, threading tiny cowrie shells onto a length of twine. *Little Fairy, come and sit by me.* The girl hops up onto the piano stool, her legs pressing against the woman's thin dress, her mottled feet dangling above the

32

pedals. *Curve your hands. Up, up, like a cat stretching. Remember how I showed you before? Good.* The woman lays her own hands over the girl's, pressing each key down. An old song from the woman's homeland, carried close to her heart. The rhythm is faltering, but they manage at least to play the notes in the right order. *The moonlit sky was bright as day and rippled like the icy waves.* They sing together as they play, the girl repeating the words and notes until she remembers them. *Treacherous lies, whispered echoes, sealed the bargain on our sorrows.*

Later, when the girl is asleep, the woman slips outside into the darkening evening, across the pebbly grass, past the pink stars of stonecrop sprouting between rocks, to the curing house her husband had built brick by brick during the first blissful weeks of their marriage, when she had spent hours watching him work, drinking in his beauty. But she's not thinking about him now. She's thinking about the horse hairs and the people who must have intruded onto their island to bring them here. Will they try to take the girl? What are the risks of running away? Both of them out on the water for hours, vulnerable, in that rickety boat. Where would they even escape to?

She weaves between the last few ribbons of black flesh hanging from the ceiling and locates the cubby hole the girl thinks is a secret, the place where she hides her little stash of sea fripperies. The woman hopes to discover only seashells, dried-up starfish and crumbling whelk eggs, to reassure herself with the innocence of this childish hoard. But there, near the top, disguised beneath fragments of smooth-edged sea glass and a jumble of whorled shells, is something. The woman has seen it before. In another life she had owned it, treasured it. All the breath leaves her body. A decorative hair comb made from ivory mother-of-pearl. The last time she had seen it had been the day of the girl's birth, the day the girl's father had died. She had thought it gone for ever to the bottom of the ocean and now it's back, mocking her. With shaking hands, she pushes it into the cubby hole, arranges the shells and glass on top, and runs to the beach. She vomits on the sand, half choking, half crying, getting it in her hair. She goes to the water's edge to wash it.

The hushing of the waves usually soothes her, but tonight the sea sounds sinister, as if many voices are whispering the girl's name. In the cottage, the girl is peaceful, her deep, even breaths calming the woman. This, I imagine, is the moment she realizes the depth of her love for the girl, surrendering to it only in the moment it is threatened. She puts her hands over her ears to try to block out the whispering, but she can still hear it in the cup of her palms, like the sound of the sea in a shell. She knows that, wherever she goes now, the voices that call the girl's name will follow her and she will have no peace.

7

Scottie: Surfing

Jasminder's shift pattern had switched to lates, so on the day my down-regulation injections were due to start, I was up first. I'd deliberately avoided opening the laptop since the other night, knowing I wouldn't be able to resist looking at the photo of the island, and not wanting to trigger another episode, but I still hadn't sorted out the house insurance, so I sat on the sofa and fired it up. I ran my thumb along the crack in the casing, caused when I'd knocked it off the kitchen counter. I supposed I was lucky not to have ruined it. It took only a few clicks to renew the house insurance, not much of a distraction, and Jasminder still wasn't awake.

Looking at the photo of the island again would be a bad idea. I opened the browser history, the website still listed, a few lines below the insurance company. I moved my finger across the mousepad, the cursor hovering over the link. I knew I should focus, try to give all my energy to the FET because, as much as I was dreading it, I didn't want to fail Jasminder or our remaining embryos or the mother I still was in my heart. I opened the webpage, clicked on the photo. *An island of St Hía.* The cottage, that tiny grey smudge. The misty cliffs, the churning seas. The taste of peaches and sand on my tongue. My arm twitched. *One-breathe-in, two-breathe-out.* I opened a new tab, removing the island from my line of vision, and searched again for the St Hía archipelago, ignoring the pages I'd already read, scanning the results for any new information I could find, anything that might tell me the name of the island in the photograph.

About a third of the way down the page I found something I hadn't seen before. The Marine Mammal Protection Society website, a thumbnail image of seals on a rocky beach and the text, *St Hía archipelago: volunteers needed for seal survey.* I clicked on the link to open it, thinking it might have the names of some of the more remote islands where the seals presumably lived, perhaps the name of what I was already beginning to think of as 'my island', and was surprised to see the call for volunteers was recent, just a few months ago, the seal survey they were conducting starting in a few days. The article quoted a marine biologist, Dr Ellie McMullen, from the University of Adelaide, explaining that she'd been running annual seal surveys on the archipelago for almost a decade and every year she needed a team of volunteers to help her with the count. No experience needed. There was none of the information I'd hoped for, perhaps another picture of my mystery island or a map I could try to match to my photograph, only pictures of seals lolling around on beaches and a smiling, blonde-haired woman I presumed was Dr McMullen.

I clicked on the photograph out of idle curiosity more than anything and it opened a blank email, from me to her, the cursor blinking, waiting for me to fill the white space with words. What if I sent her the photo of the mystery island? If she was there every year counting seals, she might be familiar with the more remote islands in the archipelago and be able to tell me which one it was. I typed a few habitually apologetic words. *Sorry to bother you . . . could I possibly ask a question . . . photo attached . . .* and clicked send.

I was a million miles away, thinking about my mystery island and with half an eye on my email inbox for a reply, so I didn't even notice Jasminder had come downstairs.

'Sorry,' he said. 'Didn't mean to make you jump.'

I slammed the laptop lid shut. 'Insurance is sorted.'

'Always good to know,' he said, going through to the kitchen and pouring himself a glass of orange juice, 'that we're okay to burn the house down.'

Jasminder sounded upbeat, happy, which only made me more miserable. The box of IVF supplies was on the counter and he opened it, busying himself arranging syringes, vials and alcohol wipes.

'I can do that myself,' I said, sounding harsher than I'd intended.

'Don't shut me out, please. We're in this together.'

He was right, and in the early days it had felt like we were a team, however bad things got. But now I just felt so lonely with it all, no matter how supportive he tried to be, and I knew I'd never be able to explain it to him.

'I just meant I have to do it myself anyway when you're on earlies or days so it's better if I do this one too, to get used to it again.'

Jasminder watched me as I cleaned my stomach with an alcohol wipe and drew medication up into the syringe. I hoped he didn't notice the faint tremor in my hands. I didn't know why I was shaking. I'd done this hundreds of times before. I pinched the flesh on the lower part of my stomach between my thumb and forefinger, plunged the needle in and depressed the syringe. It hurt more than I remembered. A pinprick of blood flowered on my reddened skin. Jasminder passed me a cotton-wool ball and I pressed it against the wound.

'Painful?'

'A little.'

I tried to think back to the first time I'd done it. How full of hope I'd been, despite my fear of somehow getting the injections wrong. Now I felt nothing but dread at the prospect of another failure.

'Just have faith, Scottie,' said Jasminder, dropping the used syringe and needle into the sharps box. 'I know I keep saying this, but I feel so strongly this is going to be the one that sticks.'

He saved me from having to reply by kissing me on the forehead. It had begun again, weeks of surfing on hope and dread. I didn't know if I could stand it.

I waited for Jasminder to go to work, then checked my emails and saw that Dr McMullen had already replied. *Sorry, no clue which island it is. There are literally dozens of islands in the archipelago and we only survey the southern ones. But, hey, you could always come and count seals with us next week and maybe figure it out while you're here? Plenty of locals with more knowledge than me. We've got space. I'm dropping huge hints here. We honestly do need a few more willing bodies.*

I reread the information on Dr McMullen's webpage. Counting seals sounded like a fun thing to do, but I couldn't just go running off to the middle of nowhere, no matter how strongly I was drawn to the island in the photo. No matter how much I wanted to get away from needles and toxic hope and will-o'-the-wisps. The cottage, the looming cliffs, the pale strip of sand. I couldn't go. Of course I couldn't go.

Jasminder was making a chicken sandwich after his late shift, still in his half-blues, his face full of earnest concentration.

'I need to tell you something,' I said.

He glanced up from the bread board. 'Are you okay? Are you having side-effects from the meds?'

'I thought I could do this. I wanted to do it, for you. But I can't.'

Jasminder put down his jar of mayonnaise. 'Can't do what? You're not making any sense.'

'IVF. FET. Fertility treatment. This.' I gestured at the family-sized room we were standing in. 'Any of it. It has to stop.'

He blinked at me. 'It's just the hormones talking,' he said. 'It's always worst in the first few days. You'll feel better in the morning.'

'No. I won't.'

He stared at me for a long moment, then came towards me and put his hands on my shoulders. 'I'm sorry. We can pause it if you're not feeling up to it right now. Pick things up in a few weeks, or a few months. We can phone the clinic in the morning and −'

'No,' I said, my voice cracking. 'I want to stop for good.'

I watched his face, watched the tightness blooming around his eyes.

'I know it's hard,' he said. 'But we have such a great chance this time with the new protocol. And Dr Lakewell says the endo scratch has had very positive results with patients who have a similar history to us. This is the one, Scottie. This time it's going to work. Just this round, please. Then I promise we'll stop if you still want to.'

I felt like I couldn't breathe. I twisted my body away more dramatically than I'd intended, releasing myself from his grip, his hands left suspended in mid-air, half clenched. He unfurled them, his long fingers that I loved, and showed me his palms, a gesture of appeasement, even though he was the wounded one.

'I'm not trying to hurt you, Jasminder, but I just can't handle another failure.'

I didn't have the words to explain about all the ghosts I was carrying around in my heart. How I didn't have room for any more. How could I expect him to understand when he didn't even know about the ghost that weighed the heaviest of them all?

'Not having another round, Scottie, is the one way to guarantee a failure. We have three embryos waiting for us. Let's talk about it in the morning when you've had some sleep. I'm on a rest day tomorrow. We can go out somewhere nice.'

I twitched, from the centre of my solar plexus. We paused, waiting to see if it would develop into a full-blown episode, but it didn't.

'I'm catching a flight in the morning.'

I watched his face flicker as he absorbed this information.

'A flight where?'

'The Outer Hebrides. Then a ferry to St Hía. It's a chain of islands in the Atlantic. I've volunteered to help with a seal survey. It's all arranged.'

'I don't . . . What? You're going on holiday? Why would you book a holiday in the middle of IVF?'

'It's not a holiday. It's just something I have to do.'

Jasminder reached forward as if to grab my shoulders again, or shake me, but then changed his mind. 'Okay. I see what this is. It's another bullshit fantasy about your past, isn't it? Like the time on our honeymoon or when we went to that cave in Wales. Wouldn't it be easier to write to the adoption agency and, bonus, not wreck our last chance of parenthood for the sake of some stupid pipe dream?'

He snapped the lid back on the olive spread.

'You've got it all wrong,' I said. 'The pipe dream is this. This house with its nursery and family room. My job with its maternity benefits and flexi-working. The pipe dream is us.'

'And when you've finished counting seals, what then? Are you coming back? Will we start up treatment again?'

I was silent in response.

'You're being so cold, Scottie. This isn't you.'

I didn't know if Jasminder was right, because I didn't know who I was any more. Perhaps there was another me, a pre-infertility me, who was kinder. But I had lost her. We both had.

'You know what?' he said, in the measured voice he used for arguing that usually infuriated me but now was just making me sad. 'If you do this, you're really only hurting yourself.'

He went upstairs, leaving his sandwich behind. I should have followed him and told him I was sorry for hurting him. I should have told him I was hanging on by a thread and couldn't risk letting go. I should have told him there were things about me he didn't know. I should have told him about the secret ghost in my heart. But I sat at the kitchen counter, letting a cup of peppermint tea go cold, listening to the scuff of his feet on the carpet, the clank of the pipes as he ran the shower, the soft thud of the wardrobe door.

8

Charlotte: The Beach

Helen always believed I was afraid of the ocean, but the truth is I dreamt about it my whole life. Not the treacly brownish-grey sea that enclosed our island city, or the polite waves of tourist beaches, but an ocean that beat with a wild, inconstant heart. I had seen a lot of seas and oceans in my life, some wilder than others. A few had called to me, but in the end, I had found all of them wanting.

Helen's mistake had been understandable because on the one and only occasion they took me to the coast – a long and hot bank-holiday day trip to celebrate the removal of my back brace – I screamed bloody murder when they tried to get me to go any closer to the water than the shingle car park abutting the beach. They had bundled me back into Phil's rusting Austin Allegro for the endless journey home, snaking along A-roads crammed with glittering cars, Helen chain-eating barley sugars in a furious rhythm of *crunch-crack-swallow*.

Phil was his usual jokey self, as if the trip hadn't been an unmitigated disaster, but I saw something else in the line of his shoulders, in the faint tension of his movements as he checked mirrors, indicated, changed gears. Something close to sadness, but deeper and more complex than my just-turned-ten-year-old self could grasp. Six months later he would be dead, robbed of the chance to be thought of as my dad, to stop being just Phil, and I sometimes wonder whether in that moment he knew he never would, and that was why his sadness leaked out through the set of his shoulders, no matter how many jokes he told.

It hadn't been the sea that had frightened me as I stood by the neatly spaced white stones marking the transition from car park to sea wall. The saltiness in the air, the crying gulls, the rhythmic beating of the waves on the beach had sent a thrill through me and I had jumped out of the car as soon as Phil had pulled into the parking space. What had horrified me, what had stopped me jumping down from the sea wall onto the beach, was the sand. Immediately beneath the wall the sand was dry and pale, billowy, jumbled with day trippers and windbreaks and beach towels pinned down with books. But beyond that the receding tide had left a vast swathe of wet, rippled sludge. Children were playing in it, building sandcastles, digging moats, and the sand stuck to them darkly, clinging to their legs and swimming costumes. That was what prompted my screaming fit, followed by a bout of inconsolable sobbing. The thought of getting that wet sand on me, of it touching my skin . . .

But the sea. It had spoken to me from beyond the uncrossable chasm of wet sand. Bluish grey, shifting, twinkling, vast. I could hear its call. It stayed in my ears for months, woke me in the night, permeated my dreams. Over the years, I came to understand that the sea I had glimpsed on the other side of that vast, rippling expanse of sand was not the ocean of my dreams, not the ocean that beat with a wild, inconstant heart. But it had woken me, alerted me to the presence of something – a different ocean – buried deep in my past.

9

The Girl: The Whirlpool Cave

The girl has a secret friend. I have the clearest picture of him in my mind. A skinny, curly-haired, knobbly-kneed boy who arrives dressed in stolen clothes and with his hair full of sand. He visits the girl only when the woman is busy, when she's stamping around in the washtub or scrubbing the kitchen floor. How he arrives on the little island is a mystery, but the girl looks forward to his visits. It is during one of the boy's trips to the island that the girl gets the horse hairs on her dungarees and the tiny seed of doubt about things she has believed for as long as she can remember is planted.

On the day of the horse hairs, she boulder-hops across a winter wet beach, breaking the cardinal rule about staying away from the water in spirit if not by the letter of the law. She keeps one hand on the cliff face for balance, the rocks slippery with bladderwrack and the bright green algae she knows as mermaid's hair. She gets black tarry stuff on her plimsolls, and the scent of rotting vegetable matter and brine lies heavy on the air.

The boy is sitting above her on a ledge near the base of the cliff, his dangling legs encased in a shimmering rainbow skirt. The girl wonders whose washing line he has stolen it from. *I don't know how to climb.*

He sighs. *Put your foot on that rock. Nae, this one. Then the*

foothold there, aye, and your right hand here and I'll pull you up.
Her desire to follow, to have the company of the boy, is stronger than her natural timidity, her fear of heights. She obeys his instructions, all sounds and sensations receding into the background as she focuses on not falling. Right hand, left foot, left hand, right foot. He grabs her hand, yanks her up, and they're on the ledge together, the girl flattening her body into the cliff face. The boy has sand trapped in his curls, like flies caught in a spider's web. The cliff is not quite vertical. They climb in single file, the boy barefoot and bare-chested, the hem of his rainbow skirt scrunched up in one fist as he clings to the cliff with his other hand.

The girl looks up, and the boy has disappeared. Instead, there is a thin sliver of negative space shaped like a crescent moon. Her tummy flutters at the way the gap sucks in the daylight, repelling and fascinating her in equal measure. The boy has slipped into the darkness. She hesitates, afraid to go in but even more afraid to try to climb down the cliff by herself. She's level with it now, and there is the boy's hand, a pale smudge reaching out from the blackness. She takes it, and squeezes through the gap.

It's as dark as the girl could ever have imagined. She can't see the cave walls but feels their closeness, their dampness. She is still holding hands with the boy. *Touch your other hand to the cave wall. There'll be light soon enough.* She puts her trust in him, and they shuffle along. *A wee step to your right. Now wait, it's narrow here.* He stops and she crashes into him. She senses him turning to face her, although she can't see his face. He takes hold of her hands and walks backwards, gently pulling her with him. She whimpers as they inch through the tiny space.

He drops her hands, and she senses him moving away from her. A breeze on her face informs her she is now in a large space. She blinks as her eyes adjust and finds she can see. The walls of the cave glow with a greenish luminescence, an eerie half-light, reminding her of the fairyland of the woman's bedtime stories, a fairyland inhabited by creatures with blackened teeth and a fondness for boiling children's bones in a cauldron. They're standing in a large chamber, partially submerged with seawater. The green light is coming from somewhere underneath the water, flooding upwards in emerald shafts that diffuse and disperse as they hit the surface, culminating in the soft glow coating the walls of the chamber. *There's a hole,* says the boy, *in the cliff, under the sea. The light rises up through there.* His voice echoes faintly, in rhythm with the amplified hush-hush of the water.

She crouches by the edge of the emerald sea. *Why's it green?*

The boy, hunkered down beside her, rolls his eyes. *It's where Enys Wolvygyen is, aye. The Island of Radiant Light. Down on the bottom of the sea.*

He is teasing her. There is no such thing as an island on the bottom of the sea. He trails his fingers through the water; the light swirls and settles. It doesn't seem to burn him. She dips in the very tips of her fingers, ready to snatch them away at the first indication of pain. When she retracts them, water drips off, shimmering into the green. She tries again, up to her knuckles, then her wrist. She sweeps her

47

hand, pushing the water with her palm, the green light moving with her. Still she doesn't burn.

The sea is waking up, becoming restless, receding from the cave walls before surging back. *We have to move,* says the boy. *Scoot onto this rock, here.* They scramble up, her plimsolls slipping on the damp surface.

What's happening?

He grins at her, his teeth radiant in the cave's glimmer. *Dinna be afraid.* The sea is collapsing in on itself, some unseen force sucking the water away from the centre and spinning it around. *There's a great rock under the sea, very deep, near to the hole where the green light comes up. When the tides and currents are just right, it makes a whirlpool.* As the water spins, it rattles, and the rattle echoes off the cave walls and becomes a hiss, a rasp, a breathy laugh.

The cave is a negative space and they're inside it. Now there is more negative space, at the centre of the whirlpool. This fascinates the girl, and she leans out a little, hoping to get a better view. The boy shouts a warning, a fraction of a second before her foot connects with a patch of mermaid's hair, but it's too late and their hands are wrenched apart, both falling, her ankle scraping agonizingly across rock, a moment of seeming weightlessness in the air. The boy cries out, and she has one last fleeting impression of him, crying, holding a hand to his bloodied forehead as she is sucked into the vortex.

A great, rushing noise fills her ears and everything is silent, although she can feel the thunderous noise of the whirlpool vibrating through her body as she spins. But it's not spinning, not really, more like whisking eggs in a bowl, up and down and round and round and back and forth all at the same time, and the world is getting greener and greener as she descends towards the light.

She passes into a tunnel of rock. Water is everywhere, getting into her nose, her throat, her lungs. She grates her elbows and knees against the rock as she falls into the light, which is no longer green, just the colour of ordinary light and then she is outside, free of the cave, free of the whirlpool, floating in the sea. It rages around her, churned up by the encroaching tide, sucking her under. Her head breaks the surface and she can cough and breathe, but then she is pulled under again. Pain pulses along her spine. And now the sea burns, searing her arms and legs as it prepares to smash her bones against the rocks. This is how she is going to die.

A flash of something beside her, silvery pale. In the last fragments of her consciousness, she thinks the boy has come to save her. She is propelled upwards out of the sea with a force so great it expels the water from her lungs. She can breathe. She takes huge, thankful gulps of air. Somehow, she is both lying on the water and moving through it. The sun warms her face, as she bumps towards the shallows. She lifts her limbs and sees she is not burnt but has scraped the skin from her arms and legs as she fell through the tunnel of rock.

You saved me, she croaks, through salt-swollen lips. But when she rolls over in the shallow water, it is not the boy's face she looks into, but the amber eye of a horse.

10

Scottie: Luck

The little ferry, *Lucky Spirit*, ploughed up a skein of froth as it skirred across the surface of a flat calm ocean. I climbed onto the safety barrier, my knuckles gripping cold, salt-scoured metal. Wind pummelled my face, unravelling my ponytail, blowing my hair into my mouth. I tasted salt and Jasminder's cheap supermarket shampoo. I could see now that the calm had been deceptive. Close to the ferry, the sea was agitated, jostling wavelets slapping up against the hull. I pressed my thighs into the top of the barrier, settling my weight into it, and let go, leaning out dangerously far, metal digging into my thighs, my shadow skimming across the water. Beneath those surface wavelets, beneath my shadow, I imagined the patterns of tides and currents and creatures, sweeping back and forth in perpetuity.

My thighs grew numb against the barrier and my nerve evaporated. I hopped down to the safety of the deck and wandered inside to the cramped passenger cabin, looking for somewhere to stow my suitcase while I peed. There were a dozen or so other passengers, most of them young, lounging around in beanies, music-festival T-shirts and scuffed trainers, tapping the screens of their phones. I wondered if they were islanders going home or whether they had come to count seals. Or if, like me, they had other reasons for travelling to this remotest of remote places.

A couple, with a girl of about four, a toddler boy and a baby, had arranged themselves and their luggage across the narrow space leading to the unisex toilet on the opposite side of the cabin. The woman, younger than me, had a sea-green headscarf knotted through her hair and a towel thrown over her shoulder. She held the grizzling baby in her arms. I faltered, trying to plot a route to the toilets that didn't take me past them, but I was too slow. The woman spotted me, swivelled her knees to one side and beckoned me past.

'You're all right, we didna start yet.' She brushed her lips to the baby's forehead. 'Did we, bub?'

Her accent was a strange hybrid of Scottish and Cornish I supposed was a result of the colonization of the archipelago I had read about, settlers leaving their homes to make new lives on a scattering of far-flung desolate islands in the middle of an endless ocean.

'It's fine,' I said, backing away, searching for an escape route.

A group of bird watchers sporting excessively large binoculars had formed a gaggle beside me, blocking my way. The woman squeezed into her chair, raising her knees to give me space. She was supporting the back of her baby's head with her hand. I wondered what it felt like, to hold your baby's head, such a tender, intimate gesture, and found I couldn't even imagine it. The woman nudged the man with her foot and he swung his bag up from the floor onto the empty seat beside him, barely breaking concentration from whatever was on his tablet screen. She smiled to encourage me through the gap they'd created, then frowned because I still wasn't passing and her baby was hungry, wailing now, and it was all my fault.

I bolted back onto the deck, back outside to the endless glittering calm. I had to get away, as far away as I could, from bird watchers and seal counters and mothers cradling their babies' heads. Had to get far enough away so nobody would hear what was about to happen, nobody but the birds, the fish, the deep hidden tides. My suitcase tipped over, slapping onto the wooden deck. I collapsed onto my hands and knees as I reached the bow. It was coming — there was no stopping it. *One-breathe-in, two-breathe-out, three-breathe-in.* The feel of the wood beneath my fingers, the cool breeze, the taste of shampoo in my hair, the soft rocking motion of the ferry. I focused on each of these things in turn, inhabiting the sensations, emptying my mind of all else. It worked. I pulled it back. I didn't howl.

Jasminder had taken me to the airport in the end, hugged me stiffly at Departures. Overnight, his anger had receded, replaced by the hope that, once I'd had time to reflect, I'd change my mind. *I shouldn't have rushed you. Take all the time you need, Scottie. Take time to heal. Things will seem brighter soon.* I hadn't known what to say. I didn't deserve his under-standing. I wanted to return the hug, to tell him everything would work out, but he had too much false hope already, so I let my body go slack in his embrace and when he finally let me go, I slunk through the gate to security and didn't look back. I told myself I was running towards something, towards the glimmer of the past that had danced for so long on the periphery of my memory. Jasminder, when he was angry after I first told him I was leaving, had accused me of lying to myself. I was running away from the future, he said, and for what? A pipe dream, an imagined past that had probably never existed. But it was the future, the one we had dreamt of for so many years, that felt like a fantasy to me. The truth was, both the imagined past and the imagined future were filled with ghosts. The differences between them were not so great.

There was a snaking pain in my upper back, beneath the scar on my spine. I felt empty, like a husk, at risk of crumbling away, like the brittle, fragile past. The air was damper, saltier than it had been before. I let it settle around my shoulders, imagined it seeping in to soothe the pain in my back. I inhaled it, smelt it in my hair. I checked my phone. Just one text message from Helen, composed with characteristic formality: *Dear Charlotte. What an earth are you doing? Poor J is distraught. Love Mum.* I didn't respond.

The endless glittering sea was broken, finally, the horizon scattered with fragments of coastline. The ferry skirted around an island that was little more than a rocky outcrop, a disused lighthouse perched on gunmetal rocks, the colour of the ocean softening to slate-grey, then green. After so much endless sea, now the archipelago hurtled towards me at breakneck speed, long low waves pushing into shallower water, unfurling onto rocks and sandy coves. As the ferry entered the harbour, to one side there was a strip of sandy beach and to the other a high concrete breakwater extending around in an arc, the space between littered with yachts and pleasure boats at anchor. This was Lugh, a settlement of brightly painted cottages sprawling uphill from the harbour, bordered on each side by sheep-dotted fields and a scattering of industrial units. It was nothing like the mossy, craggy island from the photograph. The ferry chugged and spluttered into its berth and I stood on deck, waiting for the other passengers to offload their rucksacks and toddlers and oversized binoculars, taking in the ramshackle fishing boats with tangles of green and orange nets, the piles of lobster pots and crab creels, the tatty stands selling buckets and spades and rubber rings, the stink of old chip paper. I waited for a flash of recognition, a moment of clarity, but there was none.

The Breezyneuk Guest House was supposedly only a short walk from the quayside, but it took me twenty minutes of shin-bashing suitcase-wrangling along narrow, cobbled streets to find it. It was a pink-washed townhouse, festooned with window boxes and hanging baskets. The proprietress, a tiny, brittle-looking woman with unnaturally red hair, sighed when she opened the door and saw me standing there.

'Um, I have a booking? Charlotte Scott-Bains?'

I had a headache, a dry, scouring pain in my temples, and the scar on my back hurt.

'Well, I suppose you'd better come in. Call me Nest. Like where birds sleep. One of the seal people, are you?'

I smiled my agreement and signed the guest register.

'I see you'll be here for Thora's Burning,' she said, frowning at my booking as if it was an inconvenience.

'I'm sorry?'

'The burning of the Bride Witch. Just a wee festival we put on in the spring. Something to look forward to, aye?'

The chintzy pink floral curtains and lingering background smell, a combination of Rich Tea biscuits and cat pee, were aggravating the pain in my head. I followed her up the winding stairs, trying not to scuff the skirting board with my case. The bedroom, thankfully, was a few degrees less pink than downstairs. I dumped my case on the bed and Nest furrowed her brow in silent disapproval. I pulled a printout of the photo of the mystery island from my jeans pocket and unfolded it, smoothing out the creases. 'You wouldn't happen to know which island this is, would you?'

Nest squinted at the photo without touching it. 'What do you want to know for?'

'Just some personal research.'

'I canna say, dearie. Perhaps some of your seal people will know.'

'You can't narrow it down at all? There's a dwelling. See?' I pointed to the grey smudge of cottage. 'Someone must live there or have lived there once.'

'Aye, to be sure. But the northern isles were abandoned decades ago. Canna blame the poor souls. A harsh life it was.' Nest shivered, the very thought of living on one of the remote, isolated islands too horrible to contemplate.

'So you think this is an island in the north of the archipelago? Is there a ferry I could take or –'

Nest laughed gustily, as if I'd said something hilarious. 'Oh, you'll nae find any soul willing to take you that far north. It's bad luck.'

'But –'

'Dinner is served between six thirty and seven thirty

p.m., but I do ask guests to let me know,' said Nest, slamming shut our conversation about the island. 'You're nae one of those vegans, I hope. I canna cater for vegans without notice. The front door is locked from ten thirty. Pick up a key on your way out if you're going to be late.'

Nest clip-clopped down the stairs in her child-sized patent-leather Mary-Janes. I brushed my teeth and took a shower beneath a lukewarm trickle of water, wondering what Nest had meant about it being bad luck to go to the north of the archipelago. I lay down on the bed, the photo of the island on the pillow beside me. My mouth flooded again with the taste of sand and peaches. *A northern isle. An island of the north.* I listened, inside my own mind, for the melodies of a lullaby, the hushing of the sea, but only sleep came.

The Woman and the Girl:
Tales from the Hollow Sea

It should be a happy time. Before the white horse hairs, before the mother-of-pearl comb. Before the day the girl had lain down beside a horse made of sand. Their bellies are full, the curing house still filled with desiccated ribbons of black flesh hanging from the roof. But the woman is preoccupied. She can't stop thinking about the dying shriek of a slaughtered whale. About a sea pink with blood. About accusations spat at her by people she had once called her friends. *Witch. Murderess. Baby-thief.* Only one is true.

One night, a dream comes to her. In the dream, the woman is standing in a blood-red sea, the girl beside her, their skirts floating on the surface. They are singing. An ancient, beautiful song in a strange language the woman does not understand. She tries to stop the words tumbling from her mouth, but finds she cannot, as is sometimes the way with dreams. The girl, hand icy in the woman's, sings with a faint smile of anticipation on her face. Cold creeps up through the woman's veins, thickening her blood. In her free hand she is holding a red-stained gaff. Even as she sings, her teeth chatter and her limbs shake. She wants to go back to the shore, to take the girl to the safety of their cottage, but the sea pushes against her legs, grabbing, greedy, holding her in place.

There are shadows in the water, moving around them, dark blurs breaking the surface, dipping under. The song has called them, she understands, and they have come for the girl. The girl is no longer singing but laughing with excitement. The shadows move closer, faster. The dark blurs are fins, silhouetted against the red sea. The girl lets go of the woman's hand, wades towards the shadows. And still her song comes, faster, faster, the sound of it filling her head, deafening her. The girl does not look back, and as the dark shapes surround her, caressing her, cajoling her beneath the surface, finally the song breaks and the woman screams and rushes forward, the blood-sea relinquishing its grip at last. But she is too late. The girl and the shadow-fins have disappeared, the sea rushing in to fill the spaces they have left. Somehow it is night now, although moments before it had been day. All that's left is the reflection of the stars on a crimson sea.

The woman's dream stays with her, all through the day. She writes it down in her journal, perhaps hoping the memories will lose their power when transcribed onto the page, where it waits for me, waits three decades for me to find it.

When the girl has gone on her daily treasure hunt, the woman riffles through boxes of junk, lifts mattresses, reaches into the spidery space behind the Welsh dresser. Eventually, concealed beneath a pile of sheet music in the piano stool, she finds what she is looking for.

A book, swaddled in brown paper. A gift from Sam, before he had become too frail to deliver their groceries. She remembers the day he had given it to her, the same day she and the girl had tried to rescue a seal pup. *She's nae who you think, the wee lass*, Sam had said, as he tried to press the book into her hands. *She's nae* what *you think*. The woman had been angry then, no matter all the things Sam had done for them. She hadn't even unwrapped the book, much less read it. She had written scornfully about Sam and his superstitions in her journal, but she was lying to herself. The real reason she didn't read the book was because she didn't want to know the truth.

But now the truth is catching up with her. She removes the book from its brown-paper wrapping. *Tales from the Hollow Sea* by Lucyna Richmond-Whyte. The first thing that strikes her is the picture on the cover. It's a picture she's seen before, one of the paintings she'd given to Sam to destroy, years before when the girl was still tiny. The painting is of a curly-haired child aged four or five, sitting on a rock, looking over its shoulder at the artist. The child has a fin on its back, glowing with coloured light, its face at once familiar and unfamiliar, both the girl and not the girl. The woman had begged Sam to take the painting, had wanted never to see it again. A hard ripple of anger shudders through her. She opens the cover and begins to read.

By the time the woman reaches the last page, dusk is curling in through the windows. Some of the stories she knows, fanciful tales of singing shells and sea-bears and sea-serpents she'd heard from Sam, or from her long-dead husband when they were newly married, drinking hot chocolate around a fire at midnight. But one of the tales in the book, with its carefully referenced footnotes, seems more tangible, as if it could step off the page and into real life. As if it could answer questions the woman had long ago decided not to ask.

A noise from outside, the girl singing as she skips along the pebbly path. The woman shoves the book back into the piano stool and busies herself lighting the stove. The door opens, the girl hops through, still humming her little tune.

Fairy, it's almost dusk. Why are you so late?

The girl answers with a question of her own. *Why is my hair dark and your hair light?*

The woman flinches, thinking again of how the islanders had called her a baby-thief. *It's just the way of things. Now run along with your chores before supper.*

The girl takes the witch's broom from its place in the corner, swishing it listlessly across the floor as the woman lights the kerosene lamp against the encroaching dusk. She pauses in her work, puts a hand to her hair, pinching a curl between her thumb and forefinger, stretching it out straight along the length of her nose before letting it spring back. *Why is my hair curly and your hair straight?*

The woman, warming a pot for supper, glares at the girl. *It's just the way things are. Now stop asking silly questions and finish sweeping the floor. I'll not tell you again.*

The girl sweeps, sulkiness settling around her shoulders. *Swish, swish, swish.* She leans against the broom. *Did my papa have curly hair?*

For a moment, the woman can't breathe. The girl has never asked about her father before. She finds herself unable to summon a lie. *No*, she says, in a voice that doesn't sound like her own. *But his hair was dark, like yours.*

The girl considers this information without comment, returns to her sweeping. *Swish, swish, swish.*

After supper, the woman sends the girl to bed. When she is sure the girl is asleep, she re-wraps *Tales from the Hollow Sea* with trembling hands. She chides herself. It's only a fairy-tale, after all. An old man's superstition. But still she goes to the wall in the far corner, behind the piano, and jiggles out a loose stone she has never got around to repairing. She doesn't ask herself the questions that should be foremost in her mind. Why, if it's only a fairy-tale, has she forbidden the girl to speak her own name aloud? And why has she told the girl the sea will burn? She slides the wrapped book into the space, replaces the stone and promises herself she'll never think about it again.

12

Scottie: Sorrow

I lay awake in my bedroom in the Breezyneuk, the sheets hot and twisted beneath me, a humming streetlamp outside my window, the air heavy with salt. *Ten-breathe-in, nine-breathe-out, eight-breathe-in.* I was used to thoughts intruding, forcing their way into my mind in the early waking hours. Usually it was the faces of my ghost children, always just in shadow. But tonight it was a never-ending film reel of fuzzy ultrasound images of the hollow space inside me, space that should be lush, fecund, but instead was my own personal desert. A mockery of the baby scans I saw on social media, accompanied by excited updates. *My baby is the size of a plum, a pear, a butternut squash.*

I gave up trying to sleep and went for a walk, the streetlamps blinking out as dawn broke over the town. The lanes twisting up the slopes of Lugh were a mix of quaint shuttered cottages, independent shops and a closed-up market. I walked down the hill, following the sound of plashing waves and ropes clanking on metal to the quayside. It was full of cheerful fishing boats with names like *Maria Jayne* and *Sea Goddess*. I bought a coffee in a Styrofoam cup from Paulo's food van and sat on a bench overlooking a huddle of moored fishing boats to drink it. Men in fluorescent bibs and trousers were starting to arrive, ready to go out for the day's fishing. My phone whirred and vibrated from within the depths of my bag. It was Helen, ambushing me with an early-morning phone call. Against my better judgement, I answered it.

'Jasminder's going out of his mind, poor soul.'

'I'm fine, Mum. Thanks for asking.'

'Are you, Charlotte? It doesn't seem like a very "I'm fine" thing to run off to God knows where in the middle of your IVF.'

'I'm not having any more fertility treatment.'

She was silent for a moment. I nearly said another Big Fat Negative would break me, but I didn't want to cry down the phone.

'All right, then,' she said. 'So, what are you going to do? Adopt?'

'I don't want to adopt, Mum.'

Even if I did want to, what self-respecting social worker would approve the Incredible Howling Woman as an adopter? My empty coffee cup rolled away in the breeze. I chased it along the quayside, phone in hand.

'Have you discussed it with Jasminder? What does he think about all this?'

'He's respecting my space, Mum.'

'Are you running, Charlotte? It sounds as if you're running.'

I put my foot on the coffee cup, breaking it into pieces. 'I'm not running, Mum.'

I returned to my bench, cradling the fragments of Styrofoam, cold coffee dregs on my fingers.

'You're going to look for them, aren't you?'

'Look for who?'

'Don't be obtuse, Charlotte. I know you've been wanting to for years. Look for your birth parents, if you must,
and then you'll have your DNA family, someone to com-
pare noses with, see whose eye colour you have and where
you got your beautiful curls from. You needn't have waited.
You could have done it before, you know.'

I imagined her sitting on her little patio with a blanket
over her knees, surrounded by the last of the winter pan-
sies, drinking breakfast tea she made with loose tea leaves
in a little teapot. All those years she'd had alone after Phil
died, making tea for one. It broke my heart a little bit.

'Oh, Charlotte. You've already started, haven't you?
This is what your wild-goose chase to the middle of
nowhere is all about.' She sighed. 'I suppose I always knew
this day would come.'

'Are you giving me your blessing?'

Her silence was almost palpable, even over all those
miles. She would be smoothing her grey-streaked bob,
adjusting her Alice band, as she always did when something was upsetting her.

'Not my blessing,' she said eventually. 'You don't need
it. I doubt it will give you what you're looking for even if
you find them. I know a thing or two about wishing for a
biological family.'

I couldn't ever remember Helen speaking aloud her wish
to have biological children, although I supposed I had
always known it, tangled up with my unspoken fear that I
was nothing more than a consolation prize, a sticking plaster for Helen and Phil's own infertility. That if they had
been able to have children naturally, they would never have

adopted me. I didn't want to do that to a child, to make them feel they were second best.

'Do you ever think about the children you never had, Mum?'

'Charlotte,' she said, her voice softening, 'the only thing you need to know is that I wouldn't change a thing.'

I walked to the marina to meet the seal-count volunteers, still half hoping I might grasp hold of a tangible memory, something to say I had been here before, but there was nothing. The volunteers were easy to spot, all fresh-faced and pristine in newly minted waterproofs. A woman in her early thirties, blonde and elfin and holding a clipboard, greeted me with a dazzling smile. I recognized her from her photograph on the webpage of the Marine Mammal Protection Society as Dr Ellie McMullen.

'Charlotte Scott-Bains,' she said, displaying a perfect set of white teeth to match her Australian accent and making a mark on what I presumed was a list of names. 'Everyone else is here. So glad you could make it. We were short a volunteer and there you were with your lovely email. I do love a bit of serendipity.'

'I go by Scottie,' I said.

Ellie patted the shoulder of a goateed twenty-something man standing beside her. 'This is Noah, my research assistant.'

'I'm pleased you're here too, Scottie,' he said. 'Ellie's schedules get out of whack when we have the wrong number of people and it makes her very tense.'

Ellie elbowed Noah good-naturedly in the ribs and

reeled off a list of names, *Simon, Louella, Travis, Alison, Ricky*, but I couldn't affix them to faces.

'Thanks so much for volunteering, guys,' said Ellie, tucking a stray hair into her paisley-patterned headband. 'Those who've been before, you know the drill. Newbies, I promise you're going to have such a fantastic time. So, who knows the difference between the grey seals we're interested in and the common seals we're not? Anyone?'

'Like the difference between dogs' faces and cats' faces?' said a statuesque red-haired woman with a Home Counties accent.

I was only half listening, wondering what the best way would be to go about tracking down the location of my island.

'Right, Alison,' said Ellie, 'but remember, the commons are much smaller than the greys and don't have their annual moult until August. The greys have their moult about now, which means they'll be hauled up on the beaches and super-easy to count. We'll be surveying from the boats, without ever going ashore, to avoid disturbing the seals. Our mantra is, if the seal is aware of your presence, then you're too close. For safety, each team will have at least one navigator with extensive knowledge of the prevailing tides and currents. We've hired a few local friends to help us out.'

We waved awkwardly at a huddle of what I presumed to be islanders standing a few feet away.

'The forecast is good,' said Ellie, 'but the weather and sea conditions can turn in seconds, so listen to your expert and don't argue if they say you need to come back. And wear your bloody life jacket at all times.'

Ellie divided us into teams for the day. I was with Alison and a white-haired, sun-creased local man, whom Ellie introduced as Tony. She assigned us to Sorrow, Lugh's sister island across the bay. We were to complete a full circumnavigation, counting seals at several documented haul-out sites, as well as any stragglers.

The sea was calm, with a faint, hypnotic ripple. Tony took us south in his small wooden motorboat, avoiding the rocks that enclosed Lugh harbour, then around the Sorrow peninsula, a narrow sandbar crowded with lolling seals. Alison took photographs, and I made a tally in my notebook, so we could cross-reference them later. Tony was a man of few words, or perhaps he didn't know what to say to us, these two women from a different world. He turned his boat north, towards the east coast of Sorrow. It was wilder than Lugh, less sheltered, with cragged walls of rock and stony coves. Not as wild as the island in my photograph, and much larger, but it heartened me to know that not every island in the archipelago was a carbon copy of Lugh.

'Such a beautiful day,' said Alison, tipping her face up to the sun. 'Is it your first time here, Scottie?'

A good question.

'Yes. My first seal count.'

'It's my fifth. I was here the first few times years ago when Ellie was getting started, but I took a break to have my little ones. It's amazing to be back. I mean, I miss my babies *sooo* much, but it's lovely just to get a few days of peace when I can have a shower without little hands tugging at the shower curtain. You know?'

I nodded, but I didn't know and never would.

'What about you, Tony?' Alison tried to draw our taciturn skipper into the conversation. 'Any kids?'

Tony's face broke into a crumpled smile. 'Four,' he said, 'And seven grand 'uns. Best thing I ever done.'

'Are you a fisherman, Tony?' I asked him, trying to steer the conversation into neutral waters.

He shook his head. 'When I were a lad, I worked on the trawlers. Switched to inshore after I became a family man. Run my own sea-school now I'm getting on.'

Alison snapped a photo of Tony at the helm, making him flinch. 'How old are your grandchildren, Tony?'

'Five almost grown and two wee lasses. Four and seven.'

'Such a lovely age,' said Alison.

I rehearsed different answers in my head for the question I knew she was about to ask me. I usually answered with *Not yet* or a breezy *We're still trying*, but that wasn't even close to the truth any more. If I said, *Sadly not,* would that shut her up? Or, *Actually, Alison, I'm infertile?*

'What about you, Scottie?' she said. 'Have you got children?'

In the end, I went with the simplest option.

'No.'

The word broke into pieces on my tongue but Alison didn't even notice.

'Still plenty of time,' she said. 'Live your life before you settle down. My cousin had her first at forty. Get established in your career. What do you do, anyway?'

'I'm an admin assistant.' I'd been off sick for months, ever since our last will-o'-the-wisp, that faintest of faint

71

lines on a pregnancy test. It was hard to imagine going back to my little office job. It felt as if it was from another world. 'But I'm thinking about a career change.'

I didn't know why I'd said that. Anything to avoid talking about babies.

'Are you thinking of becoming a conservationist? Is this work experience?'

'Maybe.'

'I would love to be a conservationist,' she said. 'But having kids makes it hard. You're so lucky to have your freedom.'

'Tony,' I said, 'I know Lugh is ancient Celtic, but do you know where the name Sorrow comes from?' I wasn't that interested, but it was the only thing I could think of to ask him that didn't involve babies or grandchildren.

'Aye. From *a Ilha das Tristezas*, the Isle of Sorrows. Named by Portuguese whalers shipwrecked here two century back.'

Tony's eyes were blue, but there was a hint of Mediterranean in his skin tone and something else I couldn't quite put my finger on – the angle of his cheekbones or the slant of his nose, perhaps – that made me think he might be descended from those whalers.

'There's an island I'm trying to find. Maybe you'll know it.' I retrieved the printed photo, already fraying at the edges, from my pocket and held it in front of Tony's face, the wind ripping at the edges of the paper. He muttered something I didn't quite catch.

'There's a haul-out site somewhere along here, I think,' said Alison, squinting at Ellie's map.

The boat's engine hummed smoothly, as Tony brought her about.

'Can you tell me anything about it, Tony?'

'Aye, it's likely an island in the north. Up in the Hollow Sea.'

My stomach did a flip. The Hollow Sea. A place with a name. 'Is it possible to go there?'

'You'll nae find any soul who'll agree to take you,' he said, turning his face away, his accent growing stronger. 'And why in the heavens would you want to? It's bad luck. A cursed place, you ken.'

Tony held the boat steady, as we scanned the coast for the haul-out site. The sea was littered with rocks, turning it to white foam, and beyond, in the lee of the cliff, was a beach, also strewn with rocks.

'Bad luck? What does that mean?'

'Miss,' said Tony, pointing.

I followed his gaze and there were the seals, a group of maybe twenty, sprawled across the sand and rocks, a few dipping in the surf. Alison began snapping away and I tallied up.

'Tony, I very much want to find this island.'

He looked me straight in the eye this time. 'I canna help you, Miss.'

'All done,' said Alison.

'I'm sorry,' I said. 'I lost count. Give me a sec.'

Two, four, seven, eight, eleven. But my eye was drawn to the cliff face, to a semi-circle of black at its base, and, above it, stark against the rock, a painted white cross.

'Tony,' I said, 'what's that? There on the cliff? Is that a church?'

Tony bobbed his head.

'Aye, Miss. The Chapel of Our Lady of Sorrows. A sea cave used for shelter and then for worship by the unfortunate whalers. Course it's abandoned nowadays, has been for . . .' he sucked in air through his teeth '. . . half a century, give or take.'

'There's some seals we missed counting, just on that little bit of beach to the left,' said Alison.

I scribbled in my notebook, not caring much if the number of lines matched the number of seals. I was more interested in the chapel-cave. It tugged at me, that black, empty space in the cliff wall. My back twitched. The space, the emptiness, spoke to me. It wasn't the same as when the photo of the island on my laptop screen had crashed into my consciousness. Nothing so dramatic. This pull was gentler, a nagging sense of something buried somewhere deep inside me. I didn't know what it was. But it was something.

13

Charlotte: Shattering

I remembered the day Phil died as a confusion of sensory detail. Crunchy peanut butter on toast. Creamy milk in a glass, washing away the bits of peanut from my mouth. Phil winking at me as he tied his tie. His forest-scented aftershave. I wanted to wink back, I was warming to him, but I couldn't get my eyelids to operate independently from one another. That's the last thing he saw of me, probably, sitting at the dining table, toast in hand, eyes screwed shut.

And then, after school, the synthetic-sweet new-carpet smell in the hallway, my school shoes, shiny with a T-bar buckle stowed next to Phil's for-best loafers on the shoe rack. My school skirt, tartan pleats stretched over my knees. A hole in my sock, big toe wiggling in its new-found freedom. Coloured light filtering through the stained-glass insert over the front door. White light flooding in, sucking up the colours. Silhouettes in the doorway. Words, words, words spoken in hushed tones. A single anguished sob. Helen coming apart, her body folding, falling, disconnecting.

And then, she saw me, a little thumb-sucking huddle on the carpet, and she stopped herself coming apart. A smashed vase putting itself back together again, shard by shard. I don't know how she found the strength, but she did. *Charlotte, dear*, she said, *be a good girl and go and play in your room.*

Her voice was perfectly normal, perfectly calm, as if nothing were wrong. Flashes of wallpaper through the banisters as I ran upstairs to the princess-y bedroom she had decorated for the daughter she expected to get, the daughter I wasn't, the room that had never until now felt like a refuge. She'd done it for me, pulling herself together like that. I recognized her sacrifice, in an abstract sort of way, even at my young age. It was the start of a bridge between us, perhaps, the beginning of us becoming mother and daughter.

But there was another version of this memory, a nightmare that came in the early hours. In this version, Helen doesn't pull herself together. I watch from my spot on the carpet as her body shatters, glass-like smithereens exploding out in beautiful slow-motion through the dusty light, like a universe expanding, and she can't stop it, can't knit herself together, can't find her centre of gravity to pull everything back in.

I am left alone in the hallway, the fragments of her body caught in my hair and clothes, scattered all around me, another mother lost, and I am an orphan again.

14

The Girl: Cat's Cradle

The day in the girl's life I think about most is the one when she meets the boy for the first time. A day of such simple, childish pleasures. A new friend, a game to play, a gift. She had no idea her world was turning on its axis.

It happens just a few weeks after she had left her little island for the first time in her life, when the woman had taken her to the blackfish hunt on Lugh and she had been stared at and whispered about by all those strangers. Her belly is full but, still, she is out of sorts as she dawdles down to the shore, dragging her feet on the sandy path. That morning, the woman had been singing in her sleep, a song that had raised the hairs on the girl's arms and neck and made her ache inside. She had got out of bed and pulled back the curtain separating their sleeping spaces, had stood beside the woman in moonlight made milky by salt-encrusted windows. She wanted to comfort her, reach out to touch the damp tendrils of the woman's hair spread across the pillow, but lost her courage at the last minute.

She tries to recreate the song in her mind, now, to sing a few notes into the salt breeze, but the melody is already lost to her. She is so distracted by the process of trying to arrange the notes of the song in her head, she doesn't even notice the boy until she is almost upon him. He is sitting on a rock, cross-legged, his back to the sea, a bundle of tangled seaweed in his lap. She utters a little cry and pulls up short. There has never been a visitor to the island before, except when Mr Sam used to deliver the groceries. She doesn't know whether to be afraid or excited, so she settles for gawping at the boy. He is wiry, wearing a yellow top with a bow at the neck she recognizes as belonging to the woman, stolen, perhaps, from the washing line strung between the cottage and the curing house.

The boy grins at her. *What's your name?*

She hesitates. *I'm not supposed to say it out loud.*

He wrinkles his forehead. *Why?* When she doesn't respond, he hops off his rock and comes towards her, his thumbs and fingers hooked in the crisscross of seaweed strands. *How can we be friends if you'll nae even tell me your name?* His accent is strange, reminding the girl of the unwelcoming islanders at the hunt.

She would like very much to have a friend, but the thought of breaking the rule, of saying her name aloud, fills her with fear. *It's too dangerous.* She takes a step back as he nears her, but only one step, curiosity overcoming her shyness.

He extends the tangle of seaweed towards her. *The witch woman told you that? That it's dangerous to say your name aloud?* She nods, but secretly she is troubled. She knows the word *witch*, of course, had heard it muttered about the woman by the sullen islanders on the day of the hunt. But the woman does not have a cauldron or a black cat or a pointed hat and, so far as the girl knows, her broom doesn't fly. *I'm seven and two months,* she says, a sort of consolation for not telling the boy her name.

Do you want to play Cat's Cradle? She doesn't know this

game. Who would she have played it with? *Like this,* he says, coming face to face with her. His hair is damp, springing into curls where it has dried. He turns his wrists, tilting his palms to slide the seaweed over her fingers. The girl fumbles, the cradle collapses, but he doesn't seem upset. He starts popping the air sacs on the seaweed. *Pop, pop, pop.*

You're killing it, says the girl.

He looks amused. *It's just seaweed.* But he tosses it away.

Who are you? she asks. *Where have you come from?* He pinches his lip between his teeth.

If you'll nae tell me your name, he says, *why should I tell you mine?*

She has a peach in her pocket. Beneath its furry skin the peach is squishy, ripe for eating. She takes a slurpy bite, juice running down her chin. The boy watches her. She holds the peach out to him. He observes it with interest as if he has never seen one before. He nibbles at the orange flesh uncertainly, then grins and sinks his teeth into it. The girl is alarmed. *Don't eat it all!* The boy shears off a chunk with his teeth and hands it back to her reluctantly. He has got sand on the flesh, and as she eats what is left, the crunchy grains get between her teeth.

The boy saunters away, hopping from rock to rock beyond the tideline, the forbidden zone where she cannot follow.

She tracks him as best she can, a sticky-fingered shadow, taking a parallel route, keeping her toes an inch from the darker sand. *Why did you come here?*

He is standing one-legged on a rock, his arms out for balance. *I saw you. At the blackfish hunt.* He hops down, inspects a length of driftwood, rejects it, and picks up another, long and thin like a spear.

Where is your boat?

He turns the spear this way and that in his hands. *I havna got a boat.* She knows he's lying. Boat is the only way to get here.

He scratches some lines in the wet sand with his spear. A word, unfamiliar. The girl spells it out in her head, trying to imagine how the letters would sound. *That's my name,* says the boy. *Now you write yours.*

She takes the spear, feeling the weight of it in her hands. The woman has never told her she cannot write her name, only that she must not speak it. *I'm not allowed on the wet sand.* He scoffs at this, and the girl feels ashamed. She wants to step over the line, to use the driftwood to scratch letters in the sand with this strange boy. But she is afraid. *The sea can burn,* is all she can provide, by way of explanation.

Did she tell you that? he says. *The witch woman?* She wants to tell him not to call the woman *witch,* but she can't quite muster the courage. He holds out his hand. *It'll nae burn you while I'm here. I promise it's safe.*

But she doesn't quite trust him yet, so she stays on the dry side and leans across the tideline to scratch her name in neat, squarish letters. S-U-S-A-N. She mouths the word, remembering the shape of her name on her tongue. She wants to say it aloud, to hear it, but the woman has told her it's cursed, so she's afraid.

The boy is not afraid. *Susan,* he shouts, running in circles shaking the driftwood spear. *Susan, Susan, Susan.* Nothing bad happens. *See?* he says. *The witch woman is a liar.*

The boy runs down the beach, their letters forgotten. She follows, although the beach is tapering off and soon there will be no dry side to keep to. She likes the boy, likes being called Susan, likes the sensation of being on the cusp of something new, the having of a friend. But she's also unsettled by his presence. She is a calm sea, usually, but now waves of some emotion she doesn't have a word for are rippling through her.

The boy has found a deep drift of shells, thrown up by tens of thousands of successive tides. He jumps into it barefoot, shouting with delight. She watches him with curiosity. She has no frame of reference for such unbridled joy. *Come on, Susan!* he shouts. *Come on!*

She wants to, but the drift of shells is on the wrong side of the tideline. The drift is deep, she tells herself. Her feet wouldn't be touching the wet sand beneath. Perhaps it is permissible. She runs to the drift, and jumps in. They kick through shells, like mainland children would kick through snowdrifts, laughing until they ache. The boy lies down on the shells and scissors his legs and arms back and forth. The girl does the same, not minding the sharp edges of the shells on her skin.

They lie on the shell drift staring up at the clouds. *I forgot*, says the boy. *I brought you a wee gift.*

She sits up, shells caught in her hair. *A gift? For me?* She has never received a gift before, except occasional jars of chocolate spread and strawberry laces and faceless dolls from Mr Sam.

Wait here. He trots away to where the cliff angles out into the sand, cutting off their part of the beach from the next.

Can't I come?

He turns, shaking his head. *Promise me you'll nae follow, Susan. If you follow, then I'll nae give you the gift.*

She sulks, but acquiesces, beguiled by the promise of a present. The boy is back soon, carrying a bundle of cloth resembling oil spilt in water, shimmering with all the colours of the rainbow. He opens the bundle, retrieves an object and holds it out to her.

She accepts it reverently, turning it over in her hands. *What is it?*

A comb, to wear in your hair. Made of mother-of-pearl.

She presses her fingers along the sharp tips of the comb. The girl knows what mother-of-pearl is, has touched the silky smoothness inside many a shell, but she has only the vaguest conception of decorative hair combs. Nevertheless, she is touched by the gift. The boy steps forward and shows her how to fix the comb in her hair. The prongs catch and pull at her scalp, and she sways her head, enjoying the weight of the comb there.

It's a secret, says the boy. *You canna show it to the witch.*

The girl bites her lip. *Why do you call her a witch?*

He doesn't reply but touches the comb in her hair. *Have you never wondered why the witch has light hair and you have dark? Have you never wondered about that?*

The truth is, she has never thought about it, just as she has never thought deeply about the rules for keeping away from the sea or not saying her name aloud. She fiddles with the comb to conceal her confusion. She doesn't want the boy to think she's stupid.

They bid their farewells. *Will you come again?* she asks, feeling suddenly tearful.

Aye. He grins. *Aye.* And then, with a further admonishment not to follow him, he runs behind the cliff and is gone. She waits a few minutes, expecting to hear the engine of a boat but, when she does not, she follows, hugging the edge of the cliff to avoid the tideline, telling herself it doesn't count as a broken promise because she waited and she didn't agree not to follow for ever. She comes to the other side of the beach, and there is no boy, no boat, just a cloud of white foam drifting in the surf and some footprints in the wet sand. At first, the boy's, but then they disappear and there are only deep, U-shaped marks, two left, two right, two left, disappearing into the sea.

15

Scottie: Blackfish

Ellie had arranged an afternoon in the Blackfish Tavern for the seal-count volunteers, so we could get to know one another. The pub was filled with clouds of bittersweet smoke, making my eyes sting. The smoking ban hadn't caught on in St Hía. I ordered a mineral water at the bar and squeezed between two shiny American college boys whose names I couldn't remember. Alison and another woman were talking about school catchment areas, the college boys were discussing American politics, and Ellie and Noah were deep in conversation about seal-counting schedules. I pushed my glass back and forth between my index fingers, thinking about my island, about the abandoned northern isles, about the Hollow Sea.

'So,' said Ellie, noticing I wasn't talking to anyone and taking pity on me, 'how was your first seal count?'

'Good. Great.'

'Any luck in tracking down your mystery island?'

'Not so far. The most I can get out of anyone is it's probably in the north.'

'Oh, yeah?' She nodded, glancing down at her schedules. 'That would make sense. They're weird about the north and their little haunted islands. Seriously, though, Scottie, those are dangerous seas. We don't take the seal count up there for a reason. Way too risky. You be careful.'

Some musicians were setting up right behind me and I shuffled my chair forward to give them more room. 'Tony said something about the Hollow Sea and it being bad luck to go there?'

'Yeah,' said Ellie, taking a sip of her lager. 'They're a superstitious bunch. But the Hollow Sea — if that's where your island is — *is* dangerous. One of the most intense tidal races in the world. Whirlpools, standing waves, shipwrecks. It's got the lot. Reputedly unnavigable, but I reckon that's probably an exaggeration.'

Ellie raised her voice a little as the musicians began their set, a solo violin in a melancholy key. 'It has unusually strong currents, plus a narrow strait between two islands that speeds up the flow, and some pretty unique ocean-floor topography . . .'

A piano joined in, harmonizing with the violin. I half twisted in my seat so I could see the band while still talking to Ellie. The singer, a slight woman wearing a leather mini-skirt, gripped the microphone, swaying, her knuckles white in the smoky gloom, silent, letting the piano and violin soar around her.

'Anyway,' Ellie was saying, 'the upshot is that on a flood tide, if the currents are just so, you get this lethal bloody maelstrom . . . Oh, shit.' She frowned at the piece of paper in front of her. 'Noah. Hey, Noah. The schedule for tomorrow's all messed up. Sorry, Scottie, give me a sec.'

My gaze was drawn to the curly-haired piano player, the rhythmic motion in his arms and shoulders as he played. I thought I recognized him as one of the local experts Ellie had hired for the seal count. The woman began to sing, her voice clear, unembellished, a lament about restless waves, lost loves and shipwrecks. There was something about the song that tugged at me, the way the dark shadow of the chapel-cave in the cliffs at Sorrow had. I closed my eyes, letting myself fall into the melody, letting it sweep me along, flying over ocean and coves and cliffs to a little cottage with sea holly around its front door.

A blast of cool air hit me as a door opened somewhere, shouts flying in from outside, the band stuttering into silence. I opened my eyes. The patrons of the Blackfish were moving, seemingly as one body, streaming past me to the doors. The band exchanged glances and abandoned their set, leaving their instruments and mics where they stood.

'What's going on?' I asked Ellie.

'Shit,' she said, springing out of her chair without answering my question.

Snippets of conversation flew through the smoky haze. *On the beach* . . . Ellie and Noah headed for the exit, swallowed into the streaming crowd, followed by the shiny college boys and the rest of the seal counters. *Dozens of them.* A deep sense of dread churned in the pit of my stomach. I ran after the crowd, trying to make sense of the jumble of conversations. *Dying . . . dead.* The crowd advanced along the waterfront, taking me with it. We climbed a shingle ridge, pebbles slipping beneath our feet.

'Oh, holy Christ,' said Ellie, and Noah made a sound that was half sigh, half whistle.

I caught my breath, a chill unfurling through my body. Cast up on the beach like so much giant flotsam was a pod of whales, trilling to each other as the outgoing tide foamed around their tail fins.

Ellie and Noah took charge, shouting instructions and organizing the milling crowd into teams. They were long-finned pilot whales, Ellie explained, prone to mass strandings. The whales had black skin and looked like oversized dolphins, except instead of long smiley beaks their heads were shaped like melons. Their trilling was soft, constant, unsettling. As the tide receded, more whales appeared, marooned on the shelving sand, the ocean pulling back around them, churning over their fins as they headed up to the beach through the shallows.

'We need wet towels,' Ellie said, 'or sheets to protect them from the sun, and a few of those old-fashioned wind-breaks if we can find some, because there are some neonates here and they'll dry out quick. And tarps or canvas sheeting. Dig trenches under their pectoral fins.'

I crouched beside a whale, spreading my fingers across her hide, her skin warm from the spring sun. She had a patch of pale grey pigment just below the fin on her back, and there was a brackish, seaweedy scent to her. Sand blanketed her eyes and I washed it away, cupping seawater in my hands. The whale's fin was nicked and jagged. An old soul, wearing her battle scars. She took a breath, rattling along the length of her body before juddering out of her blowhole with a weak sigh. The beginnings of a howl twitched in my solar plexus, yanking back my torso and head. It couldn't happen, not here with all these new people. I closed my eyes, my hands still on the whale's flank, and tried to remember what my counsellor had taught me, to focus on achieving stillness, just in the moment. *Ten-breathe-in, nine-breathe-out, eight-breathe-in, seven-breathe-out.* The howl subsided, but I could sense it there, lurking.

I opened my eyes to see the curly-haired piano player holding a soaking-wet Thomas the Tank Engine beach towel. He handed it to me, and I hoped he hadn't noticed my twitch or my mini-meditation or heard me counting my breaths. We spread the towel across the whale's body.

'You're one of the seal people?'

His tone was cool, just scraping acceptable levels of civility.

'I'm only a volunteer,' I said, 'I don't know anything about whales.'

He smiled thinly, half amused by my demurral.

The vet, a crumpled man in his fifties, arrived, rubbing sea-spray from his spectacles with the sleeve of his anorak. He followed Ellie to the whale with the Thomas the Tank Engine beach towel. Ellie touched the whale's eyelid gently, making her blink.

'Good,' said Ellie. 'She's still alive and we need to keep it that way. This is a senior female and I think we should refloat her first. Once we get her into deeper water, hopefully the other whales will follow.'

'That's speculation at best,' said the vet.

'Sure, but I'm pretty good at speculation,' said Ellie, calmly. 'We need to triage every whale on this beach, so we can focus on the ones that have a chance of survival and get ready for when the tide comes in.'

The whale emitted another shuddering breath. The piano player knelt beside her and started to dig beneath the fin on her right side – the pectoral fin, Ellie had called it – with his hands, reminding me of the way his arms and shoulders had moved when he was playing the piano.

'Don't be taken in by these people,' Ellie said, her mouth by my ear. 'Thirty years ago, they were still driving the whales up onto this beach on purpose to slaughter them. It only stopped when they realized there was more profit in whale-watching than whale-hunting.'

It was difficult to imagine the St Híans taking part in such a barbaric practice. But there was something routine about the way the islanders interacted with the whales. They worked steadily, getting the job done without fuss or much conversation. When one of the whales took a final shuddering breath and died, the seal-count volunteers and tourists wasted time hugging each other and crying but the islanders didn't pause, just split and filtered into other teams. I admired their pragmatism, their work ethic, but the idea of once having hunted these beautiful creatures was repellent. I knelt beside the piano player, scooping up sand with my bare hands. He acknowledged me only by shifting on his knees a little, to make more space. His fingers were thin and pale, and he was wearing blue nail varnish. I tried to match the rhythm of his movements, so our hands wouldn't collide. The sand was rich and thick and clung to my hands and forearms.

'It was never about profit,' he said.

I looked across to see if he was talking to me. 'I'm sorry?'

He pushed his hair back from his face, trapping sand in

the curls. The wind lifted his fringe up from his brow and I saw he had a scar there, faint, jagged and thin. He was about my age and his voice was soft, his accent that rhythmic Cornish-Scottish fusion.

'The blackfish hunts. She was wrong when she said they were about profit.'

Spots of heat crawled across my collarbone. 'I don't think Ellie meant you to hear that.'

'We respect the blackfish. They've always been important to us, always been in our stories. But before the mainlanders started coming and spending their money there were years when the fishing was bad and people went hungry.'

I suppressed the urge to ask him if he had ever taken part in a whale hunt himself. 'You don't have to defend yourself to me. I'm not Ellie.'

'Aye,' he said. 'Your intentions are entirely honourable and in nae way patronizing.'

'Doesn't Ellie pay you to help out with the seal count? Isn't it a bit hypocritical to take part if you think we're all here on some kind of eco-crusade?'

He stood up, unrolling his body with the looseness of someone ten years younger, and offered me his hand. I ignored it, getting up by myself, regretting my decision as my knees and back creaked into life.

'Jesus Christ,' Ellie was saying to anyone who would listen. 'Is there no one here who can organize a few boats?'

'I'll do it,' said the piano player, in the same cool tone he had used with me, and he strode down the beach reeling off names of boats and their skippers.

I dampened down the beach towel, dug under the whale's other pectoral fin, and filled the trenches beneath her fins with water, to help keep her cool. She was still breathing, those intermittent, rasping breaths. The sky had faded from blue to a washed-out pink. It would be dark soon.

Ellie came and crouched by me.

'Right, Scottie. Here's the lowdown. We're gonna keep as many of the whales as possible alive until the morning tide. See the whale just over there, the one with the nick right at the top of its dorsal fin? I'm assigning you to be its best friend. You sit with it, keep it calm, talk to it, make sure its skin doesn't dry out. Easy-peasy. Can I count on you?'

The whale Ellie was pointing at was a few metres away, wedged against a rock.

'Can't I stay here with this one?' I said, suddenly possessive of my whale.

Ellie leant towards the whale and gave her a pat. 'This old girl,' she said, 'she's super important, because I reckon she's the matriarch of the pod. If we can get her back out into deep enough water, maybe the others will follow. It's better if me or Noah sits with this one.'

'But she knows me,' I said. I looked at the whale's eye looking at me and stroked the side of her head. 'She knows me, Ellie. She's calm with me. Let me stay with her. Please.'

Ellie's face twitched, a tiny tremor by her right eye.

'Ellie, are you all right?'

She laughed softly. 'I'm a pinnipedologist, not a cetologist. I wrote an essay on whale strandings when I was an undergraduate and that's the extent of my knowledge.' She patted the whale one more time. 'Don't tell anyone I'm winging it, will you? These idiots will have us all eating whale meat for supper. It's gonna be a long night so chin up.'

My whale, my new best friend, whistled. I sat by her head and stroked her skin. I thought about the life she had lived, traversing her underwater world, her bond with her family so great that, if Ellie was right, they had followed her onto the beach and near certain death just to be with her. For hours I stroked her and whispered to her, nonsense things mostly, and hoped it was a comfort.

The sensation of time slowing down, when you're awake and alone in the dark, is what I remember most from that night. I talked to my whale, dozed a little, got up and stretched, made sure her towels were still wet. One of the American college boys brought me a blanket and food. Each whale Ellie thought had a chance of surviving had someone like me, someone to keep them calm through the night. We spoke to our whales, not much to each other.

By the time the tide began to edge in, we were ready to start helping the whales back into the water. Ellie had found me a wetsuit from somewhere, which I had wrangled myself into in the pub toilets. She coached us to ease the whales onto canvas tarps, working in teams, folding their fins down and rolling them onto their sides before righting them again.

The tarp and the whale inched out into shallow water as we waded in, taking our places alongside her flanks. Me, Noah and some other seal-count volunteers whose names

I'd already forgotten. The breaking waves tried to push us back, as if the sea didn't want the whales to return.

'Make sure her blowhole stays above water or she'll drown,' said Ellie, from the beach. 'Now rock her. Gently, gently. We need to restabilize her and get her breathing to return to normal. Work in shifts. Use the tarp to support her. I can't believe they don't have any floats. It's basic equipment, for Chrissake. She might need several hours to get reoriented. Swap out if you need to. We don't want anyone getting hypothermia.'

We floated her into waist-deep water, turning her body so her bulbous head faced out to the ocean. Other whales were being refloated, a jumble of bodies – whales and humans – in the surf. The piano player and the woman who had been singing in the pub were also in the water, supporting a young whale. The woman's face was delicate and angular, streaked with makeup. She stroked her whale and sang to it, the same song she had sung in the pub, about shipwrecks and lost loves.

Cold seeped into my knees and hips. The current pushed against my body, trying to encourage us back, back to the beach and certain death for the whales. Why did the sea not want them? I twitched, my head snapping back. *Ten-breathe-in, nine-breathe-out, eight-breathe-in.* Noah paused his conversation with one of the seal volunteers – Louella, I remembered finally – about the merits of marine-biology degrees.

'Need a break, Scottie? It's okay if you're getting tired.'

No, I wouldn't be the weak one. I wouldn't leave her. 'Just a bit chilly.'

'It's brass monkeys all right.'

The piano player was staring at me. He had noticed, then. The twitch before, on the beach, and the one now. The counting of breaths. I stared back, to let him know I didn't care what he thought. He held my gaze for a long moment, then returned his attention to his whale, splashing seawater on its skin.

We went slowly, rocking our whale, supporting her with the tarp, removing it occasionally to get a sense of whether she was oriented enough to swim, inching into deeper water. A small motorboat, the *Lazy Daisy*, manoeuvred alongside us with Ellie on board.

'Is she ready, guys?'

Noah nodded. 'I think so, boss.'

We stepped back, withdrawing our supporting hands, letting the tarp drop from beneath her, wading backwards, trying not to splash. The *Lazy Daisy* advanced, the shifting drone of her engine barely audible above the sound of waves slapping the hull. The whale remained upright, her dorsal fin a curved sail against the brightening horizon. The *Lazy Daisy* nudged a fraction further away from the shore. The outboard dipped and purred. The whale glided a little further out. In one fluid motion, she flicked her tail flukes and slipped below the surface. I could just make out the V-shaped wash as her body cut through the water. There was a smattering of applause. I prayed she was following the *Lazy Daisy*.

I sat on the quayside wrapped in a blanket eating warm croissants. Ellie came to sit next to me, lighting a cigarette.

'I know I shouldn't,' she said, slanting the pack in my direction.

I shook my head. Closer to the beach, by the shingled ridge, the piano player and the woman singer were sitting together, legs touching, smoking roll-ups.

'That man,' I said. 'Who is he?'

Ellie followed my gaze. 'Who? Oh, you mean Kenver Pellow, the bloke who organized the boats? Known him for years. Oh, God, he didn't give you a lecture about whale-hunting, did he?'

Kenver Pellow and the singer were taking it in turns to swig from a silver hip flask.

'He did, actually. He seemed to have a pretty low opinion of us. Especially considering he works for you.'

'Honestly, he's harmless. Take no notice.'

A low groan came from the last remnants of the crowd on the beach. The tide was rushing up the sand in rhythmic surges of white spume, and it was bringing whales. I ran onto the sand, *No, no, no, no, no*. One had the same grey saddlepatch of pigment as my whale. Her tail fin thrashed over broken shells and she squealed.

'Why are they swimming back onto the beach?'

'It's because of her.'

Ellie pointed to my whale. My old girl, who I'd soothed and talked to all through the night.

People were scrambling into the sea, trying to push the incoming whales back out before they beached again.

'She's old and maybe sick too,' said Ellie. 'Whatever the reasons, she's come onto the beach twice now and the rest of her pod is following her. I don't think she's viable.'

Not viable. A word used to describe embryos that weren't good enough for implantation. A word I hated with a passion.

'We can refloat her again,' I said. 'Maybe it'll work next time.'

Ellie rubbed my arm.

'Scottie, love. Do you understand what's happening to these whales while they're on the beach? They're suffocating under their own weight. Their organs are getting crushed. Their skin is blistering in the sun. It's slow torture. And her distress calls are encouraging the other whales onto the beach. There's no hope for her now.'

'Are you sure?' I said, tears stinging my eyes. 'Because I thought you were winging it.'

Her face reddened but she let it go. A seagull swooped down, pecking at the whale's eye. I shouted at it, waving my arms, and it flew away, but it would be back. The vet arrived, carrying a rifle.

'Jesus,' said Ellie, only a slight waver to her voice betraying her emotions. 'Let's at least use the chemical option.'

'We dinna have enough of the right drugs. And even if we did, they'll be harmful to the environment once the carcasses start to decompose. This is the quickest, most painless way.' He pursed his lips. 'Unless you want to open a vein and let her bleed out. I've seen it done.'

'I bet you fucking have,' Ellie muttered, under her breath.

I remembered Ellie's warning not to be taken in by these people. How, only a generation ago, they had been driving the whales onto the beach and slaughtering them. I thought

97

about how the sand must have run red with blood and shivered.

'Right then,' Ellie said, snapping back into business mode. 'Let's get as many of these whales as we can into the water. No need for them to witness their family members being shot.'

When it was time, I knelt beside my whale and put my hand on her flank. 'Hello, old friend,' I said.

Kenver Pellow crouched beside me, gently folding a towel over the whale's eyes. The whale took a rasping, shuddering breath.

Even though I was expecting it, the rifle report made me jump out of my skin.

16

The Woman and the Girl: The Hunt

One autumn morning, when the woman sees the pillar of black smoke in the distance, all the way from Lugh, she knows what it means and what she must do. Sam hasn't come with the groceries for weeks and she will not be able to eke out their meagre supplies for much longer. She hesitates over whether to take the girl with her. Which is the greater risk? To leave her alone on Bride or to reveal her to the St Hians and the torrent of gossip that will undoubtedly ensue? It seems safer to keep the girl by her side, so they hurry to the slipway, board the little fishing boat, and follow the smoke across the Hollow Sea.

As they draw closer to Lugh, they are surrounded by dozens of small wooden rowing boats filled with young men, buoyed up with raucous good cheer, moving in the opposite direction. A great number of the boats have gone out through the neck of the bay, skilfully maintaining a loose circular formation beyond the harbour walls. The girl spots the source of the smoke, a smouldering beacon situated at the top of a hill.

They're the last to arrive, having come the furthest. The woman swears under her breath as she searches for a mooring. Eventually, she finds one, on the south side of the harbour.

Is it a carnival? Is it a fair? The girl has read about summer fairs in the books Mr Sam brings her from the library.

No, not a carnival, the woman says, more harshly than she intended. In truth, she is trying to push a memory from her mind. Another life, another harbourside rippling with excitement. The day she had first seen the girl's father. She shakes away the memory and hurries the girl along the bustling quay.

Carlos Trevelyan, a cheery stallholder at Lugh market, a man she had once purchased oranges and lemons from, steps across their path. The woman, gone so long without social niceties, hesitates as she summons an appropriate greeting, but Carlos folds his arms across his chest and hawks out a greenie, his saliva bubbling on the cobbles. A woman whose son she had taught to play piano crosses herself and mumbles, *Witch.*

A woman she doesn't know joins in, hands on hips. *I'm nae one for rumours but we can see it with our own eyes. The barren witch has a wee child.* A small crowd gathers. The woman's skin burns. The girl presses her face into the woman's body, covering her ears with her hands. *How did you do it, witch? Did you cast a spell or murder them in their sleep? Did you poison them with one of your wee potions?* The woman retreats into her mind, blocking out the jeers, trying to dodge around the growing crowd of people shouting insults.

Thora? Thora? Is it really you? A man, elbowing his way through the crowd.

Antonio? Her husband's old crewmate from a lifetime ago.

Hey, hey. Leave her bide now. He spins to face the mob. *Any folk who truly think Miss Thora's a murderess had better fetch the constable or let peace sit on your damned tongues.* A disgruntled mutter runs through the crowd, but they disperse. Antonio has a string bag of peaches swinging from one hand. He must have been shopping at the market when the beacon was lit. He puts his free hand on her shoulder. *It's been awhile, Miss Thora, to be sure.*

She nods without speaking, certain that words would betray her. Antonio looks older, the laughter lines around his eyes deeper, a scattering of grey through his hair. But she supposes, to him, she must look older too, although the natural paleness of her hair disguises the silvery-white streaks at her temples. It must be a decade or more since she has seen Antonio. She tries to settle on a specific occasion and can only recall that terrible day at the market when she had screamed dreadful words at her former husband and his new wife, when she had ripped away a tiny piece of skin from her enemy's scalp with her bare hands. No wonder the islanders suspect her of having done them harm.

The girl stares solemnly at Antonio from behind the woman's legs. *So, this is the wee lass.* Antonio smiles at the girl, taking in her dark hair, her curls. *She favours her mother, to be sure.* The woman swallows. She is grateful Antonio doesn't enquire how the girl has come to be in her care.

Antonio, have you heard from Sam Pentreath? He . . . visits us sometimes but we've not seen him awhile.

Antonio frowns. *Sam Pentreath, eh? I didna know he was visiting you. Miss Thora. He had a stroke.* The woman's hand flies to her mouth. Antonio touches her elbow, then snatches his hand back, his face reddening. *He's nae passed, Thora, but he'll nae be the same man again.*

A needle of shame pricks at her, for all the times she has been short-tempered with Sam, for all the crates of groceries loaded and unloaded, for the terrible secret he had carried to protect her and the girl. Was the stroke her fault? She had expected so much of Sam, had never even considered his ageing years. She crushes the thought into nothingness. She does not possess the luxury of sentimentality.

The crowds around them move as one down towards the beach, shouts and hollers flying up, the ring of boats at the harbour entrance jostling into position. *It's happening, Miss Thora,* says Antonio. *The wife'll have my guts for garters if I miss it.*

The woman wishes they could stay awhile like this, old friends catching up. *Of course,* she says. *Go. Go.*

Antonio holds out the bag of peaches. *For the wee lass.*

The woman opens her mouth to object, but Antonio thrusts the bag into her hands and disappears into the throng. She waits a respectable moment, then tugs on the girl's arm as they follow the milling crowd past the tavern to the beach.

The boy is there, somewhere. I imagine him standing on a barrel outside the Blackfish Tavern for a better view of events to come, his hair wet and tangled with sand, dressed in clothes pilfered from a washing line. Does he see the ugly crowd on the quayside, take note of the whispered accusations and hostile glances? Does he see the girl for the first time and know immediately in his heart who she is and what he must do?

The woman and the girl come to the beach, eyes straight

ahead, ignoring the mutters of islanders as they pass. The woman feels the heat of a gaze on her back and turns. It is Uffa Denbigh, another old crewmate of her husband's, the one whose eyes had seemed to change from grey to blue to green with the shifting of the sea, eyes that had always lingered over her, making her stomach ache and not in a good way. She remembers with a chill their last encounter, how it might have ended badly for her if Father Carvalho hadn't intervened.

The crowd hums with excitement. *Blackfish coming,* says Uffa to the girl.

Leave us bide, Uffa.

He crouches, bringing his eyes to the same level as the girl's. *Blackfish, they calls them, little woman, and they's black, to be sure. But they's nae fish. They's a monster.*

They're here, they're here, someone shouts. The woman is warm with a dreadful thrill of anticipation. The crowd stills at the head of the beach, gathering in restless groups, expectation crackling in the air. Beyond the bay are the rowing boats, eight or ten men in each. Motorboats would make their job easier, but tradition and a fair fight are important. Their task is to herd the blackfish into the bay, a job for men with the patience of saints. And there, just visible in the distance, a scurry of white on the surface of the water, a flock of blackfish swimming in tight circles, herded by God and forbearance into the hunting ground.

The boats fall into formation, a solid wall in the path of the blackfish. Each time the beasts turn towards open seas, a barrier of rowing boats and oars hems them in, forcing them to turn again and again into the shallow bay. The crowd watches, tongues held and breath held, as the rowing boats make a half-moon shape behind the blackfish, sealing off the neck of the bay. Flashes of black carve through the churning white as the panicked blackfish's fins and bulging heads break the water. They thrash like giant eels as they approach the beach. The men in the boats toss out their casting stones and beat against the sides and on the ocean's surface with their oars, the flock thrusting up spray from their blowholes. The whaleman, the leader of the hunt, stands up in his boat, raises his spear and brings it down on a blackfish at the rear of the flock. A bright spume of blood flares, the injured creature rising out of the water in a fright before swimming at a pace towards the beach. The flock follows its wounded brother as sheep follow the Judas ram to the slaughterhouse.

The islanders run as one down the sand and into the shallows. Uffa Denbigh runs with them, holding his gaff high over his head. The woman and the girl run too, though with less conviction, stopping before they get to the water. *Stay here,* instructs the woman, giving the girl the bag of peaches to hold. *Do not move.* She doesn't need to remind the girl the sea can burn. The girl pouts, but obeys, craning her neck for a better view. The blackfish thrash in the shallows, roiling up clouds of sand, the beach a churning mass of people, foam and black fins. Uffa, selecting his prey, leaps into the surf with a screech that turns the woman's blood to ice, bringing his gaff down in an arc. She wants more than anything in the world to turn her gaze away, but she must observe, learn. The blackfish wails. Uffa crouches beside it, takes a knife from his belt and makes a single, swift cut, severing the whale's backbone. Its tail fluke curls upwards then crashes onto the sand. All along the beach, islanders are slaughtering the blackfish. The surf turns pink, then red.

The woman's face grows warm; her breath quickens. There is a swirling sensation in her belly. She must act now before she loses her nerve. She grabs Uffa by the arm. *Give me your gaff!* Uffa, amused by this development, laughs and tosses it to her. She grips it in her hands, learning the weight of it, feeling the coldness of the metal, and wades out to where an unclaimed blackfish lies nickering like a horse in the surf.

Uffa is beside her, wiping his bloodied blade on his trousers. *In its blowhole, Thora,* he says, his breath a flame in her ear. Full of the fire of the hunt she takes aim, crashing the gaff down clumsily, injuring the blackfish's head, the wound not deep enough to hook with. She tries again and this time the hook sinks cleanly into the blowhole. Uffa passes the woman his knife, the handle damp with his sweat. He points to the spot just above the dorsal fin, and she plunges the knife down. The blade snags on the backbone, the woman grunts and twists to no avail. *Pull it out, Thora,* advises Uffa, *and start again.*

There is a tumult of noise in her head, yet all without seems silent, distant. The woman allows Uffa to help her, pressing his body into hers, stretching their arms out and gripping the knife together, one of Uffa's hands above hers, one below. They crouch together, less awkwardly than one might imagine, for there is a natural grace in the kill. The stink of Uffa's sweat prickles her throat. They draw the blade down, one clean, sharp movement that ends the blackfish's misery once and for all. The girl watches from her place on the sand, rapt.

The woman stares down at her blood-spattered hands, the vigour and courage that sustained her through the hunt fading like sea mist on a summer morning. She slits the blackfish along its belly, pulls out its guts and rummages inside the steaming-hot carcass, locating the liver and kidneys and cutting them out. She draws off the blubber and meat into thin strips ready for salting or drying. She is heartsick, weak, the wave on which she had crested long since broken into nothingness. She carves her initials into the side of the blackfish, staking her claim, TJF, and relinquishes the blade to Uffa without a word of thanks. He wipes it across his thigh, before crouching down to flense the carcass of his own slaughtered blackfish.

The girl, colour high and bright on her cheeks, hops onto the initialled carcass of the blackfish and dances a little jig, knowing her stomach will be full for weeks, months to come. The woman barely notices, can only think she might never want to eat again. Uffa steps close behind her, indecently close now the hunt is over, his breath on her neck. He pushes her hair away from her ear and whispers, *How do you sail the Hollow Sea, Thora? Do you calm the tides with magic? Tell me.*

She twists away from him. *What nonsense,* she cries scornfully. *Magic, indeed! You never thought it was magic when my husband sailed the Hollow Sea.*

Uffa nods once. *Aye, that's true, but he grew up here and you didna.* He grabs her arm, leaning in with poisonous breath.

We know what you did, barren witch. We know what you did to our friend and his dearly beloved wife. We know you stole the bairn. He laughs, the heat of his breath landing like a chill on her skin. He points to the girl, still dancing her jig on the carcass of the blackfish. *They'll come for her, you ken, now she's growing. One day they'll come for her.*

The woman twists away with a grunt. *Who? Who is they? What do you mean?* But Uffa only stares at her, his lips thin and ugly, his jaw misshapen with anger. His eyes, as ever, reflect the colour of the ocean. Except now, instead of blue or grey or green, Uffa's eyes are red.

17

Scottie: The Burning

I was almost to the end of my three-week stay in St Hía and no closer to finding someone who would agree to take me to the Hollow Sea to search for the island in my photo. It was festival day, what Nest referred to as Thora's Burning, and Ellie had given us the afternoon off. I wandered down to the quayside beneath yards of fluttering bunting, dodging throngs of excitable children and harassed parents. A girl of six or seven wearing a witch's hat, even though it was months until Halloween, the sort of hat I had made at school with cardboard and crêpe paper when I was a child, careered into me, depositing a blob of sticky pink candy floss on my jacket.

'Betsi,' snapped a tired-looking woman at least a decade younger than me. 'Get yourself here and behave. Else Thora'll come and steal you away.'

The little girl, chastened, ran back to her mother as I scraped candy floss off my sleeve. I bought a Portuguese custard tart from the market and sat on the quay wall to eat it. The sea was like glass. Movement came only beneath the surface, where the ripples appeared warped, as if reflected in a mirror. I wanted to dive down, to touch the underwater ripples, to capture their essential intangibility and make it real, as if by doing so I could bring my forgotten past into reality too. The weather had been good for most of my stay, but still I could think only of this as a place lashed by storms. I had just a few days left in the archipelago and I still hadn't found my island.

I checked my messages and there were two voicemails from Jasminder on my phone. They felt like an intrusion into this world he would never be a part of. The first, from the day before yesterday. *Call me, Scottie, please. No pressure. Would just be good to hear your voice.* No 'goodbye', no 'love you'. Jasminder's voicemails were always short, functional. The second voicemail was only a few minutes old. *Come home, Scottie. We can stop if you want. No more IVF. You're the only thing I need.* He was lying. He didn't want to stop. He wanted a child more than anything. More than he wanted me? I had thought so, but now I wasn't sure.

I finished my custard tart and walked to the Blackfish Tavern, past a group of young men who were putting the finishing touches to an impressively large bonfire on the quayside. Inside the pub Noah, Ellie and some of the other volunteers were drinking beer out of plastic cups and dancing to fiddle music. Noah gave me an overly affectionate hug. He was drunk. They all were. One of the American college students whose name I still couldn't remember was wearing a witch's hat, grimacing as he gulped a pint of dark brown liquid.

'Oh, man,' he said, 'that sucks. How do you people drink this?'

Noah downed the last of the evil-looking liquid in his plastic cup. 'I'm going to the bar. Anyone want anything? Scottie, can I tempt you to a pint of Thora's Special Brew?

Only served once a year at festival time and tastes like a baboon's arse.'

'That comparison begs a certain question,' said Ellie.

'When did I taste a baboon's backside? A gentleman never tells.'

By the time Noah got back with the drinks, the pub was packed and I was beginning to feel claustrophobic and twitchy. 'I think I'll go and see the sand sculptures,' I said. 'Catch up with you later?'

'I'll come with you,' Ellie said, breathing beer fumes over me. 'You shouldn't drink baboon's arse for the first time unsupervised. I feel responsible for your safety.'

As we jemmied our way through the crowds to the beach, cradling our plastic cups of witch's brew, I asked Ellie who or what Thora was.

'Just the local witch of yore. The locals invoke her name to get their kids to behave. Like a darker sort of Santa Claus. They'll be chucking her effigy on the bonfire later. Which I guess means the kids can start to run riot again. At least until Christmas.'

The beach had been scrubbed clean since the day of the whale strandings, the carcasses of the dead whales cut up and removed for burial in a less scenic spot, but nothing could scrub my memory of the image of my whale, sand in her eye, her tail thrashing over shells, the report of a rifle shot. Now, instead of the suffocating bodies of pilot whales, the beach was littered with sand sculptures.

'Wow,' said Ellie. 'These sculptures are incredible. Even better than last year's.'

The nearest sculpture was of a girl sitting beside a giant

spiral shell. It was hard to believe something so exquisitely detailed could be created just from sand. The sculptor, a woman with flowing grey hair, explained all the sculptures were based on local myth and folklore.

'Inspired by the tale of the singing shell,' she said.

'It's incredible,' I said. 'How long did it take you?'

The woman twisted her hair into a headscarf. 'It was a fair early start this morning, my love. That's all I'll say.'

'All this effort,' said Ellie. 'And tomorrow they'll be washed away by the tide. I don't think I could do it.'

The woman leant across the sculpture to smooth out some imperfection she had noticed in the girl's hair. 'I choose to think the sand remembers, so they're never truly gone.'

I liked this concept, but Ellie rolled her eyes behind the woman's back, and we moved on to the next sculpture, a tooth-and-claw merman writhing on the sand, his face twisted into a scream.

'Wouldn't want to bump into one of those on a dark night,' said Ellie.

At the far edge of the beach, down by the waterline, Kenver Pellow was kneeling next to a sand sculpture, his back to me. His shoulders were moving the way they had when he had played piano and, I remembered, when we had dug sand together from beneath a whale's fins.

Ellie tugged at my jacket. 'Look at this one. It's beautiful.'

The sculpture that had captured her attention was of a woman sleeping on her side in the sand. Naked from the waist up, she had an exquisitely crafted fin between her shoulder blades. I had to agree with Ellie. The sculpture was breathtakingly beautiful. I looked around for the artist, but no one was there to claim her.

'What legend is this?' I asked Ellie. 'What creature is she?'

Ellie shook her head.

'A fin on the back isn't one I've ever heard of but I'm no expert and the lore here is pretty unique. Listen, I'm gonna head back to the pub for a bit. Make sure no one's getting alcohol poisoning. If you're all right?'

'Of course. Go, go,' I said. 'You don't want your last day of seal-counting schedules getting screwed up by witch's brew.'

She gave me a brief wave and headed back across the beach, her red jacket threading through the crowd, her loose hair whipping out behind her in the wind. She looked happy. She'd never mentioned having children, so I assumed she didn't. If Ellie could be happy without children in her life, why couldn't I? Why did being childless make me feel so worthless and purposeless, even when I envied Ellie for her career, her passion and her freedom?

I wandered between sculptures of hook-nosed witches and dolphins and sea-serpents, but nothing was as beautiful as the woman with a fin on her back. When I reached the last sculpture, Kenver Pellow was still kneeling beside it, concentrating so hard he didn't notice me. His sculpture was a child, sitting on the sand, looking back over its shoulder at the sea. I watched in silence as he worked on the detailing of the child's hair, using a tiny scraping tool that flashed silver in the sun. Satisfied, at last, he stood up, his limbs long and loose, and wiped sand from his hands onto his jeans. I walked around the sculpture, to the ocean side, and saw the child had a fin on its back, like the unclaimed sand woman sculpture Ellie and I had seen. Kenver noticed me, finally, and, for the briefest of moments, he was completely still, absorbing my presence.

'It's extraordinary work,' I said, crouching beside the sculpture, resisting the urge to reach out and touch it. 'Did you make the other sculpture too? Of the woman with the fin on her back?'

He nodded.

'And they're from a local legend?'

'Aye. Hollow Fins,' he said, in the same icy-polite tone he had used during the whale stranding. 'A local version of merfolk.'

I stood up, almost spilling my witch's brew.

'I dinna know why you emmets drink that poison,' he said.

'Emmets?'

'Emmets, aye,' he said. 'Tourists.'

I downed the last of my pint. 'But I'm not a tourist.'

He leant across his sculpture, brushed his fingers along its back, repairing some imaginary flaw, a wordless dismissal of me.

A group of chattering spectators descended, encircling the fin-child. I loitered on the edge of the group as he explained the legend of the hollow-finned people. With a larger audience he was animated, engaging, enjoying his own tale of finned mermaids and mermen, living in an underwater kingdom, riding white horses born of sand

and sea foam, enticing unwary travellers to fall into their whirlpool.

The light was changing, a tonal shift into that indefinable space between daytime and dusk, a faint curve of translucent moon on the horizon. A procession of children wearing homemade witches' hats was making its way along the quayside, escorted by men wielding flaming torches. A drumming troupe snaked alongside them, their drums slung low around their waists, beating a marching rhythm. In the middle of it all, an effigy as high as a house, paper wrapped around a wooden frame. A bride, in white, her hair made of fluttering yellow crêpe paper. The Bride Witch, Nest had called her. Thora.

People all around me were chanting, *Burn the witch. Burn the witch.* The bonfire was lit, the hiss and crackle of flames, the scent of woodsmoke, spitting embers, the mesmerizing sway of the smoke against the darkening sky. *Burn the witch.* The crowd moved as one and I moved with them, as I had on the day that we had stumbled out of the gloom of the Blackfish Tavern onto a beach scattered with pilot whales. The heat from the fire brushed my skin. The procession arrived, the drums softening to a background rumble, the effigy carried by many hands towards the flames.

A girl of seven or eight, dressed in black, the only child not wearing a witch's hat, performed an energetic dance routine before crouching in front of the fire, facing the crowd. She held a stuffed cuddly toy, a dolphin or perhaps a whale, in one hand and a plastic knife in the other. *Free the bairn. Free the bairn.* Kenver was chanting with the crowd. *Burn the witch.* The little girl sprang up, making stabbing motions with the knife at the stomach of the toy whale. *Free the bairn*. The girl flung down her props and ran to her mother, as the effigy, the witch in white, was pushed and pulled onto the fire, held upright with ropes. For a moment, the flames seemed only to caress her, and the crowd held its breath, before the paper caught. She went up in seconds, fragments of her yellow crêpe-paper hair and her white gown winnowing into the sky with the smoke.

I stood with them, the good people of St Hía, and watched the Bride Witch burn.

The children were all at home in bed, the bonfire had burnt down to embers, Thora the Bride Witch was ashes and the pub had closed its doors. Warm with alcohol, I went down to the beach, a half-drunk plastic cup of Thora's Special Brew in my hand, to get a last look at the sand sculptures before they disappeared into the sea. The moon was full and bright, illuminating the waves that lapped at the base of Kenver Pellow's sculpture, the fin-child soon to return to the sea for ever. I thought about the long night I had spent on this beach, talking to a whale. I thought about the witch with yellow hair, burning. I thought about my mystery island and its little grey smudge of a cottage and how short a time I had left to find it. I thought about Jasminder, and the babies we would never have. The scar on my back pulsed. I remembered how I had danced once, twisting and stretching my body, like the little girl in front of the bonfire.

My torso twitched and jerked. I balanced my cup on the sand, the sea washing over my trainers. I stepped forward,

forward, forward, the water at my knees, my thighs. I thought about my last ever dance class, the day before my surgery, the wave routine I had performed. Could I remember the steps? I moved my feet against the weight of the waves, I swayed my body, my arms. Eyes closed, I bent and dipped, matching the patterns of the waves, not caring about the freezing temperature. I arched my back, as much as I could post-surgery. I trailed my hands in the water, losing myself in the rhythm.

'I'm all for interpretive dance, but it's nae very sensible to go into the water half-cut and alone in the middle of the night.'

I twitched and stumbled out of my dance move. Kenver Pellow, standing on the beach, shining his phone torch in my direction.

'You scared the crap out of me. I was just —'

'Dancing. Aye, I saw.'

He pointed his phone light at the sand and picked something up. The scraper he had used to create the fin-child. He put the scraper in his pocket and looked up at the sky. 'The Fish Moon,' he said.

I waded onto the beach, my feet cold and uncomfortable inside my drenched trainers. 'I don't know what that means.'

'It's what we call the March full moon.' He took a roll-up from his tobacco pouch and lit it. 'There's an old St Hían tale that the moon is a sea and that great shoals of breal — that's mackerel to you emmets — swim in it. When the breal feed they create a disturbance that makes it seem as if the sea is boiling and that's what makes the patterns you can see on the moon's surface.'

I burst into drunken laughter, although his story wasn't funny.

'Aye, well,' he said, seemingly not offended. 'March is the month the breal start to migrate back into our waters so it's good luck anyways, to be standing beneath a Fish Moon.'

'I'll take all the luck I can get,' I said, hugging myself to try to get warm.

'I dinna think I copped your name before.'

'Scottie Scott-Bains.'

'Aye,' he said. 'The woman who's searching for an island. Well, dinna go back in the water, Scottie Scott-Bains. You're too drunk for swimming and likely too drunk for dancing.'

Before I could answer, before I could ask how he knew I was searching for an island, he had turned his back on me and was walking up the beach, his roll-up a tiny glowing dot in the darkness.

18

Charlotte: Dancing

The last time I had danced was the day before my scoliosis surgery. Helen had been ironing a tablecloth, wedged between the dining table and the ironing board.

I'm not going, I said to her from the hallway.

Don't be difficult about it, Charlotte. Please.

The tablecloth was the Sunday-best one. A gravy-smeared roast potato had dropped off my fork during Sunday lunch, a dramatic splatter pattern arcing across the pristine whiteness of the cloth. Helen had surveyed the crime scene with an air of weary forbearance and stuffed the tablecloth straight into the washing-machine, before we'd even had our apple crumble and custard, and hung it out on the line overnight. The next morning, before school, I had gone out into our narrow little garden, stood in the shade of the neighbour's rowan tree, and sniffed the still-damp tablecloth, inhaling the fresh, dewy scent of it. Now I was home from school and the tablecloth was clean and dry, returned to its virgin state. Helen was folding it with maddening precision, spraying it liberally with starch, pressing each crease with a steaming iron.

It's my body and I don't want an operation. You can't make me go.

I think you'll find I can make you go, she said, the steam puffing up around her face.

I don't need the surgery. I'm happy as I am. You're the one who says I shouldn't care what people think.

She sprayed the tablecloth and ironed in another fold. I hated the burnt-starch smell, hated that it was sucking the soft, sweet, dewy scent out of the tablecloth.

Of course you shouldn't care what people think. But the curve in your spine needs to be sorted out now while you're still young.

Why? Because it makes me ugly? Shouldn't you love me even though I'm not perfect?

The tablecloth was getting smaller, smaller than it needed to be to fit into the drawer in the sideboard, but she kept bringing the edges together neatly and running the iron along the seam.

I refuse to have this conversation with you, Charlotte.

Her face was tight and unhappy, and I knew it was about more than my habitual truculence, which she'd had years to get used to. Today would have been Phil's birthday. A part of me knew I should say something nice. Something about Phil maybe — *Dad loved the smell of freshly ironed linen, didn't he?* — but I couldn't bring myself to do it. I was simmering with teenage rage. Angry that she was so old, that my friends would snigger behind her back and ask me how my granny was. Angry that I was an only child, that I didn't have a brother or sister to act as a buffer between us. Angry at being second best to the biological children I suspected Helen would have preferred to have if she could. Angry that I had been thrown away by my birth family, and even though I knew it was unfair to blame her for that, I couldn't help myself.

You're not my real mother, I said. *You can't tell me what to do.*

The tiniest of flickers passed across her face. She stared at the tablecloth, wanting to fold it one more time, but there was nothing left to fold. It was satisfying, seeing a crack in the façade she had maintained so faithfully since Phil died. I understood she cultivated it for my benefit, to prevent herself from falling apart, but I poked at it anyway, a compulsion like picking a scab even though you knew the wound would take longer to heal.

Dad would never have made me have an operation I didn't want.

There was a moment, the tiniest of nanoseconds, when she was frozen, and then she gave the tablecloth one last blast of starch and placed it reverently in the drawer.

Charlotte, she said, her voice calm and measured, although she was still staring at the sideboard, *go and get changed or you'll be late for your dance class. You don't want to miss your —* She cut herself off, stopped herself saying *your last ever dance class* because, as the doctors had said, there was always hope. *You don't want to be late.*

I thought I might carry on picking at the scab. Tell her I had no intention of going to my dance class. That if she was going to force me into a surgery that might well mean I could never dance again I would skip the last hurrah, thank you very much. Maybe it would be easier not to go, not to have to endure the pity of my contemporary-dance friends, or the cool gazes of the pale pink ballerinas, everyone feeling sorry for the girl who might never dance again. I had a routine to perform to my classmates, one I'd been working on for weeks. I'd choreographed it myself. A dance of the sea, my body moving from calm ripples, to churning foam to crashing waves, to water trickling back from a beach. I loved performing the dance, the sensations it created in my body. I wasn't graceful, I'd never had the poise of a ballerina, but in this dance, it seemed not to matter. I felt something as I danced, as my body flowed in the shapes of waves, the emotions of the sea rushing through my limbs. If I danced it one more time, I thought, maybe I could try to remember the feeling, keep it close.

I went up to my bedroom, took off my tie and my crisp school shirt and stood in front of the full-length mirror on the wardrobe door in my plain teenager's bra. I felt disconnected from myself, my own body becoming strange and unfamiliar as I approached adulthood. I twisted around to stare at my back in the mirror. The curve in my spine had grown more pronounced over the years. But it had changed less than the rest of me and that, perhaps, was why I wanted to keep it. It was mine, something I had brought with me from my forgotten life. Giving it up would be relinquishing the last thing I had from *before*, the last part of the real me. I threw myself down on the bed, burying my wet face in the pillows. There was a knock at the door.

Go away. Don't come in here.

But she came in anyway, sitting beside me on the bed until I had calmed down enough for her to put her hand on my shoulder.

My poor, poor Charlotte, she said. *I know.*

I sat up and she touched her temple to mine. We stayed like that in silence for a few minutes. I wanted to tell her I was sorry for being a cow, but I was still crying too much. I was happy that for once she'd understood something that mattered to me, that the curve in my spine was too much to lose. For a brief moment, I fantasized about a brand-new mother-daughter relationship, like the one my friend Tabitha had with her mum, who was also her best friend, whom she could talk to about boys and sex and shopping, about her deepest feelings. Helen squeezed my hand.

I miss him too, she said.

W-what? I said, wiping snot from my nose with my arm.

Your dad. I miss him too. It's hard, but at least we have each other.

And that was my fantasy dead and shrivelled, like the last of Helen's geraniums, before it had even begun. I cried harder, and Helen put my school jumper around my shoulders and held my hand and this time I let her.

19

The Woman and the Girl:
The Seal Pup

When the girl is five years old, she finds a seal pup on the beach, sprawled spiky-furred and exhausted in the aftermath of a winter storm. She runs to the cottage in a cloud of breathless excitement.

Leave it bide, says the woman, scarcely glancing up from her pickling jars. *Its mother will come back for it, or it will die. Either way, it's not our business.*

The girl has never experienced hunger, not yet, so has the luxury of being soft-hearted, but she knows better than to argue with the woman. She completes her chores, sweeping the front step, drawing water from the well, scrubbing the breakfast dishes, folding the clean towels, still stiff with the soap powder that can't be rinsed out no matter how much the woman stamps around in the washtub. Eventually, when the woman is occupied with her crocheting, the girl sneaks back to the beach.

The seal pup is still there, facing the ocean now, as if it wants to get back there, but she can see it's exhausted, its rear flippers hanging limp on the sand. *It's okay. I won't hurt you. Where is your mammy?* There is a crust of dark red blood on its flipper. She sits, huddled in her duffel coat, by the line of tangled seaweed marking the forbidden ground beyond, but unable to bring herself to leave the pup to die alone on this cold, unforgiving beach.

The woman prepares supper, the last scrapings of a fish and seaweed stew. There is day-old bread too, which she heats through to disguise its staleness, inhaling its nourishing, yeasty scent. She hopes Sam will visit soon. She has made a beautiful blanket that he will be willing to trade for groceries and, in turn, sell at the market on Lugh. The woman strongly suspects the value of the trade is unfair, in her favour, but she dares not mention it to Sam, in case he asks for more. She is unkind about him, out of his hearing, when only the girl is present, not wanting to reveal how much they rely on him, but inside she is silently grateful. She knows they would not survive without him.

Perhaps, if it is a day or two to wait until Sam comes, she could find time to make some hats, scarves and mittens. She has some leftover chocolate-brown wool, and a good supply of the raspberry-coloured yarn Sam procured for her last summer in exchange for a bumper batch of glass jars filled with dried and powdered seaweed. The woman and the girl had made pretty labels for the jars, proclaiming their therapeutic properties. Red ragwort, good for arthritis. A tea infused with mermaid's hair for gout. A generous tablespoon of powdered bladderwrack in a stew would add flavour and lower the blood pressure. Over the years, the woman had learnt to be creative with her claims, but nobody had complained, or at least not that Sam has told her about. *Bladderwrack has sold out, Miss Thora,* he would tell her. *And I only have one of the kelp infusions left.* If that old cow Denella Carvalho could stomach a cup of mermaid's hair tea and imagine that the swelling in her foot had subsided, all well and good.

The girl is late for supper. The woman is irritated, but only mildly. She supposes it is to be expected, with the seal pup on the beach. The woman has observed, with grudging admiration, the girl's attempts to stay away from the beach all day, to obey the woman's instructions to leave the pup to its fate, when every fibre of her being is calling her back to it. When she has finished her meal and the girl still has not returned, the woman grabs a torch, hoping the battery will last because she has no spare, and heads down to the beach, carrying the girl's congealing supper with her.

The girl is a dark, whimpering huddle on the dry sand, the pup a few yards closer to the ocean, a bundle of skin and bone crying for its mother. It sounds disturbingly like a human child. The woman pushes away a memory of the day the girl was born, how she had slipped screaming and bloody into the woman's hands on this very beach. The girl hears the woman's approach, gasps and claps her hand across her mouth as she calculates how late she is for supper, how angry the woman will be.

We must be patient, says the woman. *Its mother may still be nearby.*

They retreat up the beach, concealing themselves behind a rock. The girl, with a blanket around her shoulders, eats her supper. When she has finished, they sit together without conversing. The only sounds are the gentle surf and the rhythm of their breath, which, as the night grows colder, merges with the surf so that it's hard to tell one from the other.

When the light has completely gone, the woman switches on the torch, instructs the girl to stay where she is and goes to the pup. It starts to yip, trying to scramble over rocks to escape from her, tiny jerking motions rippling through its body. The woman crouches over the pup, whispering in a voice so kind and soothing it feels foreign on her tongue. She slides her arms beneath its tiny body and scoops it up. It stinks of musk and salt, like a dog that's been swimming in the sea, but worse. The girl is by her side as she carries the pup back to the house. The woman can tell that the girl longs to reach up and touch it, but she is trying to contain herself.

Shall we fill the bathtub with water so it can swim? says the girl.

Don't be silly.

The girl's face falls, the woman pricked with guilt at her own short temper. She softens her face, her voice. *Fetch the bathtub anyway. We'll make it into a bed.*

The girl beams, the reprimand forgotten. The bath is made of tin, not heavy at all, and the girl fetches it in by herself from the storehouse as the woman riffles through her towels – not that they have many – and selects two that have greyed over the years, fraying at the edges. She lines the bathtub with them and puts the seal pup inside. It doesn't struggle, resigned to its fate, perhaps, or somehow knowing they mean it no harm. It shits all over the towels and the fishy, musky smell is so vile there's a brief moment when the woman thinks she might vomit. The pup will just have to manage with the plain tin of the bathtub. The girl comes with a blanket, a good one the woman had crocheted herself. The woman takes a slow breath in lieu of snatching the blanket from the girl's arms.

It's used to being outside in the cold, she says. *It won't like being too hot.*

What to feed it? The woman has no idea. She offers it water from the well and dried fish, but it only stares up at them with its frightened, melting eyes. In the darkest, dustiest corner of the larder she finds formula baby milk and a plastic bottle, left over from when the girl had been a baby. She warms it on the stove, stirring in the last of their butter to enrich it. She makes up a bottle, surprised by how quickly she falls into the rhythm of sterilizing, mixing, getting the temperature just right. She nudges the pup's muzzle with the rubber teat, but without success. It only cries.

By the time Sam arrives in the morning, creaking under the weight of the groceries, the seal pup is wheezing, strings of mucus hanging from its nostrils. *You've got yourself a wee kettle of fish there,* says Sam, as he hefts the crate onto the table. *A bit ripe, too, heh? What you bring it in the house for?* Sam shows her his age-blunted, tobacco-stained teeth, in what she assumes is supposed to be a cheery smile. *Unless . . . You're nae planning on eating it?*

The girl crouches by the tub, touching the pup's muzzle. *It's burning. The sea's got inside it.* She is trying to be grown-up, holding back her tears. The woman notes her serious eyes and wiry limbs, wondering when it was that the girl had transformed from a feral toddler into this tiny adult-shaped being full of secrets and compassion.

Brought you something, says Sam.

The girl tears herself away from the seal, knowing she is expected to be polite. *What, Mr Sam?*

Sam pats his thighs. *Canna seem to . . .* He pulls out his trouser pockets. *Nae there. Hmmm, now where could it . . .* He pats his torso and his backside, then takes off his cap and peeks inside. *Nae sign of it, young Miss. I canna think . . .* The girl giggles, despite herself. *Maybe I left it on the slipway. My old bones are aching. Could you go down and fetch it back for me?* The girl looks to the woman for permission. *Be quick . . . but don't run. And remember . . .* the girl is already halfway out of the door, forgetting her coat . . . *the sea can burn.*

Heh, Sam says, unloading boxes of breakfast cereal and powdered milk and tinned beans onto the table. *Still nae letting the young miss into the water? A wise choice.*

The woman fetches the basket of blankets and jars of powdered seaweed. *Will this do?*

Sam squints at a jar, holding the label to the light. *Aye. It'll do nicely. But how long do you think you can keep the wee miss away from the sea when it's all around?*

The woman folds a blanket into Sam's crate. *It really isn't your business, Sam. She nearly drowned. I'm just trying to keep her safe.*

The seal pup's breath has deepened to a slow, rhythmic rattle. It's going to die, here in this strange and frightening place, and the woman wishes she had been stronger, that they had left it on the beach.

Nearly drowned, was she? says Sam, picking up the crate full of blankets and jars.

The woman is irritated. *Why else would I want to keep her away from the water?*

Sam puts on his cap and picks up the crate, lips stretching back, showing his teeth again. *And how is nae saying her name meant to stop her drowning? Now dinna misunderstand me, I agree her name should never be said, but why lie to yourself about the reasons, you ken?*

The woman is furious now, but she owes Sam everything. *I don't care for the name, is all,* she says, in a soft, calm voice.

I brought a gift for you too, Miss Thora. Sam takes a small, wrapped package from his pocket. *All you need to know about the young miss you'll find in this book. Read it with care, that's my advice.*

The woman refrains from responding, knowing she will be unable to soften her sharp words. Sam had saved her once, towing her dead husband's boat out into the Hollow Sea and scuttling it. He hadn't even blinked, hadn't even questioned what needed to be done. And they need him still, need him to carry on being kind. Her vision blurs with furious tears.

When she doesn't reach for the book, Sam places it on the table. *Tales from the Hollow Sea,* he says, with a nod. *Aye then. Good day to you, Thora.*

The woman digs a hole on the beach, as deep as she can manage in the wet sand, getting hot and sweaty despite the chill in the air. The seal pup's body is lighter even than the night before, a sack of bones. She places it gently in the hole. The girl watches solemnly, from behind the imaginary barrier of the tideline. She has chocolate spread – the gift from Sam – smeared around the corners of her mouth. The woman asks the girl if she wants to say something about the pup. The girl seems surprised by this suggestion, thinks for a few moments, leans as far forward across the tideline as she can, and says, *I'm sorry your mammy didn't come back for you.*

When the seal pup is decently buried, the girl sits on the sand with a thoughtful expression on her face. *Why isn't the sea burning you?*

The woman rests on the handle of her shovel and wipes sweat from her face. *Who says it isn't?*

The girl points at the woman's shoes. *Your feet are wet,* she says, *but it's not hurting you. And you touch the water when you're gathering seaweed.*

The woman steps across to the dry side of the beach. *I'm a grown-up, Fairy, so it's safer for me. But the sea can burn anyone.*

20

Scottie: Sea Mist

I arrived at the marina ten minutes late and hung-over. The grinding-glass sensation in my temples at least distracted me from the realization that it was my last day in St Hía and I hadn't discovered a single concrete fact about my past. The thought of going home, to face up to a childless future, either with Jasminder or alone, made me sick with dread.

Everyone had already left on their assignments. Only Kenver Pellow was still there, leaning against a railing and smoking a roll-up.

'You're late,' he said, handing me a life jacket. 'Ellie's assigned us Brengy, Ronan, St Columba and Cathansay. It's a long trip so let's be away.'

I didn't have a word to describe how his cool appraisal made me feel, but I knew I didn't relish the prospect of spending an extended period alone with him. What would we talk about? I suppressed a sigh and followed him along the pontoon to where his boat was moored. It was a rigid inflatable, with an aluminium floor, and looked to me like the sort of boat you might go diving from.

'Sea slight. Clear skies. Should be fine, but the weather can turn on a sixpence here, so you'll follow my instructions while you're on my boat.'

'Of course,' I said, mirroring his coolness. 'How long will it take us to get there?'

He shrugged. 'It's a fair trip to be sure.'

He took us north. The sounds of the sea, splashing waves, screaming gulls, poured in, filling up the silent space between us. The sky was marbled grey. I shivered, glad of the waterproof I was wearing beneath my life jacket.

'Did you grow up here?' I said, trying to take my mind off the increasingly rough sea, my stomach rolling with every wave.

He nodded, but didn't elaborate, the wind pushing his curls from his face, revealing the thin white scar on his temple.

'I haven't seen you around much outside seal counting.'

'I live on St Mertheriana, so you wouldna.'

The third largest island in the archipelago, to the north-west of Lugh, I remembered from my guidebook.

'Are you a fisherman?'

'I do this and that but, aye, sometimes I go out on the boats.'

'Who told you I was searching for an island?'

'Word gets around,' he said, his hand moving involuntarily up to his temple and touching his scar.

'Everyone I've spoken to seems to think the island I'm looking for is in a place called the Hollow Sea, but no one will agree to take me there.'

'Aye, well.'

'Would you take me there if I asked you?'

He shook his head.

'Please,' I said. 'It's my last day. I'm leaving tomorrow.'

'Nae chance.'

'We're heading north now. How much further can it be?'

'It's nae a question of distance. The Hollow Sea's a dangerous place. And it's bad luck.'

I burst out laughing. 'I didn't take you for superstitious.'

'Nae superstition,' he said. 'Just good sense. There's a whirlpool –'

I cut him off. 'Ellie's explained all this.'

'Did she, aye? Well, then, you'll ken that the number of ships and boats sitting at the bottom of the Hollow Sea speaks for itself.'

I stared out at the ocean, swallowing my frustration. *One-wave-breathe, two-waves-breathe, three-waves-breathe.*

'What's your interest in this mystery island?' he said. 'You're nae here for seals.'

'What makes you think I'm not here for the seals?'

'There's three types of people who come to St Hía to count seals, and you're none of them.'

'I don't think you know me well enough to judge what type of person I am.'

The wind was rising, blowing Kenver's hair back from his face, the scar on his temple more pronounced than ever. 'To start,' he said. 'You're the only seal counter I've ever met who didna have a conniption when they found out about the blackfish hunts.'

'It wasn't done for fun, right? That's what you said.'

'Type one,' said Kenver. 'The Ellies and the Noahs, smug professionals here to save the wildlife from the locals who've been existing with it just fine for centuries.'

I snorted laughter. 'They're not that bad. Ellie's lovely.'

'Aye, Ellie's doing important work and I'm fond of her,

but she thinks we're all eejits because we dinna have degrees from fancy universities.'

'Maybe I'm type one, then. I've got a degree.'

The swell was rising with the wind, making me queasy. 'In what?'

'Ceramics. From Anglia Ruskin.'

'You're a ceramics artist?'

'Not any more. I'm an admin assistant now.'

This seemed to amuse him, but he refrained from comment. 'Type two,' he said. 'The gap years. You're a wee bit too long in the tooth to be on work experience. Nae offence.'

A large wave hit the boat, sending my stomach into my throat.

'Should we go back? It's getting rough,' I said, sliding my hand beneath one of the grab handles on the side of the boat.

'We're fine. She's built for seas like this. Type three. Bored suburban housewives. Like the lass with the freckles.'

'Alison. Well, there, you see. You've got me all wrong. I'm the very epitome of a bored suburban housewife. I'm just another Alison.'

'Fed-up middle-class lasses running away from their bairns and pretending they're still living free lives. That's nae you, Scottie.'

A free life. I couldn't remember the last time I'd gone out with my girlfriends and not had to endure an evening of endless conversations about their children and how fucking tired they all were and how I wasn't allowed to be tired even though I hadn't had a good night's sleep since our first IVF ended in a Big Fat Negative. I couldn't remember the last time Jasminder and I had done anything spontaneous, ruled as we were by cycles and medication and saving every penny for IVF. I turned to stare at the waves so Kenver wouldn't see the tears that welled up. I wasn't like Alison at all, and never could be.

'It's not a free life,' I said, but my words were lost to the wind and the sea.

One-breathe-in, two-breathe-out.

'Sorry,' he said. 'Didna mean to upset you.'

'I'm not upset.'

'Aye.'

'So, you were right. I'm none of the three types. Do you get a prize?'

He blinked, surprised by my ferocity, then smiled and nodded at a point beyond my shoulder.

'Look.'

A seal with a mottled face was peeping up from the waves, observing us with interest.

'Hello, girl,' said Kenver, softly. 'Scottie, meet Seena.'

The seal was small, with a mottled face and dark, liquid eyes. It dipped beneath the water, resurfacing next to the boat.

'Is it tame?'

'Aye,' said Kenver. 'She's tame. But prone to nipping tourists, so keep your fingers in the boat. Seal bites can be nasty.'

Seena rotated her body in the water, presenting Kenver with her belly.

'Take the tiller, will you?'

I scooted across and kept the tiller steady while he leant over the side and petted her.

'Did she escape from somewhere? How can she be so tame?'

'Seena's a local celebrity and she's an old lady so be polite to her. I remember her from when I was a lad.'

Seena nudged his hand with her head. Kenver patted her.

'But how did she get so used to people?'

'Ellie wouldna agree, but there's seafaring tales going back centuries of seals saving shipwrecked sailors by nudging them into shallow waters. Curiosity on the seal's part, maybe, but many a sailor had reason to thank a seal for their life. Seena's nae the first. That's enough, Seena.' Kenver scratched her head one last time. 'We canna spend all day here playing with an overgrown Labrador.'

He took the tiller from me. I knelt at the side of the boat, where Seena was showing off, tumbling and twisting in the gentle waves, and trailed my fingers in the water. 'Seena,' I said. 'Come here, girl. I won't hurt you.'

'I wouldna do that,' said Kenver. 'She'll bite you.'

Seena swam straight to me, bumping my hand with her head.

'Amazing,' said Kenver. 'I've nae seen her respond to an outsider like that.'

'Good girl, good girl. Why are you so friendly, Seena?'

'The story goes,' said Kenver, 'that a young widow found a stranded seal pup on the beach. She took it home and cared for it. Loved it as if it were her own child. But she knew it was best for it to go back to the wild, so when the time came, she took the pup down to the sea and released it. Overcome with grief and loneliness, she ran into the ocean intending to drown herself. But she didna drown. Her skin and muscles rippled. Her body broadened. Her limbs contracted, becoming flatter and wider. Silky fur grew across her skin. Her face lengthened, whiskers sprouting out. The strength of her maternal love had transformed her into a seal, and she tumbled joyful in the waves before diving down to be with her pup.'

Seena nudged my wrist one last time before darting away. I watched her dipping in and out of the waves.

'You know your story's bullshit, right? The idea that you can make yourself a mother through sheer force of will. That if you want something badly enough magic will happen. It's fucking bullshit, Kenver. There are some things you just can't make happen, no matter how hard you try.'

He was momentarily silent, taken aback by my outburst. 'It's just a wee legend. Naught to upset yourself with.'

'Your St Hía myths and legends aren't exactly progressive, though, are they? Women shape-changing themselves into motherhood. Burning witches. Christ, Kenver.'

'You're thinking of Thora, aye, from the festival? A murderess. A spurned wife who killed her husband and his new wife and stole their bairn.'

'Let me guess. The baby-thief was childless. And how did she become a witch in this story? A childless, baby-stealing witch. It's not even very original.'

'You're being oversensitive. Naebody's saying all childless women steal bairns.'

'Did the good people of St Hía really toss her on a fire?'

'O' course nae. They used to light fires for the blackfish

hunts to signal to the surrounding islands when a pod of whales was close by. A new tradition got merged with an old one is all. Naebody kens what happened to Thora.'

I looked up at the marbled sky, so he wouldn't see the emotion on my face.

'Haven't we got seals to count?' I said. 'We should get going.'

Brengy, Ronan, St Columba and Cathansay, the northern-most islands of Ellie's survey. The waves were angry, foaming around rocks. I recorded six seals hauled out on the south beach at St Columba, nine on Cathansay and thirty-two on Ronan, which was little more than a scree of rocks and sand. As we readied ourselves to head around to the beaches on the northern edge of St Columba before finishing up with Brengy, the light changed suddenly, from grey to pink, the wind dropping away to nothing, the sea becoming flat calm. Everything was silent.

'What is this?' I said. 'How can it be so still?'

Kenver opened his mouth to answer, but we were swallowed by mist, unfurling all around us, appearing from nowhere. It was so thick I couldn't even see Kenver's face. There was nothing but pinky whiteness all around.

'Nae need to panic. It'll clear.'

But I could hear the tension in his words.

'What if we hit a rock?'

The mist muffled our voices. Kenver dropped the speed of the boat, moving as slowly as possible to keep us away from the treacherous rocks of St Columba. 'We'll nae be hitting any rocks. We've got a radio, lights and a foghorn.

I'm going to plot a course right through the middle of the channel between Brengy and St Columba. We'll be safe – there's naught there to hit.'

'Is this even normal? For a mist to come down so thickly? The weather's been so nice,' I whispered, as if speaking aloud in this still and silent half-world would somehow be bad manners.

'Aye, it's been a pretty spring, but spring on land and spring at sea are very different seasons. Can you fetch the foghorn? You'll find it just down there by your feet.'

'Got it.'

'Signal once every two minutes, one long blast. And in between blasts, listen out.'

'For what?'

'Anything you wouldna expect to hear in the middle of an empty ocean.'

I signalled with the foghorn, the sound blasting into my ears. I couldn't see my watch, so I counted to one hundred and twenty, and signalled again.

The fog between us swirled and ebbed and I glimpsed Kenver's face, a study in concentration as he worked his navigational magic. The fog was dampening his hair, pulling out the curls. I trusted him, but at the same time, the blindness was terrifying. The screeching of the foghorn rolled away into the whiteness. I followed Kenver's instructions, listening for the sound of another boat, waves crashing against rocks, but there was nothing. It grew cold, all the sun's warmth sucked away into the mist. I began to shiver, my teeth chattering, my fingers frozen around the foghorn.

And then, out of nowhere, a trigger. The cold whiteness enveloping us made me think of my ghost children in waiting, the three remaining embryos in their liquid-nitrogen-filled container. What would happen to them if I didn't go home? Those embryos, mine and Jasminder's, made of the two of us, suspended in the cold fog as their time ticked away. A letter from the clinic every year to remind us, as if we might forget, how long we had left before they stopped being potential children and became will-o'-the-wisps instead.

I felt a powerful urge, then, to run home, back to Jasminder, back to hormones and injections and bruises and scans and the hope that sustained us through each treatment cycle. The hope we'd surfed on for years. How could I leave them? But reality crashed in. The thought of another failure, another loss, was too much to bear.

One-breathe-in, two-breathe-out, three-waves-breathe, four-waves-breathe and it wasn't working, the howling was coming like a train and Kenver was saying something to me, *Scottie, sound the foghorn, for fuck's sake,* and there was no stopping it now, a wave ripping through me, shearing every grief-packed atom from its mooring. I couldn't hold it in no matter how much I counted my breaths, so I just let the howl come. *Scottie, Scottie, what's wrong?* and still it kept coming. Kenver, close to me, hands on my shoulders, panic in his face. The scent of him flooded over me. Tobacco and chewing gum on his breath, deodorant, laundry detergent, the yarn of his sweater, his shampoo, the oil on his scalp, the glittering fish scales embedded in his fingertips.

And then it was over, my madness swallowed by the mist

and the mist swallowed by the sun, leaving me empty and shaking beneath a blue sky. Kenver relinquished his grip on my shoulders.

'Jesus, Scottie,' he said, unable to disguise the tremor in his voice. 'What was that? What's wrong with you?'

I had lost all sense of direction, all sense of where we were. The boat collided with something just beneath the surface, slamming us both against the side. The engine cut out. Kenver swore, scrambling up, but we bounced free from whatever we'd hit. The boat was spinning and skating across the water, pushed and pulled along by a foaming sea, chasing the receding mist. To either side of us were islands that seemed to be walls of rock stretching up into the sky, white flashes of seabirds whirling against dark cliff. Kenver continued to swear rhythmically under his breath as he tried to get the engine going. The sea roiled and roared, swirling along like river rapids, skimming us from rock to rock.

'Where are we?' I had to shout to be heard over the roaring of the sea.

Kenver barely even glanced at me as he answered. 'The Tanguy-Tanick strait.'

I remembered Ellie's words in the Blackfish Tavern on the day of the whales. *Unusually strong currents . . . a narrow strait between two islands . . . a maelstrom.*

The engine burst into life. Kenver grabbed the tiller, the motor straining as it fought against currents that didn't want to let us go. Escape seemed an impossibility. I closed my eyes and muttered a silent prayer, the sea still hurling us from rock to rock.

And then it was over. The currents relinquished us, and we were floating in calm water, the roar of the maelstrom fading into the distance. Kenver was staring at me, ashen-faced. 'Scottie —'

'Sssh.' I put my finger to my lips. I was listening, as if we were still gliding through the fog. The thrum of the outboard, screaming seabirds, all the sounds of the ocean coming alive as the fog receded ahead of us, as we came out of the strait and the sea opened up. Greys and greens. Waves churning over rocks. The taste of rain, peaches and sand on my tongue.

The rhythm of the waves was different from anything I'd heard before and yet, at the same time, it reminded me of something. These were the waves that had tugged at my soul, sung to me my whole life.

'This is the Hollow Sea,' I whispered.

Kenver nodded, his face pallid and miserable. Behind him, the last few wisps of mist were dissipating, curling up to meet the clouds, an island materializing from within.

'Is this Brengy?' I stood up, stumbling a little, enchanted.

'Scottie, sit down, for fuck's sake.'

'Kenver, is this Brengy?'

'Nae,' he said eventually, in a hushed voice. 'It's Bride.'

21

Charlotte: Scars

After my back surgery, I couldn't dance, so Helen encouraged me to walk. It wasn't the same. I missed being able to create curves and waves with my body, but I did enjoy the solitude, the opportunity to be away from Helen's constant observation and the bedroom that still felt as though it belonged to somebody else after all these years. At first, I walked the streets around our own. Neat, straight rows of terraced houses with front doors that opened onto the pavement, so as you walked past you could catch glimpses of the life inside, a lamp clicking on, a television blaring, clothes strung up on an airer. Each street was named after a dead male writer and a small wood: Shakespeare Grove, Dickens Grove, Shelley Grove. As a young child I had accepted the street names without question, but as I grew older, I found them incongruous, not least because any trees, anything green of any kind, were hidden away in narrow back gardens.

As my back healed and I grew fitter, I walked further, branching out into the surrounding well-to-do suburbs where Helen had grown up, before she had, as her own late mother had described it, 'married down', then fallen on even harder times when Phil died. My favourite place to walk was the Shires, a network of winding streets where moss grew in the cracks in the tarmac and all the houses looked different, with front gardens and driveways, and there were blossom and fruit and conker and pine trees to track the seasons.

Most of these streets were named after breeds of horse. At first, not having any experience of horses, I didn't realize this. Of course, I had heard of Shetland ponies, but didn't connect this to Shetland Street. Clydesdale Avenue might have been named after a bank, and Friesian Avenue had always amused me. Imagine living in a street named after a breed of cow. But one evening, grudgingly sitting downstairs with Helen watching telly, there was a news report about the famous Lipizzaner dancing horses, and I thought of taking the bus to school along Lipizzaner Avenue and it all fell into place. I found a book on horse breeds in the library and suddenly walking down Percheron Road, or Appaloosa Avenue, or Haflinger Close took on a whole new meaning. And although my library book showed me the colours and markings of the different breeds, in my imagination they were all white, like the Lipizzaners and the Camarillos. With each new street I walked, I imagined myself riding a beautiful white horse along a beach. Sometimes, if I had walked long enough, I would go to bed with that image in my mind, and as I fell asleep, my white horse would dance into the surf, going deeper and deeper into the ocean as I clung to his mane, as the gentle waves washed over me.

I suppose that's what I was thinking about, white horses and beaches and gentle waves, the night I turned into Oberlander Road, thinking I would walk the full length of it and then cut through the cemetery, which would bring me back to the dead-author Groves where I lived and still have time to do my homework. And because I was thinking about horses, I didn't see Simone Hayden and the others in the bus shelter until it was too late. They were from my year, but we weren't friends. They lived on the Shires so seemed impossibly wealthy to me, but what separated us more than anything was social status. They were the popular ones, the ones with the most fashionable clothes, the ones who breezed through life with a confidence and assuredness I could only dream about. They'd never been mean to me, we just existed in different universes, and I was happy to keep it that way. It was too late to turn around and crossing the street would make me look like a coward, so I stared straight ahead and hoped they wouldn't notice me.

Nice school uniform chic, said Simone, as I passed the bus shelter to a chorus of giggles.

Thanks, I said. *That's the exact look I was going for.*

Simone was wearing ripped jeans, a midi top, big hoop earrings and white trainers with platform soles. She looked amazing, but even if I'd been wearing the exact same outfit, I would have seemed like a charity-shop reject next to her.

Hey, aren't you the girl who had to have her back cut open or something? This was Simone's sidekick Emma, who I couldn't remember ever having spoken to in my life.

Yep. That's me.

Emma was holding a bottle of White Ace cider in one hand, and a cigarette in the other. *Cool,* she said. *Have you got a scar?*

Simone rolled her eyes. *Well, of course, she's got a scar, you*

147

dim bint. She had a fucking operation. Simone took the White Ace from Emma, wiped the neck of the bottle with her sleeve and offered it to me. I shook my head.

Aww, said Emma. *Are you not allowed to drink on a school night?* There was no real malice in it. It was just the way they spoke to everyone, including each other.

Show us your scar. Simone took another swig of cider.

Fuck off, I said, hoping to win points for bad language.

Oh, go on. Pleeease, pretty please. Don't worry about the boys, we'll stand here to shield you. Simone and Emma positioned themselves between me and the three boys in the bus shelter. Two of them, who I didn't know, were having a loud discussion about the relative merits of Wolves and West Bromwich Albion. The third, Sheldon Marshall, was drinking cider from a can, smoking and hiding beneath his floppy blond fringe, pretending not to look in our direction. I tied my cardigan around my waist and undid the top few buttons of my school shirt, shucking it down over my shoulders so Simone and Emma could do their scar inspection and I could get home, more self-conscious of my plain white schoolgirl's bra than I was about my scar.

Fuck, said Simone, which I took to mean she was suitably impressed.

It's ugly as hell, said Emma, but Simone shushed her, and they turned back to their cider and Benson & Hedges.

Bye, Uniform Girl, said Simone, letting me know our brief social interaction had come to an end.

One of Sheldon's friends was shaking a bottle of White Ace. *Watch out, Simmers.* He laughed, releasing his thumb like a winning Formula One driver. Simone and Emma jumped up onto the seat inside the shelter as foamy cider sprayed over my newly buttoned-up shirt, soaking right through to my bra.

Piss poor aim, Marky-Mark, said Simone.

I started walking back along Oberlander Road towards the cemetery, wondering how I was going to hide the smell of cider from Helen.

What a waste of booze, Emma was saying, in the distance, as I pushed down the latch on the cemetery gate and slipped inside.

The cemetery was cool and quiet, full of shadows and yew trees. Ordinarily, I liked to read the names on the old, abandoned headstones and imagine the life of the person buried there. *Ethel Singleton, darling wife of Robert Singleton. Albert Pimm, beloved father, son and brother.* What would they say about me if I died? Beloved daughter? Was I beloved to Helen? I was surely a disappointment to her, not the pink-loving little princess she had dreamt of. Perhaps she wished she had sent me back, regretted getting saddled with me, especially after Phil died and she'd had to raise me all alone. But tonight I was late, it was getting cold, and my shirt was wet, so I didn't linger, taking the most direct path across the cemetery to the Groves.

Hey, Uniform Girl. It was Sheldon Marshall, catching up to me with long, lanky strides, his cigarette a tiny burning sun in the fading light.

What do you want?

He pushed his fringe away from his eyes with his non-cigarette hand. *Did it hurt?* I kept walking, wishing he would go away. *Whoa, slow down a bit. I'm trying to talk to you*. I stopped dead, and Sheldon took two more of his deceptively casual strides before doubling back to face me.

I have a very high pain threshold, I said, which wasn't true.

You must be brave, he said, offering me the filter end of his cigarette. I inhaled carefully, praying I wouldn't choke. *I'm Sheldon.*

I nodded. *I know. We're in the same year.*

He grinned. *Do you have a name, Uniform Girl?*

Not that I'd expected him to know it, but it annoyed me all the same that he didn't.

Charlotte Scott. He took another drag of his cigarette. *Charlotte Scott. Your name rhymes. Ha-ha.*

I started walking again. *You don't say.*

He laughed, not at all offended by my prickliness. *You stink of cider,* he said, falling in beside me.

Yep, thanks for that, I said, even though it hadn't been his fault.

Sheldon sort of sideways stepped in front of me, holding up his hand. *Stop, Charlotte Scott.* He laughed at his accidental poem.

I have to get home, Sheldon. His fringe had fallen across his eyes again, and he shoved it back. He gave me his cigarette. *Hold this.* Sheldon took off his sweatshirt, revealing his grey school shirt underneath. *You can wear this,* he said. *So, your parents don't smell the cider.* He pulled the shirt over his head without unbuttoning it.

It won't fit me, I said, trying not to look at his naked torso, freckled and thin in the narrow strip of fading sunlight between the shadows of yew trees.

Nah, he said. *It'll do if you put your cardigan on over it. They won't even notice.* He handed me the shirt. *C'mon, Uniform Girl. I'll avert my eyes.* He covered his face theatrically. I shimmied out of my cider-soaked shirt and into Sheldon's cleanish one. I could smell cigarette smoke on it, and his boy deodorant, which wasn't ideal, but it was an improvement. I had thought it would swamp me, but it was too tight across the chest, and I was more aware than ever of my changing body, fastening my cardigan to disguise the straining buttons.

Sheldon was back in his sweatshirt and lighting another fag. *You can give it back to me at school,* he said, and I opened my mouth to thank him just as he leant over and kissed me. His mouth was warm on mine and tasted of cider and cigarettes. My mind raced. Would he be able to tell I'd never been kissed before? Was I doing it right? What did I taste of? Had I brushed my teeth after dinner? The kiss made me feel warm inside and a bit shaky. He broke away gently.

See you at school, Uniform Girl, he said, turned and strode back towards Oberlander Road and the bus shelter, a slight bounce in his walk, leaving me holding my cider-soaked shirt in one hand and a cigarette burning to embers in the other.

At school, the next day, when I tried to return his shirt, Sheldon pretended not to know me.

22

The Woman and the Girl: Susan

Before the woman becomes too afraid to speak her name aloud, before she makes the rule forbidding her to step across the line that divides the dry sand from the wet, Susan is free to do as she pleases. She is tiny still, and fey, a toddler, clumsy on land but slipping in and out of the shallow waves with the grace of a seal, her hair slick with seawater. The woman tries her best to mother the child, to pack away her guilt and care for this cuckoo in her nest. I believe she tried her best. I have to believe that.

It had been easier when Susan was a babe in arms. She cried and screamed and drank the formula milk Sam delivered fortnightly with the groceries, and she pissed and shit, and all this the woman coped with, as much as it left her exhausted and wrung out. She knew it was just the way babies were. It wasn't personal.

But as Susan grows, begins to crawl, laugh, speak, sing, toddle, swim, every action she takes seems, to the woman, to be a rejection, a judgement on her maternal abilities. If the woman tells Susan to sit and eat her dinner nicely, she will run squealing around the cottage until the food is cold and then refuse it altogether. *Nasty.* If the woman tells her to brush her teeth and get ready for bed, Susan will dance naked on the beach or hide in the curing house or squeeze the last of the precious toothpaste supply out onto the sand. If the woman tries to hug or kiss her, Susan will push her away. *Nasty, nasty, nasty.* She tells herself this is just how toddlers are, it will pass. But deep inside, in a slithering knot in her stomach, she nurses her darkest fear, that she is a bad mother, could only ever be a bad mother and that is why the universe took all of her own babies.

One late-summer evening, the woman is bathing Susan in front of the hearth, in the tin bathtub filled pan by pan with water heated over the stove. Susan is a squirmy little minnow, slippery with soap. The woman scrubs Susan's back and rinses the suds away with a jug of lukewarm water. Something about Susan's back is not right. It must be the way the child is sitting. The woman blinks.

Lean forward, Susan, she says, and for once, miraculously, Susan obeys. *Now sit up.* The woman runs her finger up Susan's spine, over each single vertebra, taking care to move her hand in a straight line. Susan giggles, ticklish, leaning into her knees, turning her head to blink over her shoulder at the woman. Soap suds in her wild curls, eyes shiny dark, droplets of bathwater sparkling on her face. The woman's breath catches, and she is flooded with a sense of déjà vu she cannot account for. She pushes it to one side.

Keep still, Susan. As still as you can. If you're a good girl, you can have a biscuit before you go to bed. Susan is instantly a statue. A biscuit is a rare treat, but there are a few left in the packet of custard creams Sam brought for them at Easter, carefully rationed, going soft now but still edible. In the upper portion of Susan's spine, between her shoulder blades, a bump, a curve that shouldn't be there. *Does your back hurt, Susan?*

Susan shakes her head, wriggles free, splashing soapy

water over the hearth. *Bissit! Bissit!* The woman wraps Susan in a towel, but she hurls it onto the floor and dances naked around the cottage. *Bissit, bissit, bissit.* The woman keeps her promise and gives Susan a custard cream.

Be a good girl and eat it nicely, but Susan runs out of the cottage, waving the tiny yellow rectangle aloft like a prize.

That night, the woman lies awake, listening to the hushing of the summer waves. Usually they soothe her, but tonight they whisper behind her back, muttering half-heard answers to half-formed questions. Two things are on her mind, twisting around one another, like a rag having the water wrung out of it. The hump forming on Susan's spine may need the attention of a doctor, but that would mean a trip to Lugh and all the unwanted attention that would ensue. And tangled around that thought is another, the powerful rush of déjà vu she had experienced when Susan looked back over her shoulder in the bathtub, with her gleaming eyes, wayward curls and wet face.

At first light, she goes outside to the store where they keep the washtub and the bathtub and everything else that won't fit inside their tiny living space. In the furthest corner, covered with a sheet, a stack of her late husband's canvases. They had been in the cottage when she had returned, reluctantly, to Bride. She had tortured herself with them for days before opting for distance over destruction and removing them to the store, never to be seen or thought about again. She remembers a time when all her husband had painted was her, but those paintings are missing, destroyed, she supposes, when he cast her out. The ones beneath the sheet came later. There are only three, all signed with her husband's initials, CF, at the bottom right corner in his unmistakable cursive. The first two are similar. A dark-haired woman sitting on the beach, wrapped in a rough-knitted shawl, staring out to sea with haunted eyes. In one, her belly is hidden, invisible beneath the chunky wool of the shawl. In the other, she is pregnant, her belly a huge moon, the edges of the shawl falling loose around the sides. She had once thought this dark-haired woman her bitter rival, but she doesn't linger over bad memories.

The third painting is the one she's interested in. It shows a naked child sitting on a rock, one of Susan's older sisters, she presumes, a restless sea in the background. The woman knows this rock, walks past it on her way to harvest limpets or sea lettuce. She shivers. The child in the painting is glancing back over its shoulder at the artist, its face framed by a mass of dark curls. The woman's half-memory, of stumbling across this canvas when she returned bitter and grief-stricken to the cottage on the day Susan was born, was what had caused the dizzying sense of déjà vu when Susan had looked over her shoulder in the bathtub.

But there is another detail to the painting, a detail that tugs at the second thread in the knot of things that had kept the woman awake through the night. The child in the painting has a fin on its back. The fin is hollow, filled with shimmering light, located just between the child's shoulder blades. The woman has heard the legend of the Hollow Fins. Her husband had told her, sitting by the stove on a winter's night drinking hot chocolate. Shape-changing merfolk who lived in an underwater kingdom beneath the Hollow Sea, who travel to the 'up-above', the realm of land-dwellers, riding horses born from sand.

The woman doesn't believe in fairy-tales. But she does wonder about the placement of the fin in the painting. It's the same spot between the shoulder blades as the slight hump she'd noticed on Susan's back. When the woman's husband had painted her, he had mythologized her hair as kelp forest and shifting tides, so perhaps in his new life, with his new family, he had done the same with his older daughter, so that the misshapenness of her back was transformed into something beautiful, a fin that pulsed with light. It was of no consequence to the woman, but if Susan has the same abnormality, then it must be congenital, and what will it mean for her, living out here in isolation with no hospitals, no doctors, no surgeons? Susan's deformity is slight, barely noticeable. Perhaps it will not grow. There is nothing to do but wait and watch. She places the sheet back over the paintings. She will ask Sam to take them, to destroy them. She doesn't want ever again to see these reminders of the new life her husband made for himself.

There are other things of her husband's in the storeroom. Shiny aluminium tubes of paint, brushes, nubs of chalk and shards of charcoal, a tin of varnish. She gathers some of them up into one of the plastic crates she uses for drying seaweed, and goes down to the beach, where Susan is swimming, a slick little seal in the surf. She watches Susan for a few moments as she dips in and out of the waves.

Susan. Come and put on your clothes. We have work to do. Susan dives into an incoming wave, and the next and the next, the sea lifting her off her feet. Her absence of fear, her unfailing belief that the sea will cocoon her, touches the woman somehow. She swallows her habitual irritation and sits down on the sand.

The sea breathes with a musical rhythm, swishing and receding, a gentle one-two, one-two beat. White curls scurry across blue-grey waves. As the sun moves across the beach, the woman's shadow lengthening on the sand, the beat of the waves accelerates and amplifies, drowning the child's rippling laughter. The white scurries intensify, giving the impression that something is moving under the water. The woman jumps to her feet.

Susan, come back now. It's getting rough. Susan disappears beneath the surf and the woman holds her breath until the child resurfaces, at the edge of the white scurries. Susan submerges again, and this time she does not reappear. The woman waits too long. Susan has swum safely in this water for as long as she could toddle down from the cottage onto the sand under her own steam. The woman has been lax with safety, driven, perhaps, by her ambivalence over the strange cuckoo child in her care, but she has never had any reason to doubt Susan's natural affinity for the water.

There is still no sign of Susan, and the sea is louder. The one-two rhythm almost sounds like her name. *Suu-san, Suu-san*, the white froth angry, clamouring. The woman runs to the edge of the water, the sea creeping around her ankles, her knees. Her skirts float and billow around her. Her cries of the child's name, *Susan, Susan*, harmonize with the song of the waves. *Suu-san. Suu-san.*

Something brushes against her leg. Chest deep now, almost to the scurrying white, and some combination of sunshine and water is forming tiny glimmering rainbows that dip and dive. The coldness pushes the breath from the woman's lungs. She wonders how Susan can tolerate it so casually, and now the woman's hair is floating on the surface, the weight of the water tugging at her scalp. Amid the white rage, a tiny elbow appears, then disappears. The woman reaches forward, the strength of the waves almost lifting her off her feet. Susan's arm surfaces, and the woman grabs it, tugging Susan close to her own body. Susan is panicking. She whips her body and bites and pummels her fists against the woman's ribs, as the angry white current plucks and pinches at her limbs. The woman somehow manages to fold Susan's body into hers, and sculls backwards against the current, towards sand and safety. For a few minutes, the current around them is so strong that the woman thinks they will not make it. And then she is shin deep in calm water, and Susan is wailing and coughing, and behind them the sea is sparkling blue.

Stop crying. Susan, stop crying. But Susan is inconsolable. She bites the woman's arm, and the woman cries out in pain, releasing her. Susan runs back into the water, back towards the deadly current and the white and the rainbows. The woman is too quick for her, too strong, scooping Susan from water to air, pinning down her kicking arms and legs, carrying her back to the cottage.

Susan manages a few tear-choked, hiccupy words. *Play. Friends. Play.*

Inside, the woman enfolds Susan in a clean towel. *Susan, hush now. You almost drowned. No more playing in the sea ever again.*

Susan shakes her head. *Friends*, she says. *Play.* But at length she is all cried out, and the woman marvels at the snottily breathing bundle in her arms and wonders if she might not have some affection for this cuckoo child after all.

In the afternoon, when Susan is quite recovered, they take the crate of paints and brushes and paint a mermaid on the deck of their little fishing boat. The woman chalks down the outlines, and takes responsibility for painting the mermaid's shimmering tail, looking-glass and the shells to cover her breasts. Susan paints the mermaid's yellow hair, the rock she sits on and the squiggle of blue waves. She doesn't pay much attention to neatness, but the woman overlooks it. The boat rocks in the gentle breeze and, as she paints, occasionally the woman glances up to catch a flash of white on an unfurling wave, or a shimmer of rainbow disappearing into the blue. And sometimes it seems as if the hush-hushing of the sea is calling *Suu-san, Suu-san*, and although the woman knows it's just her imagination, she shivers, thinking it would be best for Susan to stay away from the sea, at least for a while.

And perhaps there is no need to keep calling her Susan, a name the woman has never cared for, a name chosen by her bitter enemy. The woman has all but abandoned her own names. The one foisted on her by the islanders, which had never felt like her. But also the name that had been given to her by her parents, the name that had belonged to a shining, hopeful girl. Both of those versions of her are strangers now. Perhaps in time the child can become a stranger to the name Susan. A nickname, then. What would suit this fey child? Susan is tired, fractious. It's past time for her nap. The woman reaches out and takes her hand.

Come then, Little Fairy. Let's get you home for supper.

23

Scottie: Bride

The little jagged-edged island of greys and greens that had haunted me had a name. Bride. Looming cliffs, milky-gold sand, the white churn of the ocean. The colours so vibrant, so rich compared to the yellow tones of the photograph that had drawn me here. I searched for the smudge of grey, the cottage, but it was hidden by the slopes. Even though I couldn't see it, I didn't doubt its presence.

'You have to take me to Bride.'

'Nae,' Kenver said, his voice calm but ice-cold. 'We're nae going there.' His hand on the tiller, turning the boat around, taking us south.

'I have to go there. Please.'

'We're going back. I need to check the boat for damage.'

'Bride is the closest land, isn't it? Check the boat there.'

The breeze riffled his hair. Kenver's face was pale, the scar on his temple paler.

'Kenver, I'm sorry if I scared you but I need —'

'*Scared* me? Have you any idea how dangerous that was? You come on someone's boat, you let them know if you have a — a —' he stuttered, searching for the right word. 'A *medical* condition. Jesus, Scottie. I canna believe you.'

'That's not fair,' I said. 'You've seen me using my breathing techniques.'

He didn't reply, or even look at me. He was taking us south, back towards the strait.

'I'm sorry. I thought it was under control. I would –'

'Control? *Breathe, breathe, one–two, waves, waves*? That's your method for controlling it? Whatever *it* is? Nae really working, Scottie.'

'– never do anything to put you at risk.'

'But you did. You put both of us at risk. And now you want to go on a day trip to some fucking island? It's nae Disneyland.'

Bride was receding into the distance, the sea around us wrinkled grey silk.

'Remember the song you played? On the night of the whales? The first song of your set in the Blackfish Tavern. Shipwrecks and lost loves.'

Kenver nodded reluctantly.

'When you played the melody on the piano, it took me to this island. I could see it as clearly in my mind as I can see you right now in front of me.'

I took the creased photograph out of my pocket and showed it to him. He turned his face away, unwilling to look.

'I was adopted. Not as a baby, as a little girl. Old enough to remember. Not much. Sounds and smells and tastes. Impressions. Nothing tangible. But when I saw this photo-graph for the first time, when you played that song, it felt like . . .' I groped for the right description. 'It felt like home.'

'It's naebody's home,' he said, staring into the distance, back towards the twin islands. 'Bride is nae a good place. We're lucky it was an ebb tide and we came through the strait in one piece.' I grabbed his hands. 'Kenver, I'm begging you. This will probably be my only chance to go there. Please.'

He wrenched himself free and sighed. Where before he'd refused to look at me, now his eyes were locked on mine. I waited for him to speak, but he did not. He simply took the boat to starboard, turning in a wide circle.

'Are we . . . ? You're taking me? We're going to Bride?'

'For as long as it takes me to check the boat. Nae a minute longer.'

I could have hugged him.

On the west side of the island, a slipway, carpeted in bright green algae. Kenver manoeuvred alongside it.

'It looks slippery,' I said. 'Is it safe?'

He sighed, still angry with me, but he moved his boat away, following the coast to a sloping beach, located midway between the towering cliffs on one side of the island, and the green slopes on the other. For the first time, I saw the cottage, at the confluence of grass and sand, as if its grey stone walls grew up out of the land itself. My heart somersaulted. Kenver took us into the shallows and we hopped out of the boat. It scraped on sand and shells as we dragged it onto the beach.

'Half an hour,' he said, crouching by the hull, running his fingers along it, as he might a lover, his jeans stained dark blue by the sea. 'While I check the boat.'

I shrugged off my life jacket, still shaky after my episode. The beach smelt of rain and mud. The tide had set down thousands of shells in eerily deliberate and unnaturally geometric patterns across the sand. They shifted beneath my feet, splintering and crunching. The tideline was a jagged row of seaweed, driftwood and mermaid's purses. I stepped over it, onto soft, fine sand. I turned to see Kenver, kneeling by his boat, watching me. I raised my hand, but he didn't respond, returning to his damage inspection.

Gulls glided low and silent across the beach, their shadows falling on the drifts of shells, like ghosts. I wandered along the sand, waiting for a memory, something to explain why Bride had called to me. Had I had a life here, parents who abandoned me as easily as they abandoned this island? I lingered awhile, watching the sea, waiting for a storm, but there was nothing. No flood of memories, no sudden moment of recognition. Just the smell of rain on sand and the sigh of the waves, but it wasn't enough.

The cottage was nestled where the beach sloped up to meet the grass. As I drew closer, I realized that 'cottage' was perhaps too generous a description. The dwelling was single storey, walls constructed of grey stones rip-rapped together. The mossy slate roof was completely caved in on one side and the chimney was crumbling. There were two small windows, each made up of four panes of salt-caked glass, miraculously still intact although several of the panes had cracks running across them and the frames looked as though they would disintegrate at the slightest touch. I tried to peer inside, but the glass was so opaque I might as well have tried to see through the stone walls.

On the other side of the cottage there were two semi-derelict brick outbuildings. There had been a garden here, bordered by a low stone wall, but it had run wild over many years, and was now a choking thicket of spiky coastal plants.

The cottage's lichen-stained front door was rotting and swollen into its frame. Was it the front door from my dreams? Scraps of white paint peeled away from the wood, but there was no sea holly around it, no flowers planted by the path. I honestly didn't know. I pushed at the door, bits of rotten wood breaking off beneath my fingers, but it was stuck fast.

I sat on the sandy, stony ground, staring at the cottage, waiting for an epiphany, but none came. Had I really been so naïve to think everything would just slot into place the moment I made landfall here? I'd come so far, waited so long, and still all I had were glimpses and impressions. Jasminder had been right the whole time. I was chasing a fantasy.

The storm came out of nowhere, just as the earlier fog had done. One minute all was still, then the sky had turned black and a wind was hurtling down from the slopes, like a train, pushing blades of rain into my face and snatching away my waterproof as I untied it from around my waist. Kenver was there, next to me in the blinding rain, also seemingly come from nowhere. He shouted something I couldn't hear above the screaming wind and took hold of my arm, dragging me towards the cottage door. I shouted that the door was stuck, but my words were lost to the storm. He pushed the door once, then stepped back and kicked it, the rotten wood splintering and calving away, and then we were inside.

The cottage smelt of the island, of sand and sea, but also of decay. The rain was pouring in through the missing half of the roof, but we were at least partially sheltered from the wind. Kenver tripped over something and swore. I wiped away the rainwater that was streaming off my hair, but I couldn't make out much in the gloom. Kenver flipped on his lighter, casting flickering shadows on his face. His hair was rain-soaked, flattened to his skull, making him seem smaller, vulnerable.

'We'll have to wait it out,' he said, touching my arm. 'Jesus, you're soaking. What happened to your coat?'

'Lost it to the storm.'

His lighter flickered out, plunging us back into darkness.

'Put this on.' He pushed his jacket into my hands.

'I'll be fine.'

'If you can stop your teeth chattering for a whole minute, I'll maybe believe you.'

Kenver's jacket smelt of salt and tobacco. It reminded me of the rush of sensory detail during my episode on his boat, when I had smelt his skin, his hair. I twitched. I sensed him watching me in the darkness, waiting to see if I was going to have another episode.

'It's okay,' I said, after a moment. 'It's passed. There's no need to call the men in white coats.'

We sheltered as best we could in the end of the cottage that still had a roof, but there was almost as much nature inside as out. The light shifted from black to dark grey. The spiky coastal plants were growing inside, had reached in through tiny gaps in the walls. Sand had blown through the missing roof and was piled up in dunes around rotting chairs and table legs. Two bedframes poked out from a particularly deep drift along the wall at one end. I sculled sand away from one and touched scraps of sheets and blankets. There was a clothes rail, shreds of material clinging to metal hangers. Next to one of the beds, shells had been glued to the stone wall in a spiral pattern. It was clear the cottage had been abandoned, its occupants leaving in such a hurry they hadn't even packed. And now Nature was taking it all back, absorbing all the leftover fragments of those lives until one day there would be nothing left. I felt a sense of overwhelming sadness for the people who had lived here, for their leftover fragments. And still I had no idea if any of those fragments were a part of me.

'I'm sorry,' I said.

'For what?' Kenver was flicking the lid of his lighter up and down.

'For getting us into this mess. We're well overdue now. You don't think they'll send out the lifeboat for us, do you?' The thought of people risking their lives because of my stupid fantasy was too much to bear.

'I saw the storm coming. Radioed to let them know we'd shelter here until it passed.'

'Oh,' I said. 'Good.' I sat down on a sand drift, drained of energy.

Kenver offered me his hip flask.

'It'll warm you up.'

I sniffed whisky fumes and took a swig, trying not to grimace. I was sure I'd read somewhere that drinking alcohol was a bad idea when you were freezing, that it redirected the blood away from the vital organs to the optional ones or something along those lines, but I was past caring, pleasant warmth sliding into my limbs. 'How long has this place been abandoned?'

'Thirty year, more or less.'

He went to the window, kneeling on the deep sill formed by the thick stone walls, peering out through the salt and grime, but I doubted he could see much.

'So, what was that?' he said. 'On the boat? I dinna mind telling you it scared the shit out of me.'

'I don't owe you any answers.'

Outside, the rain had slackened a little, but the eaves still rattled in the wind.

'Aye, you kinda do. The day's nae over and you've already nearly sunk my boat and got me stranded in this shit pile during a storm.'

He finally got his lighter working again. He lit a roll-up, the end of it glowing in the dark. He came and sat beside me. 'Smoke?'

It had been years since I'd smoked. I took one, leaning towards him to light it from the tip of his, and inhaled cautiously. 'It's hard to explain.'

'I'll nae be leaving anytime soon,' he said, indicating the water pouring in through the roof.

Smoke was flooding into my lungs, filling the empty spaces inside me.

'Have you heard of post-traumatic stress disorder?'

He nodded.

'Well, it's not that. But similar. I don't think it even has a name. A trauma response triggered by . . . I'm not sure what triggers it. I thought it was . . .'

My throat filled with bile. He let the silence hang between us. Something happened then, something broke inside me.

'I'm supposed to be pumping myself full of hormones as we speak, ready to have a frozen embryo transferred into

168

my womb. Six years of trying and they can't find anything wrong with either of us.'

I exhaled through pursed lips. Spoken aloud, it sounded so small, so insignificant. This huge weight I'd been carrying around, reduced to a tiny little feather of nothing. Now I'd started, I found I couldn't stop, the taste of ash and whisky on my tongue.

'I told my husband I couldn't do it any more and ran away. I thought . . . I thought if I came here and discovered my past, the future wouldn't matter so much. I thought if I could find my birth parents – it sounds ridiculous because if they're not dead then they abandoned me – I might be able to make them love me again. I wanted to know if I had brothers and sisters. I wanted – I know it's selfish – to know someone who had the same DNA as me.'

I dragged my fingers through my hair, which was drying in thick clumps.

'It disna sound selfish to me.'

'Shit, I need a tissue.'

I wiped my face on my sleeve.

'And now you've seen it?' he said. 'Your mystery island. Do you still think it's where you're from?'

I could sense his gaze on my face in the gloom. 'I'm not sure. There've been a few moments when something's nagged at me, seemed familiar, like your song in the Blackfish. But I haven't had any stunning epiphanies.'

'Maybe the past's nae all it's cracked up to be, aye?'

'I could say the same about the future.'

He lit another roll-up. 'What'll you do now, then? Head back to your wee life in the suburbs?'

The sand I was sitting on was damp, the chill seeping into my legs and hips.

'I don't know if I can see a future for that life without children in it.'

'Your husband must miss you.'

'If my husband knew who I really was, if he knew the things I'd done, I doubt he'd want me back anyway.'

I waited for Kenver to ask me what I meant, but he simply smoked his roll-up in the darkness. I buried the remains of mine in the sand and Kenver offered me another. We sat in silence, smoking and taking the occasional swig from the hip flask.

'Storm's over.'

I'd been so focused on my own personal pity party I hadn't even noticed, but Kenver was right. Instead of screaming wind and battering rain, there were waves scraping across shells and the cries of seabirds. I looked around the cottage in the newly unfurling light. It was a single room, the part we'd been sheltering in the sleeping area, with the other end a rudimentary kitchen and living space. So far as I could tell, beneath the debris of the fallen roof and the tumbling-down chimney, there were a table and chairs and a miraculously still standing Welsh dresser with its doors swinging off, a few chipped cups hanging from hooks. An old-fashioned stove was set in a hearth surrounded by fire-blackened stones. There was no sign of a bathroom or anything approaching plumbing or running water.

Kenver was staring around the room. He touched the scar on his temple and then looked at his fingers, as if he expected to find blood there.

'How did you get that scar? You keep touching it.'

'Fell and hit my head on a rock when I was a lad. Nae recommended. We should go and check on the boat, aye?'

I didn't want to leave, knowing that if I did I would never come back. But I had to face the bitter truth. There wasn't a single thing in the cottage or on the island I recognized, not a single memory jogged. Not even the faintest nagging sense of familiarity. I was out of time. How could I have been so stupid to think I could make a reality from my imagination? It hadn't worked for the future, so why should it work for the past?

I turned to bolt, to run away again, as I always did. But there, against the far wall, something beneath a pile of fallen stones and slates. What was that? I crossed the room, pulled at the debris, sending up clouds of dust and sand, making both of us cough, shunting bits of stone and broken slates onto the floor.

'Scottie, c'mon. We need to get back through the strait before the flood tide comes in.'

The item beneath the debris was a piano. For a moment, I couldn't breathe. Was this the trigger that would bring everything flooding back? It was in an advanced state of decomposition. Parts of its casing had come apart, exposing the inner workings, and the keys were discoloured and uneven, like a set of decaying teeth. I was a dancer, not a musician, but even if I had been, this piano was long past being playable. I spread my fingers across the keys, the alternating dark and light stripes part of a language I didn't understand. I remembered Kenver playing piano in the Blackfish Tavern, how the melody had flown me high above sea and rocks to a tiny stone cottage with a white-painted front door. I lifted my hands into arches, my fingertips moving across the keys. I pressed down. Of course, the notes didn't play. There was only the soft thunking of a hammer hitting dead string and the crunch of sand grinding in the works.

I hummed something. A hint of a melody, slow and mournful. Just a few bars, a few moments and then it was gone. Into the silence came an image, a glimmer. Perhaps a memory, perhaps a fantasy. A girl aged six or seven, standing on a beach by a tideline littered with seaweed, driftwood and mermaid's purses, cradling the empty husks of whelk eggs against her body, tucked up against the winter chill in a scarf that had been knitted to look like the keys of a piano.

'What was that tune you were humming?' Kenver was wax-pale in the post-storm light.

'It's the song you were playing in the Blackfish,' I said. 'On the day of the whale stranding.'

'Nae,' he said. 'It isna. Where'd you learn it? Tell me.'

I tried to hum it again, but the melody had gone, dissipating like the mist, leaving behind only an aching sense of something just out of reach. Kenver crashed through the broken door, catching splintered wood on his jeans, and I saw the shadow of him pass by the salt-layered windows. I didn't care. I had a new fragment, a new piece for my puzzle. And perhaps it was the tiniest of brittle shards. But it was something, and I was going to grab hold and not let go.

PART II

Stories

24

Thordis: Death

Before she lost herself, subsumed herself to the care of the cuckoo child, before the child even existed, the woman had had a name: Thordis, named for the god of thunder.

Now she stands, shells and stones beneath her feet, the oar in her hand rough against her palms. A muffling cocoon of silence, but beyond it, wailing. The oar is from the little rowing boat. But why is she holding it? Why is she here, standing on this shell-scattered ground? She remembers a crunch, a thud, soft squelching. Her throat is raw, her chest burns inside. A thought fragments in her mind, ripping through the veil of silence. She can hear the everyday rhythm of waves crashing onto rocks, the incessant, screaming gulls. She observes the paddle end of the oar. It's stained russet, covered with some lumpy grey matter she can't identify. She flings it down with a cry of disgust. There's blood on her hands, she sees now, and on her jeans too, drying stiff in the sun. She touches the back of her head and winces, the hair there wet and clumped together. Her fingers come away red. The rasping sound of her panicky breathing syncopates with the breaking waves.

Her focus has been drawn by the tiny space in front of her, the space that was occupied by her hands gripping the oar. Now her perception broadens. She is standing in the garden of the cottage where she used to live, on Bride

Island. It is unkempt, the coastal plants overgrown, a spiky tangle that had once been a thing of beauty. The ugliness is the product of years of neglect and it hurts her heart. She didn't want to come back to this place, hadn't planned to, had been looking, at last, to the future. Faint grooves appear along her forehead as she struggles to map the happenings that have brought her here. They are there, in her memory, in the background, but they have the sense of a dream just forgotten and she is unable to grasp the strands.

There's a body on the ground, a few feet in front of the discarded oar. How could she not have seen it before? Its head is caved in, a shimmering mess of red and grey, but she knows who it is, knows the weft and weave of him. Her mind maps the lines from her bloodied hands to the bloodied oar to her former husband's bloodied body. She shakes her head. It's inconceivable that she might be responsible. She cannot look at his destroyed face, of course not. But if she focuses only on his arms, his back, his hips, his oilskin-clad legs, the angles and curves she knows so well, perhaps he might be sleeping, lain down here for a nap in the once-beautiful garden she made for him.

The pieces of her memory flock together to form a picture she doesn't want to see. His formerly handsome face cragged from years of exposure to the salt and sea, dark with rage. The oar in her hand, her slight body blocking the path, determined not to let him pass. Her foot had slipped on a stone and then she had been on the ground and he was bearing down on her in a fury. She had groped for the oar and swung it up, connecting with his chin, and he had roared with pain, spitting blood, and that moment was enough for her to spring to her feet, oar in hand, and then the image shatters again and she falls to her knees.

There is a surreal patchwork quality to her memories, as if they had happened to someone else a long time ago and she is merely remembering by proxy a story she has been told. She had brought the package across from Sorrow for Merryn, the woman who had stolen her husband. Merryn had torn it open greedily, barely even pausing to say thank you. What had been inside? Not documents, as Thordis had been expecting. Not a passport, or even a stash of money. No, something else she can't quite picture, but she remembers having been angry that she had taken such a risk to deliver an item that seemed so insignificant. But Merryn had wept with joy, cradling her new-born child against her body, still not saying thank you, and then Cadal had come, striding across the island towards them in a fury, and it was all wrong, he wasn't meant to be there, and Thordis had picked up the oar and shouted to Merryn to take the children to the boat.

Thordis uncurls her body, hollow as a whelk-egg case floating away on the tide. She paces back and forth in the neglected garden. Merryn. The ruiner of the garden, the ruiner of everything. Perhaps it was Merryn who had caved in his skull, pushing the oar into Thordis's innocent hands as she fled. She had stolen everything else from Thordis, so why not this too? She shall tell the police constable on Lugh of Merryn's crime and all will be well. But Merryn is not here, only Thordis, and she has blood and brains on her clothes and her fingerprints are all over the oar that was surely the murder weapon.

A far-distant wailing. A seagull? Thordis checks to make sure the sound is not in fact coming from her. Reassured, she follows the high-pitched squall, leaving behind the broken body of the man she once loved. Still loves, if truth be told. Deep in her heart she knows what the sound is. She does not need to see it to understand, but she is shrouded in a fog of denial. Whatever has happened, she, Thordis, daughter of Jonas, is innocent, a victim of circumstance. A martyr even, one might say. There are not many who would bend over backwards as she has for the benefit of their arch enemy. She follows the wailing sound through the crevasse leading to the east beach, picking her way along the narrow strip of slippery boulders that fringes the looming cliffs.

The east beach is a crescent cove shelving into rock-strewn waters. Beyond the rocks the ramshackle fishing boat is still at anchor, where she had left it, but there is no sign of the little rowing boat. Scattered between rocks are chunks of splintered wood and floating coils of rope. On the sand in front of her, the matching oar to the blood-and-brain-smeared one she has left behind. And still that wailing, the shrillness of it bleeding into her ears.

She wades into the shallows, the weight of the ocean seeping into her jeans, washing Cadal's blood away. She pushes aside pieces of the splintered wood, the remains, she realizes now, of the rowing boat. There is no sign of Mer-ryn or her children. Pushing through waist-deep ocean, a flash of yellow in the water. There, wedged between two rocks, is Merryn's baby, its face still birth-crumpled, its yellow blanket uncurling with the motion of the waves. The tide is coming in, the baby's face barely above the surface.

As Thordis reaches down to pluck the child to safety, the fog of denial that has protected her dissipates, and she is clear-headed for the first time since coming to on the west beach with a bloodied oar in her hands.

Cadal is dead. His wife and children too, the rowing boat dashed onto rocks as Merryn tried, with only one oar, to get her daughters to the safety of the fishing boat. She might tell the constable that Merryn had murdered her husband and fled with the children, but the baby is a complication whose presence cannot easily be explained. What mother would desert her new-born child? It will surely be discovered that Merryn and her children have drowned and for this Thordis will be blamed. After all, it was she who had procured the ill-maintained rowing boat that had been their undoing.

I imagine that, at this moment, Thordis has the most awful thought she's ever had. It is fleeting but that won't prevent it from haunting her for the rest of her life. *What if*, she thinks, *what if Merryn's baby was to drown too, sent straight to Heaven with its mother and sisters?* The pretence that Merryn had killed her husband and run away back to wherever she had come from would be easier to maintain. Thordis could give her statement to the constable about the terrible tragedy she had stumbled upon and go back to her almost-contented life in her little house in St Bridget's Lane with its view of Lugh harbour from the bedroom. It wouldn't even be difficult. Just a gentle push to release the baby from the rocks and the sea would take care of the rest.

Go on. Go on and be with your mother and sisters. There's no life for you here, no kin.

The baby stops wailing. At first Thordis thinks only that her ears have become numb from the incessant noise. But she can hear the hushing of the waves, the calling seabirds and her own rasping breaths. The baby waves its little arms, perhaps soothed by the gentle lap of the water, not understanding the sea's fast-approaching role in its fate. While the baby was wailing, it was a thing, a nothing, an inconvenience. A symbol only of Thordis's personal suffering, a proxy for Merryn who had done her so much harm. But the gurgling snaps Thordis to her senses. She plucks the baby from its cranny between the rocks, ripping away the sodden blanket, and folds the child into her chest.

The baby grizzles now it is out of contact with the sea and, as Thordis staggers to the shore, it resumes its shrieking. Thordis stands for a moment, panting. She has nothing dry to wrap the baby in, nothing to warm it. She does the only thing she can think of and carries the squalling bundle back to the cottage, to the place where so many of her own babies died, and sets a fire to warm them both.

25

Scottie: Spaces

I called Jasminder on the landline, so I knew he was probably sitting at the kitchen table when I told him I wasn't
coming back. I could picture the emotions passing across
his face, the tightness around his eyes, the slight sag of his
shoulders. His fingers absently rubbing his shaving stubble,
the way they always did when he was dealing with bad
news. When his father died. When he flunked his first sergeant's board. When each of our embryos failed to burrow
into the space inside me. I should have felt guilty, but I
didn't. I didn't feel anything. I had no emotion left in me. I
could think only about Bride, the cottage, the Hollow Sea
and what I might find out about my past.

'Tell me you're joking, Scottie,' he said. 'Please.'

He was using his police officer's voice. Soft, controlled,
assertive. I knew it was bullshit.

'I've made up my mind. I'm staying here.' I hated the
defensive tone that had crept into my voice. 'It's over.'

'What's over? IVF? Us? Explain what you mean.'

'Don't interrogate me, Jasminder, please. I'm not one of
your suspects.'

He paused. I listened to him breathing.

'I'm sorry. I just meant didn't you hear the message I
left? I said we could stop IVF if you wanted, so please can
you just come home?'

He took a breath, as if he were about to say something else, but remained silent. The space between us was vast, uncrossable.

'I can't live that life, Jasminder. I can't live a life that's full of child-shaped holes.'

I twisted and knotted Nest's nylon bedspread in my lap as I talked.

'Our life, the life we had, it was supposed to be full of children. There are too many reminders of what we've lost.'

'We could move to a new house. Make a fresh start? You always liked those houses with the big bay windows. There's one on the market. I saw the For Sale sign. In Milton, which is a good area.'

I couldn't bear the note of hope in his voice. Jasminder always had a practical solution to everything. There wasn't a problem that couldn't be solved with a new house or a new job, an extra injection, another round of treatment. But it wasn't just about our house and its empty bedrooms, or my admin-assistant job, with its flexible hours and great maternity leave I would never have a use for. It was about us and the children we were meant to have.

'Milton has good schools, or so I heard,' I said bitterly.

'Scottie –'

'It's not about the fucking house.' I imagined my words imprinted on his face, like a slap. 'It's us. Scottie and Jasminder. We're the ones full of child-shaped holes. Us. Every time I see you, or think of you, it reminds me of a child we'll never have. I can't live like that.'

'Oh.'

His voice was very small. He no longer sounded like Sergeant Bains of the Yard interrogating his suspect.

'You can have the house.'

'Jesus. I don't care about the house. You think it doesn't hurt me, seeing every single day the rooms I thought our children would be sleeping in? The garden they were supposed to play in? You're not the only one who's lost something, Scottie.'

I listened to him swallow. 'I'm sorry,' I said. 'I know.'

There was an ocean of silence between us and I didn't know how to cross it. Nest's nylon bedspread caught on my engagement ring, making a run in the fabric. 'The only thing I want is the rest of the money from our IVF account. It should be enough.'

'Enough for what? You at least owe me an explanation of what you're going to spend it on.'

Part of me didn't want to say, afraid that speaking it out loud would lessen its power. Or, even scarier, make it real. But Jasminder was right. I owed him that, at least. 'I've found a property on an island. It's a bit of a wreck but I'm going to do it up and live there.'

'Do you have any idea how crazy that sounds?'

But maybe crazy was the point. I was tired of following the rules. Waiting for stability, security, a mortgage, a permanent job. And what had that got me? One Big Fat Negative after another and a secret that was rotting me from the inside out.

'I'm doing it, Jasminder, and nothing you say is going to change my mind.'

He would be rubbing his hands across his chin again, the

slight scratch of his fingers across his five o'clock shadow. I didn't tell him my other reason for wanting to stay. For wanting to live on Bride. I hoped, given enough time, the wisp of melody would come back to me, or other memories would push themselves up into the light. Perhaps I was wrong, still chasing a fantasy. But I was becoming more and more certain that the answers I needed, the answers to my past, to why I'd been given up, were on Bride.

'Oh, do whatever the fuck you want,' he said quietly, and the phone clicked as he hung up.

The old me, racked with guilt, would probably be booking a ticket home right now to Jasminder and a life full of ghosts. But Jasminder didn't know me, didn't know what I'd done. How could he ever hope to understand why I had no more room in my heart for ghosts? No, I had to focus on Bride now. Perhaps there I would find ghosts too, but right now the ghosts of the past felt safer than the ghosts of the future.

Tony Oliveira's Marine Training School was a wooden shack, right on the Lugh waterfront, painted gunmetal grey. Tony wasn't in his office, but I found him next door, in M & R's Boatyard, squinting at the hull of an upturned wooden boat.

'Heard you found your wee island, Miss.'

'I did.'

'Ever caulked the hull of a boat?'

I shook my head.

'Then you're just in time for an education. Cornish Cove

boat, this is. A beautiful thing. Now, we'll need to roll the caulking cotton into balls, just like your granny would roll up her knitting yarn.'

'I'm going to move onto Bride, Tony.'

He burst into astonished laughter. I had a sudden flash of him as a young man on a fishing trawler, his blue eyes and his Mediterranean skin, his hair lush and dark instead of white and receding.

'Why in the name of all that's holy would you want to do such a thing?'

'I need to be somewhere remote for a while. Get some space.'

It was the truth. Half of the truth. Tony looked puzzled.

'Dwelling canna be fit for living in after all these years. Now, what we want to do is to get this cotton deep into the seams.'

Tony pressed the cotton into the spaces between the planks, pinching each loop with a caulking iron, a sort of flat chisel, and knocking it in with a wooden mallet.

'It's semi-derelict. But I'm going to restore it.'

'Tap-tap. Like a heartbeat. How do you plan to get to and from?'

'That's where you come in,' I said.

'Nae.' *Tap-tap.* 'It's nae for me. Like I said.'

'The islands are all haunted, right?'

'I dinna believe in ghosts, Miss, but I'm also nae much interested in becoming one. Ready to have a try?'

I was ham-fisted, fumbling with the caulking iron and the mallet, and my loops were all different sizes.

'Nae bad,' said Tony. 'For a first attempt.'

'I want to sign up for lessons with you. Study for my seamanship exams. When I'm qualified, I'll buy my own boat. But if in the meantime you could provide a taxi service so I can get the cottage fit to live in, I'd be grateful.'

'I'd be lying if I said your coin wouldna be welcome, but that's a dangerous sea, you ken.'

'Dangerous,' I said, 'but not unnavigable with the right local knowledge.'

He sighed, and nodded reluctantly.

'Teach me what I need to know, Tony. Please.'

He tapped in more caulking cotton.

'I'll think on it. Nae promises. You should think on it too. How you're going to get the people and equipment you need from A to B. That's if you can persuade any folk to risk crossing the strait.'

'Tony –'

'Sssh, please. Need to listen. Canna tell if the cotton's gone in deep enough otherwise. Hear that? Beautiful.'

'Tony, you knew which island it was when I showed you the photo, didn't you? You knew it was Bride?'

He had the grace to look sheepish. 'Ach, I thought you was a journalist or some such poking around in the past.'

Bride had a past. A past worth poking around in. I felt sick with anticipation.

'Why would a journalist be interested in Bride?'

'Best nae dwell on ancient history.'

I was starting to get tired of St Híans' habitual secrecy about their precious northern isles.

'I'm worried someone might have a claim to Bride, or

to the cottage. I could do all that work only to find it belongs to someone else. If I knew who last lived there, it would help me track down any interested parties.'

Tony seemed to accept this argument and held up his hand for quiet while he dredged for memories.

'The family that lived on Bride drowned. The fella, his pregnant wife and their two wee girls. Lost to the Hollow Sea.'

At last, some concrete information. Instead of continuing with his story, Tony busied himself using a blow torch to heat up some gooey black stuff in a metal can.

'But was there —'

'Now, we're going to seal up the seams with pitch,' he said. 'Old-fashioned, some might say, but oftentimes the old ways are the best.'

I sensed that if I asked more questions, Tony would clam up, so I took a tiny brush and copied him, painting along the seams of the boat. We had almost finished when Tony exhaled through his teeth and spoke again.

'Cadal Fernandes was his name. A fisherman. Crewed with him when we were lads. The wife, I only met her the once, but she seemed a nice enough lass. Now what was her name? Mary? Merry?'

'They all drowned? All of them? No survivors?'

Tony inhaled, as if he was about to say something else, then nodded, wiping the pitch from his hands with a rag.

'Nigh on thirty year ago, maybe closer to forty, it happened. The beginning of the end for folks living up in the northern isles. Too dangerous, too lonely out there, with nae one to save you if you needed it. Shook people up it did.'

My body twitched, as if I had been punched in the solar plexus. I didn't even care if Tony had noticed. There wasn't a place for me in this story of a drowned family with no survivors.

26

Charlotte: David

My first ghost child was more fully formed in my heart than the ones who came later. A face I could picture clearly, untameable curls, a cheeky smile. A life, a future mapped out before her. A name, the name I chose for her, carried in my heart but never spoken. She was made in a different place, this first ghost, a place of warmth and darkness, not a place of harsh light and gleaming steel, like her brothers and sisters. The child I sacrificed everything for.

Before I was an admin assistant, I had been a ceramics artist. My studio, rented from an arts cooperative, land-locked, where I made and remade the sea with clay. My trademark white clay, unglazed. Abstract curves in empty spaces. To my customers, the shapes might be anything. A foxtail, a toadstool, a galloping horse. I didn't mind, they could choose. But I knew each piece was part of the sea that whispered to me in the night.

David. A wrong turning into the studio. *These are amazing. What are they meant to be?*

His eyelashes long and pale behind his glasses. I liked them. *You decide. Whatever you think they should be.* My favourite piece. *Rag.* Tiny woven strands of clay, a tattered edge. Bleached ragwort floating on the rag end of a wave.

I get to pick the meaning? That's a big responsibility. Those eyelashes, almost brushing his cheeks when he blinked.

Taking his time. Different angles, crouching down, noting where the light and shadows fell, eyes watery blue with concentration. *A wave. I think it's a wave. Kind of a weird wave, true, but a wave.*

I shrugged, feigning nonchalance. *Whatever you like.* But he was the first, the first who had ever guessed correctly. He bought *Rag*, paling a little when I told him the price, but he handed me his credit card without blinking. I noted the name on it: David Farrier. He backed through the door cradling the bubble-wrapped sculpture in his arms like a new-born.

He came back the next day to invite me for a drink. I paid. He had bankrupted himself to buy *Rag*. We laughed a lot. The laughter made me feel strong and free. It hushed the calling of the waves. He was a social worker. I liked that. He wanted children, lots of them, and I liked that too. I went to see him play bass guitar in his indie cover band, the Fractal Caterpillars. They were terrible and I liked it. On our third date, we missed our dinner reservation when he stopped to chat to an old homeless woman. I didn't mind about dinner.

In the years that came after, I tried not to talk about David because when I did those were the stories I found myself telling. How kind he was, how funny, how much he cared about old homeless women. The stories I could tell without my throat buckling. I didn't talk about the time he left dozens of voicemails – in turns angry, pleading, cold – because I hadn't called him from my friend Angela's hen party. Or how he would buy pints two at a time and knock them back all night until he slumped glassy-eyed over the table, or how, when he started to sober up, he would get mean and tell me I should get a proper job and earn more money, that my sculptures were worthless pieces of crap.

I never told anyone about when we were on our honeymoon in Edinburgh and he wanted to go for a takeaway and I wanted to go to the taxi-rank, how he gripped my wrist so tightly and for so long, telling me he didn't want to have to divorce me, but he would if I didn't start being more reasonable. My wrist was red and swollen for days. I never told anyone when I started keeping money in my shoes when we went out, as he had a habit of picking a fight, taking my purse and leaving me to find my own way home without any money. Or if I didn't want sex, he would push me out of the bed and make me sleep on the floor, or his habit of putting me out of the house in the middle of the night dressed in my pyjamas, leaving me to spend the night alone in the garden because I was too ashamed to ask the neighbours for help. I never told anyone how he would put his hands around my throat and pull me around the house as punishment for some imagined slight. Or how he told me I was the abusive one, because I pushed him once in the chest, trying to stop him pulling my hair. And I believed him, so I stayed silent and full of shame. I tried to be a better wife.

And then, one day, two lines on a stick. The child I had longed for, and all I could do was sob in the bathroom because she deserved better, better than both of us. David was in a good mood that night, wanted to go for a drink, was irritated I had spent so long in the bathroom, that I was pale and blotchy. I told him I wasn't feeling very well and was going to bed. *Just one drink,* he said, in his most reasonable voice.

But it was never just one with him. *Not tonight. Go with one of your mates.*

He took hold of my wrists, pressed them against me, pressed himself against me, pinning me to the wall. *Be nice, Charlotte, for once. One drink with my wife is not much to ask.* His eyes, behind his gold-rimmed glasses, were the same as I remembered them the day he came into my studio, taking his time to interpret *Rag*, the only person who had ever known it was a wave.

Rag was on the mantelpiece. He released my wrists, turning, striding across the room, and he picked *Rag* up, held it high over his head.

David, no. I was frozen to the wall, my hand going to the white stick in my pocket, as if it were a talisman, a charm. *We can go for a drink. You were right. A drink together would be lovely.*

He shook his head. *Too late, Charlotte. You should have been nice.* He brought it down, smashed it on the stone hearth, my precious rag of a wave from an unknown sea, shattering into dozens of pieces. *You make me do these things, Charlotte. If you weren't being such a bitch, I wouldn't have had to do that.* He fetched the dustpan and brush and swept up the pieces of my heart. I didn't move from my place by the wall.

Why didn't you just leave, Charlotte? I imagined that's what people would say if I told them the truth. Why not just keep your baby safe by leaving? And that's why I never told, because I'd never have the words to explain how paralysed I was. The studio was struggling and David was helping me manage my finances, so most of my money was in his account. I was ashamed of being a bad wife, ashamed of leaving a marriage after Helen had used the last of her savings to pay for our wedding, ashamed of the person I was when I was with him.

You don't need to worry any more, David had said, holding me in bed when we were first together. *You've got me to look after you now.* I had not known I needed looking after.

My first ghost. Not even a baby, just a cluster of cells. A girl? My heart said yes, but I'd been wrong about so many things. I did the only thing I could think of to keep her safe. David never even knew. I didn't know I was giving up my only chance to be a mother, but if I had known, I would have done the same thing. She didn't deserve parents like us.

The first will-o'-the-wisp to haunt my dreams, and I was the one who had snuffed out her light.

27

Thordis: Birth

Thordis makes it safely through the Tanguy-Tanick strait, sticking as close as possible to Tanick's rocky coast, where the waters are calmest, grateful for the ebb tide. She moors the fishing boat at anchor in a cove on the east coast of Bride and rows to a thin sliver of rocky beach at the southernmost tip of the island. She tells herself it's safer this way, less exposed than mooring at the slipway on the west beach. But, in truth, the thought of crossing the bay from the west, of glimpsing the little cove and breakwater, of remembering how her heart would once have soared at the sight, is too much to bear.

The footpath around to the west side of the island is treacherous, the waves snapping at the narrow band of rocks and boulders between the ocean and the cliff face. Thordis tucks her parcel under one arm and, using an oar from the rowing boat as a walking pole, picks her way across the boulders, beneath the clamour of nesting seabirds, around the southern tip of the island.

Is she afraid? Is she racked with regret and bitterness, wishing she had never agreed to help Merryn? Both are possible, but I prefer to think not. She grieves, I'm certain, for the future she has given up, her years of careful saving squandered and all to help the woman who has taken everything from her. But she is resolute. She has a promise to keep, a parcel to deliver, an escape plan to execute. Her path was set from the moment she saw the marks on Merryn's wrist, the wary shadows in the faces of Merryn's daughters. It is perhaps the only truly selfless act of her life. She empties her mind, focusing only on finding her footing on the uneven ground, trying not to scrape her arm on the cliff face, leaning into the oar for balance. Thordis mutters as she bangs her shin on a rock, but she comes without incident to the south-western beach, where a natural break in the cliff forms a grassy crevasse through which she can walk to reach the cottage from its south side.

She exits the shelter of the crevasse, into a whipping wind that fills her eyes with tears. Here is the cottage that had been her home for so many years, something so familiar made foreign by the passage of time. Her garden, the place where she had buried so many of her children. The shock of seeing it again winds her but only for a moment. With the oar under one arm and the parcel under the other, she strides out to the cottage. She will not be cowed by memories. She is observing, with a sort of dull rage, the disarray of the garden, and wondering at the strangeness of knocking on the door of what used to be her own house, when a bone-chilling scream comes from the beach.

Merryn, her enemy, is on the sand, crouched at the edge of the sea, her skirts hiked up over her knees.

She looks towards Thordis calmly and says, *You're too late, Thora. You've come too late.*

She has blood on her thighs. Thordis does not know whether this is a good or a bad sign. Merryn's older daughter watches impassively, a half-full bucket of sea lettuce in her arms. The younger child plays on the sand, making patterns with shells.

Come inside the house, Thordis says, *where you'll be more comfortable*.

Merryn rocks on her haunches and screams. Thordis dispenses with the package and kneels beside her enemy. She takes Merryn's hand because it seems like the right thing to do. Sea-spray is skimming in off the waves and hitting their faces. If the frequency of Merryn's screams is a good measure of the frequency of her contractions, then the child will be born soon. She sends the older girl to fetch pillows, blankets, towels, a bowl of water and soap for washing. She would have preferred to go herself, to take a moment inside to gather her thoughts, but Merryn is gripping her hand so tightly, crushing the bones together, that she cannot free herself.

Thordis tries not to think of the time when their positions were reversed and Merryn was sitting by her bedside, pressing a cool washcloth to her forehead, whispering soothings to her. It seems at once as if it were only yesterday and yet it is also the distant past.

Merryn, where is Cadal? When is he coming back? But Merryn only wails. Thordis looks between her enemy's legs and sees the baby's head crowning. *Your baby is coming, Merryn. I can see its head.*

Merryn sinks back on her haunches, panting. The waves become fiercer. Thordis positions her body to shield Merryn from the spray. She is doing it for the child, she tells herself, the child that should have been hers. The toddler hums a little tune as she collects her shells, unconcerned by the angry sea. The older girl returns with pillows and towels, but perhaps the moment for these has passed. Thordis can't think what she might use them for.

The spray is needle sharp, shrapnel pummelling her back. Merryn bellows, and the baby's head appears, cocooned in blood and gunge. Thordis's fingertips are white, starved of blood, Merryn's ragged fingernails digging into her skin.

GIVE ME BACK MY HAND, BITCH.

Merryn lets go, grunting, and Thordis's fingers tingle, the blood rushing back into them.

One more push, Merryn. One more push. Thordis cups her hands beneath the baby's head and Merryn bawls once more as the contraction shimmers through her. The baby slides, glistening, into Thordis's hands. A little girl. Another girl for Merryn, when Thordis has none.

Merryn collapses onto the sand. The baby is silent, unmoving, a bluish tinge to its skin. Thordis slaps its bottom and it begins to cry and turn pink. She holds the baby up, intending to use her own body as a buffer against the spray. But the blossoming storm is over before it's even begun, as if its only purpose had been to accompany Merryn's baby into the world. The sea is flat and still, barely a ripple scraping across its surface. The only evidence of the wind is the white towels, which have cartwheeled down the beach and lie strewn across the rocks. Thordis places the baby on Merryn's chest.

Your daughter, she says.

Merryn whispers the child's name over and over, as if it is a talisman. *Susan. Susan. Susan.*

★

Thordis cuts the umbilical cord with a knife sterilized in the embers of the stove, washes the baby, fumbles with a nappy and swaddles it in a blanket. She washes Merryn too, as best she can, and helps her into a clean nightgown. She buries the afterbirth and umbilical cord in the garden, as far away as possible from where her own babies are buried. When she returns to the cottage, Merryn has the baby at her breast. Its sisters are sitting at the table, eating bread and butter. Thordis looks away, full of dull rage.

I should go.

The baby has quieted to a soft grizzle and Merryn lays it in a woven basket lined with a blanket that she probably doesn't know was crocheted by Thordis, years before, intended for her own children.

Did you find it? Did you bring it?

In the excitement of the birth, Thordis has forgotten all about the package. She fetches it in from where she had dropped it on the sand. Merryn snatches it from her grip, ripping away layers of brown paper and plastic, all the while saying, *Oh, oh, oh*. It makes Thordis want to strangle her.

Merryn's prize is a piece of fabric, shimmery with the rainbow colours of an oil spill. Merryn buries her face in it, inhales, then shakes it out and holds it up to the light. *But you came too late, Thora. Why did you come so late? You were supposed to come before the bairn was born.*

Thordis is speechless with rage. A skirt? This is what she has risked so much for? Through the window, she notes the position of the sun in the sky, the barely perceptible change in the quality of the light. *I must go now,* she says. *Before he comes home.*

Merryn drops the skirt into her lap. *Nae, dinna go. I can travel. I just need to rest first.*

Thordis glances through the window, anxious that Cadal might already be anchoring his boat. *It doesn't seem sensible,* she says. *I shall bring the boat back another day when you've recovered from the birth.*

Merryn pushes herself up off the bed, grimacing. *See?* she says. *I can do it. Thora, I canna stay here another day. There might still be time for Susan if we hurry.*

Thordis doesn't understand what Merryn means, but she picks the baby up and places it in Merryn's arms. *Then we shouldn't delay. The boat is on the east beach. Do you have bags?*

Merryn shakes her head. *We want naught from this place. Chesten, Delmai, come along. We're . . .* she swoons, suppresses a whimper of pain . . . *we're going on a trip.*

The five of them, two women, two little girls and a babe-in-arms, stumble out of the cottage and across the uneven ground towards the crevasse, Merryn clasping her baby and the skirt that looks like an oil spill to her breast. The older girl holds the hand of the younger, each with a thumb in their mouth. Merryn has slid the mother-of-pearl comb that had once belonged to Thordis into her hair, where it shimmers prettily. She notices Thordis staring at it. *Thora, I'll keep my promise. When we get to the boat, you shall have the comb.*

Thordis remembers the oar she had used as a walking stick. They will need it to get back to the fishing boat, and most likely Merryn will need it to keep her footing as they traverse the boulder-strewn base of the cliffs. Thordis still thinks it foolish, to attempt to travel in such circumstances, but Merryn has a fierce light in her eyes.

Hurry, says Merryn. *It mightna be too late for the bairn.*

Thordis turns back to retrieve the oar.

The older girl, Chesten or Delmai, Thordis doesn't know which, takes her thumb out of her mouth and points. *Papa.*

Thordis sees him, a backlit silhouette of rage storming up the beach from the breakwater. Her body floods with dread. *Merryn, take the children to the east beach. I'll catch up.* Merryn doesn't move. Thordis scoops up the oar. *Merryn, GO.* The baby begins to cry, shattering Merryn's paralysis and she moves, stumbling across rocks, whimpering in pain, clutching her baby to her chest, before disappearing into the crevasse, followed by her older daughters.

How long does Thordis wait on the edge of her once beautiful garden, with the oar in her hands, for her former husband to cross the beach? Only moments, surely. He is sprinting, fuelled by rage and fear. He is shouting Merryn's name, and *Nae,* and *You bitch.* But in my imagination, his passage across the beach happens silently and in the slowest of slow motions. And in the long moment as Thordis waits, oar in her hands, a memory floods her mind and pushes out all else.

Thordis Jonasdottir, as she was known then, sixteen years old with long plaits she could sit on, cleaning the tables in her mother's little café on the quayside at Tvífjallahöfn. A British trawler moored alongside. A boy on deck gathering up a tangle of nets and holding the damaged parts up to the evening half-light, squinting at them and threading them between his hands with an easy rhythm she couldn't stop watching. And she had felt changed, some-how, just by watching him at his work, in a way she didn't fully understand.

But now things are no longer in slow-motion. He is speeding across the beach, possessed by rage and fear and violence. Thordis finds time, even in that moment, to reflect and wonder at the person he has become, or perhaps he always was. In the end, she chooses to remember the beautiful young man on the deck of a stern-ramped trawler called *Miss Molly*, his pleasing hands and the way he played the violin.

Thordis raises the oar in the air and stands her ground.

28

Scottie: The Library

It was Ellie and the other seal counters' last day in St Hía and they were all cheerfully bundling aboard the *Lucky Spirit*, the little ferry that had brought me here what felt like a lifetime ago, and which I should have been embarking too, to head back to a life full of child-shaped holes.

'Give me a hug, you mad, crazy woman.' Ellie flung her arms around me as if we were old friends, not just acquaintances of a few weeks. 'How on earth are you going to do this, Scottie? Even I balked at going that far north for seal surveying and here you are, thinking you might live alone on an island there?'

Not just an island. *Bride.*

'Why didn't you include the Hollow Sea in the seal count?' I said. 'I'd have thought it would bug you to have to leave some islands out.'

'Oh, I don't know. Maybe because of the shedloads of paperwork that's generated when you start drowning volunteers?'

'Oh. Ha-ha.'

'Not really joking, Scottie. The advice I got was that the currents made the islands of the Hollow Sea more trouble than they were worth. If we wanted to include the northern isles we'd have to survey from the air. I didn't have the funding for that and there were very few documented haul-out sites in the north, so I decided to exclude them.'

'Everything's under control,' I said. 'And the weather's been glorious.'

'But it won't always be,' said Ellie, tucking her hair into her headband, the way she had the first time we met. 'How are you going to cope in the middle of winter when no one can get on or off your little island for weeks at a time?'

'It's just something I have to do.'

Ellie frowned, but it was the plain and simple truth. No matter if I spent all my money, no matter if I failed, no matter if I ended up running away again with my tail between my legs, I had to do this. The *Lucky Spirit*'s engine started. Noah and Alison were up on deck, and I waved at them, squinting into the sun. Ellie adjusted the straps on her rucksack and gave me a final quick squeeze. 'Don't be a stranger.'

Lugh Public Library was in a converted house at the top of the hill overlooking the harbour. It smelt of old paper and the perfumed carpet powder you put down before vacuuming. The solitary librarian, a woman in late middle age with pink-streaked hair and a badge with her name, Minerva, in embossed silver, took me upstairs to what had once been a child's bedroom and showed me how to use the microfiche reader.

The *St Hía Herald* archive went back a hundred years or more, but I plumped for thirty years ago as a reasonable place to start, scanning headlines for mention of a family drowned in the Hollow Sea. After hours of searching, going back through ten years of headlines about the arrival of a new police constable, the building of a schoolhouse, storms and shipwrecks, shortages of bananas, fishing quotas, births and weddings and deaths, I found not a single mention of Cadal Fernandes, his pregnant wife and their two little girls.

The shipwreck and drowning of an entire family seemed like something that would make the local newspaper. Might Tony have been wrong? Or, more likely, not entirely truthful. St Híans and their frustrating secrecy. For want of something better to do I carried on working backwards through time, not even knowing what I was looking for, another five years, another ten, my eyes moving across the magnified pages almost in a trance.

I clicked to a halt. A word, a name, a photograph. I wasn't even sure what had caught my eye. I checked the date on the newspaper: 1973. Over forty years ago. I clicked back, a frame at a time. A headline on the tiniest of tucked-away articles. *Lugh Resident Wins Piano Prize*. A few lines about a boy from Lugh who had won second prize at a music festival on the mainland. A photo of him beaming and holding his certificate. Next to him a slightly built blonde woman. The photo was blurred, of such low resolution I couldn't make out their faces clearly, but I guessed the woman was in her early thirties. The caption read: *Luis Trelawney, with proud piano teacher, Mrs T. Fernandes*.

Fernandes. The same surname as Cadal, who had purportedly drowned in the Hollow Sea with his family. I wondered how common a name it was in these parts. It sounded like it might be Portuguese, and I thought of the shipwrecked whalers who'd built a chapel in a cave on Sorrow. There was a stack of directories in an archive box beneath the table. I pulled out the phone book, only a year out of date, and flicked through to the Fs. No one called Fernandes was listed. I returned to the photo on the fiche. There was something about the woman that nagged at me. Mrs T. Fernandes, living on Lugh, teaching piano forty years ago. How was she connected to Cadal Fernandes, if at all?

I scrolled back further in time, my arm aching as I turned the dial, my eyes flying across the pages. I was over fifty years in the past, about to admit defeat, when I found it. The article was brief. *The marriage of Mr Cadal Tomas Fernandes of Bride, St Hía, and Miss Thora Jonasdottir of Tvífjallahöfn, Iceland, took place on Saturday afternoon at the Chapel of Our Lady of Sorrows, Sorrow, Father Leopoldo Carvalho officiating.* A photograph accompanied the article, over-exposed, with the dark hollow of the chapel-cave behind them, but of decent enough quality to see their faces. They were so young, looking for all the world as if they were dressed up for a school dance. He had a hangdog smile, a too-big suit and a carnation pinned to his lapel. She was radiant, in a simple white dress with daisies in her hair. *One-breathe-in, two-breathe-out.*

The date of Cadal and Thora's wedding was 1961, seventeen years before the fictional date of birth recorded on my adoption certificate. If Thora was as young on her wedding day as she looked in the photo, she would have been in her mid to late thirties when I was born. And she played the piano, just as whoever had last lived in the cottage on

Bride had played. My fingers moved involuntarily across the desk, as though across the keys of a piano, as if they might recover, in this little room full of outdated technology, library catalogues and phone books, the melody I had lost and found on Bride the day of the mist.

Tony had told me Cadal's wife was called Mary or Merry, but he hadn't been sure. No, it had to have been Thora. Cadal and Thora Fernandes, my birth parents. I had found them at last. My stomach cramped. I couldn't breathe. Found them, but lost them too, sunk to the bottom of the Hollow Sea with all my hopes of finding my birth family, of finding someone with my DNA. The blank space of my past would never be filled.

I held onto the desk, steadying myself. I felt as though I was in a dream space, somewhere between elation and grief. My breathing exercises weren't working. A howl was unfurling from deep inside me, in this tiny library where everyone would hear, where people would come running to see what the matter was and find me curled up on the floor and the news would be all through the archipelago in an instant. I couldn't stand the thought of it, so I bit myself hard on the hand. It worked. The howl turned to mist. I stared at the neat row of indentations on my skin.

With shaking hands, I printed off the photograph of Cadal and Thora. I studied their faces, trying to see myself in their features. Minerva the librarian came upstairs.

'Sorry to disturb,' she said, 'but we're closing in five.'

She glanced at the photo of Cadal and Thora on the table.

'Ach,' she said. 'If you're researching the Bride Witch,

you only needed to say. We dinna have much in our archives here. Just a paper about the evolution of the festival over the years, but if you're interested in the witch herself, then Samson Pentreath's your man. I'd be happy to put you in touch. Sam'll talk the ear off anyone who'll listen.'

The room was very quiet. Very still. I remembered the little girl with the candy floss who had run into me at the festival, her mother's warning: *Thora will come and steal you away.* I remembered the near-poisonous Thora's Special Brew. I remembered the paper effigy of a bride burning on the pyre. I remembered Kenver telling me about a murderess who stole her ex-husband's child.

'Thora Fernandes was the Bride Witch?'

Minerva frowned. 'Aye,' she said. 'I thought you knew.'

29

Thordis: The Chapel-Cave

Thordis goes to the chapel-cave on Sorrow. She had known as soon as Merryn had come to her, puffy-faced and pleading, that this would be the hiding place. Thordis has no desire to visit the chapel-cave again. She has long abandoned her happy memories to the whims of history. But she has made a promise. True, it was a promise made reluctantly, and to her bitter enemy. But Thordis, at least as I imagine her, is a woman of her word.

She lands the rowing boat on the shallow sloping beach and scrambles over rocks slippery with algae to reach the chapel, rubbing her oar-blistered palms with her thumbs. A parched sort of anger throbs through her body, as if she hasn't drunk enough water, or has drunk too much wine. At the entrance to the chapel-cave she hesitates, wishing she could run back to her little house on Lugh, with its neat parlour and tiny spinster's bedroom. But she has a promise to keep. The last time she had been here, the chapel had flickered with the light of a hundred candles and their voices had sputtered off the cave walls. This time, as Thordis slips inside, she is swallowed by darkness. Where before she had held a posy of daisies, now she grips a torch in her chilled hands. The only sounds are her breaths and the steady drip of water.

Everything has changed. The cave smells of sea and age

and loneliness. The walls had been painted with frescoes on her wedding day but now are covered with green algae and graffiti. Thordis stands on something hard, turning her ankle. She swears, passing the torch beam in front of her feet, illuminating a crumbling plaster statue of Baby Jesus, of the sort that had once adorned every nook and cranny of the chapel. Beyond it, condom wrappers, spent matches and an empty spray-paint can. It feels like only yesterday that she and Cadal had stood on this very spot and made their vows to one another, but it was a lifetime ago.

She had thought she might not be able to find the hiding place, but memories are flooding in now, unbidden and unwanted. A wan English hymn sung in their reedy, embarrassed voices. A pop song played on a tinny-sounding tape recorder. Thordis comes to the apse, where they had stood with Father Carvalho, his dog collar shining in the candlelight. She angles her torch to the left and up a little and there it is. The same pale-faced Madonna with her Child, sitting on a natural shelf in the rock, the plaster pitting and crumbling away. Could it really be this easy? Could Cadal have had so little imagination? But she supposes it is possible that Merryn has no knowledge of this place. She sets the torch on the ledge, so it shines into the space behind the Madonna and Child. She reaches inside, at first touching only air, her hand suspended in a dark space. She stands on tiptoe, stretching her whole body from torso to fingers. The barest brush of something against her fingertips. It might have been her imagination. She flattens her body into the rock, finds it within herself to stretch a little more and then, yes, this time she is certain. Plasticky rustling, the corner of something. It has a seam, a folded-over edge of some kind that she clamps between her fingers. It comes easily, in the end, catching a little on the Madonna and Child, but not tearing. A clear plastic bag and, inside that, brown paper sealed with packing tape. She had expected documents. A passport or money. But the item inside is large and soft. She squeezes it gently, battling the urge to rip open the paper there and then. Despite her many faults, Thordis is an honourable woman and it's not her parcel to open.

She tucks it under her arm, stumbles out of the chapel-cave and across the slippery rocks, and rows back out to the ramshackle fishing boat she purchased from Sam. He charged her less than it is worth, she is certain, but still it has taken all her savings and she tries not to think about how much longer she will have to wait now, before she can go home to Tvífjallahöfn. All the while her dread is rising because the package and the boat must be delivered, yet there is nowhere in the world she wants to visit less than Bride.

30

Scottie: Footprints

'You picked a day for it, Miss Scottie, aye,' said Tony, wiping his brow and squinting up at the sky.

We were heading north, always north, the sea on either side of us scattered with rocks and skerries that kept the water continually restless, even though it was the clearest of blue summer days.

'Yes, it's going to be beautiful. But the sea here never sleeps, does it?'

We were in the *Ella Mae*, the Cornish Cove boat Tony had been caulking when I had gone to the boatyard to ask for his help. He had equivocated for a week or more before finally agreeing to teach me to skipper a boat, to teach me everything I needed to know to travel safely across the Hollow Sea.

'Aye, it never does. How's school?'

I had spent much of the last two months, when I wasn't trying to sort out building permits and delivery logistics, sitting in my room at Nest's, squinting at the second-hand laptop I had bought from Roberta, the R in M & R's Boatyard, and wishing for a better internet connection, as I worked through my seamanship courses.

'Going well. I've finished and passed general seamanship, parts of the boat, collision regulation, latitude and longitude and, damn, what's the other one? Oh yes, knots and tacking. And I've made a start on weather, charts and allowing for tidal set and drift.'

'Aye, well,' he muttered, seemingly less than impressed with my progress, 'you'll need all of that. But safety, aye, make sure you dinna forget safety.'

I thought about the first time I had travelled this far north, the sea mist, the blaring foghorn, the sound of my howling, my shaking limbs, the scent of Kenver Pellow's hair, his pale-sick skin, the crunch as his boat had hit a rock. I hadn't seen him since. Now that there was no more seal counting to be done, I supposed he didn't have much reason to come to Lugh. I wondered if he was still angry with me. Did he even know I had remained in St Hía? Or did he assume I'd left with Ellie and the others, slinking back to my sad little childless life in the suburbs? I felt sick with embarrassment about what he must think of me, spilling the intimate details of my life to someone I barely knew.

In the near distance, I could see Ronan to the west and St Columba to the north-east, shimmering on the horizon. I'd taken this trip a dozen times or more in the two months since I'd decided to stay in St Hía, but it always made my stomach tighten in anticipation, crossing the sea that had taken the lives of Cadal Fernandes, his wife and children. I tried not to think of them there, dead at the bottom of the sea, but they were beginning to invade my dreams, pushing away my will-o'-the-wisps. If they were part of me, I wanted to remember them, to remember my life with them, not their deaths.

'Come and take the helm, here,' said Tony. 'It's a good day for navigating a tidal race.'

'Me? Tony, no. I'm nowhere near ready.'

'Ach, ready as you'll ever be.'

I put my hands on the wheel, trying to remember the running commentary Tony had provided each time we'd passed through the Tanguy-Tanick strait. Tanguy, to the west, had a deep channel close to its coastline relatively clear of rocks and underwater topography, creating a safer path through the strait, away from the tidal rapids and the rocks of Tanick.

'Can we not just go around the other side of Tanguy or Tanick?'

'Aye, course we can . . . if you dinna mind adding two maybe three hour in each direction, and then there's Gisela's Pillar to contend with as you come back around, and she's a tricky one. Almost as many ships taken by Gisela as by the Hollow Sea, I wager, if you add them all up. But, aye, we can choose that route if you prefer, Miss Scottie.'

I didn't bother replying. He knew I wasn't going to add hours to the journey when I had so much work to do at the cottage.

'Ach,' said Tony, as I took *Ella Mae* into the strait. 'She's gentle today. A wee lamb.'

He was right. The tidal rapids were no more than a white scurry on the water, but I wasn't taking any chances. I hugged the Tanguy coastline, beneath clouds of the ink-backed gulls Tony called Black Annies, hoping there weren't any rocks just beneath the surface I'd forgotten about. And still I could feel it, the tug of the tidal race on the *Ella Mae*, trying to draw us in. My palms sweated as I gripped the wheel, Tony watching me and watching the Hollow Sea.

'You're a natural, Miss Scottie,' he said.

Then we were through, the Hollow Sea relinquishing her grip, and there was Bride, rising out of the ocean. My heart leapt.

The cottage renovation had come on a mile. Tony had introduced me to Roberta and her husband Matty from the boatyard, an American couple who had stopped off in St Hía a decade ago during a transatlantic sailing trip and never left. Being incomers, they were unencumbered by St Hían superstitions about the northern isles and were more relaxed than most about the prospect of navigating the Hollow Sea. The irony wasn't lost on me that if I'd met them earlier in my trip I might have found Bride sooner, but I didn't dwell on it.

Roberta, who had once been a bothy-repair work-team volunteer in the Scottish Highlands, had rebuilt the chimney using original stones painstakingly retrieved from the piles of debris, rip-rapping them together, with me as her trusty apprentice. The cottage had a new metal roof, shipped to Lugh from the mainland and transported in stages to Bride in the *Ella Mae*, costing a huge chunk of my budget. Now all that was needed was to remove the piles of sand and mouldering rubbish from inside the cottage, the installation of a new door, windows, gutters and soffits, and to repoint the stonework. Most of these tasks I planned to do alone, or at least to try.

As the weather was beautiful, I decided to work on the exterior wall, preparing it for repointing by scraping and brushing away the old lime mortar between the stones. I worked methodically, a cloud of summer midges tracking my movements, losing myself in the rhythm of the work, the way

I once had when sculpting clay and would get lost for hours in the creation of a single piece. By the time the sun reached its highest point in the sky, I had finished a tiny section of the east wall. I mixed the lime mortar, smoothing it into the gaps. The sensation of the mortar drying and tightening on my skin made me realize how much I missed working with clay.

I took a break to eat the packed lunch Nest had made for me and reapply my insect repellent. Sitting in an old camping chair in the coastal jungle of a garden, I stared up at the new roof and the rebuilt chimney. It wasn't yet completely water- and windproof but already the cottage was starting to look more like a home and less like a ruin. I sensed an emotion blossoming in me as I sat there in the wild coastal garden, my aching limbs stretched out in the sunshine. It took me a few minutes to identify it as hope. It seemed unfamiliar, even though I had surfed on hope for many years, waiting to become a mother. But this version of hope was new, lighter, a shaking-off of a burden. I hadn't realized the weight of the old toxic hope I had lived with for so many years.

I finished eating and went into the cottage. The first time I had been inside, with Kenver during the storm, it had been wild, the cottage reclaimed by Nature, made as much a part of the island as the beach or the clifftop. I liked that idea, of not imposing too much order, but I also needed to live in it so some tidying up was necessary. Roberta and I had cleared away the debris at the chimney end of the house as we had searched for and picked out the stones we would use to rebuild the chimney, but most of the rotting furniture remained and decades' worth of sand still covered the south end of the cottage.

I tried to make sense of the scraps of a life left behind. Tony had told me the island had been occupied by Cadal Fernandes, who had drowned in the Hollow Sea with his pregnant wife Mary or Merry, and their two little girls. It made sense, the fragments of a life left here to be reclaimed by the island because there was no one to come and pack them away. How did that fit with the wedding photograph of Cadal and Thora I had found in the library? How did it fit with the story Kenver had told me about the child-stealing murderess, the Bride Witch, so reviled by the islanders they burnt her effigy on a pyre?

When Kenver and I had sheltered here, the sand had been virgin, untouched by humans. But now there was the pattern of our footprints, tracking across the cottage and, over them, the footprints left by Roberta, Matty and me as we worked on the renovation, each track a palimpsest, covering but not erasing Kenver's and my movements on the day of the storm. The stories I was learning about this place were similar, tracks and footprints and palimpsests laid over the top of one another. I was beginning to wonder how I would ever unravel them.

I needed to get back to work. I'd been lucky with the weather but there was no knowing how long it would last. I lingered inside, drawn by the promise of treasures to be discovered beneath the sand. The rotten old piano had already been removed, carted outside and dumped in a pile of rubbish eventually to be transported back to the on-islands for disposal. I had felt a pang as Roberta and I lifted the pieces of it into the wheelbarrow. I briefly entertained the fantasy that touching it again, the damp, peeling pieces of it, would bring back to my mind the lost melody, the one that had sent Kenver crashing angrily through the door and onto the beach, but there was nothing. The piano had been dead to me.

I decided to give up on the walls for the day, fetched the shovel and began filling Roberta's wheelbarrow with sand. It was damp and heavy, a dull ache spreading up my spine and along my shoulders. I trailed my fingers through each barrowful, checking for items that might have belonged to the people who had once lived here, as if I might be able to reconstruct the past from whatever tiny fragments the sand gave up. I found pieces of mouldering fabric, the remnants of sheets and blankets and clothing, but the only solid items were a broken cup, a teaspoon and an egg timer. I touched each one, hoping they might trigger a memory, as the piano had, but there was nothing.

A subtle change in the quality of the light, a barest shift in tone from yellow to blue, told me Tony would be here soon, in the *Ella Mae,* ready for me to guide her home across the channels and currents of the Hollow Sea. I decided to dig out one more barrowful. As I sifted through the sand in the wheelbarrow before taking it outside to dump it, my fingertips grazed an object. A tiny frisson of excitement prickled in my belly. It was a shell. A perfect pale pink spiral burnished by the sea, completely smooth to the touch. I placed it in my palm. Exactly the sort of thing I might expect to find buried in sand, but it felt emotionally warm to me in a way the teaspoon and the spatula had not. I took it outside and held it up to the late-afternoon light and I could see that, at its broadest end, someone had drilled a tiny perfect hole, for threading the shell onto a chain or a cord. It had once been worn as a necklace or a bracelet.

I put the shell into my pocket, packed up my work tools, securing them in case the weather turned overnight, and walked down to the beach to wait for Tony. The shoreline was littered with treasure. Razor shells, mermaid's purses, driftwood. I turned and saw my own footprints on the damp sand and remembered how I had felt playing in the snow, the first winter of my new life with Helen and Phil, when I had seen my own footprints, my own mark on the world for the first time. The past, whatever it was that lay beyond that moment in the snow, was still intangible, no more than an aching emotion in my chest, but now so was the future. Where once it had been signposted with the rituals and land-marks of motherhood, now it was a blank page. There would be no first steps or first words or first days of school. I would never take my child rock-pooling, prodding sea anemones in the name of science. I would never taxi my child from sports clubs to dance classes. Would never hold a feverish child in my arms wondering whether to call a doc-tor. I would never supply cookies for exam revision, or disapprove of a boyfriend or girlfriend, or comfort a broken heart. I would never grieve for all the different versions of my child as they grew into adulthood. I would never be an empty nester because my nest would never be full.

Another Scottie, the mother I might have been, seemed close to me in that moment, but I couldn't quite touch her.

I heard the soft chug of *Ella Mae*'s engine as she came into view around the bay and I ran down to the slipway to meet Tony.

31

Thordis: Merryn

Thordis is baking an apple cake, the type of cake her mother used to bake and serve in her café. The smell of warming batter permeates through the house. She has never had her own oven before, never had the luxury of being able to cook whatever she wants whenever she wants. Never had a shop she can walk to, to buy ingredients to bake a cake just because she has a whim. It's a small thing, perhaps, baking a cake, and Thordis has no idea how it will turn out, but the fact that she is here, in her tiny rented house in St Bridget's Lane on the upper slopes of Lugh, sends a slow-burning flicker of pleasure through her.

Thordis has been in the house for only a month but is more or less settled. Downstairs, she has her tiny kitchen, the walls of which she has already painted buttercup yellow, and a living room with a settee, a table to eat at and a chestnut-brown upright piano she bought for a song from a house clearance. It has a better tone than the one in the church hall, which Father Carvalho had permitted her to use for lessons in return for playing at daily services. She will continue to play at church, because Father Carvalho has been kind to her, but knowing she can do so out of choice rather than obligation is something she treasures.

Upstairs, an airy bedroom and a bathroom with a claw-footed tub to soak in. She had chosen the house because it had only one bedroom, which was all she needed. A spare bedroom would only have served to remind her of all she has lost. And she will not be here for ever. She has scrimped and saved and cleaned other people's bathrooms and out-houses for years, and even after renting the house and buying the piano she has a little left over. In a year or two, she will be able to afford her passage back to Tvífjallahöfn.

She has an hour or so of free time, before her next pupil arrives, so she curls up on her settee – her very own settee in her very own sitting room – and opens her copy of *Jane Eyre*. Of course, Lugh Library is very small and has only books in English, but she enjoys the challenge of reading in her second language. *Jane Eyre* is her favourite so far. Thordis imagines she can see something of herself in Jane, in her spirit and her passion and her imagination. Thordis pauses, between chapters, and considers how far she has come. She feels something, an emotion that is hard for her to identify. Not happiness, exactly, but something close to it. Acceptance, perhaps. Contentment. Neither of those is quite right, but whatever the emotion is, Thordis wel-comes it, perhaps for no other reason than that she has created it herself.

In the late afternoon, when the last of her pupils has per-formed their scales, played their halting waltzes and minuets and promised to practise every day for a week, and her cake is cooling on a rack on the worktop, Thordis dusts and vacuums. She was never a natural homemaker, but this is a home she has made herself, and keeping it neat is her way of expressing her pride, not just in her home but in how far she has come.

Thordis is stowing the vacuum cleaner beneath the stairs and is planning to eat a slice of cooling apple cake and then, perhaps, to read a few chapters of *Jane Eyre* in the bath, when there is a knock at the door. She has no more pupils for the day, and no close friends, because Lugh is a place where you will always be an outsider no matter how long you live here, so she considers ignoring it, pretending not to be at home. She tuts when the knock intrudes again, louder, ruder, more urgent. She turns the latch, preparing to tell whoever it is that she doesn't want to buy any dish-cloths, doesn't need her gutters clearing and, no, she doesn't care to chip in a few coins for a new swing set for the chil-dren's playground.

But when the door swings open, it isn't a charity col-lector, or a hawker. It's Merryn, her hair pinned up in a complicated swirl with the mother-of-pearl comb that had once belonged to Thordis. Merryn's hand is raised in a fist, poised to knock on the door again. Beside her, two little girls holding hands. Thordis swallows a cry of disbelief that her enemy should dare to sully the hard-won peace she has found on Lugh. She sees, through Merryn's unbuttoned blue coat, that her enemy is pregnant again, seemingly due to give birth very soon.

Come to rub my nose in it? says Thordis, despising the shrillness of her own voice. *You mothers, you think your hearts open like flowers when you give birth, but you don't have a care for a woman like me.*

Merryn's face is blotched and puffy, as if she has been crying. *Please, Thora, let me in. I dinna have much time. He thinks we're at market.* Patches of red heat prickle along her collarbone from beneath her dress. Her voice is soft and calm. It matches the way she moves her body, her gentle, precise motions. Thordis observes, not for the first time, that wherever she has angles – ribs, hip bones and elbows – Merryn has arches, cambers and softness. Her pinned-up curls gleam in the late-afternoon sun, in a way only dark hair can. So many things to envy.

Merryn checks behind her again, biting her lip. She pushes up her coat sleeve, holding out her left forearm to Thordis. The veins at her inner wrist are the same greenish blue as her coat. But they are bruised, the veins. They have ruptured, the blood seeping out beneath the skin, turning it black and purple. Merryn releases her coat sleeve, then repeats the same motion with her right arm. Another bruise, almost identical in shape. Thordis knows what those bruises mean. Is shocked by them, even though she shouldn't be. She had once worn the same bruises. But she had always thought of Merryn as charmed, in some strange way protected by her ability to bear children. She had never even considered her as a living, breathing woman, vulnerable like her.

Thora. Merryn has her pride. She won't beg. *Thordis. I must talk with you.*

It sends a chill up Thordis's spine to hear her true name from her enemy's lips. She lingers for a moment, wishing Merryn would take her children, run away and never return. Then she steps backwards into the house, beckoning Merryn to follow. They sit on the settee, mother, daughter and daughter, uninvited. Thordis remains standing, unable to bring herself to sit in the presence of her enemy.

Merryn's hands fall unconsciously to her pregnant belly. The youngest child, on the cusp of leaving toddlerhood, points at the apple cake and turns to her mother. *Yum, yum,* she says.

Hush now. Be a good girl. Dinna be rude.

The children resemble their mother, which Thordis is grateful for. She has dreamt about them and, in her dreams, they favoured their father, had the faces her own children might have had if they'd lived. There's something else too, in their faces, a faint shadow, the same shadow she now sees in Merryn's face. *They may have a slice of cake.*

The resistance of the dense sponge against the knife is satisfying. She offers none to Merryn, a childish act she knows, but she has so little power she must grab at anything she can. The first slices of the first-ever cake she baked for herself, gone to her enemy's children. Thordis's mouth twists into a wry smile.

Say 'Thank you', Merryn instructs her children.

The older girl obeys, tearing her eyes away from the cake to look at Thordis as she speaks. Thordis lies to herself that they are not Cadal's eyes. The younger girl has buried her face in her slice, spilling crumbs on the settee, but Thordis is past caring.

What do you want from me? she says, wishing she could keep the bitterness out of her voice.

I must leave him, says Merryn. *For my children's sake, I canna stay.*

Thordis wants to say unkind things, like *You've made your bed, now you must lie in it* or *This is karma, you husband-stealing harpy,* but she refrains. *I don't know why you're telling me this.*

She breaks off a chunk of the apple cake and pops it into her mouth.

Because you're the only person who can help me, says Merryn.

Why should I help you? You stole everything from me.

Merryn laughs, a bitter mirthless sound. *Stole from you? Thordis, I only set you free.* She tugs down the neck of her dress, revealing a red triangular burn just below her collarbone. *Because you know, Thordis. You know. Dinna you know?*

Thordis feels weak now, not just in spirit, but in body too. She sinks into the carver chair by the table, the one she has lovingly sanded and polished after finding it at the same estate sale as the piano. *You've found out the hard way, just as I did. But I still don't understand how you think I can help you.*

Merryn hugs her coat around herself, as if she is cold, although the room is warm. *My daughters are old enough to —* Merryn stumbles over her words, composes herself. *Old enough to travel now. I've made plans. I canna tell you what they are, but I've made plans. Cadal has hidden something from me. Something very valuable. It's nae on Bride, I'm sure of it. I've searched high and low. I canna leave until I find it. But you know him, Thordis. You know him better than anyone. Where might he have hidden something so that it could nae easily be found?*

Thordis licks cake crumbs from the corners of her mouth. *What item?*

Merryn demurs. *Something of great value to me. I simply canna leave until I've got it back, nae matter the consequence. Tell me, Thordis, please. Tell me where he would have hidden it.*

When Merryn brushes a curl from the toddler's forehead, Thordis is suffused with silent rage, as if Merryn herself is somehow to blame for Thordis's lost children, for all the curls she will never brush from foreheads. Thordis doesn't want to help Merryn, this woman who has taken so much from her. But she can't forget the bruises, the burn, and she understands, too, that there are other scars to be reckoned with, ones that can't be seen, scars that Merryn's children and their new sibling will wear on their hearts as they grow. Her heart comes to a decision before her head does.

That used to be mine. The hair comb you're wearing. Merryn's hand flies up to it, a flicker passing across her face. So, she hadn't known, had thought it a gift from Cadal to her.

I'll gladly return it to you, says Merryn, *but nae yet. In case he notices it's gone.* Her eyes are drawn to the clock above the mantelpiece. *He'll be waiting at the quayside. I canna be late. Will you help me, Thordis?*

Thordis thinks about the hair comb, about Cadal's smile as he gave it to her, his shaking hands, his borrowed, too-big suit, his crooked tie. *I'll help you find your precious item,* she says.

Thank you, Thordis. Her gratitude is less satisfying than Thordis had anticipated. Merryn is up, helping the toddler thread her arms into her jacket, as the older girl licks crumbs from her fingers.

When will you come for it? On next market day?

Merryn is buttoning her coat. *Nae,* she says. *I canna leave Bride again without him suspecting. You must bring it to me.* Merryn is herding her girls to the door, leaving in unseemly haste now she has extracted Thordis's promise.

Must I? Must I bring it to you?

Merryn either misses or chooses to ignore the sarcasm in

Thordis's voice. *Aye. Between the spring and neap tides. Come in the afternoon when he'll be out on his boat. Dinna tarry, Thordis, please. For all our sakes, I must leave before the bairn comes.*

Thordis is about to object, to point out she doesn't even have a boat, when Merryn flings her arms around her, taking her by surprise so there's nothing she can do to defend herself against the unwanted embrace. And then it happens. A kick. Merryn's baby kicks, and Thordis feels it. She cries out, and Merryn releases her. She is smiling, looking happy for the first time since she knocked on Thordis's door. *The bairn says thank you too.*

And then they are gone, the three of them, hurrying down the lane hand in hand to meet Cadal at the docks, and Thordis is left alone, pressing her hand to her belly, to the hollow space inside.

32

Charlotte: Leaving

Sometimes the waiting was worse. The day I left David, he hadn't even touched me. He was down the pub, and I was at home, waiting. I had a bath, sinking down into the whispering bubbles as far as I could so only my nose and mouth broke the surface. I wallowed for an hour or more, draining the cold water and topping up with hot, unwilling to leave its amniotic comfort. I dried myself and my hair and put on my pyjamas. I had a pair, specially chosen for the evenings David went to the pub, that almost looked like they could be a tracksuit, something you might wear outside, in case he put me out in the garden again, in case I had to stay out there all night. I lay on top of the duvet in the spare bedroom, curled up in the foetal position. It felt safer than the bed we shared. I waited, listening for his key in the lock.

He came in around eleven thirty, crashing around. I heard the kitchen tap run as he got a glass of water. I needed to move from the spare bed, because my presence there required an explanation, but I was paralysed. So I waited, and I waited, and eventually the sound of drunken snoring rattled up the stairs. I crept down to the lounge, taking a double step over the creaky stair tread, but I needn't have bothered. David was comatose on the sofa, his mouth hanging open, his neck cricked up on the sofa arm. I stood watching him for a few minutes. I knew there'd be no waking him. A thought came into my mind, the single most terrible thought I'd ever had. I could get a knife from the kitchen and plunge it into him, right into his heart, and he would never even know. Something broke in me then, my own imagined violence triggering what David's actual violence never had. I called Helen, for the first time in almost a year. She would still be up, I knew, doing her crossword.

Hello? She sounded tired.

Mum. It's all I said. I could have said, *I'm sorry, Mum, for not having called you for so long,* or *David's in a drunken stupor on the sofa and I seriously considered killing him,* or even *How are you, Mum? Just ringing for a chat.* But I said none of those things. Just *Mum* once.

What's he done? she said. *Are you safe?*

She drove two hours through the night, and when she arrived, I was sitting on the stairs, all cried out, still in my tracksuit-style pyjamas. She looked older, more brittle than I'd ever seen her. She observed David in his paralytic state on the sofa and although her jaw stiffened a little, she made no comment. She moved efficiently around the house, packing a few things, locating my passport, driving licence and bank cards, while I stayed in my spot on the stairs.

Is there anything else you want? This lamp? This photo frame? This bowl? There's plenty of room in the car. But I didn't want anything from that house, not a single thing, so she coaxed me to the car, switching off the lights as she left.

David never woke or stirred. I dozed in the front seat as

she drove us home. It was almost light when we arrived, but she put me to bed in my childhood room. The walls weren't pink any more, and there were plastic boxes full of Christmas decorations stacked up in the corner.

Sleep, she said, pulling the blankets up to my chin. She laid her hand across my forehead, as if I might have a fever. *Sleep now, Charlotte,* she said, and I did.

33

Scottie: Samson Pentreath

Samson Pentreath was a guest of honour at the St Hía Story-telling Society's August meeting in Sorrow's village hall. I took the water-taxi that ran between Lugh and Sorrow several times a day. The east coast of Sorrow had been wild, a place for seals and sea caves and crashing waves. But the west coast, sheltered by Lugh, had a sweeter nature, with a scattering of modest stone cottages on gentle slopes. A pretty fishing village, houses with pink-tiled roofs rambling up a hillside. In the bright sunshine it could have been the Mediterranean.

Using the map Minerva the librarian had drawn for me, I found the village hall without too much difficulty. Rows of chairs were set up in a semi-circle around a staging area with a chair and a microphone, a respectable crowd of mainly pensioners milling about a kitchen hatch where tea was being served. I sat at the back, near the door. The woman next to me was knitting, the clacking rhythm of the needles strangely soothing.

I was the youngest in the room by about twenty-five years, or at least I thought I was, until I looked up to see Kenver Pellow adjusting the mic. I hadn't seen him since the day we had sheltered from the storm on Bride. My stomach did a slow flip. His eyes flickered up and he saw me through a gap in the chairs but didn't acknowledge me.

He switched on the mic and tapped it. 'Testing one-two. Can you all hear, aye?'

The audience muttered its assent.

'We've a real treat for you today. Our most venerated storytelling elder, Samson Pentreath.'

'Ach,' tutted the knitting woman. 'Nae Sam Pentreath again.'

She didn't join in with the restrained applause that rippled around the room as Kenver assisted a tiny, white-bearded man to get out of his wheelchair and shuffle to the staging area with the help of an ornate wooden walking frame.

Samson Pentreath, the man I hoped would be able to tell me all about Thora Fernandes, the Bride Witch. His right foot dragged on the floor as he made his way to the microphone. My neighbour tapped my arm with a needle. 'Tells the same bliddy story every time. As if we dinna all know every word of it by heart. Wish I hadna come now.'

He eased himself down onto the chair. 'My name is Samson Pentreath,' he said. The right side of his face drooped fractionally and his voice was muffled at the edges, but his words were clear enough. 'And it's been my name for ninety-three year. I'm going to tell you "The Tale of the Hollow-Fin Wife". And dinna be thinking it's a fairy-tale, because every word I'm going to tell you is the truth.

'Many years ago, there was a fisherman. A fractious fellow. And he had a barren wife, which made him even more fractious, because what he craved more than aught in the world was a son and heir. One fine summer's day, the fisherman was out on the Hollow Sea, fishing for breal, when the sea grew wild, heaving him in one direction and the next, plucking him from his boat, submitting him to the furious domain of the ocean.

'Tossed and pitched and stirred around he was, imbibing great quantities of water and burning salt. When he saw lights moving through the water, his first thought was that he had drowned and was in Heaven. The light was many colours at once and it flitted and tumbled in the surf. Enchanted by its beauty, the fisherman dived down, desperate to find its source, and there he spied a mermaid riding a white horse beneath the waves. Her hair twisted and swayed with the currents. Her tail shimmered all colours of the rainbow. On her back she had a fin, pulsing with light. And then he knew she was nae a common mermaid, but a maiden of the Hollow Fin clan.

'The fisherman was afraid for the Hollow Fins have a fearsome reputation, but the maiden had a kind face and he begged for her help. She took pity on him, bade him mount her horse and carried him up to the shallow waters close to his home.

'The fisherman lay on the sand, his clothes stiff with salt and his limbs stiff with tribulation, convinced he had dreamt the Hollow Fin maiden in his half-drowned state. Then a sound came to him, a soft, pulsing murmur soothing to the ears. At first, the fisherman thought 'twas the sound of an animal, yet a moment later it had the quality of singing. The longer the fisherman listened, the lovelier and eerier the noise became, calming his half-drowned heart.

'There in the surf was a woman on a white horse, a creature of exceptional beauty, singing a song. She didna have a fishtail, but human legs draped in a skirt all colours under the sun, but the fisherman was sure as sure as can be she was the Hollow Fin maiden who had saved him. "Who are you? What is your name?" he said. At that, she clicked her tongue at her horse, and trotted into the sea. "Nae, nae," said the fisherman. "Dinna leave. Stay a while. Let me thank you for your kindness." But she wouldna stay and the fisherman witnessed an extraordinary transformation. The waves began to lick at the edges of the woman's skirt, and it shimmered and rippled, seeming to grow liquid at its edges, moulding around her legs, and then she was a mermaid once more. The white horse dived beneath the water, the fin on the maiden's back pulsing with light. The fisherman watched, enchanted, until they were a faint glimmer disappearing beneath the ocean's surface.

'The fisherman returned home but found himself even more dissatisfied than usual with his barren wife. He couldna purge the memories of the Hollow Fin maiden from his mind. He came each day to the beach to stand in the shallows, hoping for a glimpse of her pulsing light. One early morning, when the pale moon was still in the sky, he recalled the song she had sung to heal him, and an idea came to his mind. He waded waist deep into the ocean and began to sing, hesitantly at first, a few lines he could recall from a childhood lullaby, then a folk song and a raucous sea shanty. But still she didna come. Humiliated, he turned to go home, when a soft animal cry came from behind, sending through him a sensation he had nae words to describe, and there, emerging from the waves, was the Hollow Fin maiden on her white steed. Her tail softened and shimmered, changing shape, becoming legs draped in a skirt of shifting colours.

'Quite taken with her beauty and her miraculous power, he was, and he thought her a fitting replacement for his barren wife. He stepped close to her, his blood in a frenzy, took her shoulders with trembling hands, and declared his true and abiding love for her. She kissed him, or he kissed her. The precise order of things is of nae relevance. It matters only that they professed their love for one another and lay down on the beach that morning.

'Presently, the fisherman's wife came to the beach in search of her absent husband and when she saw him lain down with the Hollow Fin maiden she cried out in anguish. The fisherman flew into a rage, driving her away. The Hollow Fin maiden kenned she had been deceived, but as she made to leave, to return to Enys Wolvygyen, her underwater home, the fisherman snatched up her skirt of many colours. Without it, she couldna leave, would drown if she rode her horse beneath the waves in her human shape. She begged, she pleaded, she cried, but the fisherman was set on making her his wife and wouldna be moved. The white horse pawed at the surf, whinnying for its mistress, but as day passed to night, it had nae choice but to return to the underwater kingdom alone. The Hollow Fin maiden became the fisherman's wife and bore him children, but she never stopped looking for her magical skirt, never stopped dreaming she would one day be able to return to her white horse, and her home beneath the sea.'

Samson Pentreath bowed. I joined in with the applause,

although I hadn't liked the story much. St Hían folklore wasn't getting any more progressive.

'Same old, same old,' muttered the woman with the knitting. 'The daft old fool. What kind of storyteller knows only one tale?'

It was time for a tea break, my fellow audience members buzzing to the kitchen like flies. I went to the staging area, intending to offer to get Samson Pentreath a cup of tea.

'Hello, Mr Pentreath,' I said, my hand extended in greeting. 'I'm –'

Samson Pentreath glared at me, the friendly smile on the left side of his face fading. 'Get away. Get away! You're nae welcome here. Oh, go away.'

His voice was weak, trembling, but there was no mistaking his fury.

'My name's Scottie, Mr Pentreath. Minerva the librarian was supposed to tell you I was coming.'

'Get away! You left the wee 'un. You canna take her now. You're too late, lassie.'

He swung the walking frame aloft, miraculously staying on his feet, and thrust it at me, one of its legs connecting with my shoulder. The force of it took me by surprise and I staggered back, knocking a chair over. Kenver came from somewhere, putting his hand on Samson Pentreath's shoulder, whispering soothing words, lowering the walking frame to the floor. I was shaking but no one else seemed fazed by his outburst.

'Dinna take nae notice, dearie,' said the knitting woman. 'It's about time they put the old duffer in a home.'

My shoulder hurt. There was a smear of floor dust on

my T-shirt where the walking frame had connected, and a corresponding red mark on my skin.

'Let's get you home, Sam,' I heard Kenver say, as he helped the old man back into his wheelchair.

No one seemed interested in me or my shoulder. Kenver opened the exit door with his back and pulled the wheelchair through, without asking me if I was okay, or even saying goodbye. The walking frame had been left behind.

'Oh dear,' said the woman. 'He'll be needing that.'

I picked up the frame, wondering how someone as old and incapacitated as Samson Pentreath had found the strength to wield it as a weapon. I followed them outside and saw Kenver rolling Samson down the hill. I called, but they didn't hear me or pretended not to. I balanced the frame on my good shoulder, half jogging to catch them up. By the time I was close enough that they could no longer ignore me, Kenver was turning the wheelchair into the forecourt of a little cottage with pink-washed render and palm trees around the door. Kenver, propping the front door open with his foot, saw me holding the frame and visibly exhaled.

'You'd better bring it in,' he said.

The front door opened into a dimly lit living room. Kenver was transferring Samson, who seemed to be asleep, into one of a pair of burnt-orange armchairs draped with stained antimacassars. There was a coffee-table made from a tree trunk, an ancient television in one corner and a floor lamp decorated with what at first I thought were gargoyles but, as my eyes adjusted to the light, I realized were tooth-and-claw merfolk of the type that had made Ellie shiver at the sand-sculpting festival.

Every surface was crammed with Toby jugs and ships in bottles and bone china figurines. Sailors and monkeys and dolphins and shepherdesses with their lambs. The room smelt of candlewax, dust and old man's aftershave. There was a painting, mounted on the wall in an ugly frame: a child with a fin on its back, sitting on a rock. One of the Hollow Fin folk from Samson's story and, I was certain, the inspiration for Kenver's sand sculpture of the finned child at The Burning, which already seemed like a lifetime ago.

Kenver tucked a blanket over the old man's lap and folded up the wheelchair. 'If you're staying, could you maybe put the kettle on?'

His face was neutral, inscrutable. If he was still angry with me about the incident on his boat, I wished he would just say so.

The kitchen, on the other side of a beaded curtain, was littered with cups and bottles. I filled the kettle and set it on the hob while I hunted for clean teacups and tea. Next to the cooker was a well-stocked but dusty spice rack, and on the other side, a set of shelves crammed with jars. I searched for any that might be tea leaves, but they were altogether more exotic concoctions. Powdered bladderwrack, the label written in careful calligraphy with a tiny exquisite sketch of black seaweed. An infusion illustrated by an underwater kelp forest. Red ragwort accompanied by a smiling seal pup. The label for the Mermaid's Hair Tea showed a mermaid sitting on a rock drinking out of a giant cup.

I found some loose-leaf tea in one of the cupboards and

a metal tea strainer in the shape of an elephant. There was no milk or lemon in the fridge, but I found a tin of browning sugar lumps in one of the cupboards. I put the tin on the tea tray and carried it into the living room. Samson Pentreath was awake.

'Well, hello, dearie,' he said, as if his outburst in the village hall had never happened. 'What a treat to have a visitor.'

I put the tea tray on the coffee-table. 'I'm Scottie. Minerva the librarian said you wouldn't mind answering some questions.'

'Aye, you're the lass who's taking up residence on yonder Hollow Sea. You can call me Sam, dearie. We're all friends here.'

Up close, the difference between the right and left sides of Sam's face was more pronounced and I could hear the effort it took for him to speak clearly. Kenver declined a cup of tea and went outside for a smoke.

'Can you be mother? My fingers are giving me gyp today.'

Ordinarily that would have made me bristle, but I gave Sam a free pass and picked up the teapot. 'Do you take sugar, Sam?'

'Nae me. Sweet enough already. Now, what was it you wanted to ask me? I'm ninety-three year old and I've lived in St Hía my whole life, so there's nae one who knows more than me.'

The new Sam seemed bright as a button, a million miles away from the confused, angry old man of twenty minutes ago.

'I'm interested in what you know about the Bride Witch. About Thora Fernandes.'

'Worried she's going to haunt your little island?'

I smiled diplomatically.

'Well, it's stuff and nonsense. There's nae such thing as witches. I'm surprised you think different, a modern lass like you.'

'I heard she murdered her ex-husband and his new wife and stole their child for herself.'

He leant forward in his armchair, suddenly grave. 'And who told you that? Young Kenver? Well, he's got his view and I dare say he's entitled to it. But he was only a laddie when all this happened, so he dinna know the full tale.'

'And Tony Oliveira told me something different. That Cadal Fernandes drowned in the Hollow Sea, with his wife and daughters.'

'Antonio. Nice lad. Had a soft spot for Miss Thora the size of a Fish Moon.'

Tony Oliveira and his secrets. He had known about Thora the Bride Witch and had chosen not to tell me. I shouldn't have been surprised. It wasn't the first time he'd been less than forthcoming.

Sam tapped his temple with a gnarled finger. 'When I was a young man,' he said, 'fishing was my game. But it's a hard life.'

I sipped my black tea, grateful for the sugar, wondering how best to get Sam back on track.

'I got too old, you see, to carry on. So, groceries became my trade. I delivered all over the archipelago, and I made a tolerable living out of it too.'

'Did you deliver groceries to Bride, Sam?'

Sam took a slurp of his tea, liquid clinging to his moustache.

'For a time, for a time. Lovely lass, that Thora. Her real name was something else. Foreign. Unpronounceable. Dinna mind admitting I had a soft spot for her too. The wee lass must have buried a half-dozen of her bairns in that wretched garden she made, the poor barren soul, but she never let it break her.'

Half a dozen bairns. I dwelt on that for a moment, trying to comprehend the enormity of it. I wondered how it felt to grieve for such tangible losses, compared to my own intangible ones. I had no frame of reference for it. *One-breathe-in, two-breathe-out*. I was not going to have an episode in front of Sam.

'But motherhood wasna meant to be for Miss Thora.'

There wasn't a comment about motherhood or the lack of it that I hated more than 'It wasn't meant to be'. As if God or the universe saw me as a worse bet than all the mothers out in the world who neglected their children or worse. I would never believe as long as I lived that I wasn't meant to be a mother. It was circumstance, not Fate, that had got in my way. I gave Sam his second free pass of the afternoon.

'I'm confused,' I said. 'If Thora wasn't a witch or a murderess and Cadal and his wife – Merry, was it? – didn't drown, what did happen?'

Sam peered into his teacup, as if he were consulting the tea leaves for the answers.

'I'm getting to it. Two wives, he had. And when it came

to push and shove, neither of them stayed. Make of that what you will.'

Sam was silent, head down, for so long I was worried he had gone back to sleep, but then he snapped into lucidity, leaning forward in his chair to be as close to me as possible.

'Aye,' he said eventually. 'Thora left an' all. Took the wee girl with her. Back to the north, I reckon, whence she came. Played beautiful on the piano.'

Took the wee girl with her. A girl. Thora was *a poor barren soul*, but somehow, she had also had a girl. A sick, spaced-out feeling in my temples, a twitch in my torso. *Played beautiful on the piano.* Sam slumped forward in his armchair. The effort of talking to me had worn him out.

Kenver came back into the room. 'Scottie, you should go now. Sam's exhausted.'

I didn't want to leave. I wanted to ask Sam more questions, to unravel all the threads of the story and weave them back together, to try to get it all to make sense. Sam reached across the coffee-table and grabbed my hands. His skin felt paper-thin, as though he might tear if I held on too tight. He stared at me, his wrinkled face cracking with an emotion I couldn't identify.

'Merryn, my love,' he said, 'you're too late to fetch the wee girl. She's already gone.'

34

Thordis: Uffa Denbigh

Thordis's last piano lesson of the day is complete, her final pupil gone home, and she is alone in the church hall, tidying up her sheet music, dreaming of the day when she will have saved enough money to move out of Denella Carvalho's attic, when she hears the door swing open behind her. She turns, expecting to see Father Carvalho, but it is Uffa Denbigh, leering at her with his sea-coloured eyes.

Good day to you, Thora.

His voice is soft and all the more alarming for it. *And to you, Mr Denbigh.*

He walks towards her across the wooden floor. *Come now, Thora,* he says. *Nae need to stand on ceremony. We're old friends.*

They had never been friends, but Thordis forces a smile to her lips. *Of course,* she says. *Uffa.* He stands a few yards away from her, a respectable distance, but she doesn't drop her guard.

Your old man is expecting another bairn, says Uffa. *With his lovely new wife. But I expect you already knew.*

Thordis is utterly still. She can't let Uffa see that the news has crushed her heart. *Why should I care about that?* she says, but a slight wobble in her voice betrays her.

There, there, poor Thora. Two for two and nae a bairn for you.

He takes a step closer, just one step. *We all heard what you said to them. The threat you made. Naebody's forgotten. Nae even the ones that send their wee girls and boys to learn their piano.*

Thordis counters Uffa's step forward with a step back, bumping her hip against the piano lid. *What do you want, Uffa?*

He crosses the last of the distance between them with one stride and puts his fingers under her chin, forcing her to make eye contact. *The question, Thora, is what do* you *want? You married the wrong crewman but it's nae too late.* Uffa's breath is poisonous. Thordis whips her head away, but he reaches around to the back of her neck and slides his fingers into her hair. *Dinna be unfriendly, Thora.* His body pressing against hers now. *I dinna mind that you're barren. Cadal was a fool.* She has nowhere to go, trapped between Uffa and the piano. He buries his face in her neck, one hand reaching down for the hem of her dress.

Leave me bide, Uffa. Please. Her voice is a whisper.

Dinna fight it, Thora. But Thordis couldn't fight, even if she wanted to. Her limbs are frozen. Her brain is frozen. Uffa's hand is between her thighs.

The hall door opens, flooding them with winter sun-light. Father Carvalho. Thordis is hot with relief and shame. Uffa doesn't even flinch. He removes his hand languidly from between her legs. Straightens his cap. *Afternoon, Father.* Under his breath, to Thordis, he says, *I wouldna want to fuck a barren whore anyways.* He exits the hall with the air of a man out for a Sunday stroll.

Are you all right, Thora? says Father Carvalho.

Quite all right, thank you. She straightens her clothes.

246

Perhaps, he says, *you should lock the door when you're here alone.*

Thora nods. *Yes,* she says, her voice hardly shaking. *In future, I think I will.*

She waits until later, until she is alone in her attic room at Denella Carvalho's house, before she cries.

35

Scottie: Kópakonan

My first day living on Bride, in the cottage that had haunted my dreams for so long. In command of my own destiny, the proud owner of a skipper's qualification and a second-hand rigid inflatable boat called *Banana*. The cottage was near enough wind- and waterproof. The sand had all been swept away. The only thing left to finish was the pointing on the stone walls, which I could do at my own pace, and to decide whether or not to rebuild the brick outbuildings or just clear the rubble. I had learnt so much, achieved so much in just a few months. I should have been elated. But I felt nothing at all.

It was overcast but muggy. I walked listlessly along the beaches, then climbed the grassy slope to the clifftop, with no real intent or destination. The faint cries of seabirds grew louder as I ascended, becoming a cacophony. I reached the top, breathless and sweaty. Birds billowed upwards from the cliff face, white blurs oscillating against the hazy grey sky, then swooping down out of sight. Unseen waves battered the base of the cliffs. Crashing waves and screaming birds, a strange kind of symphony. Bride's own music.

Even beneath grey skies, the view was spectacular, sweeping out to the south, Tanguy and Tanick in the distance. Nothing else but sea and sky. Like the beach, the cottage, there was no epiphany. I pushed my salt-crusted hair out of my eyes, feeling sick and empty inside. All that effort to get here, and no answers, no revelations. All my thoughts and dreams of this place were just that. I still hadn't seen a single thing that had jogged a concrete memory, a single thing that confirmed to me this was where I came from.

A storm began, delicately enough, flickers of violet lightning on the horizon. My hair crackled. There was a moment of stillness, weightlessness, expectation, a lull before the storm, then the island began to breathe again. A breeze ruffled through the grass. Rain fell in intermittent, oversized, slow-motion droplets. The wind strengthened, shrieking, whipping my hair away from my face. The sea-birds dipped and dived with it in crazy patterns. My breaths quickened, matching the pace of the storm. My body swayed with the wind. The sea below was stirring, accelerating with the beat of the storm, the metronomic rhythm of the waves disrupted into a wild, tumultuous syncopation. I imagined my first ghost child, David's child, the one I had named, the one I had not been strong enough for, there, on the clifftop, grown and standing beside me, watching the beautiful violet fingers of light as the storm blossomed in the distance. Alice. Her name was Alice. Just for a moment, smiling at me, and then she was gone.

A throaty roar of thunder, and the lightning was no longer violet but ice-white and drawing closer. I'd been so stupid to imagine that the mother's heart I'd carried for all those years could be mended so easily. Coming here, to St Hía, my search for Bride, my absolute belief that all the pieces of the past would fall into place if only I could find this enchanted island. But I was here now, and the past was

still a jumble of half-remembered, half-imagined fragments. The storm was overhead, dazzling white fissures
ripping open the sky. A strange enervation swept through
my body, my limbs too exhausted to hold my weight. Rain
streaming down my face, blinding me, my toes at the very
edge of the cliff. The wind pummelling me. I unfurled my
arms, leant forward into it. Just one step and I could be like
the whirling seabirds, riding the air currents, free.

I sat in the cottage in semi-darkness, listening to the rain
howl down. Since the day I had sheltered here with Kenver,
from another storm, when I had hummed a few notes of a
melody and had a vision of a curly-haired girl wrapped up
in a scarf knitted to resemble piano keys, there had been no
epiphanies, not a wisp of a memory, even when I'd found
the pink shell I was now wearing on a cord around my neck.
The fragments of information I'd collected about Bride,
about Cadal Fernandes and his two wives, didn't fit together.
There were too many missing pieces. It was time to do what
Helen and Jasminder had both said I should all along and
write to the adoption agency that had placed me.

I lit the kerosene lamp. The wick was too long, casting
demented shadows on the walls. I ripped a blank sheet out
of an old notebook that had been mouldering away in the
side pocket of my suitcase for a decade or so and wrote the
letter in scrawled cursive, careful to make my words per-
functory and detached, although the emotions churning
through me were anything but. The letter finished, I decided
to work on the cottage walls to distract myself. Starting in
the north-eastern corner, where the piano had once stood,

I scraped and brushed at the old lime mortar around the stones, losing myself in the rhythm of the work. *Scrape, scrape, brush. Scrape, scrape, brush.*

One of the larger stones was loose. I jiggled it and tested the stones surrounding it, but it seemed to be the only one that wasn't sound. I decided to try to remove it, so I could see if there was further damage behind I needed to worry about. It slid out cleanly, leaving a small roughly rectangular space in the wall. There was something inside the space, something that wasn't a stone. My fingertips touched rustling plastic. It took a few minutes to work my fingers around the top of the package so I could pull it out. The wrapping was held down with elastic bands that disintegrated when I touched them. I unrolled the plastic, and then a layer of brown paper, but I already knew the item inside was a book.

I was afraid it might disintegrate as soon as it was exposed to the air, but it didn't. It was cold, but dry, free from rot and mould. The plastic and the wall had protected it well. I turned it over and examined the cover. *Tales from the Hollow Sea*, a collection of St Hían folklore by Lucyna Richmond-Whyte. The image on the front cover was the painting of a child with a fin on its back that had been hanging in Sam's living room. I wondered why someone would think to hide a book of folk tales in a wall.

I sat in my camping chair, wrapped in a blanket, and opened the book, turning the fragile, yellowed pages with care. I read the story of the singing shell that led an island girl to a shoal of breal during a famine, remembering the first sand sculpture I had seen at the Burning, which had been inspired by this legend. There was a story about a snake catcher, and another about a boy who rode on the back of a sea-bear. Sam's story about the Hollow Fin Wife was included almost word for word, a fond acknowledgement from the author to him in the back matter. There was additional detail about the legends in the footnotes, and discussions of the provenance of alternative versions of the tales, including one where a fin-child dropped his magical skirt down a well, stranding him in the 'up above' until he made a horse from sand to ride home to Enys Wolvygyen.

Something was nagging at me, but I didn't know what. Jasminder was right: I had been on a fool's errand. I wasn't going to find what I was looking for on Bride, but what was I supposed to do now? Where was I supposed to be, if not here? I extinguished the lamp, leaving a single candle burning, the room filling with the scent of kerosene and candlewax. I lay awake on my creaking camp bed, waiting for the candle to sputter out, waiting for absolute darkness to cocoon me, waiting for sleep that didn't come.

I took *Banana* across to St Mertheriana. I needed to post my letter to the adoption agency, but it was also the island where Kenver lived, and I wanted to show him the book I'd found in the wall. At least, that was what I told myself. But I also wanted to know if he was still angry with me, even though I wasn't sure why I should care. I didn't have Kenver's exact address, but the master of the tiny harbour was happy to point me in the right direction. St Mertheriana was rural, cottages scattered along winding country lanes surrounded by fields of sheep. It was a Sunday, so I hoped Kenver would be home, had not taken a casual fishing gig on one of the inshore fishing boats out of Lugh harbour, as I knew he sometimes did.

I stopped at the island shop to buy a stamp and an envelope and posted my letter, hesitating before pushing it through the slot, but then it was done and there was no turning back. I continued on, finding what I hoped was the right cottage, at a fork in the road by a lychgate, with a rose arch above the door. I opened the gate, but it was the wrong house. There were two curly-haired children in the front garden, a teenage boy of fourteen or so in a Manchester United strip, practising keepie-uppies, and a girl I estimated was three or four, who was burying a naked doll in a flowerbed with an air of deep concentration.

Sorry,' I said. 'I think I've got the wrong house. I was looking for Kenver Pellow.'

The little girl clutched her dirt-smeared doll by its hair and offered it to me. 'It's bath time.'

I had never known how to talk to young children, an affliction I always assumed would cure itself when I had children of my own. But now I was doomed to be the embarrassing, patronizing adult for the rest of my life.

'Oh, no. Has your doll got dirty?'

'Nae!'

She flung the doll down on the sparse lawn and started to sob. The boy lost control of his keepie-uppies and swore, not caring that I heard.

'Pa,' he yelled, making me jump. 'Paaaaaa.' He stuck his head around the side of the cottage, behind an overgrown butterfly bush. 'Pa, there's a lady. She made Rozy cry.'

I was backing away, keen to be gone before an enraged father arrived wanting to know who was responsible for his daughter's gulping, inconsolable tears, when Kenver appeared from behind the butterfly bush, a tool belt slung low around his hips. He ignored me and scooped the little girl up in his arms, where she sobbed into his shoulder, her doll hanging from her fist by a single, grubby lock of hair.

'What's wrong, Rozy Bear?'

His voice was so tender and kind. I tried to think if he'd ever mentioned having children, but I was sure he hadn't. I couldn't remember ever having met a parent who didn't talk about their offspring. I mentally cursed myself for making assumptions, because Kenver having children felt like a betrayal, however irrational that was.

Rozy lifted her tear- and snot-stained face from Kenver's shoulder and pointed at me. 'Lady says Doris is dirty.'

'I'm sorry,' I said, to Kenver, but he kept eye contact with his daughter.

'Rozy Bear. Dirt is good.' He touched his nose to hers. 'Dirt is *beautiful*.' He looked at me then. 'Right, Scottie?'

'Absolutely.'

'Right, Perry?'

The boy, who had one boot on his football and had been observing our little play with laconic indifference, pursed his lips. 'Whatever.'

'But just in case,' said Kenver, speaking to Rozy again now, 'why dinna you and Perry go and wash Doris's face, while I talk to the lady?'

Perry objected, but half-heartedly, and accepted the

transfer of Rozy and Doris from Kenver's arms to his own, pushing open the front door with his foot.

'I'm so sorry,' I said, from my place of safety by the rose arch.

'Dinna fret about it.' He was wearing paint-splattered jeans, a Rolling Stones T-shirt and flip-flops. There was purple varnish on his toenails. 'Yesterday she cried for an hour because Doris got stung by an imaginary bee. What can I do for you, Scottie?'

That coolness again. It was getting on my nerves. The people-pleasing side of me had a whole speech prepared, apologizing once again for having an episode in his boat, for putting him in danger, for forcing him to go to Bride, but I choked. 'I found something in the cottage I thought you might be interested in.'

'You'd better come through, aye.'

I followed him, squeezing past the butterfly bush to the back garden, a scrubby lawn littered with toys. In the centre of the lawn was a structure, about my height, a mishmash of driftwood and sea-scoured plastics, fishing net, rope and bottle tops. I circled it, trying to get a sense of its angles and curves. It was feminine, abstract, beautiful.

'You made this? It's incredible.'

Kenver stood beside me. 'It's nae quite finished. I collected all this stuff from local beaches. It's inspired by the Faroese folktale of Kópakonan, the Seal Woman. Different from our Hollow Fins, but nae *that* different. A mystical shape-changing creature held against her will by a human male. That's incredible to me, the overlapping themes of different story cultures. Did you know some of the earliest mermaid stories emerged from Syria thousands of years ago?'

A girl aged about eight opened the back door and danced into the garden.

'Hello,' she said, to me. 'I'm Kizzy. Pa, can me and Derwa play Cheerleaders?'

'Nice to meet you, Kizzy,' I said, but it felt too stiff, too formal.

Kenver ruffled her hair affectionately, her dark curls so much like his. 'One-hour max,' he said. 'Then it's time to tidy up before your ma comes.'

'You seem to have a lot of children,' I said, as Kizzy disappeared back inside.

He laughed.

'They dinna all live here. Perry and Derwa live with their ma on Sorrow and Kizzy is just down the road with her ma. The two little ones, Rozy — that's short for Rozel — and Coby live here. Coby's the bairn. My girlfriend's taken him to visit her parents.'

'I don't think I've met —?'

'Aye, you met her. Margrethe. On the night of the blackfish stranding.'

Margrethe. The woman who had sung about shipwrecks and lost loves, who had sung to the whales as we rocked them gently in the water. So much more than the singer in Kenver's folk band. I was full of bitter jealousy. Not because she was with Kenver, but because when he looked at her, he saw the mother of his children, and nobody would ever look at me that way.

Tinny pop music blared from inside the house. From the front lawn the rhythmic thump of a ball against a wall and Rozy giggling. The tiny, insignificant moments of family life that go by unnoticed by the people blessed enough to have them. Kenver went to get some beers from the kitchen. The only seating in the garden was a ramshackle swing seat. I sat on it, next to a straggly ginger cat, which stretched out along my leg.

'Push her off if she bothers you,' said Kenver, handing me an icy-cold bottle and sitting at the opposite end of the swing seat.

I opened my mouth intending to ask him about Thora, the Bride Witch, to see if he had any more information that might help me make sense of the different threads of the story. Instead, I burst into noisy, hiccuping tears I hadn't even known were in me. I hadn't cried properly since the day I had gone for a run around the salt marshes, back when I was still a potential mother. Kenver was silent, watching me. I wiped my face.

'I'm so embarrassed.'

'Dinna be.' He took a swig of his beer. 'Do you wanna talk about it?'

'No,' I said. 'I'm fine now.'

I reached inside my bag for *Tales from the Hollow Sea* and handed it to him. He ran his thumb across the cover.

'Lucyna Richmond-Whyte,' he said. 'I remember her. I was just a lad, and she was this grey-haired lady with a fancy accent who stayed here for a summer researching our stories. She spent a lot of time with Sam. We even named Seena the seal after her because she seemed like just the kind of woman who would . . .' He tailed off, a faintly embarrassed look on his face.

'Who would be so tragically desperate for a child she would shape-change into a seal?'

'I guess she went back to London or Oxford or wher-ever and published her book of stories instead.'

We sat silently for a while as he thumbed through the book, thoughts I couldn't read passing across his face. 'Where did you find this?' he said.

'It was hidden inside the walls of the cottage on Bride.'

He whistled softly. 'Is that why you came here, to give me this book? Hey . . . Coby.' He jumped up from the swing seat, a broad smile on his face.

Margrethe, the tiny birdlike singer from the Blackfish Tavern, the mother of two of Kenver's children, was stand-ing by the butterfly bush watching us, a baby on her hip. Kenver kissed her cheek and swung Coby over his head. 'Margrethe,' he said, 'you remember Scottie. She helped out with the blackfish rescue.'

She walked unhurriedly to the swing seat and offered me her hand. 'Hey,' she said, smiling, but her tone was cool, her eyes appraising me.

'Nice to meet you.'

'Scottie brought over this book of folklore she thought I'd be interested in,' he said, bouncing Coby up and down.

'Nae kidding,' said Margrethe. 'Scottie, would you like to stay for your tea?'

Her words were friendly, but her face was neutral, hard to read. I couldn't stomach the thought of a happy family dinner. 'That's kind of you,' I said, 'but the tides are calling.

Kenver, you can keep the book. Say goodbye to the children for me.'

He walked me to the lychgate. 'You used to be a ceramics artist, aye?'

I nodded, thinking about my white waves. 'I had my own studio.'

'Why did you stop? If you dinna mind me asking.'

'I gave it all up for job security and maternity benefits.' I laughed, hating the bitter sound. Kenver leant against the gate, lighting a roll-up.

'Start up again. Create something. Something just for yourself. I couldna survive if I didna have sculpture and music, I dinna think.'

'There's nowhere to get anything fired,' I said.

'Build your own kiln. I'll help you.'

'That's a completely crazy idea.'

'We all need a wee bit of crazy in our lives. Have you done aught with those derelict outbuildings? That's all the bricks you'll need. Christ, Scottie. Are you just going to sit in that cottage and rot? Make something. Disna matter if it's crap.'

'I don't know if I can any more.'

'Only one way to find out.'

I went through the gate.

'I'm glad you decided to stay in St Hía,' he said.

The sound of Coby laughing, Rozy screaming, the dull thump of the football, the clink of glass, and Kizzy's pop music followed me down the lane.

36

Charlotte: White Horses

I let Helen take care of me for a month or so after I left David. I reverted comfortably to the role of sulky teenager, though my teenage years were long gone, and she slipped into the role of nagging parent, mining me for information that was none of her business, that she didn't need to know, hadn't ever known since I'd left home, but felt compelled to seek out anyway, just because I was under her roof again. *Who are you meeting tonight? What time will you be home? What have you eaten today, Charlotte? Did you remember to switch the shower off while you shaved your legs? What are your plans for tomorrow? Oh, you've eaten the last banana.* I was evasive, taciturn, even when I didn't need to be, because that was my part in our little play.

Two weeks after I left David, she drove me to my studio, the back seats folded down, ready to load up as much as we could. She had offered me her garage for storage until I could get started again. I worried she had assumed I would start up in her hometown, or close by, but I knew I couldn't stay. It wasn't where I belonged. When I unlocked the studio, we saw that David had been there before us and everything was dust.

The arts cooperative manager heard us crunching across the remains of my life's work, like children crunching across day-old snow, and came to see. *I don't know when this happened,* he said, his face white with shock. *I'll call the police.*

I told him not to bother, because what could they do, really? David had made his point, and I didn't have the energy to make a witness statement about my own life. We swept the dust into a pile, then into a dustpan, and then into bin liners. It felt like ashes even though nothing had burnt.

But, still, I wasn't broken. I had more waves inside me, ready to be sculpted. David had emptied our joint bank account, so Helen agreed to lend me the money to start again. I refrained from telling her exactly how far away I planned to be and tried not to think about the dent in what I knew must be her modest savings. She pretended not to be disappointed when I finally told her I was heading south, far away from her, as if she had known all along.

Before I left, I walked the Shires, the streets named after horses. Oberlander Road, Lipizzaner Avenue, Camarillo Close. The horses were still all white in my imagination and when I got home, I shut myself away in my Christmas-decoration-filled bedroom and drew a white horse on my notepad, then another and another.

That was how I came to be living on the south coast, within listening distance of the sea, the wrong sea, not the sea I was drawn to, but it was better than nothing. In my tiny new rented studio by the beach, I sculpted waves, as abstract and intangible as they ever were, proving to myself that David hadn't broken me. And I started something new. A series of white equine-inspired shapes. My white horses.

37

Thordis: The Market

Drowning in calm seas. This is how I imagine Thordis feels when Cadal forces her onto his fishing boat one summer morning and puts her off at Lugh harbour with only the duffel bag she had brought with her from Tvífjallahöfn and enough money for a few nights' board. She should be in a fury, for his betrayal, for her lost children, for all she has sacrificed. But she feels nothing at all. She walks up the hill to the little clapboard church that reminds her of the church in Tvífjallahöfn where she had first played the piano so many years ago, to ask Father Carvalho for help, all the while expecting a storm that does not come. And Father Carvalho does help her, finding her lodgings at his sister Denella's house in return for cooking and housework, paying her a few extra pennies to clean the church and agreeing that she can use the church's piano for lessons, if she can find willing pupils.

Thordis sits on her narrow spinster's bed in Denella's windowless attic and draws posters by hand, by the light of a naked electric bulb. She misses the flickering oil lamps at Bride, but she doesn't dwell. Her posters are illustrated with a piano keyboard overlaid with a child's hands, in black and white. She wonders if it is her own hands that she is drawing. The hands of Thordis when she was three or four years old, slipping away from her parents to clamber up onto the piano stool after church one day and performing a passable rendition of 'Three Little Fingers' to *oohs* and *aahs* from the congregation, even though she had never had a lesson. Thordis finishes her posters with Denella's telephone number and puts them up in shop windows, the church hall and on the public noticeboard on the quayside. She charges a low rate for lessons, much lower than she is worth, but needs must. And she does find willing pupils. It takes time, because she is and always will be an outsider, an off-islander as they like to call her. Even her years married to one of their own, her years living on Bride, have not made her one of them.

Her first pupil is the young son of Denella's neighbour, and then the little girl from the top of the lane. Thordis discovers she is a patient, kind and attentive teacher, which is not how she expected herself to be. The mothers of her young pupils speak to other mothers, mention in passing how well little Luis and Coralie are doing with their waltzes and minuets, and before long, Thordis teaches lessons four afternoons a week and on Saturday mornings. She finds most of her pupils quite charming, which is a surprise to her, as she had never considered herself one to fuss over other people's children. Thordis is so busy drowning in the calm waters of piano lessons, ironing Denella's linens and keeping the church dust free, she barely thinks about Cadal and Merryn at all.

One day, six months or so after her eviction from Bride, Thordis goes to the Tuesday market. She dislikes it. It has too many people, too many noises, too many smells. But Denella has heard that oranges and lemons are available, a rare treat at this time of year, and since Thordis lives in Denella's house, in the wretched, white-lit attic, and pays only pennies in rent, she must suffer the indignity of being the errand girl, at least for now.

Thordis has oranges and lemons in her string bag, and an orange in each coat pocket just for her. Denella will never know she paid for eight oranges instead of the six Thordis will deliver to her.

Good day for it, Thora, says a voice behind her and she turns to see Antonio, Cadal's old crewmate from the *Miss Molly*, all those years ago.

A good day for what, Antonio? Buying oranges? Antonio had always been kind to her, even on the long journey from Tvífjallahöfn when she had lain miserable in the tiny sleeping quarters, vomiting into a bucket.

Antonio twinkles his blue eyes at her. *Well, I suppose so, Thora. If buying oranges is what you're about.*

Thordis touches his arm warmly. *How are you, Antonio?* She can't remember the last time she exchanged small-talk with someone. The banality of it feels comforting.

I'm a married man, now, Thora, with two wee 'uns and another on the way.

Does Antonio know of her losses? She musters a warm smile. *Congratulations to you and your wife.*

They bid their goodbyes. Thordis is threading a pathway through the stalls to get out of the market as fast as possible when she sees them. Cadal and Merryn. Hand in hand, strolling through the market with all the glowing youthfulness of a pair of promenading teenagers. She treads water, not breathing, as she watches them. Merryn has her back to Thordis, attracted by a display of lace tablecloths she could have no earthly use for on godforsaken Bride. Cadal is smoking a cigarette, his hair cut shorter than Thordis remembers. Merryn has let go of his hand to be able to rummage through the tablecloths, but he will not relinquish her completely, his free hand resting on her back, in the space between her shoulder blades. It is only when Merryn turns to hold a square of lace up to the light that Thordis sees. Merryn is pregnant, five or six months along, the fabric of her dress indecently snug across her bump.

Thordis has the strange sensation of looking into a mirror, although she couldn't be more different physically from her rival. She reaches down to her stomach, as if she might have a bump to match Merryn's, but, of course, there is only empty space. Merryn has seen her. She lowers the lace, holding it protectively in front of her belly. *Thora,* she says. *Hello.*

Cadal turns. He drops his cigarette on the tarmac, extinguishing it with a single twist of his boot, and drapes his arm around Merryn's shoulders. *Let's go,* he says.

Merryn ignores him, a brief flicker of annoyance crossing his face. She steps towards Thordis, shrugging off Cadal's protective arm, rubbing her blooming belly. *Are you well, Thora?*

Perhaps it is Merryn's question that breaks the calm, or the way she is touching her belly, dripping with maternal entitlement. Perhaps it is that Merryn has called her Thora, or that Cadal's eyes are only for Merryn, that he has barely even glanced at the woman who used to be his wife.

Perhaps it is all these things together, or merely the fact of Merryn's pregnancy, the heart-crushing unfairness of it. Whatever the reason, the storm comes. It fills Thordis, animates her limbs, makes her a crashing wave. She runs at Merryn, roaring.

In the years to come, when Thordis remembers the incident in the market, she can only conceive of herself as that wave, raging on a beach, pounding against rocks. She does not remember Merryn cringing and holding her belly, or Antonio gripping her arms, or Cadal's hand at her throat. She does not remember oranges rolling across tarmac, or the tuft of Merryn's dark hair, a scrap of papery white scalp still attached, in her hands. She does not remember the words hidden in her roar. *I'll kill you, I'll kill you, I'll kill you both.*

The storm has blown out and she is treading water, or drowning, or something between the two. She gathers up her dropped oranges, ignoring the stunned and silenced crowd around her, ignoring the empty space where Merryn and Cadal had been standing, ignoring Antonio's meaningless, soothing words, and she goes home, her memory of the unpleasant occurrence already comfortingly distant.

But everyone else remembers, remembers that she said she would kill them both.

38

Scottie: The Blackfish's Wife

The afternoon before Kenver was coming to help me build a kiln, Matty, Roberta and Tony, accompanied by a quiet man named Hector, a specialist from the mainland, came with the final delivery for the cottage. Almost a week late, because of the weather, because of the tides, but that was the way of things here. Matty and Roberta were as gracious and helpful as ever, that particular brand of American ultra-politeness that would sound insincere coming from anyone else, but I could tell what they were thinking. It was frivolous, ridiculous. A waste of money.

A piano, transported in pieces. The smallest, lightest piano I could find, and still a lumbering extravagance that had taken the last of the money from the IVF fund. We offloaded it from the *Ella Mae* to *Banana* a piece at a time, lugging the separate parts up the slipway and across the beach into the cottage. It was back-breaking, precarious work and, more than once, I thought we'd lose a part to the sea, but eventually we got all the pieces inside, and I'd developed a new admiration for whoever had transported its predecessor to the island all those years ago. Hector, who turned out not to have any sea legs, spent an hour lying down with a damp cloth on his forehead but gathered himself sufficiently to reassemble the piano and tune it.

'Play us a song, then,' said Roberta.

'Another time,' I said. 'Everyone's exhausted.'

I couldn't admit to them I had no idea how to play it. Matty, Roberta and Hector said their goodbyes, a faint accusatory whiff of disappointment in the air, and went down to the boat, Hector clearly less than thrilled at the prospect of a second trip across the Hollow Sea. Tony was putting on his jacket, about to follow them out of the door.

'Tony, wait. I want to ask you something.'

He glanced at his watch. 'Yes, Miss?'

I sat down on the piano stool, the stiff new fabric prickling the backs of my legs. 'When I asked you about the history of Bride, why didn't you tell me about Thora?'

Tony took off his cap, his face flushed. 'Sam Pentreath been spinning his yarns, heh?'

'Yarns? I found out about her at the library and asked him straight.'

When Sam had first told me there was more to the story of Cadal Fernandes and his drowned family, I'd been angry with Tony, at his secrecy and half-truths. But my anger had faded. Now I just wanted to know.

'Aye, well,' he said, finding something of great interest on the floor. 'Sam's a blathering old fool. A storyteller. Nae to be trusted with the truth.'

'What is the truth? What happened to Thora? Sam said something about a wee girl, but he also told me Thora couldn't have children.'

Tony rolled his cap into a tiny ball. 'Aye, he runs at the mouth, does Sam. Miss Thora's name's been sullied enough. I'll nae stand for people who should know better calling her a witch or a child-stealer. That's the only reason I didna say aught. It's best left in the past. There's naebody left who has a claim on this cottage, if that's your worry.' He looked at his watch again.

'There's something I didn't tell you,' I said.

'Oh, aye? What's that, then?'

I took a breath, ready to confess to him about my missing past, how I thought that the answers were here, on Bride, if only I could untangle the threads of Cadal's, Merryn's and Thora's stories. If I told him my truth, then perhaps he would tell me his, tell me everything he knew about Thora and the wee girl Sam had rambled about, the wee girl who, perhaps, might be me.

Roberta knocked lightly on the open door and poked her head around the gap. 'Sorry to interrupt, guys,' she said, 'but the tides.'

Tony shrugged a goodbye, relieved perhaps to escape. The truth would have to wait for another day.

Alone now, I swivelled around on the stool and lifted the piano lid. I brushed my fingers along the pristine keys. I pressed a few down at random, a series of jangling, discordant notes. I thought back to my first day on Bride, the day Kenver and I had sheltered here from the storm, and tried to conjure up the melody I had hummed then, when I had seen the derelict piano. I kept pressing down keys, hoping the random notes would coalesce into something that made sense. But, no matter how many notes I played, the melody wouldn't come.

I woke at dawn, my sleeping-bag twisted around me, a soft, pinkish glow rolling into the cottage. I put my jacket on over my pyjamas and went for a walk in the overgrown garden, wandering between clouds of tiny apricot flowers that had blossomed over the summer, forming drifts spilling over pathways and between stones.

I went to the ruined outbuildings, picking through the bricks, choosing the ones I would use to construct the kiln. Among the rubble, I found a piece of sea glass, blue, worn smooth by the waves. Beside it, a mermaid's purse and a dried-up starfish. I held each one in my palms for a second or two, in case they triggered a memory, but none did.

I picked up a brick to move it to my kiln pile. In the space beneath it was a comb, the sort of comb a woman would wear in her hair, with a decorated band and a row of sharp teeth to hold it in place. It was old and delicate, made from creamy-coloured mother-of-pearl. I had the faint niggling sense you get when trying to recall a name or a word you know you should remember, you know is filed away somewhere in the network of neurons and synapses, but you keep stumbling down the dead ends inside your own brain.

I went to the beach and sat on the sand, holding the comb. I committed its shape and colour to memory, then closed my eyes. I focused on my breaths, allowing my other senses to strengthen. The sound of the waves, the seabirds. The scent of sand and seaweed. The taste of salt in my throat. And the comb, in my palm, the weight of it, its sharp tips brushing against my skin.

The taste of peaches flooded onto my tongue. Crunchy sand between my teeth, laughter, the wind whipping through my curls, the scrape of comb teeth against my scalp, a wrist brushing against my face. Not an epiphany, nothing so dramatic. More a gentle lapping, shifting the sand around the edges of a memory, revealing it grain by grain. Still so much of the memory buried, but I was certain I had worn the mother-of-pearl comb in my hair before.

Kenver arrived mid-morning and I showed him the pile of bricks and the levelled-off bit of ground I'd prepared for the construction of the kiln. I offered him a Coke, but he shrugged it away, seeming not to want to waste time on idle chat. We began to slot the bricks together, dipping their edges one by one into the bucket of clay slurry I'd made that would bind them while still allowing the kiln to expand and contract with the heat. It was a hot day, sweat stinging my eyes as I worked, the slurry drying on my arms.

'One more row for the base, do you think?' he said.

'Yes, one more,' I said, dunking a brick in the slurry and balancing it in place.

'Have you heard "The Tale of the Blackfish's Wife"?'

I nodded, vaguely recalling a story with a similar title in *Tales from the Hollow Sea* that I hadn't had a chance to read before giving the book to Kenver.

'I'm going to do a sculpture inspired by it for the next festival, and I've been working on an interpretation of the story to perform. May I practise on you?'

'Sure,' I said. 'Why not?'

He pushed his hair back from his face, getting wet clay in the strands. 'One midsummer,' he said, 'about a year after her husband was lost at sea, a fisherman's widow was out collecting seaweed, her heart heavy with grief.'

He handed me another brick and I dipped it in the slurry, sliding it into position.

'A sea mist rolled in, carrying with it the voice of a man singing.'

I thought of the sea mist, how it had come down upon us in the Hollow Sea, how it had made me think of my embryos, my little snowbeans in their cryogenic white mist, how it had made me howl. Kenver paused, perhaps remembering too.

'She ran down to the sea's edge, listening to the beautiful singing. Her husband had had a fine voice, and many a night they had sat around the flickering stove as he sang love songs to her. She listened a while and with each note, each song, she became more certain it was her husband's voice coming from the mist. She waded into the sea, praying for a miracle.'

The base of the kiln was finished, and we were ready to start constructing the walls. There was sun on the back of my neck and the faint chill of wind. I placed the first brick, and Kenver placed the next, his arm brushing against mine.

'Blinded by the fog, she cried out his name, wading deeper, following the sound of her dead husband's voice. When the mist cleared, she saw a blackfish swimming nearby. At first, she was afraid, but the blackfish was singing, the melody pouring out of its blowhole. She began to weep but the blackfish swam close and spoke to her and embraced her with its fins. The blackfish was her husband, and she was overjoyed. A pod of blackfish had happened by while he was drowning, and as he took his last breath, his soul passed into the body of one of the beasts. They stayed together all night, in the shallow sea, beneath the Moon of Long Nights, husband and wife reunited.'

The clay slurry dried where it had splashed up my arms, pulling tight against my skin.

'In the morning, her husband embraced her and returned to his blackfish kin, promising to visit her once a year. The woman returned to life as a widow, telling naebody of her experience, for who would have believed her? Many moons passed: the Softening Moon, the Thunder Moon, the Gorse Moon, the Moon of Short Nights, the Bear Moon, the Moon of Many Kisses, and with each moon her belly swelled.'

Kenver trailed off, aware he had stumbled into dangerous territory. He knocked a brick into place. I touched his arm to let him know it was okay. He stood up, his knees cracking, to fetch more stones.

'Then, beneath a Fish Moon, she gave birth to a child, a strapping, healthy son. Her neighbours raised their eyebrows and gossiped behind her back and muttered as she passed by with the fatherless bairn in her arms, but she didna care. She wove a cradle for her son, taking the trouble to make it watertight, as her mother's instinct told her that her son would be in danger if the ocean touched him. On midsummer night she took her child down to the beach to wait. And sure enough, the mist rolled in and brought with it the sound of her husband singing. She waded out and introduced her husband to his son, and he was overjoyed. She set the cradle afloat, and her weaving skills had been true because nae one drop of water leaked through.'

A mother's instinct to protect her child. The thought of it tugged at my heart, not because I would never experience it but because I already had, right down into my bones, and no one would ever believe me because my children were only ghosts, ghosts of a future never to be lived.

'Having introduced her son to his papa, she set the cradle on the beach and fell into her lover's arms. In the morning they said their sad farewells and she scooped up her son from the safety of the sand and took him home. The moons passed and once again her stomach swelled. She wove another cradle, the neighbours twitched their curtains, and at midsummer she went down to the sea to introduce her husband to his daughter.

'In time, she gave birth to four sons and three daughters, each one born beneath a Fish Moon, and every midsummer she took them to see their papa, the bairns floating in their handwoven cradles, and the older children waving from the safety of the beach, for never were they permitted to come into contact with even a single drop of the ocean, for fear of what transformation might come over them.'

Kenver hadn't faltered at all in his careful dipping and laying of the bricks as he told the story of the Blackfish's Wife in his soft, musical voice.

'One afternoon, the woman was walking on the beach with her children when she spied a pillar of smoke across the bay and it filled her heart with fear. The bonfire was a signal to the islanders that a school of blackfish had strayed too close to the cove. Leaving her children in the care of the oldest brother, with strict instructions to stay inside the house and keep away from the sea, the woman rowed as fast as she could to the cove to beg her fellow islanders nae to slaughter the blackfish, fearing her husband could be among the victims, but when she arrived the sand was already stained red. She walked among the dying blackfish and heard the faint sound of singing. Her heart filled with grief, as she knew then her beloved husband had been driven onto the beach with his blackfish kin. She followed his weakening song, until she found him bleeding by a rock. She held his fin and sat with him, and as his song became softer, bubbles of blood escaped from his blowhole.

'When her husband was dead, she wept awhile and returned to her home, wretched with grief, wondering how she would tell her children. But her children were nae in the house. She searched high and low, panic rising in her chest. Then a pale mist blew in and with it the sound of children singing. She followed the beautiful melody with a heavy heart, wading into the sea to find a pod of seven young blackfish frolicking in the water and singing their favourite rhymes. *Oh, my children,* she wailed. *What have you done?* But they were excited and free, revelling in their new-found form and didna ken her heartbreak. As the mist cleared, the woman stood in the shallows and watched seven fins disappearing into the distance. She wept and wept, and every year at midsummer she came down to the beach and hoped her children would return to her, but she never saw them again.'

Kenver paused in his rhythmic laying of bricks, so I knew his story was done. The breeze was whipping up, working a chill into my spine.

'It's great,' I said. 'Cheerful.'

The truth was, I thought Kenver's story was beautiful. But I didn't have the words to explain the emotions it had unleashed in me. Jealousy, because I was always jealous of mothers, even the ones in stories. Grief, too, for her unimaginable loss. And anger, because it was a story born of a society that judged women no matter what they did. No doubt it had a germ of truth in it, somewhere way back, a poor, wanton unmarried woman or widow whose children had drowned or been removed from her in some other way, because stories always punish women who don't conform.

'That's it? That's your feedback?'

'I don't know what you want me to say. It's a good story and you told it very well.'

I had disappointed him. He kicked a few pebbles away from the kiln wall and went for a piss around the back of the cottage. When he returned, he was holding two cans of warm Coke, and we sat in the garden together, drinking them in silence.

'I'm sorry,' he said.

He took a last swig from his can, and it buckled beneath his fingers.

'For what?'

'It was a sensitive subject for you. I shoulda known better.'

'The story was beautiful,' I said. 'It's not like I expect everyone never to talk about pregnancy or babies in my hearing ever again.' I licked a few drops of Coke off the top of my can, pressing the tip of my tongue against the sharp edge. 'That wouldn't be very rational.'

'You dinna have to be rational about it. You feel what you feel.'

Something was bubbling up from deep inside me. I didn't want to cry in front of Kenver again.

'Did you ever take part in a pilot-whale hunt?'

The question I had wanted to ask him since the night we rescued the stranded pilot whales, the question I wanted to ask everyone I met here.

'A graceful change of subject.'

'I am known for my legendary conversational skills. So, have you?'

Kenver exhaled. 'Nae taken part. But I witnessed it once. I was just a wee boy. Scottie, it was brutal. I've never been able to get it out my mind. Almost thirty year, and I still remember the stench of blood and fear, the blackfish screaming. It's partly what my interpretation of "The Blackfish's Wife" is about. A way of acknowledging that the blackfish killed in the hunt had family bonds that were broken in the most violent of ways. That the blackfish feel pain and loss just as we do.'

He touched the thin white scar on his forehead. I was becoming fond of that unconscious gesture. I crushed my Coke can. 'Come on,' I said. 'Let's build.'

39

Thordis: Seed Baby

There is a baby, a secret inside her, a secret she gathers into herself, a tiny seed in the darkness. She tells herself it is because her husband can't take another loss, that she alone is strong enough to bear the twin burdens of hope and fear. And perhaps that is true, but I know her. I know the secrets of her heart, and I think she is lying to herself. She doesn't tell him about the baby because she is afraid. Afraid to know the truth about his increasingly frequent night walks, and afraid not to know. Afraid of his hands, squeezing her wrists, grinding her bones together. Afraid he might become the old Cadal, the one who kisses her sweetly on the small of her back, her spine, her shoulders, her neck, her nose, her mouth, her knees. Afraid she won't be able to keep her baby safe. Afraid he will blame her, again. All these things would be too much to bear so she doesn't tell.

She draws him a bath, pumping water from the well and heating it pan by pan on the stove until there are a few precious inches of soapy water sloshing at the bottom of the tub. He comes home, for once when he is expected. He doesn't look at her but drops his salt-stiffened clothes on the floor where he stands. He exhales as his body hits the water, drawing his knees up to his chest. She can smell the salt and tobacco odour of his skin. Thordis loves the smell of him, has always loved it, but there is something new, a changed ingredient, a note so subtle it might be the shift from shallow water to deep ocean. It nags at her. She washes his hair with a jug, combing out the tangles. She soaps his body, observing the grey streaks in his beard, the hollowness beneath his cheeks, the silvery fish scales hooked into his fingers and thumbs that cannot be removed with any amount of scrubbing. She shaves his beard, the stretch and pull of his skin beneath the scrape of the blade, revealing the untanned skin beneath.

She's rinsing away the last of the suds when he puts his hands over his face. *Did I get soap in your eyes?*

He shakes his head, his hands still covering his eyes. He can't look at the marks on her arms, she realizes, marks he made.

She continues to rinse, and when he lowers his hands he says, *I'll be better*, but she knows it's an empty promise.

She boils the kettle for tea as he dries himself, they drink in silence, and he eats a helping of leftover stew. She leaves hers, pushes it around the bowl, cannot stomach it, but he doesn't seem to notice. She dresses for bed, covering her body shyly, as if they were new lovers. Cadal brushes his teeth, spitting foamy toothpaste into a china bowl. She has watched him brush his teeth a thousand times or more, a simple intimacy, but somehow, they are strangers. She wonders how this happened, but then she glances at her arms, the fading marks there, and knows they were always thus. The Cadal she thought she had known, the Cadal she had loved, was only ever a figment of sixteen-year-old Thordis's imagination. She can't even blame him for that.

They lie in bed, their backs touching, an abyss between them.

A week later, on a soft summer night with a waxing gibbous moon, Thordis is brave. She wakes in the night, the bed empty beside her, the space Cadal had occupied still warm and full of his scent. It's not the first time he has left in the middle of the night. She has always pretended to be asleep when he comes home, has never found the courage to ask him about it. But tonight she slips from beneath the covers, throwing on her coat and shunting her bare feet into her plimsolls.

The island's songs, which have grown so familiar to her over the years, have an unworldly timbre. The soft plash of the wind rippling through sea grass, the sigh of receding waves, the calling birds, becoming a cacophony of ghostly notes tumbling through the air. It is treacherous underfoot, rocks slippery with algae strewn across her path, but Thordis does not stumble. Her feet dance to the beat of the island's song.

The gibbous moon sets early, but there is light enough from the stars to see her husband on the beach. She creeps as close as she dares, crouches behind a rock, though in truth she doesn't think he would notice her presence even if she moved carelessly, so absorbed is he in his own actions. He makes a fire, built from gathered driftwood and dried-out seaweed. The flames dance and crackle with the breeze, another harmony in the island's song. He sits beside the fire, on the soft, dry sand, facing out to the ocean, his violin at his chin. The first few notes of his song, fragile like lace, drift across the sea. It is a lullaby of the archipelago, one that Cadal has played for Thordis many times over the years, but never has it sounded more beautiful. Stars reflect on the sea's surface, dipping and curling with the waves.

A pain comes, tearing through Thordis's womb. She doesn't hear her own scream, as her ears are filled by Cadal's song. She staggers against the rock, clutching at her abdomen. It's a pain she knows, has lived through so many times. She breathes, shallowly, quickly. The pain recedes, but the next wave is coming. In the space between waves, she looks up at the beach, at Cadal, her one chance of help, or comfort, even though she knows in her heart there is none to be had.

There is a dark-haired woman on the beach, standing at the confluence of sea and sand, her skin waxy in the starlight. Beside her, a white horse, stamping in the surf. The woman is singing a wordless, beautiful song. Her voice is like a bell, beginning with just a few notes tingling into the ocean. Cadal has stopped playing, is enraptured by the woman. The pace of the song quickens, the notes flurrying out of her mouth. Her song harmonizes with the wind and breaks on the sand, like waves. The sound makes Thordis shiver, enchants her, like Cadal is enchanted, when she should be full of rage and grief.

The song ends. The silence seems loud, discordant in comparison, bleeding into Thordis's ears. The woman, who is dressed in a long, flowing skirt, kneels in front of Cadal, taking his hands in hers. They become lost in the simple pleasure of observing one another's faces. Another wave of pain and Thordis curls up on the sand, tries to make herself smaller, to make the pain smaller, but she can't stop screaming. This time they hear her.

Time becomes a haze. The only constant is Thordis's pain, which eclipses all else, a parasite that swallows her rage and fear and grief. Voices above her. Cadal. *Why didna you tell me, Thora? You shoulda told me.* And a softer voice, the woman, cajoling, soothing him, reasoning with him. Thordis is in his arms, crossing the threshold of the cottage like newlyweds, except that Thordis is bleeding, and his lover follows.

Thordis, lying on the bed. When the pain comes everything is eclipsed. In the brief moments of respite, she's aware of a small hand holding hers, a cool cloth on her forehead, soft, sweet breath on her face. His presence, too, further out, at the edges of her consciousness, brooding. When it is over, the woman, her new-found mortal enemy, washes her with warm water, changes her pyjamas.

There is daylight, the fragile light of a still, early morning, and sweet tea at her lips. Thordis is numb now. She feels no pain. A semi-coherent thought: she will never feel pain again. Soft voices arguing on the periphery. Thordis wants to go to her garden, wants to bury her child with its siblings, but the woman is worried. *She needs a doctor, Cadal.* His response muttered thickly: *Merryn, I want her gone. She dinna belong here now.*

They go to the garden, the two women. Thordis floats, numb and pain free. Merryn staggers, from the weight of supporting her lover's wife. Thordis sits. The woman digs. Together they bury what there is, the barest traces on crumpled linen.

Thordis sleeps awhile, in her bed, on fresh sheets that have appeared from nowhere. The dark-haired woman speaking soft insistent words: *Let me go, let me go* and *Where is it? Where have you hidden it? Tell me, please. Give it back.*

Thordis wakes again, later, whatever later means, and Cadal is by her side, bathed in yellow light like some biblical vision. *You must go, Thora. There's nae place for you here.* Her own childhood duffel bag, a few things thrown inside, not by her.

Merryn, puffy-faced, by the door. *I'm sorry, I'm sorry, I'm sorry.*

The tang of salt on her lips, the cool breeze in her hair, the dull ache inside her. The haze clears a little, as the boat splutters away from its moorings, and Thordis's last moments on Bride are beset with clarity. She chooses not to look at her husband, the man she once loved. Still loves, perhaps, despite it all. Instead, she turns her gaze back to Bride, clear and glorious and sparkling, and watches until there is only sea, endless sea, behind them.

40

Scottie: The Piano

The kiln was finished and we were crouched by the well pump washing clay slurry from our hands and arms. The sky shifted from blue to mauve.

'Storm's coming,' said Kenver, wiping his hands on his jeans.

'Are you sure?' The change in the colour of the sky was subtle, tantalizing. I wanted it. I wanted the storm.

'I should go,' he said. 'Before it gets bad. You'll be all right here?'

The sky was darkening fast now, from mauve to violet to a threatening purple.

'I'll be fine. Go on, go. You don't want to get caught in it.'

He shrugged on his jacket. 'It's been fun. Hey, I want something that gets fired in the kiln. Consider it payment for services rendered.'

'The very first thing I make is yours.'

Kenver looked at me intently and for a moment I thought he was going to kiss his fingers and touch my forehead, the way Jasminder always did. But he just zipped up his jacket. 'I'll hold you to that.'

I watched him half jog across the beach to the slipway, the rising wind tugging at his clothes, and went inside to the calm space of the cottage.

I lit the stove to heat some water to wash. The rain

began. On the roof at first and then, when the wind arrived, drilling sideways against the windows. It wasn't as fierce, as savage as the storm had been on the day I first came to Bride, but it had come on more quickly than I had expected and I worried for Kenver, crossing the Hollow Sea. When the water was warm enough for washing, I peeled off my T-shirt, feeling the chill in the air. The rain was hitting the windows in waves as the wind ebbed and flowed. I remembered standing at the top of the cliff, screaming with the wind across the Hollow Sea, imagining Alice beside me, my grown-up ghost child.

I was lathering my washcloth, dressed only in my jeans and bra, when there was a brief knock at the door, and it swung open. Kenver stood in the doorway, dripping water on the floor.

'Shit,' he said, raising his voice to compete with the hollering wind. 'Sorry.' He ducked out into the rain as I shimmied back into my dirty T-shirt.

'I'm decent. You can come in.'

Kenver stepped fully inside and pulled the door closed behind him, shutting out the storm.

'Is it bad?'

'A wee bit fiercer than expected. Can you put up with me a while longer?'

'Café Scottie is open for business. I can offer an extensive range of warm beer and instant noodles. Sit over here by the stove. I'd offer you some dry clothes, but I don't think I've got anything that would fit you. It's funny, there's something about you being here that seems to bring on storms.'

He didn't answer. I realized he was staring at the piano.

'It came yesterday,' I said. 'I don't really know why I got it. I can't play.'

'It must have been a job, getting it onto the island.'

'It was.'

I thought he might go over to the piano, play it himself, but he simply took the beer I was offering and levered the lid off with his thumb.

'Do you want to use the radio to get a message to Margrethe?'

'Margrethe?' He looked momentarily surprised, as if he had forgotten who she was. 'Nae, she and I, we're nae what you'd call joined at the hip.'

I removed the cap from my bottle with the opener. 'Bloody hell, Kenver. You have two children together. Won't she be worried?'

'Margrethe will be fine.'

His voice was neutral but there was a tightness to his jaw he couldn't conceal. I wondered if it was annoyance with my question, or if things were strained with Margrethe. Maybe both.

I boiled water for the noodles. He sat in the camping chair and I sat on the camp bed as we ate in silence, twisting the noodles around our forks. The storm had settled into a steady rhythm. The thrumming of the rain on the metal roof was calming, almost hypnotic. Kenver finished his noodles and put the empty pot on the floor.

'You know about my art,' he said. 'Tell me about yours.'

'Waves.'

He raised his eyebrows in a question. I told him how I

had made and remade the whispering sea with clay, hundreds upon hundreds of white waves, abstract but full of my heart.

'Until I came here,' I said, 'I didn't understand they were all waves from the Hollow Sea.'

He looked at me thoughtfully. 'Is that why you havna started up again? Because now you have waves on your doorstep? You dinna need to make them now?'

The wind was rising again, hurling the rain at the windows in angry gusts.

'No,' I said, my throat choked with tears. 'It's not that. I feel like a desert inside. My body can't create anything. My mind can't create anything. My hands can't create anything.'

The wind battered at the seams of the cottage, and once again the light from the kerosene lamp came alive, casting wavering patterns on the wall and ceiling.

'I'm barren in every sense of the word now.'

Barren. A word to turn people away. But I'd said it aloud, claimed it for myself. Kenver didn't flinch. He stood, went to the piano, and pushed up the lid.

'You created something the last time we were here together,' he said. 'Remember?'

The keyboard glowed yellowish white in the lamplight.

'I hummed a tune, Kenver. It's hardly creating. It's not like I can even remember it now.'

Kenver perched on one end of the piano stool, patting the empty space beside him. I hesitated, twirling my beer bottle by its neck.

'Scottie, c'mon.' He pressed his fingers down on the

keys, one note, two notes, a minor chord, sad and aching. 'Scottie, I beg you, dinna leave me here with my undignified arse hanging off the piano stool.'

I laughed and joined him, our hip bones pressed together. I could smell the rain on his clothes. I grazed the keys with my fingertips, but didn't depress them. His hands, then, still clay-streaked, on mine, pushing down. The thudding of a hammer against a string, discordance, the wrong notes pressed together, before we found our rhythm, our space, and my fingers learnt to respond to his touch, the gentlest of pressure. Our fingers flew across the keyboard together, and then he let go, lifted his hands up and away and I played alone. I made music from somewhere deep inside me. *The moonlit sky ripples like the icy waves, breathing wintry, moaning mists in dark and secret salt-licked caves. A winter sea, a midnight sky, a lover wailing with the tide. False promise under night-washed moon.*

When the song was finished, I felt spent and shaky. The storm had petered out while we'd been playing. I got up, banging my knees on the underside of the piano, flinging open the window, scenting the cottage with rain and sand.

'What's wrong?'

Kenver touched my shoulder and I flinched. I didn't turn to face him but stared out at the sky. 'Everything's so confusing. I don't know who I am any more.'

He didn't respond, but I could hear him breathe, sense his closeness, the smallest of spaces between us. I cried silently, unwilling to wipe my tears and draw attention to them.

The light was fading fast, all greys and ambers. Kenver

applied gentle pressure to my shoulders, to get me to turn around, but I resisted, walked away. I sat on my sad little camp bed and wiped my nose with a tissue. My hairbrush was on the bed and I picked it up, desperate for something to do, to fill up the time and space around me. My sea-and-sand-ravaged hair was a bird's nest, unbrushed since the day before. I ripped at the tangles.

'Ow. Fuck. Ow.'

Kenver took the brush from my hand. He started at the ends, teasing out the tangles one by one. I closed my eyes, listening to the beat of the waves on the sand. He moved up to the roots, the tiny beads on the end of each bristle sweeping against my skin, drawing blood up into my scalp.

'You're surprisingly skilled with a hairbrush.'

'I've got three daughters.'

The mother-of-pearl comb I'd found in the rubble of the derelict outbuilding was on the windowsill. Kenver picked it up and stared at it. He gathered my hair on one side, the teeth of the comb scratching my scalp. His wrist brushed my ear. A memory of the comb flowed in, like a wave, but I couldn't catch it and it ebbed away.

His fingers on my spine, his breath brushing the nape of my neck, just the thin material of my T-shirt between his skin and mine. He pushed my T-shirt up, one vertebra at a time, stopping when he reached my scar, his fingers resting there on the gnarled tissue. I remembered walking through streets named for horses, pulling down my shirt and show-ing my scar to my more popular schoolmates before Sheldon Marshall had kissed me with his ashes-and-cider mouth. I hadn't been ashamed of my scar, even then in my teenage years, because the curve in my spine was part of me, the only thing of my past I still had, as much as the surgeon had tried to excise it. I focused on the sensation of Kenver's fingers moving across the scar tissue, rough against rough, in the way I sometimes focused on counting my breaths or the crashing waves.

'Ach, Scottie.' He exhaled. 'What did they do to you?'

He moved his hand away and my scar pulsed. Then his lips were brushing the scar, soft against rough. He hesitated, waiting perhaps for a sign from me, and I pulled my T-shirt over my head, arching my back, so he would know it was okay, and then he was kissing my spine and I was trying not to think about how I hadn't shaved my underarms. He pushed aside my freshly brushed hair and kissed my neck.

Then we were facing one another, fumbling with belts and buttons and zips, his face serious, the scar on his temple luminous in the lamplight. I emptied my mind, purged it of everything as we kissed, the sound of our breath louder than the sea, his hands on the curved part of my belly, the calluses on the pads of his fingers scraping across my skin and the hollow space beneath it.

We fell onto the camp bed, which creaked and swayed. We laughed, sliding onto the floor, only my unzipped sleeping-bag between us and the stone. Kenver sighed, and I thought I had never heard a sadder sound.

Then there was nothing. No ghost children, no snow-beans floating in perpetual ice mist, no hormone injections, no ultrasounds of my empty insides, no undecorated nurseries, no Margrethe. No Alice. No Jasminder pressing his fingers to my forehead. No white ceramic waves smashed to dust. No storms, no seabirds screaming, no Helen ironing her tablecloth into smaller and smaller squares. Nothing but the hushing of the sea and the cool stone on my back and the spaces between us waiting to be filled.

41

Charlotte/Scottie: Jasminder

I was no longer Charlotte. I sloughed her off like an old skin, left her behind with the dust of a hundred white waves. It was the only way to feel as if I was truly free from David. He could keep Charlotte, the fragile husk he had created, could clamp his hand around her wrist and hold on to her for ever, and it didn't matter because I was Scottie now, someone new.

I rolled my new name around on my tongue. It felt strange in my mouth, unfamiliar, but in a good way. I spoke it aloud, to the mirror in my new flat, and it sounded even stranger. I grew my hair, leaving the curls to find their own meandering path. Tiny, tiny things, yet they made me feel lighter, freer. I could hear the sea from my new studio, where white waves and white horses flowed through my fingers into the clay. It was the wrong sea, a tame sea, obedient and well-mannered for the summer swimmers, but it was better than nothing. Its beach was miles of soft golden sand, littered by tourists on summer days, and then by the rubbish they left behind. I would walk along the beach at dawn, when I could shut my eyes and pretend it was the wild and unpredictable ocean of my dreams. Autumn was better. The tourists left and the sea became more unpredictable, more adventurous. It raised its voice, sometimes, above a whisper. But it would never be the wild, inconstant sea of my dreams.

I was strong, then, the strongest I had ever been. I had no idea what was coming. My ceramic waves and horses were selling enough so I could move to a bigger flat. I didn't think about David at all, didn't think about all the times I had had to hide money in my shoes on a night out, or when he had hacked off my ponytail with the kitchen scissors. I didn't think about his blue eyes or his laugh or how he'd been the only person ever to know that the shapes I produced in my studio were waves. I didn't think about the child I had given up, the child who was not yet a ghost, just the barest of glimmers I thought would fade away because there would be children in the future. Those things had happened to Charlotte, and I was Scottie now.

Then, Jasminder. A blind date I should have said no to because I wasn't ready for another relationship. I was wary of nice men. David had been nice. David had been charming and cared about old homeless ladies. But Fran, who managed the kiln I rented space in, kept on and on about her cousin's friend's lovely neighbour who was unaccountably single, and eventually I agreed just for some peace.

We met for a drink, a country pub with a roaring fire midway between our respective seaside towns. He came with a gift, a paper bag of pick'n'mix. It was all very ordinary. *You have musician's hands,* I said.

He shook his head. *Sadly not. No musical talent here.* He held them out to me for inspection, palms down, then palms up. We pressed our hands together, amused by the disparity in size. Our hands seemed to encapsulate the differences between us. His fingers were long and slender, soft and neat. Mine were rough and dry from working with clay, the nails bitten ragged, a hastily applied layer of varnish already chipping off. He had a straight double-heart line on his palm. I had a single curve.

We spent the evening tangling and untangling our fingers and sharing the pick'n'mix. At the end of the night, he walked me to the station.

I'd like to see you again, he said, when we reached the ticket gate.

I opened my mouth to reply. To explain that it was too soon, I wasn't ready, I had too much baggage.

He pressed his fore and middle fingers to his lips and brushed them against my forehead. *Scottie, whoever hurt you, whatever they did, well, they're scum, obviously, and I hate them, but they're in the past, right?*

I nodded, swallowing the tears that threatened. He could see right through Scottie to Charlotte and I hated that.

Good. Leave them there. You don't need to tell me anything. But I want you to know, I can be patient. We can do this slowly. Or not at all, if it's been a terrible date for you. Just let me down gently because it was a great date for me.

I glanced at the departures screen, but I still had a few minutes to go. *The date was . . . good.* I fed my ticket into the gate.

'Good' I can live with. Next time, the pick'n'mix is on you.

And he did that thing again, kissing his fingers and transferring the kiss to my forehead, so absurdly formal and old-fashioned I couldn't help but be charmed, and then I was through the gate and the train was at the platform and Jasminder was walking away, his back wide and comforting in his black coat, and I thought he might not have to be too patient at all.

42

Thordis: The Storm

Bride is an island of music, full of songs that ripple at the edge of her consciousness. I imagine Thordis lying awake during long, dark nights, listening to the wind purling through grass, the waves plashing back on themselves as they recede from the beach, her husband's sighs as he tosses and turns in his sleep. The songs are so loud, so insistent, she sometimes feels as if her ears might bleed. The song that calls to her most is the song of the storm.

The storms on Bride are frequent, ferocious and quick. They flare up, rage through and burn out, like forest fires. When she had first come to this island, Thordis had been afraid of the storms, but now she welcomes them. They break the suffocating tension that hangs in the air, moist and heavy, like humidity. The magical hour after a storm has blown through is when Thordis is at her most serene, floating in post-tempest equanimity. It's different for Cadal. He is immune to the storms, as distant from them as he is from Thordis, as oblivious to the crackling tension that precedes them as he is to their brief but rampant turbulence and the pacific waves of tranquillity they leave in their wake.

This storm begins at dusk, purplish light leaking through the salt-fuzzy kitchen window. Thordis goes outside, leaving Cadal to his painting. The pressure drops, the air around her falling away, and she has a sense of lightness, a freeness she hasn't felt since her first terrible loss. The wind sings, rich and ephemeral, the sound of ghostly monks chanting through the shells. The storm speeds closer, its darkness overtaking the dusk. At first, the rain falls slowly, deliberately, and Thordis imagines she can hear the tiny splash of each droplet as it smashes on a pebble or a shell. She turns her face up to the sky, the rain falling more fiercely, the wind snatching at her plaits and the hem of her dress. The storm has beguiled her, drowning the songs that haunt her.

She kneels on the beach, spreading her hands across her belly, shells digging into her knees. The child inside her, the tiny seed, is not afraid, so Thordis is not afraid. The crescendo of the storm subsumes the sound of her breaths, but she can feel their speed, their raggedness in her chest and throat. She is soaked now, with rain and seawater, but it's of no concern to her. Thordis has submitted to the storm. She lies down, inhaling the scent of rain and sand and rotting seaweed. Hail comes, white beads of ice the size of apple pips, no more painful than a midge bite as they pelt her body.

Thordis sits up, the hail growing to the size of marbles, smashing into her head and shoulders. She wraps her arms protectively across her stomach. The child inside, she knows, is still not afraid. Thordis tries to stand, but the wind and rain batter her down. The storm calls her name, *Thordis, Thordis, Thordis*, over and over again, until the syllables are meaningless sounds in the wind. *Thordis*. Cadal is there, his arms around her. Dragging her, lifting her, somehow carrying her and shielding her from the hail at the same time. Cadal, impervious to the frozen slingshots, carries Thordis across the carpet of ice back to the cottage, slamming the door against the storm with his foot.

Thordis sits on a kitchen chair, shivering, still in a stupor from the power of the storm. Cadal doesn't speak, busying himself with lighting the kerosene lamp and the stove. Is he angry? Thordis cannot tell. He fetches a clean towel, stiff with unrinsed laundry powder.

What were you thinking, Thora? He unrolls the towel, rubbing it across her hair. *God, you're freezing.* Outside, the storm is still raging, the wind hurling ice at the windows. *Stand up.* His voice is gentle. Thordis obeys. He unfastens her sopping dress and pulls it over her head, slapping it down on the stone floor. He wraps her in the towel. *Come closer to the stove. You'll catch your death.* His voice breaks. The heat from the stove coils out in comforting waves. Cadal dries her body, the roughness of the towel scraping her skin, soaking up the remains of the storm. *Promise me you'll nae do aught that stupid ever again. I couldna bear it if aught happened to you.*

Her tongue is swollen from the lashing sea-spray, her lips cracked and dry, so she can only whisper her promise. *I won't, I won't, I won't.*

He kisses her. It's like a first kiss, tender and tentative. He holds her face, presses his forehead against hers. He trails his fingers across her belly, where their seed-baby sleeps. He kisses her there, from navel to pubis. He kisses her breasts, the small of her back, her spine, her shoulders, her neck. When he has kissed every inch of her body, he takes her to bed and it is sweet.

Thordis slips into a dream of herself. She is on a fishing boat with a mermaid painted on the deck and wind chimes in the wheelhouse. In the dream, she is wearing her wedding dress and, as in life, she is pregnant, but instead of a pip, this seed is almost grown, her dress stretched tight across the ripe moon of her belly. The fishing boat descends beneath the ocean, not sinking but submerging purposefully, welcoming the seawater that flows across its gunwales.

Beneath the surface, the sea is cool and calm, sunlight refracting through the green-grey water. Shoals of silvery fish dart and flock like murmurating starlings. The boat dives deeper, bow first, carrying Thordis down into the depths, into a forest of rippling kelp suffused by ghostly light. Her hair, unfettered, twirling out above her, intermingled with the seaweed forest, stretching up almost to the surface, to the single faint pinprick of sunlight that penetrates the murky green.

She goes into the wheelhouse, where the wind chimes play a song that sounds like whales calling. Still the boat descends, and the sea around her darkens, but the strange supernatural glimmer follows her, lighting the way. She feels no fear, no emotion. Her hair grows and grows, tugging at her scalp as it coils upwards to the sun. The water is icy, leaching into her bones. Down the boat goes into a seemingly bottomless ocean.

Cadal is there. He floats towards her, his face lit with a soft, ethereal pallor. She sees instantly he is drowned. His tongue, black and swollen, flops from the side of his mouth. He says her name, her Icelandic name, the name he no longer calls her. *Thordis*. Somewhere above, the wind chimes ring faintly. A bubble floats out of Cadal's mouth.

Her abdomen is gripped by a sudden, wrenching pain. She gasps, doubling over.

It's our daughter, says Cadal. *She wants to come out.*

Thordis screams as another contraction rips through her. She feels as if her daughter is tearing her apart with her bare hands in her eagerness to escape.

Cadal pushes open her knees and peers between her legs with his dead eyes. *Here she comes, Thordis. Remember your breathing exercises.*

There is one more rippling seam of excruciating pain and then he reaches inside her and pulls their daughter out. He holds her up to show the woman, the proud, beaming father.

A healthy bairn, he says. *A wee girl.*

The child is a slippery grey bundle of fur, with clawed flippers for hands and the face of her father.

That's not my daughter, says Thordis.

The child laughs glitteringly, and then is gone, her flippers impelling her through the water, leaving a cloud of blood, placenta and amniotic fluid in her wake. Thordis sprawls, exhausted. Cadal is holding a pair of kitchen scissors.

To cut the cord, he says, soothingly.

He reaches up above her head, gathers the swirling ropes of her hair and snips. She sees her beautiful hair floating in coils, up, up past the kelp forest, past the flitting shoals of fish to the sunlit surface of the ocean above. She screams.

Screaming, screaming, and Cadal is shaking her shoulders and crying and she's still below the surface, rising, rising up from the dark into the sunlight and the sheets are covered with blood and the pain, oh, the pain, and Cadal is saying, over and over, *It's your fault, Thora, it's your fault for going out into the storm.*

43

Scottie: Sea Glass

I woke alone from a dream where I was falling through a tunnel of green light. I had slept past nine o'clock. I couldn't remember the last time I had done that, the last time I hadn't woken in the early hours grasping at the fading wisps of a dream about my ghost children. Kenver's inside-out T-shirt was hanging off the camp bed and his trainers were by the stove where he'd kicked them off to dry.

I couldn't remember the last time I'd had sex without the pressure of making a baby. When Jasminder and I first started dating, probably. I'd forgotten the freedom of committing to the moment for the moment's sake and nothing else. We'd started trying to get pregnant even before we got married and it had been thrilling at first, the heady expectation that we could be making a person. The feeling didn't last. Every period, every false alarm, month after month, my body betraying me, sex reduced to the soul-destroying ritual my fertility chatroom friends referred to as 'baby dancing'.

People told us stories about their distant cousins or high-school friends or former work colleagues who had got pregnant naturally after failed IVF or when they were in the middle of adopting, or years after they finally stopped trying. And since our infertility was unexplained, nothing wrong to be found with either of us, we held on to that hope. Even as it weighed heavier and heavier, as the months and years passed, we had carried it still.

Sex with Kenver had been so freeing, and I didn't regret it, didn't feel guilty. Not even about Margrethe. They weren't joined at the hip, Kenver had said. I didn't think about Jasminder. Couldn't think about him. Everything we had had together had been sucked dry, desiccated by infertility, our relationship a ghost now, like our never-conceived children.

I pulled on my jeans and a T-shirt and tied back my hair, my scalp tingling with the memory of Kenver removing one tangle at a time. I washed my face and brushed my teeth at the well-pump and went to look for him.

He was on the beach, down at the shoreline, making a sand sculpture.

'Hey,' I said, embarrassed by my shyness.

'Hey, yourself.'

Kenver stood up, shirtless, clumps of damp sand on his jeans and his forearms.

'It's nearly finished,' he said, gesturing at his sculpture.

It was a horse, facing out to the ocean, forelegs kicking up from the sand as they might kick through surf. Its tail fanned out behind it, sweeping across the shell-studded shoreline. It seemed impossible for something so exquisite to have been created out of sand. Its head was so detailed it appeared almost to have come from a cast. It couldn't have been further from the abstract equine shapes I used to make with clay.

'It's extraordinary,' I said.

He reached out and brushed my forearm with his sandy fingers and the scar on my back pulsed again.

'You can name it.'

I remembered the little blue piece of sea glass I had found in the ruins of the outbuilding.

'Sea Glass,' I said to the horse. 'I name you Sea Glass.'

Kenver knelt by its tail. His back pale, full of motion. Between his shoulder blades the barest hint of a curve. I hadn't noticed it the night before. I brushed my fingertips along his skin there. He became still, allowing me to explore him.

'You have a curvature of the spine.'

He turned around. 'A frequent condition in St Hía. From a common ancestor, you ken.'

I reached up and touched the white knot of scar tissue on his temple. 'Tell me again,' I said, 'how you got this scar.'

'Fell off a rock.'

A boy with curly hair, blood on his forehead and his hands, and I was falling, falling into shimmering green light.

'A rock in a sea cave,' I said.

He took my hands. His face was very still, looking at me. 'Aye.'

'The sea cave on Bride with the green pool.'

'Aye.'

My body folded in on itself, and I was kneeling on the sand. Kenver released my hands and picked up a tree branch from the tideline. He scratched his name in the sand. K E N V E R. He laid the branch in front of me. I didn't know if

I could move. He didn't rush me. He waited, a short distance away. I reached out and touched the branch, its sea-sculpted smoothness. I uncurled myself, an inch at a time. I pressed the tip of the branch into the wet sand and wrote a name. I stared at the letters, the strange alien shapes. S U S A N.

'Welcome home, Susan.'

His voice a whisper.

'How long have you known?'

He was keeping his distance, respecting my space. 'There was something about you on that first day, the day of the blackfish strandings. But I thought it was my imagination. Then we came to Bride and you hummed that tune. A melody I've only ever heard played on this island. But such a tiny scrap of a tune. I wanted to tell you, but you seemed so fragile. So, I waited. I waited for you to come to me, and you did.'

'There's still so much I don't remember. Who are my parents? What happened to them? What happened to me?'

'I'll help you remember.'

I had fantasized about this moment for my whole life. Finding my people, my home, my blood. And now it had come it didn't seem real. Kenver took my hand, leading me to the horse sculpture.

'Look, Susan, the tide's coming in,' he said.

Susan. Susan. Susan. I allowed myself to fall into the name, as you might fall into the arms of a lover. Rocking, rocking from heel to toe, displacing the sand beneath my feet. The cool waves.

'The sea can burn.'

I heard myself say it, but I didn't understand the meaning. Kenver's breath on my neck.

'I won't let it burn you.'

I was Susan. Not Scottie. Not Charlotte. *Susan*. A girl who had once scratched her name in the sand on the beach at Bride. Who had once fallen through a whirlpool. Who had once believed the sea would burn. I knelt by the sand horse, the sea swirling around me.

White horses. Twisted rags of waves, their frilled edges flicking against the horse's hoofs. I lay down. The Hollow Sea breathed and I breathed with it, foam caressing the horse, moving along its flanks, swirling around my legs, my body, my head. The space between my shoulder blades grew warm, pulsing with the beat of the waves.

I inhaled the scent of the sea, could almost imagine the sculpture moving beside me as the sea took it grain by grain. The sea was taking me too, a grain at a time, taking Susan, leaving Charlotte and Scottie behind, making them ghosts. The waves I had dreamt of my whole life whispered as they swirled around me. Sea Glass, his soft mane in my fingers and a voice speaking my name again and again. *Susan, Susan, Susan*. A howl rose up in me and I let it out and for once it felt good. It felt free.

A commotion, coming from the right of me, far away. My name. My old name. A version of me I was leaving behind. *Scottie. Scottie*. I didn't know that person. I wasn't her any more. They were calling someone else, and I wished they would be quiet because this was the moment, the moment I'd waited for my whole life. Raised voices, but I blocked them out, focused only on the waves and the sand and the heat in my back and the remaking of me, of Susan.

'Scottie. SCOTTIE!'

A voice that didn't belong here, intruding, a hand grabbing my T-shirt, pulling me up, away from the sand horse, out of the waves, the spell broken, the real world smashing its way back in. Confused brown eyes staring into mine. Jasminder. I coughed, half choking on sand and seawater.

'What the fuck, Jasminder? What are you doing here?'

His eyes tired and strained. I pushed past him onto the sand, the waves tugging at my soaking jeans.

'You can't be here. Why would you come here?'

Jasminder followed me, his jeans and trainers stained dark by the sea. Kenver watched us, his face unreadable. And behind him, Matty from the boatyard, nervous and uncomfortable.

'I've been trying to call you,' Jasminder said. 'If you'd answer your fucking phone, or your emails . . .'

He tailed off, taking in the shirtless man on the beach with me, the boats at mooring, three now including Matty's.

'I don't understand what's going on here,' he said. 'Why were you lying in the sea? The waves were coming over your face. I thought –'

'It's none of your business, Jasminder. I think I've been clear about where things stand.'

Matty was hopping from one foot to the other, desperate to put some distance between himself and whatever scene was playing out.

'Hey, buddy,' he said, to Jasminder. 'I gotta go back. My

kid, she's playing soccer. I promised to take her. We have to leave before the flood tide.'

I twisted my wet hair into a bun, dull pain pulsing along my spine.

'He'll come with you,' I said. 'He's leaving. Jasminder, please go.'

Jasminder looked at me and then at Kenver. 'Scottie,' he said. He tried to take my hand, but I jerked it away. 'Scottie, listen to me.'

'No.'

'I'm not here chasing after you. I wouldn't do that.'

'Buddy,' said Matty. 'We gotta go now.'

'Just leave, Jasminder. Please. You don't belong here.'

He flinched.

'I think she's been pretty clear,' said Kenver, in a soft, even voice. 'She wants you to go.'

'Stay if you want,' said Matty, 'but I'm leaving now.'

'Go then,' said Jasminder. 'I'll come and get my things from the boatyard later. Scottie, one of those boats is yours, right? You know how to use it? We can go back together.'

Matty threw up his hands and left, jogging along the beach back to where he'd moored at anchor, leaving behind whatever madness was occurring.

'Jasminder, please go with Matty. This is not the time for some grand romantic gesture.'

'That's not what this is.'

Jasminder had grown the beginnings of a beard and it was streaked with grey, making him look older. He stepped towards me and took my hands. I squirmed and tried to release myself.

'Let go of her,' Kenver said mildly, and I sensed him moving towards us, but Jasminder ignored him.

'Scottie,' he said. 'It's Helen.'

Time stopped. Except for the crashing of the waves on the beach. I hadn't called her for weeks, not since she'd given me the sharp side of her tongue for telling Jasminder I wasn't coming home.

'She's had a stroke. I couldn't get hold of you. That's why I came.'

He released my hands. I couldn't speak.

'The ferry leaves at two. You've got time to pack some things if you hurry.'

One-breathe-in, two-breathe-out. The sand horse was gone, swallowed by the sea.

'How bad is it?' My voice small and ashamed, lost in the vastness of the ocean.

'It's bad. You need to come home.'

'Is she —' My voice did a strange wavering gulp. 'Is she going to die?'

Jasminder looked away, not answering, which was answer enough.

Helen in her sunlit hallway, shattering into a million pieces and putting herself back together again. Driving for hours through the night to make me safe from David. In her tiny dining room, ironing her tablecloth into smaller and smaller squares. But I didn't want to leave, not now, just when I was finding out who I was.

'Okay, fine. Okay. I need to throw some things in a bag.'

Kenver's hand on my elbow.

'Dinna leave, Susan. You've only just come home. Stay here, where you belong.'

I wanted to stay. I wanted to stay so badly.

'My mother is dying, Kenver. I have to go.' I started back towards the cottage. Kenver fell in beside me.

'She's nae your ma, Susan. She's a stranger. This is your home. Your ma is here.'

'Is she?' I said. 'Poor barren Thora the Bride Witch? Or Merryn the second wife? Kenver, I have to go.'

He grabbed my wrists. My wet trainers slipped on the stony ground. I tried to struggle free, but he didn't let go, and all I could think of then was David smiling at me so reasonably and squeezing my wrists so tightly I could feel the bones crunch together.

'Let me go, Kenver.'

'I'll tell you everything, Susan, but you must stay.'

His grip on my wrists grew tighter. I felt a howl bubbling up. Not the wild, free howl of being taken by the Hollow Sea a grain at a time, but the agonizing, shameful howls of my fractured soul.

I sensed more than saw Jasminder coming towards us. He was trained in conflict resolution. He would get Kenver to see sense, that I had no choice other than to leave. But Jasminder was moving fast, faster than he should have been and there was a crunching sound as his fist connected with Kenver's jaw. Kenver staggered back, releasing my arms. Jasminder landed another punch. Kenver sprawled onto stones and shells, dazed.

Jasminder rubbed his knuckles. 'Don't put your hands on her, okay? You don't touch her.'

Kenver half crouched, panting, getting ready to run at Jasminder. I stepped between them. 'Enough,' I said. 'I do not need my honour defended by anyone.'

Kenver moved his jaw back and forth, checking to see if it was broken. 'You'll nae come back. If you leave now, you'll never come back. You need to stay so I can help you remember.'

I wanted to stay, to learn about the little girl with the piano scarf. I looked at my wrists, the red marks Kenver had left there. *One-breathe-in, two-breathe-out.*

'I'm going to pack a few things now. Neither of you follow me.'

I ran past the kiln, inside the cottage, slamming the door behind me. How could Helen be dying? She was so strong. Jasminder was wrong. She would bounce back from this. My back throbbed, along the line of my scar. My head was full of glass, my mouth paper dry. I grabbed some clothes, stuffing them into my suitcase. I started to strip off my wet things but changed my mind. They could dry on me. There was sand in my hair, in the creases behind my knees, in my mouth. Grains of the sand horse, grains of me, perhaps, as I had slowly disintegrated into the sea. I knew when I remembered this day it would seem like a dream, disconnected, the pace of things all wrong, the simultaneous sense of being in the moment and being out of time.

The door to the cottage opened. Jasminder.

'Your friend has left,' he said. 'We should hurry if we want to make the ferry.'

He came in, looking around, taking in the inside-out T-shirt flung over the camp bed and the man's socks and trainers by the stove, the knowledge of it passing across his face.

'Christ, Scottie,' he said, in a near whisper. 'This is how you've been living? In this . . . hovel? Has it even got a bathroom?'

I zipped up my suitcase. I couldn't explain it, not even to myself. I left the cottage door swinging open behind me. There was no sense to it really, a childish act of rebellion, perhaps. In truth, I was angry. Angry with Helen for having a stroke just as I was about to discover my past, angry with Jasminder for coming here, forcing me to be a dutiful daughter. Angry with Kenver for thinking I was too fragile when he could have told me everything months ago. Jasminder, always the sensible one, the rational one, went back and closed the door.

'You don't want the sea air getting in there,' he said. 'It'll ruin your stuff.'

Kenver's boat was still at its mooring. I scanned the shoreline and the cliffs but could see no sign of him. We put on our life jackets and I manoeuvred *Banana* out from the slipway. I looked back as we turned south out of the bay and maybe, in the distance, I could see a figure standing on the beach watching us.

44

Charlotte/Scottie: Beginnings

Are you sure you want to do this? Jasminder said, squeezing my hand.

I squeezed back. We were standing in my newly bare studio, the one close to the wrong sea, the one where I'd made white horses as well as waves, where I'd rebuilt from the ashes of my first studio, the ashes of my relationship with David. Light was streaming in through the stained-glass windows, made from tiny fragments of sea glass the previous occupant had collected from the beach. I had a sudden flash of memory, of the hallway in Helen and Phil's house dancing with coloured light whenever the sun hit the glass panel over the front door just so. And I thought of the light in the hallway the day Phil had died, the way it danced across the shoe rack, the textured wallpaper, the white-painted banister. For a long time when I was growing up, whenever I saw sunlight dancing through stained glass, I thought of Phil, but then it had stopped. Faded away. I hadn't even noticed, until now.

It's a bit late for second thoughts, I said. *I'm about to hand the keys back.*

He turned to face me, grabbing my other hand and pressing them both into his.

I just want you to be sure about what you're giving up. You built this place from nothing.

He blinked, the tips of his long eyelashes seeming to brush against the delicate skin beneath his eyes.

We can't carry on living fifty miles apart, I said. *I'll find something new. Preferably with a salary.*

And a water-cooler.

A computer password. And maternity leave and going back part-time when we have kids.

Jasminder wasn't much for smiling. Even when happy, he inhabited an air of studied seriousness. But he smiled then, his face lit by the coloured light flowing through the stained glass.

We embraced and went to hand back the studio keys.

45

Thordis: The Spell

Even on this island they share only with birds, relentless motion follows them. Mountainous waves, dark grey and silver-tipped, erupting, shifting the surface of the world. Their tiny cottage, the beach, the lichen-swirled cliffs. The island constantly assembles and disassembles itself in rock falls, sand drifts, streams and shifting tides. Thordis finds it unsettling, this lack of stillness. How can she root herself to this place that never stops moving? She knows she will never love Bride as much as Cadal does.

When he's not away on the *Miss Molly* or playing his violin on the beach, Cadal paints Thordis into the land- and seascapes of St Hía. She likes to watch him work, creating beauty from a blank canvas. She likes to study the unwavering concentration that suffuses his body as he paints. The stillness of his face, his eyes darting across the canvas, the way his knees creak and snap when he finally moves. Her favourite is a painting of her face in the Hollow Sea, her hair a whirlpool between the twin islands. His favourite is one of her underwater, in the deep, dark green, her hair a forest of floating kelp reaching up to the light.

The first loss comes just a few months after their wedding. Cadal is away with the *Miss Molly* and Sam had come the day before with the groceries, so Thordis suffers the loss alone, with nothing and no one for comfort. When

Cadal returns home, salt-crusted and ravenous, she tells him the news, the loss of a child he hadn't yet known was coming. He touches her hair and says, *Best nae dwell on it, Thora. There'll be other bairns. I promise.* Perhaps he was right. What was the point of grieving the loss of a child who had never been, a child she had only half suspected might be on the way. But still she cried privately in the night when Cadal was asleep.

He is at home when she loses the next pregnancy, six or seven months later. At breakfast, Cadal presses his hand to her belly to feel his son moving.

It might be a girl, she says.

Nae, Thora. I'm certain it's a wee laddie. He's grinning, his confidence infectious and Thordis wants to believe. Already she is further along than before.

She is kneeling at the stove, boiling a kettle to make their mid-morning tea, when the first lick of pain ripples through her and she feels dampness between her legs. She never forgets the slack horror on his face when he realizes he is helpless to stop what is happening. He whispers to her, *I'm sorry, I'm sorry, I'm sorry.*

In the following days, she notices a change in him, the first tiny grief lines etched around his eyes, a subtle difference in the way he looks at her, as if even then he sensed an essential barrenness in her, that she would never be the mother of his child. He sits for hours on the beach, staring out to sea, popping mermaid's purses and crushing skeletonized seaweed to dust.

A few weeks later he comes home smelling of beer, unshaven and red-eyed, his sweater filthy. *I quit the* Miss

Molly. She is too shocked to respond. *Conn was getting on my nerves,* he says, in answer to her unasked question.

But how shall we live?

He takes her hand, leads her outside, his fingers glittering with hooked-in fish scales. There by the slipway, a shiny new fishing boat. It's small, intended for one or two men to fish for breal or lobster inshore. *I'm my own boss now,* he says. *And I'll be home every night, to take care of you.*

Thordis doesn't ask him how he afforded the boat, suspecting that she wouldn't like his answer. She rubs her hand on her belly, as if by doing so she can cloak her next baby, her next tiny seed, with magic. A spell to protect them all. It is then that she sees their marriage is as delicate and brittle as the skeletonized seaweed Cadal likes to crush in his fist, a web of fissures, paper thin and translucent.

46

Scottie: The Hollow Sea

I had become accustomed to the Hollow Sea, to navigating its safe passages. The tidal race was mild today, only the faintest tug on *Banana* as we passed between the twin islands. Jasminder sat up front, staring out at the rolling grey expanse, misery etched across his back. Yesterday's storm had washed away the last of the summer. The sea, grey beneath a pearlescent sky, swelled and dipped in gentle slow-motion as Bride faded into the distance behind us.

Jasminder twisted to face me, squinting into the wind. 'You must be sorry you ever met me.'

'Why would you think that?'

'I couldn't give you a baby. The only thing you've ever wanted.'

'I never blamed you. It was both of us. Neither of us.'

He ran his hand over his fledgling beard. 'I dreamt of being a dad,' he said. 'Maybe they weren't as brightly coloured as your dreams, but I still had them. Still *have* them. Putting my new-born child in my mother's arms. Christ, Scottie. I'm her oldest son and I couldn't give her a grandchild.'

He turned away, the rest of his words lost to the wind.

'I'm sorry.'

He wiped his sleeve across his face.

'Maybe you still can have children,' I said. 'If you meet someone new.'

He laughed sadly. 'I was going to say the same to you. You could still be a mum. We couldn't make babies together. We just didn't fit. But could we with other people? I've thought about it. Haven't you? You're ahead of the game. You've already found someone new.'

I never hated our unexplained diagnosis more than at that minute, how it had left us with a splinter of hope, a tiny bright thing that had burrowed between us, a wound that caused an incurable infection.

'He and I, we're not . . . it's not . . .'

'You don't owe me any explanations.'

'No. But I need you to understand I'm done with all that. I've let it go. I'm not trying to be a mother any more. I can't . . . If it didn't happen again it would be unbearable. I don't think I could survive it.'

'What are you going to do, then? Live on that island in the middle of nowhere, in that . . . *shack*? What sort of life is that? Why hide away from the world? So you never have to see anyone else's baby? That's not brave, Scottie. It's cowardly.'

'It's not what I'm doing.'

'Isn't it?'

The wind was growing stronger. Jasminder zipped his jacket up to his neck. 'You might as well know I'm going to put the house on the market. You can have half of whatever's left over after I pay off the mortgage.'

'But you love that house.'

'It doesn't feel like home without you there.'

Jasminder selling our house, the home we had dreamt about and sweated over, broken our backs to pay for. It should have felt like a loss, but my only emotion was relief.

'And it didn't feel like home to me, without our children in it. I tried to tell you, but you wouldn't listen.'

'That's not fair, Scottie. We've got three embryos waiting for us. But you gave up on them.'

I wanted to tell him he was wrong. That letting go wasn't the same as giving up, but I was afraid my words would sound hollow.

He looked at my wrists, taking in the red marks around them, the marks left by Kenver. 'Did he hurt you?'

I shook my head, wishing the marks didn't remind me of David, of Alice, my first ghost child. I wanted to say I was sorry I had reached the end of the road first, that I had cheated him out of his last chance at fatherhood, that I just couldn't walk that path any further.

'I was pregnant once. A long time ago. When I was with David.'

Jasminder stared at me. 'You lost a baby? Why didn't you tell me?'

'No, you don't understand. I didn't lose her. I let her go.'

He was silent, taking this in.

'It wasn't a safe relationship, and I wasn't strong enough to leave him, so I let her go. I had an abortion because I wasn't brave enough.'

I waited for Jasminder to tell me I was a coward, that I was selfish, that I was a bad mother. To tell me all the things I had thought about myself over the years.

'You could have told me,' he said. 'I would have understood. It wasn't your fault.'

Not my fault. I wasn't sure if that was true. I did know that if I had been braver, I would have been a mother already. I would have had an almost ten-year-old child. Maybe not my imagined Alice, my perfect girl, but a child who needed me, a child who wasn't a ghost frozen in a moment of time.

'What was that?' Jasminder's gaze snapped away from me and he scooted to the edge of his seat, peering into the sea. 'I saw something.'

'It was probably a porpoise.'

Jasminder knelt by the starboard side, scanning the water.

'There,' he said, pointing. 'See it?'

I wasn't sure. A flash of movement, perhaps, beneath the waves.

'Yes,' he said. 'There. And there. More than one, but beneath the surface.'

The water was becoming choppy, waves slapping against the hull, spray hitting us, the boat rocking and jerking.

'Stop leaning over the side,' I said. 'It's getting rough.'

Jasminder ignored me, mesmerized by the shadows darting beneath the waves. The outboard began to labour, and I sensed our momentum slowing, as if we were being blown back. But the wind was still light, and southerly, barely lifting the wisps of hair from around my face.

'Lights,' said Jasminder. 'There are lights in the water. Look at the colours. Could it be jellyfish?'

The outboard whined. I glanced up, ready to scold

Jasminder for still hanging over the edge of the boat, but saw that he was now half standing, his mouth gaping open, pointing behind me. The engine began to smoke, and I realized we were not being pushed from ahead by the wind but sucked back from behind.

'What the fuck is that?'

Still struggling with the tiller, I half turned to see what he was pointing at. The sea was a scurry of froth, a white stripe stretching back twenty or thirty feet through the rolling grey waves. The white became more and more agitated, as I tried desperately to pull us away, but the sea was roaring now, louder than our voices, louder than the failing engine.

'It's the Hollow Sea,' I shouted, but my words were wasted, sucked into the frothing ocean.

I relinquished the tiller, knowing it was pointless. The sea tossed us around as if we were on a fairground ride. I could see glimpses of shapes moving and flashes of colour within the white, and then it seemed to fall, to collapse in on itself, the white strip of surf shifting down like land in an earthquake, turning inside out, becoming a tunnel, a whirlpool, and I knew then there was no hope. We were in it, falling through, falling down, but miraculously, for a few moments, there was space and air around me and I could still breathe. Jasminder reached out for me and I grabbed his hand. The boat tipped over, ripping us apart, my life jacket torn away, a howl ripping out of me, water in my nose and mouth, my eyes and ears, intruding, filling me, crushing me, forcing the air from my lungs, the bubbles rising up, and there were lights and rainbows and shapes and darkness and shimmering warmth spreading along my spine. I wanted to sleep, to sink into a dream as I drowned, to die in the presence of my will-o'-the-wisps and they were there, all around me, flitting just out of reach.

47

Thordis: Brides

I try to imagine Cadal through Thordis's eyes, to see the boy she loved once. But he remains distant to me, this smiling, sunlit boy in her heart. It's easier to see the monster he became. But, to honour her, I will try once more.

Her first morning on Bride. A girl still in every way that matters. She wakes, a little land-sick after the long journey from Tvífjallahöfn. The slightest of indentations on the pillow where he has slept virtuously beside her, but he is gone now. The first of many mornings she will wake alone, but she doesn't know that yet. The bed is snuggled into one corner of a large, chilly, mostly empty room. It isn't cosy, this room with a stone floor and walls and no decoration, so sparsely furnished it's barely even a home. A place to sleep, nothing more, for a single man with simple tastes. Already she is learning something about him.

He has left a bowl of fresh water for her to wash in, pumped from the well outside, and a pebble that has captured all the colours of the sunset and all the scents of the ocean. She goes to the window, hoping to look out at the sea she has listened to all through the night, but the glass is thick with salt, so it is like staring into a mist. She washes her face, brushes her teeth and plaits her hair. The faint edge of nausea in her stomach subsides as she acclimatizes to being back on solid land. She pushes open the cottage door to her first proper sight of the island in daylight, a jumble of rocks and shells, and everywhere the spikes of a sea-green plant she has never before encountered. She picks her way across the uneven ground, the hem of her skirt catching on the spiky plant, and already she knows she will tame this space and make it beautiful.

The cool morning air fills her lungs and she huddles deeper into her coat, reaching into her pocket and closing her hand around the sunset pebble. Although there is space all around, she feels a sudden rush of claustrophobia. The screeching of the flashing white seabirds seems harsher than the calls of the gulls at home, and the sky feels paler and lower. The cliffs are oppressive, looming, giving her nothing of the exhilaration and freedom she had imagined she would feel when she reached this place of which Cadal had spoken so fondly. Bride, she senses, is an island of contrasts, of conflicting geographies and discordant rhythms. Beautiful, to be sure, but also desolate, unwelcoming.

The beach to the north of the cottage is crisscrossed with narrow, half-hearted streams and littered with shells and skeletonized seaweed. She finds Cadal standing on the shoreline, his violin tucked beneath his chin. Hand on bow, fingers on strings, but the instrument is silent. He doesn't acknowledge her, hypnotized by the cadence of the waves as they scrape back and forth across the shells. The musician in her understands he is waiting for the waves to reach a certain rhythm. This is a song to be played in harmony with the sea. She pushes down a sharp prickle of jealousy and waits.

When the shift in the rhythm comes, she, a stranger to this place, does not recognize it, but life flows into his limbs, his face, and he begins to play. Tentative and melancholy, the notes wavering and breaking, then becoming a tumult. Thordis is enchanted, her homesickness forgotten.

The song ends and he notices her, his face breaking into the same crinkled smile that had caused her to climb down the linden tree outside her bedroom window and leave her old life behind. He puts his thumb under her chin. *What do you think of my island?*

There might be a petulant note to his voice, Thordis thinks, one that dares her not to fall in love with Bride. *It is beautiful,* she says, her voice catching. He opens his arms, and she steps into his embrace. He kisses her forehead and hair. He kisses her neck and her face and her mouth. His kisses turn her limbs to mist and her homesickness to a distant memory. She thinks they might lie down then, together, on the drifts of shells and rotting seaweed, but he has places to show her.

The chapel-cave of Our Lady of Sorrows. Cadal handsome and sheepish, a carnation in the lapel of a borrowed suit a size too big and a decade out of date. Thordis pretty in a white cheesecloth dress and sandals, daisies threaded through her plaits. The only guests are the crew of the *Miss Molly*, Conn, Antonio and sly-eyed Uffa, as well as Conn's wife, a formidable red-haired woman named Grainne. They land their launches on the narrow shale beach and clamber over rocks slippery with seaweed. Cadal and Conn go ahead, to meet Father Carvalho. Grainne fusses over Thordis's hair and Antonio, bringer of bowls and buckets for her to vomit in during the long journey from Tvífjal-lahöfn, holds her hand sweetly as she traverses the rocks in her inappropriate footwear.

Good luck, says Antonio, kissing her cheek.

Alone for a moment, waiting, Thordis clutches her posy of daisies and gasps with delight at the hundreds of flicker-ing candles. Does she have doubts? Regrets? I think not. Thordis was always a person who forged her own path, who didn't look back. Perhaps she thinks only of love and romance. Her processional music begins, a violin solo of *Ave Maria*, played on a wind-up gramophone. She walks into the sallow candlelight, past muted frescoes and drip-ping wax, so different from the red-roofed church in Tvífjallahöfn with its plain white walls and beamed ceiling. Cadal, waiting in the apse with Conn and Father Carvalho, turns to watch her. His face is serious, full of concentra-tion, and he rocks back and forth in his borrowed shoes. They sing an English hymn about peace, their half-hearted voices sputtering off the cave walls. Cadal and Thordis make their vows and kiss chastely.

Thordis, scarcely able to believe she is a married woman now, holds her husband's hand and reflects on how far she has come in a few short weeks, how much she has grown up. They wait, the two of them, until the others have left, muted conversations echoing into the distance. Cadal holds her face in his hands.

I have gifts for you, Thora Fernandes.

Thora. It's the name of a stranger and it gives her a funny

feeling in her stomach, to hear it from Cadal's lips, but she shrugs it off. She supposes it is easier for him to say. He leads her to a plaster statue of a Madonna and Child sitting on a shelf-like ledge in the cave wall.

But I didn't get you anything, she says.

He kisses her, to let her know it doesn't matter. *Reach in here. Around the statue.*

Behind the Madonna is only darkness. She hesitates.

It's good luck for the groom to leave a gift for his bride.

He squeezes her waist and, because she trusts him completely, she reaches in. At first, she finds nothing, her fingers touching empty space. She moves her hand downwards, and there, lodged in a tiny nook, a palm-sized package wrapped in tissue paper. She senses his excitement as she unwraps the gift.

A decorative hair comb carved from ivory mother-of-pearl. She turns it this way and that so it glimmers in the candlelight.

It belonged to my mother. And all the mothers in this family before her. My great-great-great-grandfather brought it back from a whaling expedition. And now it's yours, and one day it will belong to our oldest daughter. He puts it on for her, pressing the teeth into her scalp as he slides the comb up the side of her head.

Thordis runs her finger along the intricate carved swirls. *It's beautiful.*

There remains another item, still half wrapped in the tissue paper. Cold metal against her palm. *A key? For what?*

He folds her fingers over it. *Keep it safe and you shall see, darling Thora. We should go now.* He leads her along the aisle back to the world outside, the hard edges of the key digging into her hand.

They step, blinking, into the bright autumn light, Grainne throwing rice and the boys teasing Cadal. Grainne takes a photograph of them, still shy with one another, squinting into the sun. The photograph will be hazy and over-exposed, the only one Thordis will ever have of them together. She throws her posy into the ocean, and they watch as the current takes it.

A bride for Bride. Thordis still holds the key, grown warm from her skin, as Cadal carries her across the threshold. He puts her down and she stares around, knowing the gift must be here, wanting to please him by finding it and demonstrating her delight. What could have such a key? A music box, perhaps. Or a secret journal. At first, she doesn't see it, because the milky light can't penetrate the layers of salt on the windowpanes to reach the furthest corner of the cottage. Impatient, Cadal takes her shoulders and turns her around, steering her in the right direction. There, in the gloomiest corner, against the wall, is a piano.

Oh, my goodness. She runs to it, her delight genuine. She would never have imagined it possible to bring a piano to a place so remote. She strokes her fingers across the walnut lid, brushes her fingertips along the gleaming ivory keys. Cadal, she senses, is standing behind her, bursting with anticipation. She wonders how he could have afforded this, but she doesn't ask. Instead, she turns and jumps into his embrace. *I love it, I love it, I love it. I love you.*

Aye, he says, *I know,* and kisses her. There has never been a kiss like it, before or since. She yields to it completely. When the kiss breaks, he takes one of her plaits in his hands, rolling off the bobble with his thumb. *I'll keep you safe, Thora,* he whispers, so soft she can barely hear. *You belong to me, now.*

Surely, she thinks, we belong to one another.

48

Scottie: Enys Wolvygyen

A hand holding mine, my hair an underwater forest dancing around me. The hand squeezes mine and my first
thought is, could it be Alice? Could I be meeting her now
at the end? But this is not a child's hand. Light all around
me, intruding through my closed eyelids so I open them.
Kenver. Air bubbles from his nose, the fronds of his hair
mixing with mine, his legs enfolded in a shimmering fabric
that is all colours and none. This is what dying feels like.
This is my tunnel of light, sinking into nothingness with
only a dream of Kenver for company. Lips on mine, Kenver's breath, warm and sweet, inside me. A fin on his back,
hollow, glass-like, pulsing with coloured light. Kenver
darts away and now he has a tail, a merman's tail with a
scalloped fin, each scale a tiny glimmering rainbow in
mother-of-pearl. I reach between my shoulder blades and
there is a fin there too, slicing through my cotton T-shirt,
because in this drowning dream they haven't cut a part of
me out. I am whole again.

A horse, by Kenver's side. A white stallion with amber
eyes, snorting bubbles, tail fanning out in the current, like
seaweed. Kenver puts his arms around Sea Glass's neck,
and I put my arms around Kenver. Sea Glass dives down,
through forests of swaying kelp, leaving the sunlight behind

us, until there is a different light, a light that is shimmering luminous watery green.

Kenver releases Sea Glass to graze on the kelp forest, my feet sinking into soft sand. His breath inside me, again. Hollow Fins gather, encircling us, observing me with dark, shining eyes. A female, streaks of grey in her seaweed hair, shimmering tail fluke slicing through the water. She darts behind me, caressing my fin with such tenderness, and then she is in front of me again, her hair falling across her breasts. She touches my face, her long fingernails making indentations in my cheeks. Her eyes are inscrutable. This is Merryn, my mother. A dream Merryn, a dream mother, a mother I never knew. She sings, a few haunting notes strung together, a song without words. Without knowing, without thinking, I begin to sing too. A song of the archipelago, of Enys Wolvygyen, of the Hollow Sea, each note fragile, glass-like, pure. When the song ends, my mouth aches with the silence. *It wasn't my fault,* she says. *Thora came too late. She was supposed to come before the neap tide.* I don't understand, but when I open my mouth to tell her the only words I can speak are *Mother, Mother, Mother.* We embrace. All around us, other Hollow Fins. Flitting, murmuring shadows.

Behind Merryn, two dark-eyed mermaids, curly hair falling to their waists, one smiling, one sullen. It is like staring into a double looking-glass. The soft-faced smiling one grasps my hands and kisses my cheek. I have seen her face before, in a painting and on the cover of a book. The sullen one darts back and forth, narrows her eyes, then licks me, from my neck to my face, her tongue rasping along my skin. My sisters.

Merryn presses something into my hands. Soft, silky, I hold it up to the glowing light. A skirt, all colours and none. I understand, without being told, that wearing it will complete my transformation, provide me with a mermaid's tail to replace my useless legs, will make me whole. I hold the skirt against my body, my legs tingling with warmth. A soft song from the loose gathering of Hollow Fins around us, hungry to have me back in the fold. Kenver's thumbs in the waistband of my jeans, unbuttoning, unzipping, touching my belly with his lips. A stirring, a fluttering inside me. I understand then that I'm not barren here. A life, a future as the mother of Hollow Fin children stretches out before me, Kenver kissing my mouth, filling it with bubbles.

I wrap the skirt around my hips. A shimmering sensation in my limbs. I am coming home, at last. I look up, up through the green to the sunlit sea above and, floating, falling, there is a tiny black and orange speck. Jasminder, trapped in a drowning dream of his own, the currents stealing him away. I want to stay here, want to become the mother I was always meant to be, but the price is too high. I rip the skirt from my body, and it swirls away in the current.

Kenver is calling me, *Susan, Susan*. I push up from the ocean floor with my clumsy, human feet. Hands around my ankles, grabbing. Prickles of pain in my feet and legs, dragging me down. They are changed, Kenver, Merryn and my sisters, their fingernails turned to yellow claws, piercing my skin, their faces twisted in fury, their fins blackened with rage.

I struggle, kicking out, kicking up, but they are dragging me down and I can't breathe, I am drowning again, and I know, even if I could break free, I could never outswim them. A white blur, a whinny, snorting bubbles, and Sea Glass is there, nudging my arms, placing his body beneath mine, lifting me up, up. I grab his mane, Hollow Fin claws ripping through the skin on my legs, but then the claws are gone and I am free, my warm blood billowing out into the cold sea below me.

Susan, Susan, Susan. It is not Merryn, not my mother who calls for me, but Kenver, and the anguish in his voice nearly makes me turn back. We keep going, Sea Glass and I, up through the green and into the sunlit sea. Jasminder floating, face down, eyes closed, surely drowned. Sea Glass is gone in a flurry of sea foam, and there is an intense, rippling pain in my back, and I can almost touch Jasminder now, but he drifts away. I want to call out to him, but I have no air left in my lungs. I reach out and grab his foot.

49

Thordis: Two-Mountains-Harbour

Tvífjallahöfn. Two-Mountains-Harbour. A fishing town both sleepy and bustling. A rainy climate and a rippling grey harbour that sparkles only on the rarest of sunny days, protected on either side by twin crenellated mountains.

On this day that will change everything, Thordis is working alone in her mother's café after school, mopping the floor as the last of the day's patrons finish their meals. A wave of excitement unfurls along the quay, the remaining customers scrambling to pay their bills so they can get outside to see what is going on. She joins the throng, looking for an excuse to be late for her piano lesson. She's been finding her lessons more and more tiresome, lately, and Mr Halldorsson is prone to resting his hand on her knee as she plays. She has so far endured it because in two days she has her recital at the town hall, and in a few months the auditions for the conservatory of music in Reykjavík, her route out of this town and a life preordained as a fisherman's wife.

Snatches of conversation in the air – *British, gunboat, impounded, trawler* – from which Thordis gathers a British trawler has been apprehended fishing in the exclusion zone and is being escorted into port by a brave Icelandic naval ship. For an impounded trawler to come to Tvífjallahöfn is the most exciting thing to happen for years. Thordis weaves her way into the crowd, jostling for the best view as the trawler and gunboat inch down the fjord and make their way into dock. She jeers along with her townsfolk as the captain of the British ship, short and paunchy, is taken ashore and marched to the gaol where he will remain until a hefty fine is paid. The rest of the crew, permitted to stay on board under strict curfew, seem bemused by the fuss. One responds to the insults by removing his trousers and showing the good townsfolk his arse, and after that there is not much to see and nobody to shout at so the crowd drifts away.

Thordis returns to the café, with time enough to spare to empty the ashtrays. She has a good view of the trawler, the *Miss Molly*, from the window. Most of the trawlermen have retired below decks. Just one remains, a young man with a mass of dark hair framing the glowing tip of his cigarette. Thordis lingers by the window, finding the ashtrays there to be in particular need of wiping. The young man finishes his cigarette, gathering up a tangle of nets from the deck, damaged perhaps in the skirmish with the gunboat. He holds the nets up to the evening sunshine, squinting and threading them between his pale hands with a kind of easy rhythm that makes her kidneys fizz.

The young man falters in his work, perhaps sensing Thordis's eyes upon him. He stares directly at the café window, the ashtray Thordis is cleaning clattering to the floor. She ducks beneath the table, retrieves the ashtray, and when she gathers the courage once again to glance in his direction, he is frowning into his nets. He grants her one more fleeting look and then her brother Magnus comes marching down the quayside to chivvy her up, her lateness for her piano lesson doubtless reported by Mr Halldorsson. When she glances back, hurrying along the quayside with Magnus, the trawlerman is gone below decks.

On the second evening, Thordis is cleaning the café windows, spraying the glass with vinegar, rubbing it with newspaper until it gleams. The young trawlerman is sitting on deck with his crewmates, conversation and laughter floating into the sky. He picks up a violin and tinkers with the strings. To Thordis, it seems incongruous to have such a delicate instrument on a fishing trawler. He starts slow, drawing the bow across the strings with the same grace as he had gathered nets the previous day. Thordis does not recognize the mournful tune, but it is beautiful. It quiets the seagulls and the lapping waves. The melody quickens, his body sways with the rhythm, faster, faster, the notes no longer sorrowful but infused with a vitality that makes her want to throw down her newspaper and vinegar and dance, right then and there, on the quayside. The sun lights up a cascade of broken bow strings. It fascinates her, the idea of playing with such passion that the instrument becomes damaged, yet the music continues to grow and swell. Thordis has no doubt Mr Halldorsson would be horrified by the very thought, but she is not. The trawlerman concludes with a flourish and glances at the café, perhaps to see if Thordis is watching. She whips away her gaze, busying herself sticking posters back on the newly sparkling windows.

On the third evening, the café is closed because Thordis is performing her recital at the town hall, trussed up in her

343

best dress with all the town dignitaries sitting in the front-row reserved seats. She is about to begin, with Mozart's Fantasia in D Minor, when she glances up, searching for her parents in the audience. They are lost in the sea of faces, but *he* is there, has slipped in at the last moment and is standing at the back, by the exit doors, a recital poster crumpled in his fist. They stare at one another across the hall. *Start,* start, *silly girl,* hisses Mr Halldorsson from the front row.

She fluffs the first note, then settles, her fingers flying across the keys. She doesn't think about him until the end when everyone is applauding and she is curtsying with a bouquet of yellow roses in her arms. She looks to the back of the hall, by the doorway, hoping to see him once more, but he is gone, slipped away, returned to the *Miss Molly* before anyone notices he has broken curfew.

On the fourth evening, he comes into the café while Thordis is working, her mother in the back room doing the accounts. It's raining outside, the drops shimmering on his hair and face. The other customers grumble and bob their heads together, speculating on whether he is breaking curfew by coming the short distance across the quay from boat to café. He orders a Coca-Cola and a liquorice straw in broken Icelandic. *You're an excellent pianist, Miss Jonasdottir,* he says, in English.

I practise every day. In the church with the red roof at the top of the hill. At six o'clock. She fumbles with his change.

You must be very dedicated, Miss Jonasdottir, to practise every day. Their hands brush as she deposits the change in his palm.

It's the only time I get to be alone. There's never anybody there.

Except on Tuesdays when my piano teacher comes, and Sundays when there's a sermon. She glances into the back room, but her mother is absorbed with her ledgers.

Today is Thursday, he says. *How sad that you'll be all alone.*

She bobs her head. *Thank you for your custom.*

He comes to the church, as Thordis had known he would, at five minutes past the hour, slipping in as she practises her scales. She pauses, her hands on the keys, listening to the clop of his boots on the polished floorboards. *Why do you English steal our fish?* she says, without turning around. *We don't like people who steal our fish.*

He hesitates, his youthful confidence temporarily evaporated. *I'm nae English. And we were five mile outside the exclusion zone. I'm Cadal Fernandes. A proud St Hían. You'll nae have heard of it.*

She shakes his outstretched hand. *What a strange name.*

He smiles, not offended. *Nae stranger than Thordis. What was that song you played at your recital? The very last one, I think it was. It moved me. Will you teach it to me?*

He slides onto the piano stool beside her, squeezing his knees beneath the keyboard.

She likes the sun lines around his eyes, which make him appear to be smiling even when he is not. She plays a few bars. He studies the movement of her fingers, tries to replicate the melody, slipping out of key. *Like this, Englishman.* She places her hands over his, pressing down his fingers in sequence. He repeats the pattern, faltering. *Better,* she says. *Again.*

In this manner, a few bars at a time, Cadal learns the

melody, although no one would mistake his playing for hers. *I must go,* she says, noticing the time. *I'm expected.*

He takes one of her plaits in his sun-weathered hands, lays it across his palm, watching her face. *What does your hair look like, Thordis, when it's set free?*

It thrills her to hear her name on his lips. *That's for me to know and you to discover.*

Cadal comes every day to the church and Thordis teaches him to play the songs and melodies she has grown up with. One evening he brings his violin. *People will hear,* she says. *We shall be discovered.* He tucks the violin beneath his chin, his mouth serious, his eyes crinkled in the perpetual smile that has kept Thordis awake and restless into the early hours. He draws the bow back and forth across the strings, finding his pitch. Satisfied, he begins to play. The song she has taught him. She tilts her head towards Cadal, towards the violin, her eyes closed, leaning into the music. *Play,* he says. She brushes her fingers across the keys without depressing them, reluctant to break the spell. *Thordis. Please.* She plays. She doesn't need to think about the notes. Her fingers dance a path across the keys. To begin with, the notes from the piano and the notes from the violin are separate, rising up suspended in their own spaces, but then they touch, tendrils of melody entwining, becoming one instrument.

When the song is over, they stare at one another, breathless. Cadal takes her hands, pulling her up from the piano stool. He kisses her nose, her mouth. *Our skipper's paid his fine. We're leaving tomorrow at high tide.*

Her breath catches. *I thought we would have more time.*

He kisses her earlobes. *We'd have all the time in the world,* he says, *if you come with me.*

Thordis breaks away, a dizzy sensation in her temples. *Leave Tvífjallahöfn?* She sits on the piano stool, pressing her palms together to still the dizziness. *Couldn't you stay? You could get a job on a trawler?*

He kneels, enclosing her hands in his. *Who would have me? You said yourself they hate Englishmen.*

She has no answer. It won't matter to anyone in Tvífjallahöfn that Cadal is from St Hía, that he's not an Englishman. *But I have school. And piano practice. And my audition for the conservatory. How can I leave my family?*

He strokes her palms, his fingers glittering with fish scales. *Aye. Sweet Thordis. You're meant for better than a humble fisherman's wife. You must go to the conservatory in Reykjavík and become a concert pianist. It would be a crime to rob music of your talent. It's just . . .* he moves his thumbs to her inner wrists, to the soft green veins there . . . *it's just I thought you loved me.*

Thordis wants to touch his face, but he is holding her wrists so tightly she can't move them. *Cadal, you're hurting me. Please let go.*

For the briefest of moments, so brief that perhaps Thordis imagines it, he squeezes her wrists tighter, grinding the bones together, then releases her. He smiles, eyes shiny with tears. *How can you talk of hurt, Thordis, when you've bewitched me so, only to cast me away?* He fumbles for his violin and it clatters to the floor. *Go now, Thordis, please. I canna look at you nae more. You've broken my heart.* She runs, tearful, to the church door and he does not try to catch her.

★

Thordis, her face swollen from crying, stares out of her bedroom window at the perpetual half-light of northern summer nights, wondering why she finds herself so unexpectedly attached to Tvífjallahöfn. She has a loving relationship with her mother, but her father and brothers are distant, taciturn, existing only to fish, eat, drink beer, sleep and pay for her piano lessons. She has schoolmates, but never a best friend, never the sort of friend you could tell your deepest secrets to. And then there is Mr Halldorsson, his wandering hands and obsessive attention to technique, his ability to strip the music he teaches of every scrap of passion and verve.

How different it was to play music with Cadal. Her skin still tingles with the memory. How passionate the notes flying from his violin had been. She touches the barely there bruise on her inner wrist, faint, like the smear of the moon in the sky. Everything she plays from now on will be lacking, will be a single vine but never the forest, a drop in the ocean but never the glorious crashing waves. He had filled the empty spaces in her music. How foolish to have dreamt of the conservatory in Reykjavík, to have dreamt of concert houses around the world, when she could only produce such talentless, leaden music that it took a humble fisherman and his battered violin to complete it. If her music has no magic of its own, then what is her future if not the path she has plotted and planned and worked towards for years?

She thinks about Cadal. The sun-creases around his eyes, fissures of untanned skin revealing themselves when he laughs or frowns. She thinks about his hands mending the nets on the deck of the *Miss Molly*, and the glowing tip of his cigarette against the rain-drenched sky. She imagines St Hía and a misty tiny island named Bride, remembering the soft affection in his face when he spoke of home. Her new-found childish cleaving to Tvífjallahöfn hardly compares.

And yet, and yet, and yet.

She knows the tides, this fisherman's daughter. She knows in less than an hour the *Miss Molly* will head west along the fjord towards the open sea, and she will never see Cadal again. So as the sky blossoms to a yellowish pink she throws some clothes and a few knick-knacks into her duffel bag and opens her window wide to the fading night. She doesn't leave a note. What would she say? She thinks only of Cadal, the way he had taken her plait and placed it across the flat of his palm. *What does your hair look like, Thordis, when it's set free?*

He's waiting for her, grinning as she hops up on deck, flinging his arms around her. *Good girl. I knew you wouldna let me down.*

She doesn't look back as the *Miss Molly* chugs up the fjord, not even once.

PART III

Sanctuaries

50

Scottie: Floating

Jasminder wheezes softly as he pulls up at the hospital drop-off spaces. There is an angry bruise on his forehead.

'Give Helen my love,' he says.

'You're not coming in?'

He closes his eyes for a few seconds, then opens them. 'Of course I am. Just let me go and park the car.'

Helen, so tiny and brittle and pale in her hospital bed. At first I think I've come to the wrong bay. Her face is slack on the left side, her hair in fuzzy tufts across the pillow. I know she would hate this. She always takes such care with her hair, her neat, straight bob and her colour-coordinated Alice bands.

'Hello, Mum. It's Charlotte. I'm here.'

I don't know if she can hear me, if she's even still in there, trapped deep inside this rattling shell. Perhaps she's already grown her feathers and flown away.

Jasminder arrives with plastic chairs. He pulls the curtain around the bed then coughs, doubling over, not noticing a nurse glaring at him. I try not to think about turning his body gently on the beach at St Columba, before Matty got worried when Jasminder didn't arrive at the boatyard to collect his belongings and came looking for us. I try not to think about the sand and salt caught in Jasminder's eyelashes, the kara on his wrist glinting in the sunshine. I try not to think about begging him to breathe, to please breathe.

I squeeze Helen's hand. She moans, snatching away, her hand dropping to the bedcovers, restless, grasping, the purple bruises from the cannula stark against the sheets. I try again, and again she pulls away.

'She's angry with me.'

'It's a reflex,' says Jasminder. 'That's all.'

My wrists are swollen. They throb faintly, and there is a pattern of bruises left by Kenver's fingers. I pull down my sleeves to hide it from Jasminder. We sit either side of the bed in our plastic chairs, my dying mother a buffer between us. Jasminder coughs intermittently. We're still wearing the same clothes as when we had left Bride, torn and reeking of the ocean, stiff with salt. My head hurts, on the left side, above my ear. I touch my scalp and find a bruise there. I trace its outline, mapping the pain with my fingers. I have no memory of hitting my head. My hair has dried in salt-crusted spirals, my skin stretched so tight across my face I feel as though it might split. The scratches on my leg itch as they heal, the skin knitting together. Helen's breath begins to rattle, deep in her throat, the worst sound I have ever heard. A nurse comes to change her syringe driver and the rattle subsides.

Nurses come and go, day shift changing to night. The hospital ward seems like a place slipped out of time, with its bright lights and beeping through the night, the faint conversations of nurses, the stench of disinfectant and the relentless, draining heat. The only thing that marks the time is Helen's breathing, her gradual crescendo over the hours into another death rattle. Jasminder goes to the nurses' station to find someone, and they come, and she is quiet again. I wonder how we will know when death is coming, if we keep silencing it, but it's too terrible to listen to.

I touch her forehead, her hand, her skin papery and thin.

'You can go, Mum, when you're ready. You don't need to hang on any more. Jasminder's here. I'm not alone.'

Somehow, it's morning.

'I'm going down to the hospital shop,' I say. 'To get her a hairbrush.'

'I can go,' says Jasminder. 'You stay.'

'I don't trust you to buy the right one.'

For a moment I think he's going to kiss his fingers and touch them to my forehead, like he has done so many times before. But he doesn't.

I find a hairbrush in the shop I think she would approve of. The inside of my mouth feels like fur, so I buy a tube of toothpaste and two toothbrushes. Taking the stairs back to the ward, my mouth zinging with mint, I feel more alert, less disconnected from the outside world, as if I am back in reality for the first time in months. The world of St Hía, of Lugh and Sorrow and Bride and the cottage, of Kenver and sand sculptures, of Tony, of Sam and his stories, seems unreal to me now.

Jasminder is waiting at the entrance to the bay. I squash down my annoyance with him for leaving Helen alone.

'I managed to get a decent hairbrush. And I got you some toothpaste –'

'Scottie,' he says.

'— because I don't know about you, but my mouth felt like shit —'

'Scottie.'

'— and I feel a lot better now I've brushed my teeth.'

'Scottie.' He takes my hands.

'No,' I say. 'Not while I was gone.'

I go behind the curtain and she looks the same, lying there in the hospital bed like a tiny bird. 'I don't know how long I'm supposed to sit with her now,' I say.

'As long as you want.'

He waits with me the whole time.

We go back to her house, the neat little mid-terrace in the Groves where she had lived since before she became my mother. I shower, washing away the smells of the Hollow Sea, of Bride, of Kenver, and lie down in my old bedroom, listening to the rain dripping from gutters. I had never known her to be lax about getting the gutters cleaned before and a little worm of a thought works its way into my brain, that she'd been ill before the stroke, while I'd been off chasing ghosts. I doze for a while, among the piles of Christmas decorations. Jasminder naps downstairs on the sofa, the sound of his coughing scraping at the fragile layers of my sleep.

'What will you do now?' he asks me, in the late afternoon when we have both given up on sleeping the day away and he is wearing Helen's fluffy winter dressing-gown and washing the salt out of our clothes.

'Stay here for a bit. Until the funeral, anyway.'

He's playing music on his phone, softly in the background.

The same music he had played on a loop when his father died, a song from an old Hindi movie. Kishore Kumar singing about doomed love. It breaks my heart a little bit that he would play it now, for Helen.

'And then you'll go back? To St Hía?'

'You want to know if I'm going back to Kenver? Why does it matter? You and me, we're not together.'

He controls his face, pulling a tangled mass of clothes from the washing-machine and separating them out to go in the tumble-dryer.

'I'm sorry,' I say. 'I'm tired.'

'No problem. It's just . . . Never mind.'

'No. What? Tell me.'

He turns the dial on the tumble-dryer to set the heat and presses start, the clothes inside beginning to twist and fall.

'When I was asleep just now, I dreamt I was floating in the sea, half drowning. You were there and so was he. Your friend. You were swimming away with him, swimming away fast. I called out to you. I called for help because I was sinking under the water. And he kept swimming further and further away and pulling you along. But you came, Scottie. You left him, and you came back for me.'

He pulls Helen's dressing-gown closer around himself, although it really doesn't fit.

'Just a stupid dream,' he says. 'I'm going to shower while the clothes are drying.'

Jasminder stays until the funeral. He goes with me to register Helen's death, and to the funeral director. He helps me decide on the wicker coffin when I waver, reminds me that

Helen hated white flowers, especially lilies. He books the caterer. He sits with me while I plan the service, his church-school education giving him a bigger repository of hymns than I to choose from. He helps me write the eulogy, and on the day of the funeral, when I choke, he delivers the eulogy for me, and Helen's friends and neighbours and her third cousin twice removed from Swansea get to hear about a woman who once shattered into a thousand pieces but glued herself back together again for her daughter.

A few days after Jasminder leaves, because he has to go back to work, I start sorting through Helen's things, categorizing them into piles. 'Keep'. 'Charity shop'. 'Too nice to donate'. 'Friends might want?' When I can't find a pile to add an item to, I create a new category, until there is stuff all over the floor. There isn't much in the 'keep' pile. Helen's wedding and engagement rings and a box of family photos. I feel guilty about not finding much I want to keep, but worse than that is the knowledge that when I die, there'll be no one to sort through my knick-knacks, no one to care about old photos or family heirlooms. There'll only be a stranger arranging a house clearance, and everything I'll have gathered through my whole life will be nothing more than junk.

I'm up in the furthest corner of the loft, trying to keep the cobwebs out of my hair and manhandle a musty-smelling roll of carpet out through the hatch, when I notice a small wooden crate, thick with dust. The lid is nailed down, and I have to force it open with a palette knife, splintering the wood around the edges as I lever it off. Inside the crate, wrapped up in a bin bag and sealed with parcel tape, is a red satchel. The leather is old, scuffed, water-damaged. I lift it, gauging the weight of the contents, and undo the buckles. Another bin bag, brittle with age, protects whatever is inside. Bundles of documents wrapped in wax paper. I pull back the edges and see handwritten sheet music, letters unsent, jotted song lyrics, a journal. There are other items too. A postcard of an Icelandic fishing village. A peach stone, a blob of wax and a cuttlefish bone.

I take the items downstairs, spread them out across the carpet. Why did Helen have these? I unwrap the wax paper protecting the handwritten sheet music. There is water damage around the edges, but the notations remain clear, inscribed along the stave with blue ink.

There are two envelopes tucked in with the sheet music. One old, one new. I open the new one first. *Dear Charlotte. I never quite found the right time to give you these. I hope you can find it in your heart to forgive me. Love Mum.* The other envelope is water-stained, yellow with age. Inside, a photograph. A sheepish boy in a suit too big for him and a girl with daisies in her plaits, smiling at the camera. The original of the photo I had first seen in the archived copies of the *St Hía Herald*. Cadal and Thora Fernandes on their wedding day. I search for an emotion, and find only numbness.

When my phone buzzes, I have been sitting for hours on the lounge floor reading through song lyrics and snippets of poems and journals, and my knees are stiff, my back aching. I don't want to answer it. I'm content to stay here for ever, weaving together the last threads of my past. But I pick the phone up in case it's Jasminder checking in before the interment of Helen's ashes. The screen bursts into life. A notification. A voicemail from Ellie. I listen to her message, uncoil myself from the floor and go outside to Helen's garden, to the little patio table where she liked to sit and drink tea and watch the birds on the feeders, to call Ellie back.

Walking home from the churchyard after the interment of Helen's ashes, through the Shires, through the streets of white horses, Camarillo Close and Lipizzaner Avenue, Jasminder asks me what I'm going to do now.

'Will you sell the house?'

'Yes. I think so. I don't want to live here.'

'Will you go back to St Hía?'

The same question I have asked myself, again and again. And somewhere during grief that is like floating, and grief that is like waves, and grief that is like drowning, I have decided.

'No. Not St Hía.'

The acknowledgement, unspoken between us, that I won't be going back to Kenver. Because Kenver is a ghost of the past, just as much as my will-o'-the-wisps were ghosts of the future.

'Actually, I've been offered a job. My friend Ellie – the marine biologist I told you about – put me on to it. It's entry level, no experience needed. Working in a seal sanctuary in Ireland. Living on site, taking care of things when the sanctuary's closed to the public. Over time I'll be trained to help care for the seals too.'

We turn onto Oberlander Road, where I walked as a girl

and dreamt of white horses. Jasminder's face contracts a little. 'It sounds like an amazing opportunity.'

'It's remote. There's a village a few miles up the road, and a beach, but that's all.'

Jasminder pauses on the corner of Helen's street. He looks at his hands, his long fingers that I love, twisting his wedding ring around and around.

'Are you going to take the job?'

'I have to do something with my life. Why not this?'

'Scottie, I wish to Christ you'd stop running away from me.'

I take his hand, the way I had on our first date in the pub, tangling and disentangling our fingers.

'You're right,' I say. 'I am running away. But not from you. Just the life we had that's full of child-shaped holes. Can you understand?'

He swallows, tracing his fingers along my palm lines, but doesn't reply.

We have reached Helen's front door, navy blue with a gold knocker and a stained-glass pattern, the same door she had opened to such terrible news all those years ago. I wonder how she could have endured looking at that door every day for the rest of her life, how it didn't remind her of everything she had lost. We go inside, and the sun is coming out, casting stained-glass colour all over the hall. I think of us, Jasminder and me, how we have shattered into pieces, how we haven't been able to make ourselves whole again. How strong Helen must have been.

'You should run away too,' I say. 'You'll never heal properly living in that house, doing that same job and watching all your colleagues go on maternity and paternity leave. I don't know how you can stand it.'

He hangs his coat over a chair, switching the kettle on to boil.

'Running away,' he says, laughing softly. 'You might be on to something, Scottie. Maybe I'll do just that. Run away. Fly away. I'm free as a bird. We're both free as birds.'

He sighs and leans down to touch his forehead to mine. In that moment, I feel another kind of grief. Not floating, not drowning, not waves crashing down on me. Instead, an empty beach of pristine sand, stretched out before me, for miles and miles into the distance. The beach has no landmarks, no moments of life mapped out. There is only me, alone beneath a great weight of nothingness, to fill up that beach with footprints.

51

Scottie: Remembrance

I start my shift in the sanctuary hospital, scrubbing and disinfecting the isolation pens of the newest arrivals, including the whitecoat who had come in yesterday, her wounds disinfected with Hibiscrub and sealed with antibac spray that will stain her fur blue until her first moult. Her cries are disturbingly human. *Muuuuuummm. Muuuuuummm.*

Maggie arrives for her shift in a cloud of white breath, her beanie pulled down low over her ears. She makes me a coffee before we weigh the pup by manhandling her into a pup bag and hooking it onto the weighing scale.

'It's a godawful noise, isn't it?' Maggie says, as I pump Milton into a bucket. 'That *muuuuuum* sound the whitecoats make? It never used to bother me so much until I had my boys, but I feel things so much more, like, since becoming a mammy.'

I slosh the Milton solution around the pen. A few months ago, Maggie's words would have been a knife to my heart, but I'm stronger now.

'Poor skinny wee thing,' says Maggie, recording the pup's weight on the white board. 'She needs a name, bless her. It's your rescue so you do the honours.'

I had been the one to find her, in response to a call from a dog-walker, a tiny smudge of nothing on an empty beach, an obvious respiratory infection and a wound on her flipper. This season, they're naming all their patients after book characters, which should make it easy, but my mind is blank.

'Let's get some food down her, while you think it over.'

My idealized notions of bottle-feeding tiny white bundles of fluff have been well and truly punctured. Until they're old enough to feed themselves, the pups are fed fish soup by a tube. The little seal pup objects to everything we do, and Maggie and I both nearly get bitten. I kneel, straddling the pup's body with my knees, holding her still as Maggie pours the foul-smelling soup down the tube into her throat.

I like the pup's feisty nature and that's what brings a name to my mind.

'Pippi Longstocking?'

Maggie laughs.

'Good one. Write it up there, can you, and I'll disinfect the pup bag. Ha, she's pooped in it.'

Pippi the grey seal, the first living being I ever got to name. I hope it's a good name and it brings the feisty little pup all the luck she needs.

The sky lightens in tiny increments, from charcoal to navy to indigo. I find Jasminder on the beach, at the furthest edge of it, repairing the groynes. He likes the solitude, I think. I pause for a few minutes, watching him work. He spots me and waves.

'You've got fish scales in your hair,' he says.

'You can never have too much sparkle.'

He tries to brush away the scales with sandy fingers, but they're hooked in. We both laugh. It feels good to laugh.

'Don't take this the wrong way, but you stink of fish blood.'

'It's all glamour here,' I say, showing him my cuffs, bloodied from washing out the buckets used to feed the seals.

Around the groynes, the sea makes little swirling, foaming eddies. There is clay on my hands, drying, tightening, from the ceramic seal pups I've been making to sell in the sanctuary shop.

'Are you ready?' I say.

He reaches out and squeezes my hand. 'Give me ten minutes, and I'm all yours.'

There is a nameless island in the bay, not much more than a sandbar knitted together with grass. We take the kayaks across. I thought we might both be afraid of the water, of boats, after what happened in the Hollow Sea, but we needed to learn, as the sanctuary uses kayaks to check on the local resident seal population from a respectful distance. Aidan, the sanctuary manager, turned out to be a good teacher when he had finally lowered his eyebrows after realizing neither of us had ever been in a kayak before. We surprised ourselves by enjoying it. On a calm day, the gentle rock of the waves beneath the hull, and the rhythmic turn of the paddles, is meditative.

We kayak around the island to the south side, until we find a beach with no hauled-out seals. Four years to the day since egg retrieval, the day our embryos, the lost ones and the ones remaining in cryogenic suspension, had been made. I take out my letters, handwritten on some crumpled airmail paper I found at the back of the writing bureau. One to Alice, one to my embryos and other ghost children, and one, which Jasminder doesn't know about, to Helen. Writing them was harder than I'd thought it would be. I had sat for an hour or more staring at the semi-transparent blue sheets. In the end, I had started each one with *I love you,* and let the words flow from there. And they did flow. I didn't edit, but let the words stay as they fell onto the page from my pen. Jasminder has one letter, in a plain brown envelope, which makes me smile because it is so like him to write the most important letter of his life using the same paper and envelope he would use to write to his bank manager.

'Are you ready?' he says.

I nod, and he gets out the small ceramic bowl he has brought with him. He wedges the bowl in the sand, and we put our letters inside, my three and his one. He holds up a cigarette lighter. 'Purloined from Aidan,' he says, crouching beside the bowl.

'Do you think this is okay? Should we have got a permit or something?'

He ignites the lighter, shielding it from the breeze. 'Let's live fucking dangerously.'

The letters catch immediately, blackening around the edges, an orange flame licking up. He takes my hand. All those words, words from the deepest places in our hearts, turning to ash. We watch them burn.

We wade out into the ocean, protected from the worst of its chill by our wetsuits.

'Do you want to say anything?' he says.

I shake my head. I have no words left in me. Jasminder rests the bowl of ashes on the soft, swelling surface of the ocean. He pushes one edge of the bowl down, water swirls in, caressing the ashes at first, then taking them. Jasminder is saying something in Punjabi, a language he rarely speaks in front of me. I don't understand his words, but they have the cadence of a prayer. My tears flow freely. The bowl is clean of ashes. The ocean has taken them, gifted them to the tides, all our words and dreams and hopes and grief set free.

I ask Jasminder if he found it difficult to write to our never-to-be-conceived children.

'My letter wasn't to them,' he says. 'It was to you.'

'Oh.'

'The old you. The version of you who thought she could never be anything, never be worth anything, if she wasn't a mother. I wanted to say goodbye because I loved her. But you're someone new now. Do you feel that?'

'What do you mean?'

'It's a good sort of new, Scottie. It's not just you, it's both of us. We can grieve for our old selves while we're creating the new. You know, you haven't had an episode since we got here. I almost miss my crazy howling woman.'

I had left my howling in the Hollow Sea, in Enys Wolvygyen, in the bruises on my wrists and the scratches on my legs, in the vision of the future mother-me I had chosen to leave behind to swim back to Jasminder. I knew now that the howling hadn't only been grief for my ghost children, but also for the loss of my past selves, for Charlotte and

Susan. But I'm whole again. They are part of me, part of Scottie, part of the mother-in-my-heart. I still have to grieve, but I don't need to howl. Not any more.

Jasminder uses his thumbs to brush the last tears from my cheeks. He kisses me, on the mouth, in a way that he hasn't kissed me for I can't remember how long. I think he might be wrong, about the old versions of us being lost. Those versions of us are still here, battered, bruised. We're creating something new from them, transforming them as we heal.

There are dolphins zigzagging in the bay, silver fins cutting through silver water. We leave the beach as we found it, unmarked, belonging only to seals and seabirds.

We are at Trinity Cove. Aidan, Maggie, Tristan and I. It's the first seal-pup release of the season. Samwise, Matilda and Katniss are going home. They've grown too big for pup bags so we carry them from the van in cages and line them up as close to the sea as we can. It's rougher than I expected, and I wonder how the pups will cope with the waves, having spent so many weeks in the calm of the sanctuary's pools. They have so many challenges to come. Their first time hunting live fish, their first time finding a place to haul out, their first time meeting seals who have only ever been wild.

I remember Katniss, who had been rescued on my first day at the sanctuary, when I was wondering whether I'd made a terrible mistake because it was a million miles away from what I had thought it would be, and then this little seal pup on the beach, a bag of bones. And it was my job to take care of her. What she needed, unsentimental humans disinfecting her wounds and feeding her fish soup by a tube, was not the same thing I needed, or had thought I needed. I had wanted to nurture, to hold tiny seal pups in my arms and bottle-feed them while they stared into my eyes, and instead it was a daily round of hard graft, rinsing blood out of buckets, weighing frozen fish until my hands turned blue, scrubbing and disinfecting the pens. But it was meditative, in a way, the routine and the repetition. The physical exhaustion was satisfying and left no space for the mental exhaustion that had weighed me down for so many years. And I learnt that there was more than one way to nurture.

'Do you want to do the honours, Scottie?' Aidan gestured at the cages. 'Come on, look lively. Let's have them away before the dog-walkers descend on the beach.'

I step around a pile of flat stones someone has built into a tower and flip open the cages one at a time. Matilda comes out like a rocket, her ungainly shuffle across the sand surprisingly efficient. She glances back once, as if to check nobody is chasing her, and then she is in the ocean, and as soon as it is deep enough, she begins to swim to freedom.

Samwise and Katniss are slower, more cautious, shuffling forward a few metres, then stopping, uncertain of what to do, the yellow tags on their rear flippers bright against the sand. We position ourselves behind them, coaxing them forwards. Samwise is the first to get the idea, shambling into the ocean, just as Matilda is pushed back onto the sand by a wave. Matilda, undeterred, heads straight back in, this time swimming almost parallel to the beach, edging further out by degrees. Samwise gets the idea, following a similar path to Matilda. I lose sight of both of them, as they get into deeper water, just a brief flash of their dark heads before they dip beneath the waves. Grey seals are not social animals but, in the end, Matilda and Samwise are together, our last sight of them two little heads in the churning foam around a rock.

Katniss is still in the shallows, fighting against the waves pushing her back, back, back to the beach. A large wave comes, and I think it will push her right back to almost where we are standing, but she dives into it, disappearing into its swell, and then I see her, surfing each of the incoming waves, and she gets smaller and smaller and I search for her in the deep wide ocean, but she is gone, she is free, she is home.

There is a letter waiting for me when I get back to the house. Forwarded from St Hía by Nest, a reply from the adoption agency to the enquiry I had sent from Bride. I'm afraid to open it, but what can it tell me that I don't already know? I sit down at the writing bureau, where I have reconstructed Thordis's life, a song, a shell, a postcard at a time, and open the letter. The language is business-like. It doesn't tell me much. I skim over it, irritated to have to waste my energy on meaningless words. But there is an enclosure. A newspaper article, yellowed and fragile, protected by a plastic wallet.

A girl, name unknown, origin unknown. Aged seven or eight. Discovered alone on a beach, a shipwreck perhaps, but perhaps not. Unable or unwilling to say who she is, where she has come from. An appeal for information.

There are two photographs. One of a girl, aged seven or eight with dark curly hair, staring sad-eyed into the camera, captioned, *Do you know this girl?* The other photograph, captioned, *Do you recognize this clothing?* is of a scarf, hand-knitted, in the shape of a piano keyboard.

Thordis's story is written, pieced together, part history, part imagination. But it is as true as I could make it, true to her heart. I have one more scene to write. I have imagined it, pictured it. And it belongs, this final scene, not to Thordis, but to the girl, to Susan. To me.

52

Susan: Forgetting

She wakes alone in the dark, on a beach. A girl who has already lost two mothers in her short life and will one day lose a third. Sand is stuck to her face and shins. It smells different from the sand at home, saltier, less rainy. It scratches her as she tries to brush it off. Her rain hat is gone, her curls full of the alien sand, but miraculously the satchel is still attached where the woman had threaded the strap through the buttonholes and underneath the raincoat. Susan does not have the energy to remove the satchel, so it hangs there from her chest as she wanders into the dunes. She has never encountered such a thing as mountains of sand knitted together with grass before, and it makes her miserable and homesick.

She hunkers down in a space between some dunes. Grains of sand trickle down the slopes and she thinks of the sand timer in the kitchen at home, breakfasts of boiled eggs and soldiers. She cranes her neck, finding comfort in the familiar pattern of the stars and the pale sliver of moon that is the same as the moon she looked at last night from the window by her bed, next to a seashell-decorated wall. She cries a little, then waits. There is nothing else to be done.

At dawn, a rust-coloured dog comes to her, puts its paws on the satchel, its cold nose on her face. Susan whimpers. The dog shivers with joy.

Harley, comes a man's voice. *Harley. Come, Harley, get here, will you? What you got there? Well, I'll be . . .* Does the man who finds her have a kind face? I like to think he does, and once the dog is on its lead, Susan is no longer frightened.

I'm not seven any more, she tells Harley the dog. But that is the only information she can share. Already the patterns of the shells on the wall by her bed are fading, and what was it about the sand from before that was different from this sand?

How long will it take her to forget who she is, where she comes from, who raised her?

The truth is, not long at all.

Acknowledgements

I feel extremely blessed to have Sue Armstrong of C+W as my agent, and Clio Cornish of Michael Joseph as my editor. It's a special thing indeed to have met not one but two people who instantly understood what I was trying to achieve with *The Hollow Sea*. I'm grateful for Sue's unwavering expertise, kindness and advocacy and for Clio's unending patience and magical editorial powers, which lifted *The Hollow Sea* to the next level so many times I've lost count. Thank you also to Lauren Wakefield for her incredible cover design, and Ciara Berry, Sophie Shaw, Madeleine Woodfield, Nick Lowndes, my proofreaders and everyone else at Michael Joseph who has worked on *The Hollow Sea* behind the scenes. Thanks also to my copyeditor, Hazel Orme, for her exceptional attention to detail and insightful suggestions.

The Penguin WriteNow mentoring scheme for writers from backgrounds under-represented in publishing provided me with much-needed confidence and support. I received extraordinarily helpful feedback on sample chapters of *The Hollow Sea* from Poppy Hampson at the workshop stage of WriteNow and was later mentored by Jessica Leeke at Michael Joseph. Jessica was incredibly generous with her time, giving me the space to talk at length about the story I wanted to tell, and all the possible ways in which I might tell it. Without those conversations and Jessica's feedback on an early partial draft and outline, *The Hollow Sea* would be a very different book, or locked in a bottom drawer never to see the light of day. When Clio took over as my mentor, I was relieved to discover she was equally as kind, patient and perceptive as Jessica had been. Thanks are also due to everyone involved in the creation and administration of the Write-Now scheme, but especially Ithaka Cordia, Siena Parker and Louisa Burden-Garabedian.

While writing *The Hollow Sea* I was lucky to receive an Arts Council England National Lottery Project Grant, providing me with the time and space to write at a time of precarious employment. It also covered the costs of spending two weeks volunteering at the Cornish Seal Sanctuary in Gweek. The staff there work extraordinarily hard caring for seals and other animals and still found time to answer all my questions, for which I'm grateful. Thanks are due also to Juliet, for cake and additional support with accommodation costs.

Finding the time, space and motivation to write is always a challenge, even for those of us without children. I started writing *The Hollow Sea* at one of my favourite places, Circle of Misse in the Loire Valley, supported by my dear friends Wayne Milstead and Aaron Tighe. I finished it during lockdown with the help of Writers' HQ's online writing retreats, which were much appreciated at a time that was uniquely challenging for everyone.

Thank you to my friend Helen Salsbury for her continued warm support and her insightful feedback on an early draft. My fellow WriteNow mentees provided sage advice and virtual hugs via our WhatsApp group, as have many of my fellow debut writers publishing in 2022. There are too many to list but thank you all.

The Hollow Sea deals with topics very close to my heart and I don't think I would have ever been able to write it without my friends in the childless-not-by-choice community, who have provided friendship, support and inspiration. *The Hollow Sea* is for you. To anyone I've forgotten to thank, please forgive me or, better still, let me know, so I can include you next time.

Finally, I'd like to thank my family. The word 'families' is often used in public discourse as shorthand for 'families-with-children', but my family is no less precious for not having any children in it. Mum, Sarah and Chris, we might be small in stature and small in number, but we make it count. Dad, miss you always. Poppy, Bella, Yuki and Kiko, thank you for loving me unconditionally and giving me a reason to get out of bed when times are tough. Finally, but most importantly, Satbeer, thank you for being the best and most annoying person I've ever known and for being patient while I put the pieces of myself back together again.